VIKRAMADITYA VEERGATHA
BOOK 4

THE WRATH OF THE HELLFIRES

VIKRAMADITYA VEERGATHA

BOOK 4

THE WRATH OF THE HELLFIRES

NATIONAL BESTSELLING SERIES

SHATRUJEET NATH

JAICO PUBLISHING HOUSE

Ahmedabad Bangalore Chennai
Delhi Hyderabad Kolkata Mumbai

Published by Jaico Publishing House
A-2 Jash Chambers, 7-A Sir Phirozshah Mehta Road
Fort, Mumbai - 400 001
jaicopub@jaicobooks.com
www.jaicobooks.com

VIKRAMADITYA VEERGATHA: BOOK 4
THE WRATH OF THE HELLFIRES
ISBN 978-93-89305-67-8

First Jaico Impression: 2020
Second Jaico Impression: 2021

Page design and layout: R. Ajith Kumar, Delhi

Printed by
Trinity Academy For Corporate Training Limited, Mumbai

To
Santhosh Gopalan.
Rest in peace, my friend.

Matsya
Viratapuri
R. Yamuna
Kosala
Sravasti
Pragjyotishpura
The Marusthali
Arbuda Mts.
Kausambi
Girivraja
Magadha
Vatsa
Udaypuri
Sristhali
R. Kshipra
Dandakabhukti
Vanga
Avanti
Riksha Mts.
Ujjayini
Tamralipti
Dvarka
Anarta
Heheya
Vindhya Mts.
Mahishmati
Odra
Uttara Tosali
R. Payoshni
Aanupa Marsh
Bhrigukaksha
Tosali
Kalinga
Dandaka Forest
Sindhuvarta

Index of Major Characters

(In alphabetical order)

Humans

The Kingdom of Avanti

Aatreya	merchant of Malawa
Ajanya	commander of the Imperial Army
Amara Simha	councilor of Avanti
Angamitra	captain of the samsaptakas
Aparupa	daughter of Aatreya
Atulyateja	garrison commander of Udaypuri
Barisa	palace blacksmith
Brichcha	father of Shanku
Dhanavantri	councilor of Avanti and royal physician
Dveeja	Aparupa's companion
Ghatakarpara	councilor of Avanti; nephew of Vikramaditya and Vararuchi
Greeshma	bandit; escapee from the Dandaka Forest
Kedara	captain of the Imperial Army
Kalidasa	ex-councilor of Avanti
Kshapanaka	councilor of Avanti; sister of Queen Vishakha

Kunjala	physician at Avanti's palace
Mahendraditya	late king of Avanti; father of Vikramaditya, Vararuchi and Pralupi
Mithyamayi	Vismaya's niece; maid to Pralupi
Mother Oracle	Shanku's grandmother; head of the Wandering Tribe
Pralupi	sister of Vikramaditya; Ghatakarpara's mother
Pulyama	captain of the Imperial Army
Satyaveda	governor of Malawa province
Shanku	councilor of Avanti; granddaughter of the Mother Oracle
Sharamana	garrison commander of Musili
Suhasa	commander of the Imperial Army
Upashruti	mother of Vikramaditya and Pralupi; second wife of Mahendraditya
Ushantha	mother of Vararuchi; first wife of Mahendraditya
Varahamihira	councilor of Avanti
Vararuchi	councilor of Avanti; half-brother of Vikramaditya
Vetala Bhatta	chief councilor of Avanti; royal tutor
Vikramaditya	king of Avanti
Vishakha	wife of Vikramaditya; Kshapanaka's sister
Vismaya	chief of the Palace Guards

The Kingdom of Magadha

Ambalu	Kikata spy
Ashrava	councilor of Magadha
Asmabindu	councilor of Magadha
Bhaskara	councilor of Magadha
Daipayana	general of the Magadhan army

Diganta	councilor of Magadha
Kapila	second son of late king Siddhasena
Shirsa	commander in the Magadhan army
Shoorasena	king of Magadha; elder son of late king Siddhasena
Siddhasena	late king of Magadha
Uttama	councilor of Magadha

The Kingdom of Vatsa

Chandravardhan	king of Vatsa; ally of Avanti
Himavardhan	brother of Chandravardhan; father of Ghatakarpara
Piyusha	Shashivardhan's bodyguard
Shashivardhan	son of Chandravardhan
Yashobhavi	councilor of Vatsa

The Kingdom of Kosala

Adheepa	general of Kosala's army
Bhoomipala	king of Kosala; ally of Avanti
Gajaketu	travelling musician
Kadru	courtier of Kosala
Kirtana	courtier of Kosala
Pallavan	envoy and councilor of Kosala

The Kingdom of Matsya

Adri	garrison commander of Kasavati
Baanahasta	king of Matsya; ally of Avanti

The Anarta Federation

Yugandhara	chief of the Anarta Federation; ally of Avanti

The Republic of Vanga

Bhadraka	Vanga chieftain
Sudasan	chancellor of the Republic of Vanga

The Hunas and the Sakas

Aab'za	Saka chieftain
droiba	Huna shaman
Ga'ur Thra'akha	Kalidasa's Huna name
Khash'i Dur	chief of the Hunas
Nor'han	Saka tracker
Zho E'rami	late Huna chief; Kalidasa's father

Devas

Agneyi	apsara and chief of the fire-wraiths
Brihaspati	royal chaplain of the devas
Gandharvasena	a deva
Indra	lord of the devas; king of Devaloka
Jayanta	son of Indra
Manyu	palace-keeper of Devaloka
Matali	a deva
Narada	envoy of Devaloka and advisor to Indra
Shachi	wife of Indra; Jayanta's mother
The Ashvins	elite cavalry of Devaloka, led by Nasatya and Dasra
The Maruts	the seven sons of Diti
Urvashi	apsara of Devaloka and mistress of Indra

Asuras

Amarka	asura general; son of Shukracharya
Chandasura	asura general; son of Shukracharya
Diti	sorceress and matriarch of the asuras
Hiranyaksha	lord of the asuras; king of Patala

Hiranyakashipu	lord of the asuras; older brother of Hiranyaksha and Holika
Holika	witch queen of Patala
Laayushi	demon and servant of Paurava
Paurava	asura and first Wielder of the Hellfires
Shukracharya	high priest of the asuras
Veeshada	the thief of the Halahala

Others

Ahi	the serpent-dragon
Betaal	the Ghoulmaster; lord of Borderworld
Kashyapa	sage and progenitor of the devas and asuras
Kubera	lord of the yakshas
Shalivahana	lord of the danavas
Shiva	the Omniscient One
Takshaka	lord of the nagas
Tribhanu	lord of the kinnaras

Glossary of Indian Terms

(In alphabetical order)

aguru	oil of agarwood
angavastram	a stole or light shawl to cover the torso
apsara	a beautiful, supernatural female being in Hinduism
aryaman	possessor of greatness; also, a form of address
ashoka	a rain-forest tree
ashtapada	an ancient Indian board game
badi-maa	elder mother; a form of address
ber	jujube; Indian plum
bheri	a large drum
chakram	a throwing weapon, circular in shape
champaka	magnolia
chaturanga	an ancient Indian strategy game; ancestor of chess
chausar	an ancient Indian board game; precursor to Ludo
chillum	traditional Indian clay pipe
churail	a legendary creature resembling a human female

danava	a mythical race in Hinduism
danda	a walking stick
devadaru	a species of cedar
dhoti	traditional men's garment
ekashringa	rhinoceros
ganjika	cannabis
ghat	steps leading down to a body of water, such as a holy river
goparasa	myrrh
gurudev	master or teacher; also, a form of address
jamun	black plum; Java plum
kashayam	a brewed Ayurvedic medicine
katari	a fist dagger
kinnara	a legendary tribe in Vedic India
koel	cuckoo
ksheera	traditional Indian rice pudding
mahaguru	grandmaster or teacher; also, a form of address
mahashilakantaka	a trebuchet or catapult
mahisha	buffalo
mama	maternal uncle
mandala	a spiritual and ritual symbol in Hinduism representing the universe
manjishtha	Indian madder
naga	a legendary tribe in Vedic India
nana	grandfather or old man; also, a form of address
nishigandha	tuberose
parijata	coral jasmine
peepal	the sacred fig tree
pranaam	salutation
raj-guru	royal tutor; also, a form of address

rakshasa	a mythical humanoid being in Hinduism
rani-maa	queen mother
roti	Indian bread
rudrapushpa	hibiscus
rudra veena	an Indian string instrument
samrat	emperor or overlord
samsaptaka	a tribe of mythical warriors
saptaparni	devil's tree
soma	Vedic ritual drink
suryayantra	a heliograph
tambulam	paan; a betel leaf and areca nut preparation
tilaka	mark worn on the forehead by Hindus
til laddoo	sweet made of sesame seeds and jaggery
urumi	a longsword with a flexible whip-like blade
uttariya	a scarf-like garment draped on the upper body
vaidya / vaidyanath	physician; also, an honorific and form of address
vajra / vajrayudha	thunderbolt; Indra's weapon of choice
vajranaga	monkshood
vyala	a mythical beast
yaksha	a mythical spirit in Hinduism
yashtimadhu	liquorice

Contents

Hunt

Crouched within the ruins of the burned-out building that backed up against the river, It waited and watched, scuttling from one vantage point to the other, narrowly observing the ragged line of approaching men.

Now that the drums had ceased beating, an overbearing stillness had settled over the forest, broken only by the lovelorn call of a koel *from across the river, and the fleshy splat of rainwater falling from the eaves and branches above. In the forest, the silence was occasionally disturbed by the soft tread of the men's feet on grass, the snap of a twig under a careless foot followed by a muffled curse. Thus, the hunting party, numbering a little over two dozen men, pressed forward in pursuit of its quarry.*

It watched the hunters come through the undergrowth in a tightening semicircle, their bows half-drawn, arrows nocked and pointed at the ground, spears set at an angle in anticipation of a sudden charge. The men wielding the nets followed, ready to cast their snares if the prey exposed itself. The drummers were in the rear, their drums silent. The boar had been cornered. Their job was done.

It watched the unsuspecting hunters draw near. It arrived at a decision.

The big man. The biggest man in the group, the biggest man It had ever laid its eyes upon. The one with the long-handled axe and the hair knotted in a high ponytail.

That was the man It wanted.

Gripping the two swords between thick, webbed fingers, It got to its feet.

"The boar has taken refuge inside the garrison, your honour."

"Are the trackers certain?"

The hunters were close enough for their voices to carry to the jumble of fallen bricks and rafters.

"They are, your honour."

"Isn't it ironic for a boar to choose a barrack of the Huna swine as a hiding place?"

A small roll of mirth swelled at these words. Hearing the men snigger, It peeked from behind a pile of rubble to see that the speaker was none other than the giant with the ponytail. The man grinned and spoke again. "It's time to flush the swine out of these barracks all over again."

More smiles and a flashing of teeth. One of the hunters addressed the man who stood beside the giant.

"Shall we enter, your honour?"

The man nodded, and at a signal, the hunting party began converging towards the broken-down gate of the fortification, weapons and nets at the ready.

Your honour.

The two words had been directed not at the giant, but at his companion. Intrigued, It turned its attention to the man with renewed interest.

The man wasn't nearly as tall or broad as the giant, yet there was authority in the set of his shoulders and in the way he carried himself. Black, shoulder-length hair covered his head, which rested on a strong neck, and he had a firm jawline that ended in a chiseled chin. The ease with which the man bore his old, heavy sword told of hidden strength in those finely muscled arms.

It paused for a moment. The man had charisma. Perhaps he too should be challenged, and not just the giant.

The boar had run off to the left of the building, seeking shelter in the thickets that had sprung up around the kitchens and outhouses, where once fires had burned in pits and ovens to feed regiments of soldiers. The soldiers were dead and gone now, leaving behind a vacuum that nature was refilling systematically. Grass grew knee-high almost everywhere, creepers had laid claim to the walls and roofs, while nests, webs and cocoons festooned the corners and crevices of the derelict fort.

Now, as the hunters slipped past the battered gate, It began casting spells of ancient provenance that opened up illusory spaces in the compound—spaces that the hunters filed into unthinkingly, spaces that led the party away from the giant and his regal companion. Weaving spell upon spell, It separated the hunters into smaller groups, funnelling each group in a different direction. Once It was satisfied that its targets were well isolated, It began reeling the two men deeper into the ruins.

"I can never forget this place." It was the other man speaking, not the giant. There was a dark inflection in his voice. "It was here that Varahamihira lost his leg."

"Even those who weren't here that day remember the battle," the giant replied. "They say you fought like you were possessed. Really, how many Hunas did you strike down that afternoon?"

"I wasn't counting. It's all a blur anyway. We had lost men earlier in the ambush; we were hopelessly outnumbered. And then Varahamihira was brought down. If I had signalled a

withdrawal, the troops' morale would have broken. The only option was to not give up and keep on fighting." A pause. "Besides, there was no question of letting what they'd done to Varahamihira go unavenged."

Deep, pensive silence from the giant. The footsteps drew nearer.

It cast another spell, a whisper that rippled outward and spread, enveloping the two men. Neither heard nor sensed anything. Not yet.

"Quite some revenge you exacted," the giant finally spoke. "The men still talk of the holy Kshipra running red with Huna blood for days after."

"Once blood has been spilled, it is impossible to say whose blood it is. It's all just red." An element of pain in the man's words carried through the brittle air. "I would rather—"

Halting midsentence, the man looked around, his brows furrowing in puzzlement. The giant too drew to a stop and instinctively gripped his axe tighter, tensing as he raised his guard, eyes darting from left to right.

"What's this? What's happening here?"

Without them realizing it, the space around the two men had shifted and transformed dramatically. Where a moment ago they were picking their way through the decay of overturned furniture, discarded armour and weaponry, and fallen debris from a caved-in roof, they now suddenly found themselves in an open courtyard, swept clean and tiled with smooth sandstone. A broad, shady verandah ran the length of the courtyard's perimeter, where ornate sandstone pillars stood in brooding silence. A heavy urn made of polished brass occupied the centre of the courtyard, from which a nishigandha *shrub flowered. Sunlight flooded the courtyard from the bright blue sky.*

"Where are...?" The giant paused and looked over his shoulder. "Is that the way we came in?"

The other man glanced at the door that ought to have brought them to the courtyard. Whatever lay on the other side of the door was now steeped in inky darkness.

"I don't remember walking in..." he hesitated. "And the men... where are they..."

Raising their weapons, the two men backed into one another, scanning the courtyard for trouble. The sunlight threw the verandah into shadow, making it hard for the men to see into its depths.

"Is this for real?" the giant asked. He didn't wait for an answer. "What do we do?"

Drawing a deep breath, It shuffled out of the shadows of the verandah.

"We get out of here."

"How?"

"The same way we got in, I supp—"

It stepped out from behind one of the pillars into the sunlight. Into the second man's field of vision. He jerked his head to see better and their eyes locked.

"—who are you?"

"Huh, what?" The giant swung around. Now two pairs of eyes stared at It.

"Who are you? Where did you come from?"

It hobbled painfully into the courtyard on its gnarled, spindly legs. It offered a small, pathetic smile that was missing several teeth. Harmless, ingratiating. The men lowered their weapons by a fraction, their shoulders relaxing just a bit.

It grinned to itself. Gain their confidence, gain their confidence...

"I am a friend. I mean no ill will." Its voice was old and gravelly, as if from disuse.

"What is this place?" the giant asked. "Do you know..."

"What are you hiding behind you?" The other one interrupted sharply. "Show us your hands. Now!"

It's hands moved, and the swords came into view. They were still in their sheaths.

"Why were you hiding those swords from us?" The men had taken up a defensive stance. "Who are you? Speak up."

"These are for you." The words whistled through the gaps between It's yellowed teeth. It stretched out its scrawny, withered arms, offering the swords, hilt first, to the men. "Gifts."

"We don't need them," the giant replied, his eyes flicking over the courtyard, looking for signs of any new threats. "I have my axe and my brother here has a sword that is possibly death's dearest ally."

"I would still like you to have them."

The giant's companion eyed the swords. The unadorned iron hilts felt solid and heavy. The aged sheaths were made of brown animal hide. He stroked his moustache. "Why?"

Anger stirred in the pit of It's stomach. Patience, patience…

"Take them, please."

Still suspicious, the man took one of the swords, cautiously weighing it in his hand. He gave a mild nod of appreciation. It immediately waved the second sword in the giant's direction, urging him to take it. The giant grudgingly obliged.

There!

Eyes gleaming in anticipation, It clucked its tongue in delight. "Good. Now you can fight me with them."

The two men peered down at It for a moment, before exchanging bewildered looks.

"Is this a joke?" the giant frowned. "We are not fighting a frail old man like you."

"You will have to. That is the only way," It protested.

"This is absurd, nana,*" the other man reasoned. "Tell us what you really want—"*

It opened its mouth wide and let out a guttural snarl. "Fight me."

Before either man had the chance to respond, It changed rapidly, growing and shifting form in the blink of an eye. It added muscle and bone, gaining twice its height and nearly four times its girth so that It towered over the men by two hands. An armour of thick scales had sprouted all over It's trunk and limbs, and its slobbering mouth was suddenly full of sharp teeth that It bared at the men. It held a mace studded with long iron spikes.

"Fight me," It growled again, its fetid breath hot on the men's faces. There was nothing left of the old man from earlier.

If the men were taken aback, they barely showed it. They both stood their ground and stared back at It, defiant. It smiled inwardly. This was a good sign.

The giant flung the sword aside and hoisted his axe. His companion was about to do the same when It spoke again.

"Use the swords I gave you."

"No," the other man refused. Throwing the sword and sheath down on the sandstone, he gripped the hide-bound hilt of his own sword tight, ready to do battle.

"My swords. Or the men who came with you die needlessly." It motioned with its head in the general direction of the door. "Do it, now."

The men shot sidelong glances, assessing the seriousness of the threat. Exchanging curt nods, they looked with loathing at the creature glowering down at them with small, bloodshot eyes. Slowly, they lowered their weapons to the ground and picked up the sheathed swords instead.

"Hurry, get them out."

Riled by It's tone, the giant yanked his sword free of its sheath. The sunlight instantly caught and glinted off the blade, which was smooth and at odds with the drab hilt.

"Just remember that you asked for this," the giant said through gritted teeth. Stepping away, he put distance between himself and his companion, and circled around so that

suddenly the creature had to guard against attack from two sides.

This one is good, *It thought to itself, watching the giant.*

Or rather, watching the sword in the giant's hands.

It watched the sword weave and cleave through the air. It watched the sunlight spark off the cutting edge. It watched the dull gleam of the cold, flat metal. And It felt the disappointment well up inside its chest.

No, the giant was not the one.

It turned to face the other man, who still hadn't drawn the second sword. It grunted and shook its head in impatience. The man responded by easing the blade out of the scabbard and brandishing it, letting the power in his wrist carry to the metal. His half-turned body was perfectly poised to attack and parry, the sword's point steepled in the creature's direction.

It watched the man. And It watched the arc of the sword—which suddenly appeared to shimmer, as if with heat.

It blinked in wonder and disbelief.

Peering closely, It observed the lick of small flames on the metal. Almost at once, the sword turned orange, then red, before burning white-hot along the edges. Meanwhile, the flames continued lapping at the blade, ravenous and growing in vigour with each passing moment.

"Watch out, brother," the giant's voice rose in alarm. "Looks like sorcery to me."

With a moan of relief, It let go of the spiked mace and dropped to its knees. It's entire body crumpled, and as swiftly as it had morphed into the vile and hulking creature, It now shifted back to a black-skinned figure of medium build, with short twisting horns on its head. It stayed on its knees, docile, staring up at the man holding the flaming sword. The man switched his gaze from the sword to the creature, his brows arched in surprise and mistrust.

"Who are you?" It asked in an awed voice. "Who are you, aryaman?*"*

"I am Vikramaditya, king of Avanti," the man replied. "And that is my friend and brother, Kalidasa. Who are you, and what is the meaning of all this?"

"You are the one I have sought for so many years, good king," It answered. "You are the one destined to wield the Hellfires."

"Hellfires?" The king looked at the burning sword. "You mean this thing?"

"This and the other one." It pointed to the sword in the giant's possession. "Accept them, for they are rightfully yours."

Kalidasa examined the sword he was holding. Then, striding over to Vikramaditya, he handed his king the weapon. The moment the blade changed hands, it too caught fire, burning like its twin in the king's other hand. Vikramaditya and Kalidasa exchanged a mystified glance.

"You still haven't told us who you are," said Kalidasa.

"I am the demon, Laayushi, slave of the noble asura, Paurava, the first Wielder of the Hellfires." The creature's gaze switched to Vikramaditya. "I have been looking for you per my master's bidding. These were his swords. They are now yours."

"I don't understand," Vikramaditya gave a puzzled frown. "Who is your master, and why am I to have his swords?"

"Because you are worthy of them, good king. But I have done a poor job of explaining myself," Laayushi bowed his head. "Pardon me. Let me tell you everything there is to know about the Hellfires..."

Resolve

A constant rumble of hooves rose off the desert floor, like an undercurrent, and the dust being kicked up lingered in the dry air like a veil, shrouding Mun'h in a haze that altered the strength of the morning sunlight, without weakening the heat of the day. If anything, the haze trapped the heat, while the dust added to the discomfort by chafing the eyes and nostrils. The Huna tribesmen, who now numbered in excess of seven thousand in Mun'h alone, had taken to covering their faces with scarves and shawls almost all the time.

Over three dozen of these tribesmen, comprising *shy'ors* and warriors, sat astride their horses or stood in a loose circle, leaning on their long spears and observing Kalidasa. The man they had all come to admiringly address as *mahek* sat on a mat spread on the sand, his legs folded under him. He held his hair bunched up in one hand, gripped tight, and as the Hunas craned their necks in wonder and curiosity, he put a sharp dagger to the ponytail and sawed through it, chopping it free. Placing the severed lock to one side, Kalidasa continued tonsuring himself, cutting off clumps of hair, and then shaving his scalp until his head was rid of the last trace of hair.

Word spread and the crowd of onlookers swelled, so that close to a hundred pairs of eyes were on Kalidasa as he gathered his shorn locks into a square of white cloth, which he then folded and placed on a miniature pyre built on the sand in front of him. Not a sound escaped the watching Hunas as Kalidasa sprinkled water over his head and bare shoulders to purify himself, before getting to his feet and going around the pyre three times, pouring ghee churned from yoghurt over the stack of wood. Placing an earthen pot filled with water on his shoulder, he resumed circling the pyre, before letting the pot roll off and shatter on the earth behind him. He then set a torch to the pyre, and as wood and ghee caught and burned, he walked around the pyre for a final time, head bowed, palms joined in obeisance.

Kalidasa was nearly done when Khash'i Dur elbowed through the ring of spectators, accompanied by the *shy'ors* of three other powerful tribes. All four *shy'ors* waited patiently while Kalidasa completed the ritual by washing himself, and it was only when the giant walked up to them and bowed that Khash'i Dur inclined his head in return.

"So, you have... how do you say it... done the last rites?" His eyes crinkled against the glare.

"I have, nearly," Kalidasa glanced at the fire. It burned steadily, giving off only a few straggling wisps of smoke. "I will collect the ashes once it has cooled."

"You do this before every battle, Thra'akha? Perform your own last rites?"

"No. We do this on the day we become *samsaptakas*, when we burn something of ours, something precious to us, as a token of destroying our attachment to life. What we burn is also symbolic of our worldly body."

"And you swear never to return from battle defeated."

"We take the Death Oath," Kalidasa nodded, running a hand over his bald head. "A promise to leave the battlefield either victorious or dead. That's why these last rites. By performing them, we wipe the fear of dying from our minds. The *samsaptakas* are already dead going into battle."

Khash'i Dur nodded in understanding. "Why now?" he indicated the sacrificial fire. "I mean why again, today?"

"Before the day ends, we will be on our saddles, riding east." Kalidasa turned to look, but the rising dust obscured the far horizon. It didn't seem to matter. The giant's gaze stayed fixed on a spot beyond the curtain of dust, where the mountains began. "The battles that lie ahead will test us to our limits. I don't know what the outcome of those battles will be, but one thing is certain. I shall not live in defeat. For me, it will always be victory or death. This," nodding at the fire, "was a reaffirmation of that vow."

In the pause that followed, one of the elder *shy'ors* leaned forward and murmured into Khash'i Dur's ear, watching Kalidasa all the while out of the corner of his eye. Kalidasa strained to catch the exchange but failed to do so. The Huna chieftain nodded unhappily. Taking two steps closer, he planted a gentle hand on the giant's shoulder.

"There is talk among the men," he said cryptically, lowering his voice.

"What kind of talk?" Kalidasa squinted down at Khash'i Dur.

"The men respect you, and not just because you are the son of Zho E'rami. They are fighters themselves, and they plainly recognize the warrior in you. You have inspired them, and they believe you will lead them into the land of plenty. Yet..." the *shy'or* dropped his voice some more. "Yet, they wonder about the rituals that you practise. They see you perform your last rites; they see you hold on to the customs you learned in Avanti. And they ask why you still haven't embraced the traditions and rituals and culture of the desert."

"And thus, they question my loyalty." Kalidasa looked at

the ring of faces around him, his eyes finally settling on the three *shy'ors* who had come with Khash'i Dur. "They wonder whether I am Huna enough to be trusted."

Kalidasa smiled thinly and reached for the dagger at his waist.

"It is not that we don't trust you, Thra'akha..."

Before the chief could finish, Kalidasa drew the dagger, raising his voice so everyone could hear him.

"*Ma'a i duz'ur l'uk yahe. Ma le'a koo'b qurr hei zuh'i aa'lle.*"

I am a son of these endless sands, and I will set all doubt to rest in your minds.

Kalidasa went to the pyre, which had started collapsing into itself, the strips of old wood slowly turning to embers. Kneeling by the fire, the giant held the dagger's point over the flames. The Hunas barely moved a muscle, their eyes pinned on Kalidasa. The entire desert suddenly appeared to be in the grip of a deathly hush.

The tip of the dagger blackened and began smouldering. Kalidasa got back to his feet and held the dagger aloft, turning slowly so all could see him.

"*Urug ha,*" he announced. "*Ma le'a k'yar hriiz ei'te.*"

Look, I will wear the *hriiz* now.

Kalidasa pressed the point of the blade against his forehead, and in a quick, downward stroke, drew a deep cut that plunged almost all the way to the spot where his eyebrows met. As pain blazed from the cut, pulsing through Kalidasa's mind, the tribesmen raised their spears to the sky, shaking them and roaring the Huna war cry in unison.

"*Kul'a gwede'r. Kul'a mahek. Kul'a q'ult.*"

Raise the sword. Raise the storm. Raise the war.

The cries spread outward like ripples in a pond, catching and echoing through Mun'h and its surroundings; and as if in response, a hollow, hungry howl issued from the direction of the desert—a howl that was part pain, part rage and part madness.

The men continued chanting the war cry.

"*Kul'a gwede'r. Kul'a mahek. Kul'a q'ult.*"

Blood from the wound oozed and ran down the bridge of Kalidasa's nose. As the first drops dripped off the end and spattered on his toes, the giant blinked the pain away and turned to the western fringe of the desert, where the two *yah'bre* loomed like living nightmares, showering dust as they loped towards the Huna township, howling through awfully wide mouths crammed with black clouds and electric-white lightning.

"*Kul'a gwede'r. Kul'a mahek. Kul'a q'ult,*" Kalidasa muttered grimly to himself.

***

Thunder rolled across the sky, drowning out the young captain's words.

"What was that again?" asked Varahamihira, leaning on his crutch. He turned one ear theatrically in the captain's direction. "Speak louder, son. You are a soldier of Avanti, unless you have forgotten that. Put some heart into your words."

"Yes, councilor." Pulyama went a little red, conscious of the attention this exchange had begun drawing. The sentries standing by the garrison's gate had been listening from the start, and now soldiers from around the compound were also staring his way. "I... I was not informed you would be coming."

"Okay. But we are here now. What are you going to do about it?"

"I can... I shall ask inside if... whether you can..."

"We are councilors of Avanti, captain," Varahamihira interrupted, jerking his thumb at himself, then at Dhanavantri, standing to his right. "We can very well do whatever it is that you were considering asking whether we can do."

"Not that we are asking for much," Dhanavantri spoke for the first time, milder and placating. "We are here to meet Councilor Vararuchi. Lead us to him."

Pulyama licked his lips uncertainly. "If you will wait here a moment..."

"That will not be necessary, captain." The deep voice came from across the garrison compound, and Varahamihira and Dhanavantri turned to see the burly form of Commander Suhasa heading their way, his head bent against the slowly intensifying drizzle. "Salutations, councilors," the commander said with a small *pranaam*. To Pulyama, he added, "I shall attend to them." Addressing the councilors with another bow, he said, "This way, please."

Varahamihira fixed the commander with a cold eye, but before another word could be said, Dhanavantri nodded. Suhasa turned and struck a path across the wet compound, and seeing the royal physician follow, Varahamihira had no choice but to hobble along after them. They went up a grassy mound and reached the shelter of a verandah, just as the drizzle turned to rain to the accompaniment of a deafening crash of thunder.

"Right in time," Suhasa breathed out in relief as he brushed little droplets of rain from his big, white moustache and looked at the downpour.

"Not if the captain there had had his way," Varahamihira snorted, mopping the damp from his pock-scarred face and white hair.

"Spare the fellow, councilor," the commander replied. "Your arrival is a surprise, and the poor chap didn't know how to deal with it."

"Heaven forbid something of real significance taking that one by surprise." Shuffling his crutch around, Varahamihira faced the commander. "Are these the sort of men you command for the rebellion against the Samrat?"

If Varahamihira saw Dhanavantri wince, he ignored it. Suhasa, for his part, refused to be baited.

"Let me take you to Councilor Vararuchi," he said stoically.

Word of their arrival had reached Vararuchi, for he met his visitors at the head of the stairs, on the landing outside the room that served as his makeshift council chamber. He greeted them with courtesy, but under the circumstances, there was no space for the warmth of old. Ushering them into his chamber, he inclined his head at Suhasa, indicating that he wished for privacy.

"Can I offer you some buttermilk?" he asked, once his guests were comfortably seated.

"How about offering us an explanation of what's happening?" Varahamihira ploughed to the heart of the matter without preamble. Leaning forward, he looked Vararuchi in the eye. "How did we end up like this?"

Vararuchi sat back in his chair and stroked his moustache, appraising his fellow councilors. "Has he sent you to talk to me?"

"Does it matter? Does that change anything?"

"Has he?"

Varahamihira and Dhanavantri exchanged glances. "No," the former replied. "The Samrat will not have a dialogue with you until…"

"Until I take my demands back," Vararuchi nodded. "I know. Those were the official terms of the message I received from the palace." A smirk played on his lips. "So, why are you sitting here, talking to me?"

"Because we are not the Samrat. And because we want to try and put some of the missing sense back into this whole affair."

The words hung in the air. Outside, the rain beat down hard, stifling the rumble of thunder.

"What do you want to know that you don't know already?" Vararuchi asked finally.

"Why... why ask your brother to vacate the throne? Why push him into a corner like this?"

"Is he my brother?" Vararuchi levelled his gaze at the men across the table.

Varahamihira shifted in his seat. The action was minute, but Vararuchi caught it and smiled.

"You know what you are doing amounts to treason," said Varahamihira. "Conspiring against the throne..."

"I concede that under normal circumstances this would be treason." Vararuchi got up and went to a stand where a clay pitcher sat next to four clay tumblers. "But it is not treason because I am not conspiring *against* the throne, but rather, *saving it* from an imposter who claims Aditya lineage. I am protecting the crown and throne of Avanti." A small pause. "Buttermilk?"

Dhanavantri and Varahamihira shook their heads. Vararuchi filled one of the tumblers for himself and returned to his seat.

"Imposter?" It was Dhanavantri's turn to lean his bulk against the table and gaze into Vararuchi's face. "I remember Vikrama as a small child, walking between you and the old king, holding onto the king's fingers and yours for support. Whenever he tripped, you and the king would grab his hands to steady him, making sure he didn't fall. That is how you both showered love on him. Later, when Mahendraditya was dying, he gave each of you one of his swords, passing on the responsibility of protecting Avanti to both of you. How can someone who grew up on your and the king's boundless love become an imposter? How can someone who has been handed the responsibility of defending Avanti—a responsibility that he has wholeheartedly embraced—be termed as an imposter?"

"That was then, when none of us knew better. Today, he

knows the truth, yet he won't own up to it. That makes him an imposter." Vararuchi's lips curled in bitterness. "And all for what? Just to keep the Queen Mother's honour from being torn to shreds? The Queen Mother's honour is more important than the truth; is that the Samrat's message to his people?"

"If he protects the Queen Mother—*his mother*—it is only because of a promise he made to King Mahendraditya before the king died," Dhanavantri replied. "Vikrama gave the king his word that he would defend the Queen Mother's honour at any cost."

Vararuchi looked from the physician to Varahamihira. "And was there any witness to this promise that was made to father?" The words brought a sardonic smile to his face. "Or are we to simply believe the Samrat's word?"

"Are you implying that Vikrama is lying?" asked Varahamihira.

Vararuchi sipped his buttermilk and shrugged. "A promise is a convenient thing."

"In which case, would it not be just as convenient for him to get the Queen Mother to come out and say that Mahendraditya is his father, and that he is a true-born Aditya? There is no shame in that." Varahamihira let this settle over Vararuchi. "Isn't that all that you have been asking for, all the clarification you seek? Don't you see how easily he can give that to you, Vararuchi? Think, *think*."

"No imposter would let that kind of opportunity pass," the physician muttered.

"Absolutely," Varahamihira nodded. "Vikrama can settle this debate with one stroke of cunning, one act of manipulation, yet he will not do so. Why? Because Vikrama will not take recourse to a lie. You have forgotten that the truth is your brother's code of honour."

"And yet he will not acknowledge the truth that he is not Mahendraditya's son..."

"Because he is tied to his word, Vararuchi," Dhanavantri exploded in exasperation.

Vararuchi subsided into a grudging silence.

"What was the need for all this?" Varahamihira waved his hands around, referring to the garrison and the rebellion. "You could have come and spoken to him—or to any one of us."

"I came, and I was rebuffed." Vararuchi shook his head. "Here's something to think about. Not once was I informed of Ghatakarpara's kidnapping. Why?"

"When news first came of Ghatakarpara's disappearance from Udaypuri, we discussed informing you," said the physician. "At that time, we didn't really know what had befallen the prince, whether he was in any real danger. As you were visiting *badi-maa*, the Samrat thought it best not to bother you. He guessed you would cut your visit short and come rushing back to the palace—which was exactly what you would have done. He wanted you to spend time with *badi-maa*. Later, when we learned of the kidnapping, a rider was sent with a message to you—"

"No rider ever came to me," Vararuchi gave his head a vehement shake.

"Shanku was the one who dispatched the rider. You could ask her, except that she is somewhere in the Dandaka, on her way to the stronghold of the danavas."

Vararuchi shrugged by way of reply. Varahamihira watched him for a moment before speaking. "This is your form of protest? Raise a flag of revolt and turn the soldiers against their king when there are so many threats to Avanti's survival, when the need of the hour is to stay united?"

"You credit me with too much here, councilor. There was no need to turn the soldiers against the Samrat, for he has already lost their faith with his actions. Also, the threat to Avanti didn't seem to deter the Samrat from letting Kalidasa return to his people." Vararuchi eyed Varahamihira narrowly.

"The responsibility for Avanti's safety begins at the top, so how come I am the only one being questioned?"

"We will deal with Kalidasa and the Hunas, but we need to stick together if that is to happen," said Varahamihira.

"I am afraid that does not answer my question." Vararuchi pushed his chair back and rose. There was a finality in the way he stood, crossing his arms and looking down, that didn't escape the other two councilors.

"What will it take to change your mind about this?" asked Dhanavantri.

"You already know. The Queen Mother must issue a statement denying Indra's insinuations and clarify the matter of Vikramaditya's lineage."

The visitors got to their feet. At the door, Varahamihira turned back one last time.

"I hope this madness will end before it is too late and we all come to regret it," he said before limping out.

Vararuchi watched the councilors depart with a glum face.

***

Two murderous bolts of lightning, fast and full of anger, hurtled into the abyss, one chasing the other so quickly it felt as if they were at war. Indra, who was leaning against a high window, followed their descent until both were swallowed by the moat's yawning darkness, and all that remained was the crackling smell of ozone. In an instant, thunder crashed into the palace, amplified by the high cliffs all around, setting the crystal ceiling lamps quivering in their chains and making Narada wince. Indra himself, however, didn't even blink as he went back to staring over the cliffs, over Amaravati, in the direction of Mount Meru, which was lost from view in a dark mist of rain.

"Why isn't the garuda here yet?" he growled, his brow heavy with annoyance over his blue eyes. "Matali should have sent us *some* information, *some* news of progress."

"Perhaps there is no progress to report—"

"*No progress to report?*" Looking over his shoulder, the deva lord pinned his severe gaze on Narada. Then, turning around slowly, he faced the hall, his eyes fixed firmly on the diplomat. "Matali has been in the human king's palace for *ages* now. So has Urvashi. One or the other *has* to have found something out, right?" He glared at the four faces before him. "*Right?* Otherwise what good are the two of them?"

Indra spun on his heel and went back to staring out of the window, where the rain was now coming down in sheets, blowing over the cliffs and moving across the drawbridges at a slant before arriving at the courtyard below. Narada stole a glance at the others around him, looking for reactions, but the expression on all threc faces were closed.

"It has been more than four days since the garuda left with instructions to Matali to speed things up. And what have we got so far? *Nothing*," Indra snapped, his voice rising above the pounding of the rain. "Heaven knows what Shukracharya has been up to in these three days." He wheeled around again to face the hall, gesticulating wildly. "Why, the asuras might be moments away from striking Ujjayini—they might even be attacking the place while we stand here, wasting our time in talk. Matali's last report had stated that the human king has just *three* councilors left to help him guard his city, one of whom is a cripple on crutches. That's how vulnerable Vikramaditya is! No... *no*..." He gave his head a furious shake. "This waiting for Matali and Urvashi will not do. We have to move *now* if we are to beat the asuras to the Halahala. Takshaka. Tribhanu..." he looked at the two figures standing next to Narada. "You must leave for Ujjayini."

"As you wish, lord of the devas," said Tribhanu, the king of the kinnaras.

"Straightaway," Indra added imperatively.

The naga king, Takshaka, bowed his head. "Yes, my friend," he whispered, the words carrying in strange half-echoes, as if spoken simultaneously by many tongues.

The two lords were about to leave when Narada spoke.

"Would this be prudent, my lord?" he asked, feeling the weight of Takshaka, Tribhanu and the chamberlain Brihaspati's eyes alight on him.

"More prudent than sitting here doing nothing to stop the asuras from getting hold of Veeshada's dagger," said Indra. The deva's lips curled in a cold sneer as he sized up the diplomat. "But I wonder what makes you argue in favour of inaction? Could it be fear of the human king, or is it just the storm that is making you nervous? Or maybe you simply lack confidence in the brave nagas and kinnaras."

"Not for a moment would I doubt the courage of the nagas and kinnaras, my lord," said Narada with a quick bow at Takshaka and Tribhanu. "Both have proved themselves extremely dependable in the past by assisting us in countless battles against the asuras. Nevertheless, I am wary of Vikramaditya, even though his position may have weakened considerably from before. Why? Because nothing changes the fact that he continues to wield the Hellfires, and we don't quite know if Matali has found a way of neutralizing the threat those two swords present."

Narada sensed the naga and kinnara lords grow tense beside him, while a troubled frown graced Indra's face. "Moreover, my lord," the diplomat continued, taking advantage of the leverage he had acquired, "if we do smash through Ujjayini's defences, what would we gain if Matali doesn't know the dagger's whereabouts? The Halahala would be lying undefended, and the asuras could chance upon it and claim it for themselves." He paused. "Did you not yourself caution Jayanta against the perils of rushing in when he carelessly summoned Ahi to Ujjayini?"

"Don't remind me of that bungling fool," Indra waved a hand in a fit of exasperation. He walked over to a table on which a jug brimming with *soma* sat in a basin filled with chilled water. Pouring himself a cup, he held the drink in his hand, brooding into the dark red liquid.

Narada assessed Tribhanu and Takshaka discreetly. The former was a tall, broad-chested centaur with a lush mane running down his back. The coat that covered the kinnara's lower body and flanks was the same black as his mane and his short, trim beard. He wore gold earrings, while his arms were adorned with stacks of gold bracelets. He sported small silver bells on all four legs, tied just above the hooves. His handsome face was impassive as he waited for Indra to arrive at a decision. The naga was a different specimen altogether, distinguished by a barbed and horned snake's head growing out of a humanoid body. Not nearly as tall or as well-proportioned as the kinnara, Takshaka stood on a pair of squat, powerful legs, while his long, muscular hands almost reached down to his knees, the toes and fingers ending in curved claws. Luminous green-black scales covered his body, while the eyes behind his stubby snout were black and beady, going back and forth between Narada and Indra. The naga had a tail that trailed on the floor behind him, slender and twitching slowly in anticipation.

"There is merit in what Narada says."

The diplomat's eyes widened in surprise at the unexpected support from Brihaspati's quarter.

"It is my suggestion that we be patient and give Matali and Urvashi some time, lord," said Narada, latching on to the chamberlain's words. "Let us trust Matali to find us a way to the Halahala."

Indra grimaced and looked out of the window. The rain was so dense that Amaravati's spires had disappeared from sight, and even the cliffs were no more than shadowy outlines. The lord of the devas looked hopefully in the direction of Meru, then turned back with a shake of his head and drank the *soma* in one large gulp.

"Very well, we shall not attack Ujjayini just yet," he said, looking fiercely at Narada, as if daring him to object once again. "But the naga and kinnara armies will move as close to the city as possible, so that we can attack the moment we hear from Matali. If we have to exercise the patience of a predator, let us at least be close to our prey for a quick and efficient kill."

Narada bowed, conceding to his king's decision.

Takshaka and Tribhanu bowed as well. They turned to leave the hall without another word; one silent on his short, scaly legs, the other's hooves striking sharply on the marble floor, in rhythm to the sweet chime of the silver bells. They were halfway to the door when Indra called to them from behind.

"Bring me Vikramaditya—*alive*. I want to see him standing here, bound hand and foot, begging for mercy. It is something I desire as much as Veeshada's dagger."

***

The quiet within Ujjayini's council chamber was woven with the patter of a thinning rain falling into the lake, so a soft, sleepy hush swaddled the room like a blanket. The storm from the morning had blown over, the clouds slowly beginning to disperse in the east. Four lamps still burned in their recesses in the walls, lighting the chamber, while a fifth sat on the council table, illuminating the pile of palm-leaf manuscripts at Vikramaditya's elbow.

Other than the samrat, there was one person in the chamber, an old man with a heavily bronzed face and large calloused hands who stood at the foot of the table, hands folded out of respect. Vikramaditya assessed the man from his seat at the head of the table, his eyes gentle but firm in their enquiry.

"Do you think you can do it?" he asked.

"Most definitely," the man answered, then paused. "But do you really want this done, Samrat? There is already a shortage of iron in the kingdom..."

"I know," said Vikramaditya, his voice even, his face in shadow.

"Pardon me, but I didn't at all mean to be disrespectful, Samrat." The man hesitated, suddenly anxious. "It was just... that wasn't my intention."

"I know that too, Barisa." The samrat smiled to allay the man's fears. "You care about Avanti, and that shows in your words. And in your work as chief blacksmith of the palace. Swords, spears and axes fashioned by you have kept Avanti's pride intact over the years. Your work and your words are above reproach."

"You are gracious, my king," the man sighed with relief. "Every bit like your father."

The smile on Vikramaditya's lips faltered at the mention of Mahendraditya, but recovering swiftly, he said, "You are the only one I can trust with this job, Barisa." He cocked an eyebrow at the man. "So...?"

"I will make them, Samrat."

"As quickly as possible."

The blacksmith nodded.

"And you will do this all by yourself, involving no one else. No helpers, no apprentices, no understudies. Word of this should not go beyond the two of us. We will be the only ones to know about this—you and me. Have I made myself clear?"

"Abundantly clear, Samrat. I shall be careful. You have my word."

The king pointed to a bundle that lay on the table, wrapped

securely in coarse jute-cloth. "I thought you might need a reference."

"That would help, your honour." Barisa stepped forward and picked up the bundle. "I shall have this returned by the end of the day, Samrat."

"Very good. You may leave."

The man bowed, did a *pranaam* and backed out of the room.

Once the door had closed on the blacksmith, Vikramaditya turned back to the pile of palm leaves on the table, on which were scrawled detailed lists of troop allocations along the frontier. The samrat tallied these lists with other sets of palm leaves that highlighted the allotment of provisions for the soldiers, making certain that no regiment or outpost in Avanti would suffer a shortage of food on account of some palace clerk's oversight. Normally, this was the Acharya's or Amara Simha's duty, but in their absence, the king had taken the responsibility on himself.

A while passed and the rain petered out completely, making way for a wan sun, before there came a tap on the door. Looking up from the leaves, the samrat saw Dhanavantri and Varahamihira let themselves in, nodding their greetings to him.

"Vismaya just told us you wanted a meeting," said Varahamihira. "Did you?"

"Yes." Vikramaditya set aside the quill he was using to make notes. "Something has come up that I want to share with you."

The king picked up a scroll that was lying rolled on the table to one side. "Here," he said, waving it.

Dhanavantri came around and took the scroll from Vikramaditya. Unrolling it, he read through its contents quickly, his expression growing sombre as he reached the end.

"What is it?" Varahamihira asked.

"A formal message from the Anartas, from Chief Yugandhara," said Vikramaditya.

"They know about Kalidasa's departure," the physician explained, looking up from the scroll. "They want to know Avanti's official stand on the matter, as and when the Hunas invade Sindhuvarta. They are concerned that Avanti has not made its position on Kalidasa clear."

Varahamihira shifted his weight on his crutch and grimaced. "It is a matter of time before the other kingdoms of Sindhuvarta also start demanding answers," he muttered. He pointed to the scroll. "When did this come in?"

"Earlier this morning," the samrat said. "I sent word immediately, but Kshapanaka is somewhere outside, overseeing the city's evacuation, and the two of you weren't around." He paused and looked at the councilors curiously. "Where have you been?"

Varahamihira shot Dhanavantri a glance. "We dropped in on the garrison of Musili."

The chamber was quiet, the king taken aback, staring at the councilors. "Why?" he asked finally.

"Somebody had to talk, Vikrama." Varahamihira limped to a chair and slumped down, suddenly tired. "Somebody had to open a conversation."

Again, a silence. Dhanavantri also took a seat, placing the scroll before him.

"And? Did the talking help?" Vikramaditya asked. Putting his elbows on the table, he flexed his fingers and cracked his knuckles as he gazed at Varahamihira.

"Yes and no," the old councilor sighed. "No, in the sense that Vararuchi is stubborn and not amenable to reason. Like you," he quickly added.

The samrat remained impassive.

"But the trip was not entirely useless either," Varahamihira continued. Nodding at the physician seated across him, he said, "We figured some things out."

"Like what?"

"Like, for instance, that no matter what Vararuchi says, his problem has very little to do with Kalidasa and the Hunas."

Vikramaditya's eyebrows rose in bemusement.

"I think we must start at the beginning for this to make any sense," said Dhanavantri.

With a nod, Varahamihira settled into his chair to recount the details of their visit, and the conversation he and Dhanavantri had had with Vararuchi. The physician filled in any parts that Varahamihira missed mentioning, and before long, the samrat was fully updated on what had transpired in Musili that morning.

"All his energies are focused on the Queen Mother clearing the air about my lineage," Vikramaditya said slowly, once the councilors were through. "That is his only agenda, his *obsession*."

The councilors nodded.

"Why?" the king asked, wholly perplexed. "Doesn't anything else matter to him?"

Varahamihira shrugged. "Probably because he knows that is a weak spot. That he has you and the Queen Mother pinned down, and that you will not lie your way out of the situation. He has got you both where it hurts."

"But why?" Vikramaditya asked again, shaking his head. "*Why* this fixation with the Queen Mother? I can understand his anger at my letting Kalidasa leave Ujjayini, of feeling a sense of anguish and betrayal. Kalidasa is a grudge I understand, but not the Queen Mother."

"Yet, this is *not* about Kalidasa and the Hunas," said Dhanavantri decisively.

The silence stretched as the three men grappled with the puzzle that was Vararuchi.

"This isn't about Kalidasa and the Hunas, yet the men rallying behind Vararuchi have done so because *they* think that's what this is about—because that is what matters to *them*." Vikramaditya looked meaningfully at his councilors. "What happens when the concerns of these men have been addressed, when they have been assured that the palace is willing and capable of tackling Kalidasa and the Hunas? Where will that leave Vararuchi? Will these men still be prepared to back his demand that I step down as king? Would they then even care whether or not I am King Mahendraditya's son?"

Dhanavantri eyed Varahamihira out of the corner of his eye. "What is on your mind, Vikrama?"

The samrat straightened his back, stretching his neck to ease out a kink. "What I have in mind is very simple," he replied. "Our first job is to start winning back the support of the discontented factions of the Imperial Army—the factions that have been taken in by Vararuchi's rhetoric, and the factions that might still come under his influence. We reach out to the men and tell them that their concerns are valid, that the palace is conscious of these. We then assure the soldiers that the palace will never play with their lives, and that it has every intention of defending the integrity of Avanti against the invaders."

"You want messages to this effect to be sent to all the garrisons in Avanti?"

"Later, yes. But before that, I want to address the commanders and captains of all the garrisons in and around Ujjayini in person. Commanders of the Imperial Army, as well as those of any Frontier Guard units we have here. Include captains of the City Watch as well. And those of the *samsaptaka* divisions. I will speak to every unit chief whose job involves protecting Avanti."

"When do you want to do this?"

"First thing tomorrow morning," said Vikramaditya, rising from his seat. His shoulders were square, his eyes set on action. "If a message needs sending, why delay it?"

"And this message we will be sending… I suppose a more or less similarly worded message also goes to the Anartas as a reply to Yugandhara?" asked Varahamihira.

"To the Anartas. And to Viratapuri and Kausambi and Sravasti and Mahishmati. Let each one of our allies know where Avanti stands—firm and resolute at the frontier, ready to keep all challenges to Sindhuvarta and the throne of Avanti at bay."

"*All challenges at bay*—I like that." Varahamihira chuckled and looked up at Vikramaditya with a thin, knowing smile. "This plan of yours is good, Vikrama."

The samrat only stared back at the councilor, his expression shuttered and unreadable.

***

The banyan had been dead for a long, long time.

It stood in the middle of the broad plain, embedded so deep in the dry and dusty soil that it was immovable, its twisted trunk and roots fossilized in a way that no axe had been able to bring it down, despite the best efforts of Diti's doughtiest offspring. The danavas of old had once worshipped it as the life-tree, but with their passing, the tree had withered, as if mourning their fall, yet refusing to submit to the triumphant asuras.

A soft chuckle escaped Shukracharya's lips as he stood by the tree, running a hand over its trunk and feeling the ridged contours of the old wood under his palm. The asuras had done everything to tear the banyan—a symbol of danava resistance—down and had failed. Now the same despised tree was finally going to be of use to them, serving as a conduit between Patala and Borderworld, where the Ghoulmaster sat waiting for Vikramaditya, guarding Veeshada's dagger. Which, of course, he had no business guarding.

It was time Betaal was freed from that unnecessary responsibility.

Turning his thoughts away from the tree, Shukracharya cast his eye out into the plain, where the asura army was arrayed in a wide ring around the banyan, their horns curling proudly in the diffused half-light. The warriors were grouped in pairs, and each pair of asuras had the tips of their swords pressed against one another's throats, where the main artery was located. Their arms were rigid, ready to thrust and kill at a command, and they glared at each other, staring death in the eye. Every asura clutched a jagged javelin in his or her free hand.

Beyond the ring of asuras, further out in the plain, fifteen mutant war mahishas stood chained to heavy scaffolds. These mahishas bore resemblance to regular mahishas, but were bipedal, and had humanlike arms and trunks. The bison heads that rose from their thick, sinewy necks were crowned with big, curling horns that matched the bulk of their bodies. Asuras with long spears flanked each war mahisha, the speartips pressing into the beasts' necks. The mahishas themselves clutched broad double-headed axes that gleamed even in the dark of the plain, the axe handles cuffed to their wrists with chains. The beasts snorted and rolled their black bison eyes, stamping their hooved feet and straining at the scaffolding in impatience and anger.

"Is this the only way, mahaguru?"

The high priest turned to consider Holika, who stood to his left, along with the asura lord Hiranyaksha and a handful of asura courtiers. The Witch Queen of Patala was observing the asura warriors encircling them and the banyan in wide-eyed fascination.

"Death is the only known gateway to Borderworld,"

Shukracharya replied. "How will they find their way in if they won't die?"

"Does the human king also die before he enters Borderworld?" Hiranyaksha enquired. "Did *you* die before you made the same journey yourself, mahaguru?"

Shukracharya gave the questions a moment's thought before answering. "I cannot say about the human king with any certainty. All I know is that the Acharya, his chief councilor, helps him make the crossing. As for myself, yes, I did have to die on both the previous occasions."

Silence fell over the group and the plain.

"And it is the *sanjivani-mantra* that brought you back to life both times, mahaguru?"

"Yes. That is the role of the mantra."

"The mantra will bring these brave asuras back too, once they have helped you secure the Halahala? And the mahishas as well?"

Shukracharya hesitated. "It… that is my belief. But to be honest, I have never cast the *sanjivani-mantra* over such a large group before. I have no way of knowing the extent of the mantra's potency."

The group lapsed into silence again.

"But whatever happens, the mantra protects *you*, doesn't it?" Holika looked keenly at the high priest for reassurance. "Once you have the dagger, you *will* return."

Seeing the high priest nod, she let her breath out in relief. Hiranyaksha also relaxed visibly. "Then let us delay no further," he said.

Shukracharya stepped forward. "Brave warriors of Patala! We are at the crucial point of claiming the Halahala for ourselves, and the privilege of bringing the Halahala to Patala has fallen on your capable shoulders. Coming generations of asuras will be eternally grateful to you for what you are setting out to achieve this day. Hold your swords and javelins tight, for you will need them where we are going. Now go without fear and fight well. For Patala."

"For Patala. For asura glory," the asura warriors screamed back, not taking their eyes off one another, their swords unwavering.

Hiranyaksha waited for the roar to die down before signalling an asura minion, who struck a small brass gong. A heavy metallic clang shot from under the tree and bounded into the plain, slipping past the circle of asura warriors, who were already driving their swords into each other's throats. The ring muffled the grunts and choking sounds that escaped the dying asuras' lips, and it even softened the irate bellowing of the war mahishas as spears skewered into their necks. One by one, the asuras dropped to the dry earth, still retaining their grips on their javelins and swords, which were now tainted with the blood of their brothers and sisters. And the mahishas sagged heavily in their scaffolding, dying slowly as the blood leaked from their wounds. By the time the last echoes of the gong had dissipated into the open sands of the plain, there wasn't a single asura warrior left breathing around the plain. What remained was a crude circle of bodies, slumped and lifeless.

"The brave sons and daughters of Diti are on their way," Shukracharya said, taking in the scene with satisfaction. "I must follow them."

Still facing the plain, the high priest got down on his knees. Taking hold of his ironwood *danda* with one hand, he moved the iron-grey beard that covered his throat aside with the other. Invoking the Dasa-Mahavidyas for strength, he tipped his head back so his throat was fully exposed. He waited, gazing at the faraway stars, until Holika stepped into his view from behind, a sharp dagger in hand. She dithered, looking at Shukracharya in mild apprehension.

"Do it," the high priest said with a brisk nod. He then closed his eye.

Holika brought the dagger to Shukracharya's throat. For a brief moment, she was seized with uncertainty. Then, pressing the razor's edge into the soft, yielding flesh, she drew the dagger hard sideways, slashing the high priest's throat wide open.

Conspiracies

The turmeric-yellow flags in the hands of the heralds hung limp and dispirited, the peacock-feather ensign of Kosala lost in the curls and folds of the cloth, as if in hiding. With hardly a breeze blowing from across the Ajiravati, the air over Sravasti was still and heavy with foreboding as King Bhoomipala stood under a broad cotton parasol and surveyed the troops his generals had assembled.

"What are the numbers again?" he asked Adheepa.

"There are three thousand infantrymen, your honour," the old general answered. "In addition to that, a regiment of a hundred horsemen, and the archer brigades. Plus, we have managed raising a militia of retired soldiers that numbers around four hundred."

"We have *less* than three thousand infantrymen… and just *one* archer brigade, your honour," Kirtana clarified, looking pointedly at Adheepa. "A few hundred archers, in all."

Adheepa glared at the courtier in displeasure.

"It's the facts that count in war, not the exaggerations," Kirtana shot a glance back at the general.

"Wars are won on the back of belief, my friend," Adheepa

scowled. "An army must disregard facts and realities to fight impossible odds and gain impossible victories. An army should always be bigger than it is."

"Yes, but acknowledging the facts—"

"Alright, enough," Bhoomipala said, cutting in. Dabbing at the sheen of sweat forming on his forehead, he looked at the army standing before him, noting the listing shoulders of the men with a sour eye. No matter what Adheepa said, all he saw was a badly depleted army—barely three thousand five hundred strong—that bore an air of defeat even before it had left Sravasti for the border with Magadha.

"Will you be addressing the men, your honour?" Adheepa asked after a short pause.

"When they are all set to march," the king nodded. "Disperse them."

As Bhoomipala headed back towards the palace, the general stepped out from under the parasol's shade and signalled his commanders to get the troops back to the training grounds. He then hurried after his king, ducking into the welcoming shadow of the palace, where the young courtier, Kadru, stood in the company of a tall, dark-skinned stranger.

"Greetings, your honour," Kadru bowed.

The king inclined his head, glancing at the man with Kadru. The man immediately put his hands together in a *pranaam* and bowed.

"Your honour," said Kadru. "This is Ambalu, jewel of the Kikatas."

"Your good courtier is kind of heart and sweet of tongue," the Kikata replied with a nod in Kadru's direction. "Indeed, I am Ambalu, son of the Kikata tribe. At your disposal."

"Greetings," said Bhoomipala, looking up at his guest. "I am glad you agreed to meet."

"You want Councilor Pallavan avenged. We want Sajaya and countless other brothers and sisters who were killed in

Magadha avenged." The Kikata studied the faces around him. "There is value in cooperating against a common enemy."

A while later, they were all seated in the king's upper-floor chamber, overlooking the Ajiravati. Freshly squeezed lemon, sweetened with jaggery and cinnamon, had been served, and as he took a sip of the drink, Bhoomipala studied Ambalu. He had been expecting someone a little older to be leading the Kikata resistance within Magadha, whereas Ambalu was young, probably in his early twenties. He had the deep, mournful eyes so typical of his tribe, yet he moved with the speed and ease of youth, his muscles well developed on his lean frame.

"You know about Gajaketu?" Bhoomipala asked, running his fingers through his thick salt-and-pepper beard. "The musician?"

"The witness to King Siddhasena's murder and Sajaya's innocence," Ambalu nodded. "Courtier Kadru told us everything."

"Kosala is on the verge of declaring war on Magadha, even though the bulk of our army is at the frontier, defending Sindhuvarta from a barbarian attack. We have less than four thousand men at our disposal."

"While the Magadhan army is five, perhaps six times larger," Ambalu finished.

The king and his courtiers shifted uncomfortably.

"How many men do you have as part of your resistance?" Bhoomipala asked finally.

"Between two hundred and two-fifty."

Ambalu watched the king's jaw drop open in dismay. The Kosalan council exchanged dubious glances.

"That is hardly a number," Kirtana grimaced, scratching his broken nose.

Ambalu was silent for a moment. "There is an old saying among our people," he said. "If we can't burn bright as the sun, we can still glow like the firefly. For it is not the size of the light but its intent that dispels the darkness."

"There is wisdom and hope in what your people say," said Bhoomipala. "But one cannot ignore the size of the Magadhan army—"

"The Magadhan army your soldiers will face will not be so big," Ambalu butted in. Seeing the puzzled stares coming his way, he set his empty glass aside. "You forget that Magadha has occupied the Republic of Vanga, and to keep Vanga under his control, Shoorasena needs troops on the ground. There are over a thousand Magadhan soldiers guarding the iron mines in Dandakabhukti, while another thousand or so are stationed in Tamralipti. A further two thousand have been deployed over the republic's eighteen principalities to keep rebellions from sprouting. So, you already have four thousand less troops to contend with."

Adheepa, Kirtana and Kadru brightened and looked at their king. Bhoomipala thought that a breeze had suddenly struck up and blown through the room.

"There is more," the Kikata said, raising a finger to hold everyone's attention. "If I may ask, when do you plan to move against Magadha?"

"Probably in the next couple of days. Whenever the army is ready," the general replied.

"I would suggest a little delay, for I have information that Magadha plans to move against the kingdoms of Odra and Kalinga next." Seeing the surprise on the faces of the king and his men, Ambalu nodded. "Shoorasena wants to take the ports of Tosali and Uttara Tosali, so he can have a stranglehold on all trade to and from Sindhuvarta. Now, to move against Odra and Kalinga, he will mobilize soldiers from Vanga into action, but he will also need Magadhan troops whom he can trust completely. My guess is between twelve to fifteen thousand men. Once Shoorasena's campaign gets underway, the gap between Kosala's forces and the forces that remain in Magadha gets greatly reduced, see?"

Bhoomipala saw, and he liked what he saw. "How reliable is your information?"

"We have faith in our sources," the answer was cryptic. After a short pause, the Kikata said, "Let us not give Shoorasena any opportunity to suspect what we are planning. No beating of drums, no declaration of war. Let him think Kosala has learned its lesson from Councilor Pallavan's death. Let him think Kosala is dead on its back. Hit him when he is not expecting even a breath from us."

"We have already let the news of Gajaketu's presence here become public," Kirtana said. "Word of what he witnessed is already spreading and will soon reach Magadha. It is too late to suppress that, and Shoorasena will know we have leaked the news."

"That may have its advantages." Ambalu considered Bhoomipala thoughtfully. "Do you know who betrayed Councilor Pallavan to Shoorasena, who was ultimately responsible for the councilor's death?"

The king shook his head. The thought that someone must have snitched on Pallavan had not once crossed his mind.

"Courtier Asmabindu."

"King Siddhasena's legal advisor?" Bhoomipala gasped in shock. "It can't be. He was always loyal to Siddhasena..." His voice trailed off, disbelief giving way to doubt.

"Asmabindu betrayed the councilor, and his own colleagues, Uttama, Diganta and Bhaskara. The three courtiers were later falsely accused of conspiring with us, the Kikatas, and were executed."

"Asmabindu..." Bhoomipala whispered, struggling to make sense of it. "Why?"

"Ambition." Ambalu spat the word as if it explained everything. "With Vanga coming under Magadhan rule,

Asmabindu began nursing the dream of becoming Governor of Vanga. There were quite a few candidates for the post, so Asmabindu decided to prove his loyalty to Shoorasena and win the post as a reward. Councilor Pallavan was one of the four who paid the price of Asmabindu's ambition."

"The rat," Adheepa swore angrily. "When all this is over, we must make him pay for Pallavan's blood by flaying him alive. Till then, I hope the governor's seat he coveted is a thorny one for him."

"Despite doing everything, he hasn't got the post," the young Kikata chuckled. "The office has gone to the Vanga chief, Bhadraka, for switching his loyalties to Magadha. Word is that Bhadraka betrayed the other chieftains, hastening Vanga's fall."

"Serves the worm right," growled Bhoomipala, referring to Asmabindu.

"Asmabindu is very upset. Apparently, turning over Councilor Pallavan and the others was part of his deal to become Vanga's governor, but now that the deal is not being honoured by Shoorasena, Asmabindu is furious. He sees it as a betrayal."

"Treachery gets served treachery," said Kirtana with a smug nod of satisfaction.

"You are not getting the point," Ambalu said, leaning forward and staring at the king and his men. "There is someone is Magadha, *in the very heart of Girivraja*, who knows the truth about Gajaketu and King Siddhasena's death. This person has a grudge against Shoorasena. This is exactly the sort of person who can be of use to us."

"Are you implying that we ally with the man who has Pallavan's blood on his hands?" Adheepa gave a vehement scowl. "Never!"

"We can't," Kadru agreed.

"I am not asking that we be his friend. He used Councilor

Pallavan to further his end. We use him to further ours. If he will willingly turn against Shoorasena, help him. Strengthen him. Give him the means and the incentive." Ambalu looked entreatingly at Bhoomipala. "Allow him to help you bring Shoorasena down."

The king rolled the idea around, liking its texture. "How?" he asked cautiously.

"Reach out to him. Tell him we can deliver Gajaketu to him. He can take the credit for Gajaketu, for bringing the truth out. He can assume the part of Siddhasena's loyal man, seeking justice for his murdered king. He can become a hero to the people of Magadha. He can then ask for whatever he wants as his reward. A grateful kingdom will give it to him."

Bhoomipala ran a glance over his courtiers, who all looked very unhappy. "We are making a hero out of a villain," Kirtana mumbled. "Pallavan's soul won't forgive us."

"The objective of this fight is to defeat Shoorasena's designs," Bhoomipala reasoned. "Let us not lose sight of that."

"Pardon any disrespect, but is our objective not avenging the deaths of King Siddhasena and Pallavan?" asked Kirtana, still troubled.

"It is, but unless we defeat Shoorasena, no purpose is served," Bhoomipala replied. "Besides, we can still have our vengeance on Asmabindu, once Shoorasena has been dealt with. There are many ways of exacting revenge. We will find a way to get Asmabindu later."

"As long as that piece of scum is made to pay for his sins, I am okay with any plan," said Adheepa. The other two men nodded, reluctant, but also reassured by the king's promise.

Bhoomipala drew himself up in his seat and looked at Ambalu. "How do you propose to act on this?"

"Do you have anyone in Girivraja to whom the task of liaising with Asmabindu can be entrusted?"

"I am afraid not. Pallavan had contacts there, but by the looks of it, they are all dead."

"Never mind. I have people who can do what is necessary." The Kikata paused. "Meanwhile, though it may never come to it, let us continue preparing for battle."

***

"What do they mean they haven't seen him? *Somebody* should have seen him."

Amara Simha stared at the interpreter before switching his gaze to the five trembling Saka farmers standing before him and Angamitra. "It's one man in a desert that is flat and open… how could they have not seen him?" Gripping his battle-axe tighter, he glared at the men. "If they have him hidden away, tell them to come out with it or they will pay dearly."

"Where could they hide the prince, your honour?" the interpreter asked.

The councilor shot the interpreter a glance but turned away, knowing that the man was right. One look at the scattering of six mud-and-thatch huts that made up this scraggly Saka hamlet sprouting in the middle of nowhere, and it was plain that the place offered no scope for anyone to hold anyone captive. Moreover, these were just peasants and quarrymen, minding their own business of negotiating bad deals from the harshness of the desert.

Yet, Amara Simha was loath to take the villagers for their word.

Their search for Ghatakarpara was nearly two full days old now, and what had started as a seemingly straightforward ride east from Ki'barr had turned into a rambling and endless quest as they crisscrossed this patch of the Marusthali under a burning sun. They had come across nine Saka settlements in these two days—none as large as Ki'barr, and all poorly defended—but despite dire threats being issued to the *shy'ors* in each one of those, nowhere had anyone admitted to catching even a faint glimpse of Ghatakarpara. Now, as the sun went down on the day, Amara Simha felt desperation creeping in on him.

"Shall we be spending the night here, your honour?" the interpreter asked.

Amara Simha looked at Angamitra briefly before replying. "How far is the nearest habitation from here?"

The interpreter posed the question. Three of the villagers argued amongst themselves for a moment before agreeing. "Nearly half a day's walk to the north," said the interpreter. "A village of some twenty dwellings. But there is another village to the east, by the name of Gaiz. That one is approximately the same distance, maybe a little more. Much larger too, it seems."

The councilor heaved a sigh of exasperation. Where should they head next—north or east? Which of the two villages was more likely to have been on Ghatakarpara's path—*if* he had come this way at all? And what if the prince had been skirting the settlements to escape being seen and captured? How would any of the Sakas have seen him then? And if that's what he had done, how was the prince keeping himself alive, where was he getting the food and water to sustain himself? The questions kept piling up on top of each other, continuously nagging Amara Simha.

"Yes, we will have to spend the night here," he said finally. He could tell that the men were tired to their bones, and much as he wanted to get on with the search, rest was crucial, especially if they were to meet with resistance ahead—of which there was a steadily growing likelihood. Reports of their raid on Ki'barr would have reached the major Saka garrisons, while news of their visits to the Saka settlements would also be spreading rapidly. Amara Simha suspected that the Saka war chiefs had already begun deploying men in the towns and villages, shoring up defences, while the possibility of Saka search parties looking out for them couldn't be overruled. He had, as an afterthought, brought the *shy'or* of Ki'barr and the *shy'ors* of two of the larger Saka villages along with him as hostages, but he had no idea if any of them were important enough to guarantee him and his men safe passage. Amara Simha believed that eventually, this affair would demand a resolution with swords. That was why rest was needed.

As the interpreter relayed the decision to the frightened villagers—who then rushed to make arrangements to house and feed the soldiers, sharing what little they had so they didn't incur anyone's wrath—Angamitra went off to let his men know about the halt, leaving Amara Simha to walk to the shade of one of the huts and sit down, stretching his legs to ease the fatigue. The wound he had sustained on his back in Ki'barr still hurt, and he wondered if it had worsened in the heat of the sun. A timid little girl brought him a small basin of water, which he used to rinse the dust from his arms and face.

"I have told the men we leave two hours before daybreak."

The councilor looked up to find that Angamitra had returned. "Very good," he nodded in reply.

Squatting on his haunches, the commander of the *samsaptakas* picked up three mud pebbles that had come loose from the hut's foundation. Tossing one some distance away, he used a second pebble to try and hit the first. He missed. He chucked the third pebble at his target. He missed again. Blowing his cheeks out, Angamitra dusted his hands and sat on the ground, crossing his legs under him. Amara Simha noticed that the commander's arms had tanned deeply, while the skin on his face was stretched and red, peeling at the cheeks and on the nose. His lips were cracked from the dryness in the air. The councilor knew his own face was as ravaged from exposure to the sun, wind and endless dust of the desert.

"Which way do you think the prince went, your honour?" the *samsaptaka* asked.

Amara Simha looked at the commander with a sour smile and shrugged.

"We don't even know if he came anywhere close to where we are," he answered, looking out at the darkening desert, wondering if he would fail to keep the promise that he had made to Vikramaditya, to bring Ghatakarpara back to Ujjayini safely. An image of the king's nephew lying dead somewhere, sprawled face down and half-buried in the sand, sprang to the councilor's mind. Amara Simha blinked the picture away hastily and sighed. "We don't even know if we are looking in the right places."

"So, do we go north or east?" Angamitra asked. "North is closer, they said."

The councilor reached into the folds of his tunic and brought out a coin. "Wherever our destiny takes us," he replied. "Face up, north. Face down, east." He flipped the coin in the air.

Both men watched the bronze chip spin and rise. They watched the coin reach the top of its curve, then descend as gravity exerted its force. They watched the coin land on the hard ground, bounce once, and flip over. They watched it settle and lie in the dust.

Angamitra leaned forward to look at the coin. "Face down. East," he said. "To Gaiz."

***

The oracle lowered herself onto the bench slowly, allowing her stiff joints time to ease into position, one by one. The palace guard assigned to see to her needs held her by the shoulders, assisting her, though the oracle was tempted to tell him that if he really wanted to help, he should fetch a palanquin so she could return to her old, familiar life with the Wandering Tribe.

"Are you comfortable, mother?" he asked.

The oracle waved a hand in reply, not trusting her tongue at all, afraid that she would end up saying something ungracious and totally uncalled for. The man was simply doing his job and was actually being nice and courteous about it. She could not make him the target of her vexation with her life in the palace.

Taking out a small cloth pouch, the oracle shook a portion of crushed betel nuts into the cup of her palm. These she tossed expertly into her mouth, and as she began chewing, she contemplated the expanse of the palace lake, beyond which Ujjayini spread and unfolded, silhouetted against a gently darkening sky. The storm from the morning had washed the air clean, so the smell of jasmine filled the air, even though the terrace where the Mother Oracle sat had no flowering plants.

From somewhere in the city, temple bells began to ring, and for some reason, they reminded her of her daughter, Shanku's mother. The oracle gave this a moment's thought before concluding that almost everything reminded her of Shanku and her mother these days; she missed them both, Shanku more so as they had grown closer since she had come to the palace. That had been the only upside of coming to Ujjayini. And now even that was a thing of the past.

The Mother Oracle wondered where Shanku was at the moment, how she was faring in the Dandaka. When the girl had come to her and said that she was going into the Forest of the Exiles, the oracle had quailed, fearing for the girl, hating herself for having mentioned the danavas to Vikramaditya. She had, in a fit of irrationality, even considered concocting an omen to keep Shanku from going, a piece of fiction about some evil to come if the journey was not aborted. She could do it. She was the oracle. People would believe anything she said.

Then, an earlier conversation with her granddaughter had come back to her. Seated on a park bench, discussing Shanku's ability to vanish at will, she had told the girl how they had the freedom to choose what they wanted to do with the gifts they had each been blessed with—*the choice of doing something good with it*. Recalling those words, the oracle had suppressed her misgivings and blessed Shanku, instructing her to use her gift in the quest for Janasthana.

Still, she feared for the girl. And she missed her dearly. So much that she wondered about meeting Brichcha. Reading the spider webs, she had discerned how miserable her son-in-law was in the dungeon, lamenting his daughter's departure. They were two of a kind, she and the old warden, kindred souls, relics bound by their love for Shanku. Perhaps they could share their anguish and anxiety. Perhaps she could send the samrat a word, asking for a meeting with the man, she thought to herself as she listened to the lake lap against the palace's walls. The king would readily agree—

The Mother Oracle paused, stilling her thoughts. She listened.

She listened to the water gently striking the stone walls.

She listened. *There was something else...*

She tried to push herself up, but the effort was too much for her.

"Young man," she hailed the guard. "Quick. Help me stand."

Once she was on her feet, propped up with the guard's support, she shuffled to the edge of the terrace and leaned over the parapet.

"Be careful," the guard said, his voice rising in concern. "You will fall—"

"Shh-shhh," the oracle motioned with her hand, frowning.

The guard watched the Mother Oracle, her head cocked, listening. He peered down at the lake curiously. All he saw was the dark, brooding water, and the blur of two fish, flipping their tails and slinking into the lake's depths.

"Send word to the king, to anyone who is in charge," the oracle said. "There is a dead body in the lake."

"Where?" The guard bent sharply over the water.

"Be careful or *you* will be the one to fall in," the Mother Oracle snapped. "You can't see the body. It is not down there. It is somewhere in the lake. I overheard the fish talking about it. Don't stand there with your mouth open—go inform someone about it."

It took the guard a little while to return with three men. One of them was a short man with a slightly crooked nose and a grey beard. "I am Vismaya, chief of the Palace Guards," he said, introducing himself. "I have heard about you, mother, but we haven't met."

The oracle repeated what she had already told the guard. The chief waited for her to finish, then bowed. "Thank you for letting us know, mother." He looked closely at her. "Whose dead body is it?"

"How would the fish know?" the oracle shrugged.

"Right," Vismaya nodded. "Is it that of a human?"

"Yes. Why would I have bothered you otherwise?"

"You wouldn't be able to tell us where we should start searching for the body, would you?"

"No, the fish didn't say."

"That is alright, mother. I shall have the entire lake searched." He paused and glanced at the sky, deep purple in colour. "It is growing cold out here. Would you like to be escorted back to your chamber, mother?"

The Mother Oracle nodded. The guard offered his hand for support and they walked out of the terrace.

"Notify everyone in the palace about the body," said Vismaya to the men accompanying him. "And inform the boatmen on the Kshipra that we will need some of them to trawl the lake. They can start tomorrow morning."

"How many men would we need, chief?" one of the guards asked.

"I don't know. Five, six... How many men would it need to find a dead body in a lake of this size?" He shrugged. "Let them send as many as they can."

Vismaya turned his back to his men and looked into the lake, deep in thought. The setting sun fleetingly caught his face, and in its flares and shadows, for a brief moment Matali's features emerged, staring darkly into the black waters.

***

The rain had returned immediately after sunset, opening with the sound and fury that had marked the morning's storm, before losing its vigour and settling into a sedate drizzle that now fell on Vararuchi's shoulders as he crossed the garrison ground and made his way back to his quarters. He had chosen to eat with his men that evening, knowing that gestures like these strengthened the bonds of brotherhood and allegiance, and after nearly half-a-dozen rounds of firewater and singing and jesting, he could tell that he had done the right thing. Now, feeling the warmth of the firewater steal through his body, he smiled in contentment as he climbed the stairs to his rooms.

The smile and the contentment lasted exactly up to the door of his council chamber.

As he neared the door, a soldier stepped out from inside the chamber. The man's hair was wet and stuck to his scalp, and his clothes were damp and beaded with rainwater. His hassled expression changed to relief when he saw Vararuchi. Recognizing him as one of the guards at the main gate, the councilor eyed the man in surprise. The soldier bowed and stole a quick peek into the chamber before addressing Vararuchi.

"There is a visitor for you, your honour," he said, keeping his voice down.

A visitor? So late in the night?

"She insisted on seeing you right away, your honour. She was adamant—"

She?

"Who is it?" Vararuchi asked, approaching the door. He craned his neck to look in.

And his eyebrows rose in surprise—while his spirit slumped to the floor to lie at his feet, crumpled and joyless.

"How are you, my brother?" asked Pralupi, turning from the window to look at him. "Come right in. I believe these are your rooms."

Vararuchi nodded to the soldier, dismissing him. He then crossed the threshold and entered the chamber, shutting the door behind him.

"Nice place you have here," the princess said, casting a critical eye around, examining the room from floor to ceiling, taking in the crude architecture of the garrison, which was totally at odds with the refinements of the palace that Pralupi was so accustomed to. "Your own council chamber," she arched her brows at Vararuchi. "Not very fancy, but I imagine this is temporary. One step away from the one in the palace, am I right?"

Vararuchi stared at her. Pralupi looked at him and smiled thinly. "Right?"

"What do you want?" the councilor asked.

"Oh, straight to the point." Still smiling, the princess chuckled. "Not very chatty."

"You and I were never chatty."

"You have a point there." Pralupi came around and sat down on a chair. "Will you not sit down?"

"I prefer to stand. Actually," Vararuchi glanced at the window, "I should be retiring for the night. I have a busy day ahead, so if you can tell me what you are here for, we could both be done quickly. You could head back to the palace, and I could go off to bed."

The princess's nostrils flared in temper at the councilor's words and a retort boiled to her lips, only to be stifled at the very last moment. Swallowing her anger, Pralupi smoothened the creases on the shawl she was wearing and brushed off a few drops of rainwater from her shoulder before she looked at Vararuchi.

"I am here to help you."

Vararuchi didn't let the surprise show on his face. "In what way?"

"In your fight against Vikrama."

This time, Vararuchi couldn't stop himself from gaping at his half-sister.

"Why are you looking at me like that?" Pralupi stared back at the councilor.

A bitter smile crossed Vararuchi's lips. "You have hardly ever spoken *one* civil word to me, Pralupi. We have barely talked at all in the last ten years. We have practically been strangers to one another all our lives. I fail to understand why you would suddenly want to help me."

"Because you are my brother."

"And Vikrama is not?" Vararuchi scrutinized the princess's face.

Pralupi wrinkled her nose and dismissed the question with a wave of her hand. "He is the son of some deva. Not like you and I. We share the same father. We are tied by blood."

"You and he share the same mother," Vararuchi said flatly.

"Who cheated on our father," Pralupi spat in disdain. "She doesn't even count."

The rain had intensified a little, drumming on the tiled

roof. The councilor remained silent, wondering where this was coming from and what this was leading to. All through his adolescence, this woman had never once acknowledged him as anything more than an appendage to the palace, someone who existed on the fringes of her consciousness because he was of some value to her father, and later, after Mahendraditya's death, to her younger brother. After Ghatakarpara's birth, when Vararuchi had visited Kausambi to see his nephew, Pralupi hadn't even come out to greet him; it was King Chandravardhan who had escorted Vararuchi to meet and bless the newborn.

"How exactly do you intend to help me?" he asked.

"I'm glad we are finally talking about things that matter," said Pralupi. "For someone who was in a tearing hurry to retire for the day, you were wasting a lot of time on needless conversation."

Vararuchi crossed his arms and waited.

"Okay, what I can do for you is give you more muck to throw at Vikrama."

"I don't understand," said the councilor.

"You want to discredit Vikrama. You want to malign him, drag his name through the dirt, show everyone how unworthy he is of being king of Avanti. You want him off that throne so you can have it for yourself—"

"I do not want the throne," Vararuchi cut in harshly.

"Fine. I don't care either way. But you *do* want Vikrama humiliated. I will give you an opportunity to humiliate him further."

"How?"

"By way of another public scandal." Seeing the shock on the councilor's face, Pralupi gave a sly smile. "I'll help you strip away one more layer of respectability that makes Vikrama everyone's beloved king, a layer that makes him honourable in the people's eyes, adding to his aura of invincibility. I will have at least one more member of the council turn against him. The pieces are already set for the little game to begin, brother, and the game will commence very soon. We only need to wait for Vikrama to fall into the trap."

Unable to believe his ears, Vararuchi blinked at his sister, wondering what devious scheme she had devised, and stunned by the malice in her eyes and her words. He didn't understand this hatred—where had it come from so suddenly? What had Vikramaditya done to earn this spiteful woman's displeasure?

"You said Vikrama will lose one more of his councilors. Who?"

"I am glad you like what you are hearing," the princess said, smiling wickedly at her brother. "Eager for the details, I see. Everything will be revealed when the time is right. Patience." She paused and drew a breath. "You do realize that this help comes at a price."

Of course.

"You say you don't want the throne..." Pralupi looked at Vararuchi with narrowed eyes and offered him a smile that said she didn't believe him. "Okay... but after Vikrama ceases to be king, no matter who sits on the throne, I want *you* to promise me this in exchange for what I am going to do to Vikrama."

Vararuchi waited, not knowing what to expect.

"I want you to help Ghatakarpara become the next king of Vatsa."

The councilor was so taken aback that he stopped breathing for a second.

"How can I—"

"Oh, come on," said Pralupi, throwing her hands up in frustration. "You brothers ask too many questions. You don't think enough for yourselves. Do I have to tell you every little thing? There are so many ways of convincing Chandravardhan to agree to this. This is Avanti, and you will be its king. Just do it, brother. Like I said, I promise you a scandal you will love."

Vararuchi stared at the floor, struggling to make sense of everything. Where had the succession of Vatsa come into all this? For how long had Pralupi been nursing these wild ambitions for her son? And was Vikramaditya going to pay the penalty of having turned down the same demand that Pralupi had placed before him?

"It is late, and you have a busy day tomorrow," said the princess, rising abruptly from her seat. "I shall be in touch." As she moved past the councilor, heading for the door, she added, "The shaming of Vikrama is assured. You just have to keep your end of the bargain, brother."

The door closed, and Vararuchi heard Pralupi's footsteps go down the stairs and fade away. In the silence that followed, he heard her words ringing in his head.

I want you to help Ghatakarpara become the next king of Vatsa.

The shaming of Vikrama is assured. You just have to keep your end of the bargain, brother.

***

The fog pressed in on the asura army as it tramped through the wet, open marshland, Shukracharya and the asuras in front, the war mahishas bringing up the rear, their heavy, cloven feet churning the chalky mud so that a deep, mangled trail unfolded in their wake. Now and then, drops of rain fell on heads and shoulders from above, though whatever was above was lost in the fog. Except for the muted sound of marching feet, the silence was absolute, the fog growing dense so only the jagged curves of the lances and the tossing horns of the mahishas could be seen, thrusting and waving through rips in the drifting whiteness.

"Are we anywhere close, mahaguru?" one of the asuras

marching at the head of the column next to the high priest asked, peering into the thick curtain ahead of them.

"I don't know," Shukracharya answered, feeling the bile of irritation rise inside him.

He had always disliked Borderworld for its flat, featureless evenness. And the fog—for some reason, particularly severe on this occasion—made it even harder to tell one's exact whereabouts. It could take forever for someone to find his way around this place. And right now, the high priest's problem was compounded by the fact that he had with him an army of two hundred asuras and fifteen mahishas who were already dead in Patala. He didn't know how long the effects of the *sanjivani-mantra* would last over this army, so if they didn't find and force a way into Betaal's citadel quickly enough, there was a distinct likelihood of the mantra's powers fading, and him being left with dead asuras and mahishas here as well, for the Ghoulmaster's ghouls to quietly dispose of.

And no Veeshada's dagger to show for all the effort.

"We can't be very far," he said, more in hope than anything else.

They trudged along for a while longer, the rain increasing in intensity, as if to mark their progress. At the same time, an intermittent breeze began blowing, driving the fog before it. The chill brought a shiver to Shukracharya, but he was thankful for the breeze. If it sustained for long enough, it might help disperse the fog so they could see better—

"I smell something."

The high priest turned to the asura who had spoken in surprise. "What is it?"

"I don't know, mahaguru... but something..." The asura sniffed, seeking the elusive smell.

Lifting his *danda* high, Shukracharya called out. "At the count of five, everyone stops. One... two..." This was the only way an army that was stumbling through fog could come to a halt without crashing into itself and toppling over, cutting itself on its own weapons.

Once the entire force had drawn to a stop, the high priest turned to the asura. “Is the smell still there?”

The asuras standing nearby all raised their noses to the air, sniffing.

“It’s gone,” the first asura said, looking disheartened. “I’m certain I wasn’t imagining it—”

“It’s there,” another asura pointed excitedly as the breeze shifted. “I’m getting it.”

“Something burning,” said a third. “Burning flesh.”

“A fire.” Shukracharya’s eyes shone in relief. “A funeral pyre.”

The asuras looked at each other and grinned. Word rapidly spread to the very back of the column and a low, eager chatter took to the air.

“Where is the smell coming from?” asked the high priest.

One asura licked her finger and held it up in the breeze. “That way,” she said, pointing to the column’s left and a little behind.

In a matter of a few seconds, the entire army had veered around and was loping in the direction the asura had indicated. Where a little while ago they had looked tired and dispirited, the asuras were now bursting with energy and intent, propelling themselves forward in the belief that their quest was at its end. And sure enough, through the fog, one by one, the pyres of Borderworld came into view, burning orange and arranged in rows that went as far as the eye could see.

Shukracharya was at the head of the column when, all of a sudden, like a conjuror’s trick, the fog fell away to reveal the entire cremation ground. And rising from the centre of the ground was the gigantic banyan, its enormous trunk many dozen yards thick, the spread of its colossal canopy over the pyres a veritable sky beneath the sky.

The banyan that holds up the field of endless pyres.

The abode of Betaal, the Ghoulmaster.

"Veeshada's dagger is somewhere inside that tree," the high priest yelled, pointing. "Once the mahishas bring the tree down, the Halahala will be ours."

As one, the asuras lifted their weapons and screamed into the silence. The next moment, they were a raging torrent, racing towards the banyan, the war mahishas up in front, their massive axes raised to destroy the beating heart of Borderworld.

Disappointments

The swords were gleaming arcs in the firelight, slicing the air in great circles as the troupe of eight dancers leaped and twirled to the beat of the drums. The fire, the orange of the dancers' costumes, their turmeric face paint; everything was coordinated for effect, a yellow-orange blur of rising rhythm and movement in Vetala Bhatta's eye.

The drumming broke, tapering into silence, and the dancers pulled apart, stepping away from the bonfire with the stealth of tigers, swords drawn and poised, shields up against their chins. A reed pipe began playing, sharp and thrumming with anticipation, and the dancers tiptoed around the fire, watching each other closely. Then, at a choreographed cue that the Acharya didn't see coming, the drums rolled in fury and the dancers sprang at one another, shields coming together in a deafening crash, swords clashing with a violence that made the sparks fly. And suddenly there was fire everywhere as a band of jugglers flitted between the warring dancers, dodging swords and expertly tossing and catching brands of fire.

Fire and firewater mixed, and the spirit of the festivities spread through Uttara Tosali, setting the city alight in its celebration of a successful harvest. There was rejoicing everywhere, save for the one table that had been set apart from the rest of the feasting—the ceremonial table where Vetala Bhatta and Chancellor Sudasan now sat with Queen Abhirami and King Veerayanka, all of them pretending to be entertained by the dancers, jugglers and poets, while their minds were decidedly elsewhere.

At a sign from the queen, a heavy curtain was drawn around the table, blocking off the view and cutting out the noise, cordoning the table off from everything else—and insulating the merrymaking outside from the grimy realities of politics, the raj-guru thought to himself as he sat up in his seat. The queen waited for the attendants to refill the cups of *soma*, and it was only when they were just the four of them that she spoke.

"Let me understand this," she said, looking from Sudasan to the Acharya, before going back to the chancellor. "Shoorasena of Magadha has invaded the republic of Vanga and has put to death many members of Vanga's Grand Assembly."

"Seventeen members, good queen, including the chiefs of four of our principalities," said Sudasan.

"Yes," Abhirami said, and from the tightening of her jaw, Vetala Bhatta deduced that she hadn't appreciated the interruption. She was a stately woman, in her early forties, the Acharya guessed, her hair streaked very lightly with grey, her age showing in the lines around her brown eyes. But for her dour, unsmiling demeanour, she would have been distinctly pleasant looking.

"And Shoorasena's men are hunting for the rest of the chiefs, which is why you are in our court." The queen shot a glance at her brother sitting at her side. "Correct?"

"Absolutely, my queen," said the chancellor.

"And you, raj-guru... are here because Magadha has captured Vanga's iron mines and now also controls the port of Tamralipti."

"Yes, good queen."

"You have a shortage of iron, so your king would want us to share iron from our mines—"

"*Trade*, good queen. Not share." The Acharya knew the interruption would displease, but it was important to make that distinction.

"Trade, yes. But that would still mean giving it away," Abhirami smiled thinly.

"In exchange of something of value that you may want," Vetala Bhatta smiled, hoping the smile didn't look overly eager or enthusiastic.

"But there is nothing we want." Abhirami turned to Veerayanka again. "Is there?"

The king shrugged and shook his head. He was younger to his sister by a few years, the Acharya could tell. They shared the same long nose, broad forehead and high cheekbones. Veerayanka also had a flowing, well-maintained black beard.

"You would also like us to open our ports to you for trade," the queen said.

"To Avanti, and with your permission, to the rest of the kingdoms of Sindhuvarta."

Abhirami wet her lips with a sip of the wine and sat in contemplation for a moment, elbows on the table, her fingers crossed. The drums had fallen silent, but the sounds of revelry came in a murmur, interspersed with bursts of laughter.

"There is no confusion over what you want, raj-guru," she said at last. "But you..." she turned to Sudasan with a troubled frown. "What do *you* want from us? I mean... are you looking for military support? Do you want us to help you reclaim Vanga by overthrowing Magadha? What exactly do you seek?"

The chancellor looked at Vetala Bhatta and licked his lips. "To be honest, good queen, we were only looking for political asylum. That was all we wanted when we docked our ships in your harbour." Sudasan paused and looked from Abhirami to Veerayanka with freshly kindled hope. "But if you are willing to back a military campaign against Shoorasena and topple—"

"And why would we do that?" Abhirami asked, peering at the chancellor.

"I... don't know..." Sudasan mumbled, taken off guard. "You... just said that..."

The Acharya felt like smacking his head in frustration. The chancellor was ruining it for himself, and if he wasn't careful, he would ruin it for everyone else in Sindhuvarta as well.

"We didn't say," the queen said pointedly. "I only asked."

"Yes... good queen, yes." Sudasan took a sip of the *soma* to calm himself. "Indeed... asylum is fine. Just fine. If you could grant us that—"

"And why would we do that?"

The chancellor blinked at Abhirami, then stared at Veerayanka and the raj-guru, not comprehending. "The chiefs of Vanga and I have come here with much hope, queen and king," he said finally. "Don't turn us away, please."

"If we do grant you asylum, we will inevitably earn Shoorasena's displeasure," said Abhirami. "Why would we want that? Why would we want to cross Magadha's path when it has done us no harm? Why should we get into a disagreement that has nothing to do with us?" She turned to her brother, who nodded in support.

"The same goes for you," she said, turning to Vetala Bhatta. "When we furnish you with iron and open new trade routes for you, we are siding with you against Magadha. Why? Why should we take sides when this does not even concern us?"

"At times, it is important to side with what is right, even if there is nothing personal at stake," said Vetala Bhatta softly. "Sometimes, not taking sides is the worst mistake one can make."

"The raj-guru is right," Sudasan leaned forward in his

earnestness, forgetting etiquette for a moment. "We, in Vanga, never took sides on matters pertaining to Sindhuvarta. We genuinely believed that as long as we left everyone alone, everyone would leave us alone. Look where that has brought Vanga, good queen. I implore you not to make the same mistake."

Abhirami and Veerayanka looked at one another grimly.

"Moreover, by not assisting us or the kind chancellor here, aren't you already picking one side over the other?" asked the raj-guru.

"We simply do not go chasing after war," said Veerayanka, speaking for the first time but dodging the question entirely.

Vetala Bhatta smiled thinly at the king. "War is not prey that anyone can chase at will. War is a predator that hunts us as *it* wishes."

The siblings exchanged glances again. The Acharya wondered what was going through their minds, why there was such reluctance to commit to helping. He wished he had his spear and some privacy so he could tap into their thoughts and figure out what was locked up in there, and which keys to turn. He decided he had neither the time nor the patience for that.

"I noticed that you dance your beautiful dance with swords," he said, gesturing at the curtain. "Is that all you will ever use those weapons for?"

"In my opinion, we have made ourselves fairly clear," said Abhirami coldly, pushing her cup away and rising abruptly. Veerayanka also stood up, and the raj-guru was pleased to see that his face under the beard was suddenly red. The fire wasn't entirely dead here. There was hope.

Abhirami stared at the Acharya. "I wish you a good night's sleep. I am assuming we won't be seeing you in the morning."

"With your permission, I will probably leave very early," Vetala Bhatta nodded in reply.

Abhirami was turning away when Sudasan addressed her,

his voice quavering a little. "What about me and the surviving chiefs of Vanga?"

"You may stay here a week." The queen looked at the chancellor. "It would take you that long to stock up on provisions and get your ships in proper shape to sail again."

***

Powered by the might of the war mahishas, the axes bit deep into the tree, taking out thick slivers of wood and bark with every hefty swing. Again and again the axes descended, and at each blow, Betaal felt the tree shake, even though he knew it was just his fancy. But there was nothing imaginary about the screams coming from the ghouls who were trying to protect the tree—and failing miserably. The ghouls threw themselves on the asura army, only to be cut down by their javelins, and the ground around the banyan was quickly piling up with their bodies, thin and ripped open, part flesh and bone, part formless spirit.

Betaal let go of the attendant ghoul's hand and opened his eyes so the points of red light in the hollows showed again. He had seen enough of what was happening outside, in the field of the pyres, to recognize the threat that the asura army posed. And any doubts about this army's intent had been cleared the moment he saw who was commanding the asura force.

Guru Shukracharya, the asura high priest himself.

Betaal looked down at the dagger. It fit neatly into the palm of his hand and weighed practically nothing, a crude weapon with a hilt made of obsidian, something seemingly so ordinary and inconsequential it shouldn't have merited a second glance. Yet, Betaal could feel the full weight of its burden pressing down on him and on all of Borderworld, as he considered the implications of the asura attack.

"The tree won't be able to withstand the mahishas' axes for

long, Ghoulmaster," said the attendant ghoul. "The mahishas number more than a dozen."

"How large is the asura army?" asked Betaal.

"A couple of hundred. We are no match for their strength and their swords. We cannot hold them back much longer."

Betaal nodded, strands of fire from his flaming locks coming loose and falling away to the floor. The ghouls were not warriors, neither by nature nor by training. And there had never been a need for guards here; there had never been anything in Borderworld worth protecting, worth stealing. Until now.

"Can't we give them what they are here for?" said a second ghoul.

Betaal closed his fingers around the dagger. "Not without me breaking a promise."

"Then how shall we save the tree, Ghoulmaster?" the first ghoul asked, sounding more and more frantic. "What should we do?"

There was only one thing to do.

"Leave me for now. But keep me informed."

When he was alone, Betaal opened his fist and glanced at the dagger. Now that the asuras were at his doorstep, he distinctly remembered their coming, their ruthlessness, stopping at nothing in their greed to claim the dagger. This was Borderworld, the future of everything, where everything had already happened before. Only, as usual, he did not know what happened after this; whether the asuras prevailed, whether he was able to save the tree, whether he was able to keep the promise made to the human king. He would remember after the events had played themselves out. But by then, it would probably be too late.

Betaal held the dagger up to his hollowed eyes, looking at the hilt, polished and ink black. He waited for the light to emerge from its opaque core. And it did, a haunting, swirling iridescence, the blue scattered with pinpricks of gold and silver.

The light of destruction.

There was only one thing to do.

Closing his eyes, the Ghoulmaster raised his skeletal face and began whispering.

Wise king... Borderworld is in danger... The dagger is in danger... I fear I will fail to honour my promise... And I fear that in my failure, you *will fail to honour your promise to the Omniscient One... Come to me, wise king... Come and take the dagger back... Relieve me of its responsibility, for I can keep it no more... Come, so Borderworld can be saved... Come, so the Halahala can be saved... Do you hear me, king?... Come... come...*

Betaal stopped to listen, his head cocked. He then whispered again, repeating his plea, calling out to Vikramaditya. He listened again, this time for longer.

At last, with a futile shake of his head, he opened his eyes.

The human king was not listening. The human king was not asleep.

Betaal looked at the dagger with a troubled sigh. If the king didn't sleep soon, he wouldn't be able get through and warn the king about the danger the Halahala was in.

And he wouldn't be able to save the tree and Borderworld.

***

Kicking away the light quilt that covered him up to his knees, Vikramaditya sat up in bed with a sigh and stared at the semi-darkness of his bedchamber. He blinked and pressed his palms to his eyes, feeling the fatigue, but being unable to fall asleep. He had lain there, tossing and turning, his mind a circus of thoughts, their ceaseless chatter keeping him awake. Tired and frustrated, he now swung his feet off the bed, not knowing what to do next. Picking up a light shawl and wrapping it over his shoulders, he stepped onto the adjacent balcony, where a freshening breeze took him in its embrace and began playing with his hair.

The hour was late, and the palace was quiet, with only the guards up and about their business. Across the lake, Ujjayini was silent too, its lights winking out even as the samrat watched. The usual trills and hoots of the night birds were absent as well, and even the roll of thunder was missing from the lightning that flashed above the western horizon. The hush was everywhere except inside his head, Vikramaditya thought wryly as he breathed in deep, wishing the air would cleanse his mind of everything that was preventing him from sleeping.

The swoop of a bird low over the lake, a shadow hunting for its prey, snapped the king out of his thoughts. He tried to follow the arc of the bird, but it was already lost in the darkness. Looking down at the lake and imagining quiet ripples forming on its surface, Vikramaditya's mind went back to the dead body that was lying somewhere in its depths. It was Vismaya who had reported the Mother Oracle's message to the council, and the man had efficiently also conducted a headcount of every member in the palace, which included the guards and the palace hands. No one had been found missing or was unaccounted for, which only deepened the mystery of the body in the lake.

The samrat was wondering what surprise the upcoming search would throw up when he heard the door to his bedchamber open softly. Alerted by some primal instinct, the king tensed and took a step backwards, concealing himself in the shadow of a curtain. He then peered cautiously into the room, seeking the intruder out in the dark.

There was no need to look for the intruder.

The door to the bedchamber was thrown wide open, and light from the gallery shone in through it. Framed in that rectangle of gold was the slender silhouette of a woman, the lamplight falling softly on one bare shoulder and glinting off one of her earrings. As Vikramaditya frowned in puzzlement, the heady scent of *champaka* filled the room and came to the balcony in a gentle tide.

"My king?" the woman called in a voice that had the lilt of a songbird.

"Who is it?" Vikramaditya demanded. He had heard that voice before, but he couldn't quite place it.

"Mithyamayi, your honour. Princess Pralupi's maid."

Now he remembered that voice. The samrat entered the bedchamber. "What is it?"

The maid took a step into the room as well, her anklets chiming sweetly. "The princess wishes to see you, my king. In her chambers."

"At this time of the night?"

"Yes, your honour."

"Really?" Vikramaditya squinted at the silhouette, straining to see her better. It would help if he lit a lamp, but his feet felt chained to the spot. His eyes too refused to leave the svelte figure, as if afraid that she would be gone when they looked back. "What is it about?"

"The princess didn't say, my king." The maid's hands were graceful like a dancer's, and the king stared, mesmerized. "She only said that it was a matter of importance."

The fragrance from the *champaka* flowers was making Vikramaditya giddy. He felt trapped. He wasn't being able to think. "Let her know I will see her shortly," he said, fighting for breath.

The maid turned and left the room, and a sense of loss assailed the samrat. The shadows in the bedchamber came crowding around him, and something heavy clutched at his heart. He felt a crying need to be held close and comforted. Even the light in the gallery outside appeared to pale a little, the brightness leaching away in grief.

Shaking his head to clear the fog of despair, Vikramaditya went to a small fountain and splashed his face with cold water. As he towelled himself dry, he turned his thoughts to Pralupi's sudden and desperate demand to meet, certain that it had everything to do with Ghatakarpara and the throne of Vatsa. He reckoned it would have been best to ignore the summons and deal with Pralupi's pique in the morning, but back then, with the maid standing in the half-light, the simple act of thinking had proved daunting. And now it was too late to do anything but go and see his sister.

When he arrived at Pralupi's doorstep, the door was shut. The king rapped on it twice, then pushed it open and walked into the antechamber.

"You wished to see me, sister?" he called.

The was no response. Picking the door to his left, the samrat entered the landscaped balcony, which was lit by three cloth lanterns that had come all the way from Srivijaya. He walked along the stone pathway leading to the small pond, listening to the soft gush of the miniature waterfall and expecting Pralupi to be seated on a stone bench or the teakwood swing. But except for the birds in their cages overhead, the balcony was empty.

"Sister?" he called once again, just to make sure.

Nothing.

Guessing that Pralupi was in her bedchamber—probably asleep, he thought, hope and relief surging together—Vikramaditya was about to turn back when he caught the scent of *champaka*. The same instant, the tinkle of anklets rose to his ears, and the king knew the maid had made an appearance.

The samrat turned, and for a full moment, he was dazzled by the sight of Urvashi. The apsara stood in the balcony, halfway to the antechamber, bathed in the glow of the lanterns, one hand on her hip, the other hanging casually by her side. Her hair was done up with *champaka* blossoms, and her eyes were lined with kohl—eyes that assessed the king with a mixture of shyness and unabashed desire, challenging him, making the blood beat quicker in his veins.

"Where is the princess?" he asked, the words struggling to form themselves on his tongue.

"She isn't here, my king."

There was a teasing smile on those luscious lips now. It struck Vikramaditya that the maid had disappeared altogether. What remained was a woman of mystery.

"I thought she wanted to see me."

"*She* didn't. I did."

The apsara walked towards the samrat, the soft light intensifying the sway of her hips, throwing shadows over the flowing lines of her breasts and stomach. She stopped when she was an arm's length away, her head tilted, her chin raised, the neck arching sensually.

"Does my sister know about this?" Vikramaditya asked, his eyes narrowing.

Urvashi didn't reply immediately. Instead, narrowing the distance between them, she raised a hand to Vikramaditya's face and lightly traced the outline of his beard with her finger. "Does it matter?" she asked, fluttering her lashes. The air was heavy with the fragrance of *champaka*.

"Who are you?" the king asked, stepping away.

Urvashi smiled and immediately closed the distance again. "Whoever you want me to be, my king," she whispered, draping her arms around the samrat's neck and drawing him closer. She pressed herself to him, her softness begging to be touched, her breath honey on Vikramaditya's lips. "I can be anything you fancy."

The night went still around the king and the apsara, holding its breath as Urvashi melted into the man's body with desire, her lips brushing the king's.

"Let me be the love you yearn for," she sighed, pouring her soul into her words.

Taking the apsara by her wrists, the samrat disengaged himself gently from her clasp. "That's not possible," he said.

"Why?" Urvashi gazed up at the king with doe-like eyes, her hand slipping quickly into Vikramaditya's, her fingers entwining with his. "Let me show you," she smiled seductively, tugging him towards the swing. "Come."

"No." The samrat resisted. "I want *you* to come with me."

Urvashi bit her lip, her eyes delicious pools of excitement. "Take me wherever you wish, my king," she gave a mischievous laugh.

Vikramaditya walked out of the balcony, the apsara following close behind. They traversed two galleries and went down two flights of stairs before arriving at a door. The samrat knocked lightly, and it opened a crack to reveal the sleepy face of a maid.

"Your honour," the maid said, bowing and pulling the door open.

Stepping through, the king motioned to Urvashi. "Come."

Urvashi found herself in a bedchamber. A solitary lamp illuminated the room, and in its light, she saw a large bed hung with lace curtains. On it lay a woman, pale and thin, staring blankly in front of her. An aging matron hurried to her feet, bowing silently to the samrat.

"I wish to be left alone," Vikramaditya said to the matron and the maid.

He waited for the door to shut completely before approaching the bed. Urvashi hung back, suddenly no longer in control, no longer sure of herself.

"Come," the samrat again beckoned kindly.

The apsara went up to the bed and looked down at the woman, who showed no sign of having noticed either of them. She was beautiful, but her skin had a deathly pallor, and her gaze seemed to be looking into a precipice, into the depths of some deep, subterranean crypt. An involuntary shiver escaped Urvashi.

"This is Vishakha, queen of Avanti, the light of my life," said Vikramaditya. "She has been like this for the past two years, ever since she took a fall off a horse's back. She just lies here and stares. I have no way of knowing what she is thinking, what she is seeing in her mind—if at all she can see and think in the place she is now." The king paused to look at the queen, and in that moment of silence, the apsara sensed the pain under Vikramaditya's composure. "For a short while, she did recover, but then she fell again and went back to being the way you see her now."

"Tell me..." he turned to look at Urvashi, "...can you be her? The only woman I have ever loved—*the love I yearn for*? The one who will not speak, and not listen when I tell her that I love her?"

Grabbing her roughly by the elbow, the samrat pulled Urvashi closer to the bed. "Is there anything you would do to be her, lying like this all day, all week, all year round?" he asked, glaring into those kohl-rimmed eyes in anger. Urvashi flinched and tried to pull away, but the king wouldn't let go of her, holding her arm tight. "Would you be willing to sacrifice everything you have for this? *No, you won't*. Yet *this* is who I love," he shouted, pointing at Vishakha in anguish. "*This* is who I want to hold in my arms, who I want to sing to sleep, night after night."

A tremor ran through Urvashi and passed to Vikramaditya. The samrat blinked and let go of the apsara's arm. He exhaled, getting a hold on himself. The next words he spoke were milder, more forgiving. "You said you could become whoever I wanted you to be, whatever I fancied. No, Mithyamayi. We mustn't change like that for love; it wouldn't be love at all. If anything, it is *love* that changes us, transforms us, makes us better than who we are. When you understand this difference, you would have understood love. Go now. There is still some night left for sleep."

Without a word, Urvashi headed for the door. Turning to Vishakha with a sigh, Vikramaditya sat down by her side and gently took one hand of hers in his. He brought the hand up to his lips and kissed it, then pressed it to his cheek as he looked into the queen's face.

Vishakha didn't react when a tear from the king's eye fell and rolled down her hand, leaving its wet trail of pathos on her skin.

The samrat was lost in his torment, so he didn't notice Urvashi stop momentarily at the door and look back at him, sitting by Vishakha, holding her hand, his head bowed, his shoulders hunched.

The apsara watched the king and queen for a moment. And then she was gone.

***

Listen to my call, Samrat... the asuras are here for the dagger... I cannot protect it any longer... Come and save Borderworld from destruction, king... Take the Halahala back... I need your help, Samrat Vikramaditya... Are you listening to me?... King...?

The Ghoulmaster stopped and listened for a response. There was nothing.

He closed his eyes again and began whispering in rising desperation.

Samrat Vikramaditya... You must listen to me... the Halahala is in danger...

"The mahishas have cut through nearly a quarter of the tree, Ghoulmaster."

Betaal opened his eyes and stared at the attendant ghouls.

He wanted to see for himself, but he didn't have the courage to do so. The two ghouls wouldn't be making this up, he was sure.

"And we have lost too many of our brothers to the asuras' swords and javelins. It is hopeless trying to fight them."

"You must plead with them to stop this madness, Ghoulmaster. That might work."

"It will not," replied Betaal, feeling the helplessness, feeling powerless to do anything about it. "They are not here to negotiate. They are not here to listen to anyone's pleas. They are not here to show mercy. They are here for the dagger, and they will not leave until they have it."

"We can't let the tree fall."

Betaal nodded unhappily.

"Is the human king not coming to our help?" asked a ghoul.

"For some reason, the human king isn't falling asleep," said Betaal.

The two attendant ghouls looked at Betaal in despair.

"There is one way of saving the tree—the dagger and I will have to leave its protection," the Ghoulmaster said at last. "If the dagger is not inside the tree, what would be the point of cutting it down?"

"But if you leave the safety of the tree, how will the dagger be safe?"

"It is a risk that we will have to take for the sake of the tree and Borderworld," Betaal replied. He paused thoughtfully. "But I have an idea that might just buy us time."

Ultimatum

The sun had only just cleared the horizon, so the shadows of the garrison buildings were still long on the ground, offering plenty of shade to the men who had assembled in the central garrison's inner courtyard. In all, there were approximately forty of them, a motley crowd of commanders and captains of the Imperial Army, the Frontier Guard and the City Watch, in addition to four captains of the *samsaptakas*. The men huddled in small groups, chatting among themselves, occasionally hailing an acquaintance in another group across the courtyard. The atmosphere was friendly, but there was also nervous tension—and a spot of guarded anticipation—in the way the men kept glancing towards the main door that led to the courtyard.

Matali stood all by himself in a corner of the courtyard, by the trunk of a stout neem tree, observing the soldiers through hooded eyes. These were the men who would have to face the brunt of the attack when the Ashvins and the naga and kinnara forces led by Takshaka and Tribhanu came to tear this city apart under his master's orders. Matali smiled inwardly as laughter erupted in one of the groups. It wouldn't be funny when Avanti's dead began piling up. He almost felt sorry for these men.

"Vismaya, my friend. It's been a long time..."

Matali turned to see a man wearing the silver medallion of a captain of the City Watch approaching him with long, bounding strides. The man had a wide grin on his broad, dark face, and his arms were flung open, ready to draw Matali into a bear hug. The deva had no idea who the man was, but he was plainly a very dear friend of Vismaya's. Matali pushed a suitably pleased smile into his face, but by then, he was lost in the man's embrace.

"How have you been?" The captain let go of Matali only partially, holding him by the shoulders and beaming into his face. "Look at you—chief of the Palace Guards, eh?" He clapped Matali on the shoulders proudly before finally releasing his hold. "I heard about the appointment in Lava. That medallion suits you. Well deserved, I must say."

"Thank you, my friend. How are you?" Taking his cue from what the captain had said, Matali quickly added, "When did you return to Ujjayini?"

"Two days ago." He paused, his face darkened, and his voice dropped. "So much has happened since I left. Councilor Kalidasa is gone, Councilor Vararuchi has... well... and half the city has been evacuated. It's hard to believe all this is really happening." He paused, then brightened. "Well, at least you are chief of the Palace Guards. That is one good thing that has come out of all of this."

Matali bowed and smiled but said nothing. He wished the captain would leave him alone. The man knew Vismaya well, and Matali was afraid a prolonged conversation would throw up his lack of familiarity with Vismaya's life, setting the captain wondering about him, raising his suspicions. He just wished something would divert the man, make him go away...

"You are very quiet," the man said suddenly. "What's the matter? Aren't you happy to see an old friend?"

"What? No, of course I am. It's just that I am a bit distracted with all this..." the deva waved his hand in the general direction of the courtyard.

"Ah yes, overseeing the Samrat's security. I understand. That's why you are here."

"Actually no," Matali replied. "The Samrat wants to address senior officers of every military division responsible for the defence of Avanti. I represent the Palace Guards."

"Oh, of course." The captain turned away, but almost immediately swivelled back. "I heard that a niece of yours has come to the city?" He peered at Matali. "I didn't know you had a niece."

"I didn't know either," Matali chuckled and scratched his grey beard.

"Where did she come from?"

"Viswapuri," said Matali, refusing to volunteer anything more.

"I see." The captain looked away, puzzled. Matali cursed under his breath. This was not going well.

"This niece... what's her name?" The man had the persistence of a horsefly.

"Mithyamayi," the deva said tersely, turning away. He hoped his brusqueness would hasten the end to this conversation.

"Mithyamayi." The captain thought about it and nodded slowly. "I'm told she is now Princess Pralupi's maid?"

"Mm-hmm." Matali avoided the man's searching gaze.

"That's good." The captain nodded again, satisfied. Then, "You must come home for lunch one of these days. Dheera was asking about you." He smiled at Matali.

Surprised at the sudden change in the subject, the deva sighed in quiet relief. "I will. How is Dheera?" He hadn't the faintest clue whom he was enquiring about.

"She is well. Expecting our next one." The man made an imaginary bump in the air near his lower belly to explain himself better, before waggling four fingers at Matali.

"Nice. And oh, congratulations."

The captain grinned his thanks, then gestured towards the door. "The Samrat's address... you are in the palace. You probably know what he wants to say." He looked at Matali hopefully.

"I don't," the deva replied. "Honestly."

The captain nodded again, then leaned in closer. "Do you think what Indra said about the Samrat's father is true?" he whispered. "That the Samrat is Indra's grandson?"

A sudden flurry of activity at the door spared Matali from replying. Two commanders of the garrison marched in, shouting orders for everyone to fall into disciplined lines as the king was expected at any moment. There was a rush of feet, and the captain slipped away towards his own units with a wave at Matali. Being the only one from the Palace Guards to be present here, the deva continued standing under the tree.

The samrat walked in through the door, and Matali's eyes widened as they went to the swords strapped to the king's waist. The sword handles were plain, the scabbards made of very old leather. He had heard enough about that pair to identify them correctly—and by the murmur that had broken out in the courtyard, so had the men charged with defending Avanti.

"Silence," one of the commanders ordered. "The Samrat will speak now."

As everyone waited for the soldiers to quieten down, Matali observed Vikramaditya. The king stood with his feet apart, his back straight and his chest thrust out, arms akimbo, the hands resting lightly on his hips, right next to the sword handles. He exuded an air of confidence, the manner of a man who had mastered the misfortunes that life had sent his way. Yet, his eyes looked drawn and tired as he took in the rows of men standing before him, though his tone was friendly and accessible when he spoke. The words themselves were carefully chosen to carry the full authority of the throne.

"Brave warriors of Avanti," he began. "I have a secret to share with you, something I have never told anyone ever before." A pause for effect. "Whenever I look upon you, my chest swells with pride. Because in you, I see a love for Avanti that is so deep that the very earth is rich and fragrant with it, giving back to us its gifts for generations to come. And when I look at you, great relief and great joy course through my veins. Because in you, I see the future of Avanti, secure from all threats, strong and assured like a deeply rooted banyan in a storm. You warriors will never let harm come to this land; that is how much you love Avanti."

"Which is why, today, in front of me I see faces etched with doubt and uncertainty. And why not? You love this land very much; it is natural to fear for its future. Fear, not because some enemy threatens to come at us. *Enemies* don't rattle us. *Enemies*, we know how to deal with. Fear, because one of our *own* has changed sides, and we are not sure how to fight our own. So, I look at your doubts, and my heart skips a beat in anxiety."

"But now is the time to still the heart and silence all those doubts. For what is there to doubt? When one of our own crosses over, he ceases being one of us. *He becomes the enemy*. And as I said, enemies count for nothing—we know precisely how to deal with them." The samrat's hands crossed and went to the hilts of the swords. In one swift, smooth move, both swords were drawn from their sheaths, the high-pitched zinging of the blades loud in the silence of the courtyard.

"We will deal with our enemies—*every last one of them*—exactly the way we've been taught how to."

The samrat held the swords away from his body, and as Matali watched, fascinated, the blades burned hot and caught fire. Small gasps and whispers erupted across the courtyard, but Matali was too absorbed in studying the Hellfires to notice. He licked his lips, marvelling at Diti's creations, which were meant to bring the devas to their knees. Fortunately for the devas, no asura hitherto had been able to wield these swords and summon the malevolent powers infused in them, but now this human... Matali looked at Vikramaditya in admiration. The man knew the power of words. He also knew the power of the weapons he held in his hands. The soldiers were in his thrall.

"In some quarters, there is this feeling—born entirely out of love and concern for Avanti's wellbeing—that the palace made a mistake in letting Councilor Kalidasa leave Ujjayini. That the councilor's intricate knowledge of our strengths will work against us in battle. Warriors of Avanti..." the samrat raised his voice, simultaneously lifting the Hellfires to shoulder-level. As if in response, the flames spurted along the length of the blades. "...what intricate knowledge can stop these swords, I ask? And what intricate knowledge can stop any one of you, the hardiest and bloodiest of fighters that Sindhuvarta has ever produced? Our strength is our faith in ourselves, and our faith is limitless. That is why the palace does not fear what Councilor Kalidasa may do. That is why Avanti will not be breached."

Vikramaditya raised one of the Hellfires over his head, pointing it at the sky. "You have my word that when the time comes, we will cut down every hand raised against Avanti," he roared. "We will bury old friendships in the same battlefield where we will bury the ambitions of our enemies. *We are Avanti. We are the sun itself. Look at us, and you will burn.*"

"Avanti... Avanti... Avanti... Avanti..."

The chant rose spontaneously from the men, growing in pitch and volume, as clenched fists pumped the air and sandaled feet stamped on the courtyard's stones.

"Avanti... Avanti... Avanti... Avanti..."

The words reached a crescendo and became a furious stream of sound, flooding the courtyard and spilling out of the garrison, washing down streets and taking everyone up in its tide.

"Avanti… Avanti… Avanti…"

Before he even realized it, Matali's heart was beating to the rhythm of the chant.

***

Urvashi ran her fingers through her hair absentmindedly, spreading the scented oil in long and delicate strokes. Her feet were dipped into the water up to her narrow ankles. She sat on the steps of the bath, in a patch of dimpled sunlight, the hem of her *uttariya* trailing in the water, her eyes staring at nothing. Even the drooping flight of a flycatcher, white and showy against the mossy greens and browns of the bath, failed to stir the apsara out of her thoughts.

Can you be her, the only woman I have ever loved?

The image of the samrat, sitting beside his queen and holding her hand, returned to Urvashi.

The only woman I have ever loved…

When she had walked onto that balcony decorated with ferns and lit by exotic lanterns, she had been certain of the outcome of her mission. She was an apsara. She was more than an apsara—she was Urvashi, the most desirable of all apsaras, with hardly a rival in Devaloka. She was trained in the art of love. She had every deva lusting after her. She was irresistible.

And yet, Vikramaditya had resisted her.

For a woman who lay in a bed, as good as dead.

The only woman I have ever loved…

How was that possible? He was a man, and more than that, he was a king. He could love as many women as he wanted. That was what she had been taught in Devaloka, where apsaras fulfilled only one role—that of letting the devas love them. What kind of man could love only one woman?

The kind who sees women as more than objects of desire, who holds women in esteem.

The thought came out of nowhere, surprising the apsara, shaking her out of her reflections. It was a new idea, one that had never occurred to her before. But was it even possible, could such men even exist? The notion was so alien that Urvashi frowned, ready to dismiss it.

Then something came back to her.

It had been the day she had come to Ujjayini with Indra and Gandharvasena, the day Indra had confronted Vikramaditya with the truth about his real father. Indra's march to the palace had been stopped by Vikramaditya, and there on the streets of Ujjayini, the deva and the human king had engaged in a war of words. And in full view of Ujjayini's citizens, Indra had stunned the samrat with the secret about Gandharvasena. But when Vikramaditya rejected the deva's assertions, contending that Mahendraditya was his father, Indra had suggested a way of settling the matter.

Let us both agree that your mother's word will be final. Let us ask Queen Mother Upashruti who your father is—her dead husband, King Mahendraditya, as you claim, or my son, Gandharvasena, as I insist.

Urvashi clearly remembered sitting in the veiled box of the chariot, listening to the silence on the street that morning, as Indra's challenge rang in everyone's ears.

And she remembered Vikramaditya's answer.

I will not insult my mother by having her character put to test just because someone comes along questioning my paternity. I will not allow you to humiliate my mother in front of her people. I don't know how you treat your women in Devaloka, but in Avanti, the dignity and honour of our women is sacrosanct...

That was the kind of man who could love just one woman all his life.

"There you are." The voice startled Urvashi. She turned to see a palace maid standing at the head of the steps to the bath, looking very annoyed. "The princess is throwing a fit, asking for you. Hurry up."

The maid turned and left without waiting for an answer.

The apsara sighed. Pralupi was habitually a late riser, but today was different, Urvashi knew. She also knew she should have been better prepared. She just didn't know how.

When she finally pushed past the door to Pralupi's bedchamber, the apsara saw the princess pacing the room feverishly, her nervous energy barely contained in her tightly coiled body and clenched fists. Urvashi noticed the pile of clothes lying on the floor, crushed, damp and splattered with mud.

"Salutations, princess."

Pralupi stopped her pacing and glared at Urvashi, hands on her hips. "Where have you been?"

"I was having a bath—"

"Well, couldn't you have been quicker? You know how I hate tardiness."

"Apologies, princess. I was—"

"Enough," Pralupi raised a palm flat out. "I have no interest in discussing this further. I want you to come quicker when I call, that's all."

Then, as if none of this mattered, the princess's manner changed, her eyes brightening with excitement. "So," she asked in a tone that could be mistaken as being friendly, "how did it go?"

Urvashi hesitated, wondering how best to say this, not certain what reaction to expect. Pralupi peered at the apsara, eyes beady in anticipation, head bobbing in encouragement. "So?"

"The Samrat… declined."

"Declined?" Pralupi stared. "Declined what?"

"The Samrat declined my attentions, princess."

"Oh." Pralupi's eyes narrowed, and despite the warmth of the sun flooding in through the high windows, a chill crept into the atmosphere. Pralupi walked to a table and poured a cup of water for herself. She drank the water, then looked back at Urvashi.

"I set everything up perfectly for you, and still you failed." She paused in disdain. "If your beauty does not serve any purpose, you are pretty much worthless to me, Mithyamayi. If you can't charm a man into your arms, you must find employment elsewhere." The princess turned her back to the apsara. "Let your uncle know I will not be needing your services—"

"Princess, please wait."

Urvashi took a hurried step towards Pralupi, her mind frantic. She couldn't leave the palace without finding out the Halahala's whereabouts. What would she tell Matali? That she had failed to seduce the king, and the princess had thrown her out because of that? And Indra would be furious with her for having come so close to the human king and still failed…

"*Please* don't send me away, princess," Urvashi joined her hands in entreaty. "I will… I will try again. With the Samrat. I promise I will."

Pralupi stared at the apsara for a long moment. "You will have to try a lot harder than you have."

"I will, princess," the apsara replied with a sigh of relief. "Please, trust me."

Pralupi turned and walked off towards the window. "Ready everything for my bath. And take those wet clothes away."

Urvashi was leaving with the pile of clothes when the princess called after her.

"I don't have forever, which means *you* don't have forever.

You have two days to work your magic on the king. Two days."

The apsara left the chamber, still wondering what the princess was playing at, why having her maid seduce her own brother was so important to her. She figured it was really none of her business. She was just thankful for the opportunity the princess was giving her to get close to the king.

A king who was so different from anyone she had met before, noble yet also kind…

Two days, Urvashi reminded herself with a shake of her head. Two days to find the location of Veeshada's dagger.

***

He slipped through the fog, doing his best to stick to the thickest and densest patches, conscious that his flaming hair could easily betray him to the asuras who were hot on his trail. He dodged and sidled, continuously moving away from the tree, yet revealing himself in short flashes so that the asuras stayed interested in the chase.

The escape from the banyan had been traumatic and was achieved only by dint of a huge sacrifice on the part of the ghouls. The ghouls had come to the tree in large numbers and beset the asuras and the mahishas, fighting and falling in droves, making no impact on the attacking army, yet distracting it long enough for the Ghoulmaster to leave the tree and find refuge in the fog. With so many ghouls now gone and the tree severely damaged, Betaal realized that the architecture of Borderworld had undergone a fundamental shift, that it would never be the place it had been before.

"What is in it for you, Ghoulmaster?"

The voice came over the marsh, disembodied, needling and challenging, almost echoing his own thoughts.

"What do you get in exchange for all that you have lost today?"

Betaal didn't reply. Instead, he slid into a heavier cloak of fog.

"What has the human king given you that you are willing to bear so much for him?"

Silence.

"Why do you even care who has the dagger? Give it to us, and we shall leave in peace. You have my promise."

Betaal turned left so he could circle back towards the tree. He didn't want to get so far away that he couldn't return to it fast enough.

"I know you are in there, Betaal. I know you can hear me."

Away in the distance, Betaal saw a knot of asuras groping through the fog in search of him. He wondered if he should reveal himself just a bit.

"Okay, let me make you an offer. Hand us the dagger, and you and your ghouls can come and reside in Patala. How is that? No? Okay, if that is not good enough, here is something that cannot be beaten." A pause. "In exchange for the dagger, you can reside in Amaravati. Who wouldn't want that? Oh... you wonder how I can make that promise? Believe me, when we have the dagger, all of Devaloka will be ours to do as we please."

Betaal hovered in the fog. The dagger felt hard in his palm.

"What do you say? Amaravati for the dagger? Think about it. The asuras will not go back on their word. I, Shukracharya, promise you that."

The mahaguru himself, the ghoul realized. He should have guessed.

Betaal moved away. He did not want to reveal himself to Shukracharya.

A little while passed before the voice came again.

"Did you think about what I said?"

The Ghoulmaster tried to see where the voice was coming from.

"This is your last chance to agree." There was an impatient edge in the voice now.

"Are you there? Of course, you are there." The voice became ominous. "Very clever, I must say."

Betaal tensed.

"Hiding in the fog with the dagger, knowing you will be hard to find. Tiring us in this game of hide-and-seek." Shukracharya chuckled. "Ingenious, you think. Toying with us like this."

Suddenly the voice was angry. Very angry.

"Let us play a different game now. No place in Patala for you, no place in Amaravati. Those deals are off. You will now give over the dagger just to save the one place you have."

Betaal felt the fog grip him, cold and full of menace.

"I am ordering the mahishas to go back to cutting down your tree, *your home*. They will not stop until you have surrendered the dagger to me, Ghoulmaster."

Shukracharya paused to let what he had just said take hold of Betaal's imagination.

"New deal. Your tree for the dagger."

A deathly hush fell over the marsh. Betaal stood in the drifting fog, alone and utterly defenceless.

***

"Whose body could it be?" asked Kshapanaka, leaning out of the window to watch the man enter the water with a splash.

"It is a complete mystery," Vikramaditya replied, joining her to look down at the boatmen in the lake. A dozen of them had been searching the waters all morning, and they had almost cleared the south end of the lake without finding anything.

"A body here doesn't make sense," said Kshapanaka. "Could the oracle be wrong?"

"We know she never is."

They went back to observing the boatmen dive and disappear underwater.

"How is the evacuation going?" the samrat enquired.

"Well enough. We have managed vacating more than half of the city."

"Any resistance?"

"There is bound to be some," Kshapanaka looked at the king. "But we are handling it with as much care and sensitivity as possible." She stared at Ujjayini, across the lake. "Some of them are so adamant. There is one woman in the northern quarter, a widow. Her husband died when the deva horsemen attacked. He was a soldier in the City Watch, it seems. She refuses to leave her house; she says she would rather die where her husband lived and served. She is the only one remaining in her locality. Everyone else has left."

"Let her be, don't compel her," said Vikramaditya. "But make sure someone from the City Watch keeps an eye on her. And leave instructions that should the city come under attack, she is to be escorted to the palace. She can take shelter in the Labyrinth."

Kshapanaka nodded at the king thoughtfully. "Then there are these two households in the eastern section. Both refuse to vacate..." she cleared her throat, "...insisting they won't obey the orders of someone who... who is not worthy of being the king of Avanti."

Vikramaditya looked at Kshapanaka, then turned away.

"I made enquiries," the councilor said. "Both houses belong to families related to the garrison chief of Musili. Commander Sharamana. Vararuchi's right-hand man."

"Where in the eastern section?"

"Close to the old cattle market." Kshapanaka swatted at a passing fly. "What should we do about them?"

"Nothing," the samrat replied. "Keep an eye on them as well."

Before Kshapanaka could add anything more, the door to the council chamber opened to let Varahamihira and Dhanavantri in. The former gave a wide grin as soon as he caught sight of Vikramaditya.

"I passed the central garrison on my way here and stopped to meet some of my engineers," he said, limping quickly into the room. "The mood there is thoroughly upbeat. Your address has worked like a charm. All they are talking about is your speech—and the Hellfires, of course." Varahamihira came up to the king and clapped him enthusiastically on the shoulder. "What a superb idea it was, talking directly to the men. You have won them over, Vikrama. Watch the word spread from here."

The samrat gave a tired smile but said nothing.

"Here," said Dhanavantri, holding out a small wicker basket. "Madari made these. I thought I would bring some along."

"What is it?" asked Varahamihira.

Before the physician could reply, Kshapanaka had lifted the cloth covering the basket. "*Til laddoos*," she exclaimed. "I love these."

"Madari makes these so well," Varahamihira said, helping himself to two.

"I know you love them."

"Having them right before lunch is not a good idea," Kshapanaka smiled as she took a couple as well.

"What's the occasion?" asked Vikramaditya, popping one into his mouth, waiting for the flavours of sesame and jaggery to burst on his palate. "Mmh… delicious."

"The occasion is the grand speech from the morning,"

Varahamihira grinned. Then, turning serious, he asked, "You wouldn't have that speech written down, would you?"

"No, though I did make a few notes last night."

"A pity. But we could still use the notes to draft the message to the Anartas—"

"That won't be necessary," Dhanavantri interjected. "I had one of the palace scribes attend the speech, so we have most of it recorded."

"Excellent," Varahamihira rubbed his hands in satisfaction.

Vikramaditya walked to a nearby chair and slumped into it.

"You look fatigued," Kshapanaka observed, licking some jaggery off her thumb. "Are you alright?"

"I'm fine. It's just that I haven't slept a wink all of last night."

"Why?" Varahamihira peered down at Vikramaditya.

"So many things," the samrat said, shaking his head vaguely. "Thoughts mostly, not letting me sleep."

"Thoughts about what?"

"Well, there's Vishakha," the king took a deep breath. He looked at Dhanavantri briefly, as Kshapanaka stared out of the window. Varahamihira put a hand on Vikramaditya's shoulder but said nothing.

"Then there is Ghatakarpara and Amara Simha. There has been no news from them—or *of* them—since Amara Simha left Udaypuri and rode into the desert. What am I to tell Pralupi? She is his mother, after all, and it was my decision, sending him to the frontier. Then there is Shanku in the Dandaka..."

"Shanku is strong," Kshapanaka countered. "She can take good care of herself. She needs you to trust her, not worry about her. And as far as Ghatakarpara is concerned, Amara Simha has promised to bring him back, and he will."

"That is exactly what I tell myself too," said Vikramaditya with a sigh. "It is actually Ujjayini and its people that I am most concerned about. Some have lost loved ones; others have lost their livelihoods. I fear more are set to lose both, and it pains me to know that I am the cause of all this uncertainty. They had no part in my decision to protect the Halahala, yet they are paying the price of that decision. That is so unfair. What kind of king would do this to his people?"

"You did what was right with the Halahala, and now you are doing what is right for your people," Dhanavantri seated himself opposite the king and looked into his face. "As king, you will always be forced to reconcile opposites and balance out causes and effects. This is the lot of the king, the burden of the crown. Accept it, Vikrama."

"I have." A wry smile danced briefly on the samrat's lips. "Don't forget that just this morning, I declared war against my oldest friend, the closest I ever had. And by doing that, I have manipulated public opinion to wrest the initiative from my brother, for whom I have only had love and respect. In one morning of good work, I have lost a friend and a brother *here*," he rapped his chest where his heart beat. "The king's lot, I get it." Stretching his neck, he smiled. "It's just that being king can get a little tiring at times."

"I don't have a cure for being king yet," said Dhanavantri, chuckling softly, "but I can give you something for the tiredness. Something that will help you sleep."

"Right now," said Vikramaditya, rubbing his eyelids, "sleep would be a welcome gift."

***

"Thank you for coming, raj-guru. And do forgive us if we came across as being a trifle rude yesterday."

"Pardon me as well if I unwittingly overstepped any boundaries, queen and king."

Seated on the royal divan, Veerayanka and Abhirami nodded. "Do sit down, raj-guru," the queen said.

The Acharya bowed and took his seat diagonally opposite Sudasan and six other men who, he presumed, were the remaining chiefs of Vanga. His eyes met the chancellor's, and they nodded at one another in a silent greeting. Abhirami was conferring with her brother and a couple of her councilors, so Vetala Bhatta had the luxury of surveying the chamber, which was airy, tastefully adorned, and offered an inland view of Uttara Tosali. From where he sat, the raj-guru could see bullock carts loaded with stalks of paddy trundling to the city's granaries, while closer to the palace, fisherwomen bore the morning's catch to the market in broad baskets, trailed by noisy crows that tried to get at the fish when the women weren't looking.

"I suppose you know what this is about, raj-guru. Have you been briefed yet?"

"The men you sent to fetch me gave me a broad idea, but I am weak on the details," the Acharya looked across at Abhirami. "From what I have gathered, you have received a report of a Magadhan attack being planned on Odra?"

The Acharya and his company of soldiers had left the palace right after daybreak and had been on the road for nearly three hours when a couple of riders had caught up with them. The riders told the raj-guru that Queen Abhirami had learned of a Magadhan plot to invade Odra, and hence, she had requested him to return to the palace immediately. He had been escorted straight to the royal chamber, where they now sat in discussion.

"Yes, apparently, plans to invade Odra are at a fairly advanced stage," said Abhirami. "That is what we have gathered from the report we've received."

"How advanced are these plans exactly?" asked the Acharya.

"It seems Magadhan troops have started arriving in Tamralipti in the thousands, and Vanga's ships are being fitted and readied for war. We are told Vanga has some thirty seaworthy ships."

Abhirami looked at Sudasan for confirmation. Sudasan nodded but quickly added, "They aren't war ships, really. More trade vessels, my queen."

"But they can transport troops, can't they?"

Sudasan and his chiefs nodded.

"If I may ask, how did you come by the report?" Vetala Bhatta enquired. "To the best of my knowledge, you don't have spies in Vanga..."

"We heard about the plot from a trade ship that docked in Uttara Tosali yesterday evening," said Veerayanka, looking at Sudasan and the chiefs.

"A trade ship?" the Acharya wondered. "From where?"

"Vanga."

"Vanga?" Vetala Bhatta blinked in confusion and stared at Sudasan. "But Odra does not trade with Vanga, so what was the trade ship doing in Uttara Tosali?"

"We don't trade with anyone," Abhirami corrected. "It appears the ship was bound for one of the Southern Kingdoms but was running low on drinking water. It came here for a refill." After a pause, she added, "We make those allowances."

The raj-guru looked across at Sudasan. "What else did the ship's crew and captain say about the Magadhan war plans, chancellor?"

"We didn't even get to meet them," said Sudasan ruefully. The six Vanga chiefs shook their heads, looking positively gutted. "By the time we came to know they were here, the ship had left."

"I don't understand." The Acharya stared from Sudasan to Abhirami. "Why was it allowed to leave?"

"The masters of the dock have been instructed not to

permit visiting ships to linger for long," said Abhirami, sounding a tad regretful. "Once the drinking water had been taken on board, the ship must have been encouraged to move out of anchorage."

"Then how did the news about the Magadhan plan get to the palace?"

"Someone on the ship mentioned it to one of the guards at the dock," said Veerayanka. "The guard notified his captain, who brought the news to us."

"And by the time anyone here could react, the ship had sailed," Vetala Bhatta spoke under his breath, staring at the chamber's black granite floor, deep in thought.

"Raj-guru, you were right yesterday when you said that war is a predator that hunts us," said Abhirami. "We have done our best to avoid crossing anyone's path and picking up any fights, yet we see that we cannot always escape confrontation. You were also correct in saying we must side with what is right; it has taken the threat of an invasion for us to open our eyes to the merit of your words. Our apologies. We will make quick amends, though." She turned to Sudasan. "My brother and I open the doors of Kalinga and Odra to you and the chiefs of Vanga. You may stay here as long as you want."

Sudasan and the chiefs got to their feet, put their palms together and bowed low in gratitude. "Our most sincere thanks, queen and king," the chancellor's voice quavered with relief. "We owe you a debt of gratitude, which we hope we can repay."

Abhirami nodded and turned to the Acharya. "As a token of our thanks to you, raj-guru, we are willing to grant Avanti…" she stopped on seeing that Vetala Bhatta was not listening to her. "Raj-guru… is… everything alright?"

The Acharya lifted his head and considered the queen before turning to Sudasan. "I have a question. Ships from Vanga have been navigating these seas for generations now. So, when a trade ship sets sail from Tamralipti for the Southern Kingdoms, is it common for drinking water to run out mid-voyage?"

Sudasan looked at the raj-guru closely for a moment, then glanced at his chiefs. "It is highly unlikely," he said at last. "Our captains have a very good measure of the amount of food and water that needs to be stocked. They hardly every err in this, and moreover, rationing is very strict. It is a matter of life and death, after all."

"So, a water shortage like this one couldn't have occurred on a Vangan ship?" the raj-guru leaned forward eagerly.

"Shortages can always occur," one of the chiefs replied. "An accident, maybe. There is only so much you can budget for."

"Yes, that is true," the Acharya admitted. "Except that this ship was heading for the Southern Kingdoms, which means it was close to the start of its voyage in Tamralipti. Why would they have a water shortage so near home, less than a quarter of the way to their destination? That would be terrible budgeting, wouldn't you say?"

"What is your point, raj-guru?" Abhirami asked.

"I see the raj-guru's point," said Sudasan, looking troubled. "Also, even if the ship had been running low on water, why would they veer so far off course to come to Uttara Tosali, which is almost to the west of Tamralipti? It would be far more sensible to stay the course and go to Tosali, which lies to the south, in the general direction of the ship's destination. Coming to Uttara Tosali for a refill does not make sense."

"I still fail to see the point," said Abhirami, a little tetchily.

"The point is straightforward, my queen," said Vetala Bhatta. "A ship from Vanga docks here, purportedly to refill drinking water. Someone on that ship quietly slips your guard information about a Magadhan invasion being organized in Tamralipti, an invasion involving a fleet of Vanga vessels. Before this informer can be questioned further about the plot, the ship leaves Uttara Tosali. Going by what the chancellor and I just discussed, it is obvious that the water shortage on that ship was only a pretext for it to dock here, so that the report about the invasion could be planted."

"Somebody went out of their way to let us know that an invasion was in the offing," said Veerayanka. "What is wrong with that? We owe whoever it was our thanks."

"If that individual, whoever he is, was doing you a favour, why the need for so much secrecy?" asked the Acharya.

"Because he fears for his life," said one of the chiefs. "You forget that Vanga is under Magadhan rule, and there are traitors everywhere in Tamralipti."

The rest of the chiefs nodded and murmured in agreement.

"There are traitors everywhere, yet a whole ship and its crew is risked to let Odra know about this invasion?" Vetala Bhatta looked at the chiefs shrewdly. "You know Vanga well—who in Vanga really cares enough about Odra's fate to put himself through so much trouble and danger? Who in the Vanga you have left behind would bother what happens to Odra? Who is this remarkable and resourceful well-wisher the king and queen have in Vanga?"

The chiefs looked at one another.

"You are right, raj-guru," said Sudasan. "There is no one left in Vanga who would do such a deed in good faith. Not for Odra."

"What do you mean by that?" asked Abhirami in alarm.

"What it means is that this report is a lie," said the raj-guru.

Abhirami and Veerayanka stared. "So, there is no Magadhan plan to attack us?"

"Oh, there is. There definitely is. This report confirms it."

The queen looked at the Acharya as if he had lost his mind. "You just said the report was a lie—"

"The report that Magadha intends invading Odra *by sea*

is a lie, disinformation cleverly planted to sidetrack you into expecting and preparing for a naval attack. The actual attack on Odra will come over land, *from the west*, through the passes in the Riksha Mountains."

The chamber went so still that the laughter of children splashing in a pond somewhere nearby echoed in the silence.

"Let us look at the logic of it," Vetala Bhatta continued. "The chancellor himself said that the Vangan ships are all trade ships, poorly suited for war. They will be hopeless in a sea battle involving your superior navy, my queen. Add to this the fact that Magadha's soldiers have no experience of sailing. They can't deal with the sea, and will be in no condition to fight at the end of a sea voyage. The Magadhan army is a land army, and Shoorasena will never use it any other way."

He paused to let that sink in. "Forget the sea. Prepare to defend Odra on land."

***

Fog.

Fog everywhere. Rolling by in thick wads. Curtains of fog.

And in that fog, a voice. Faint, frail, far away.

...you hear me... must come... out of time... late to save...

The voice was somehow familiar. From a long time ago. It was also persistent.

...please come... only you can... is the last...

And then, suddenly, a face through the fog. A blur of vapour, like a phantom, like a ghost.

Like a ghoul.

A face that he had seen before. A face from a long time ago.

...running out... do you hear me...

And then the face again. Skeletal, with sharp teeth and fangs, the eyes hollowed out, dots of red light burning in their depths. And the hair on flames. Or rather, the hair *of* flames.

Betaal.

You hear me, king... at last, at last... you must come now... the Halahala is not safe... the asuras have attacked Borderworld... come now and save us... we need you... there is no time to delay... come now... the tree is in danger...

The fog thinned. The face thinned. And everything went black.

And then daylight was pouring into Vikramaditya's eyes as he blinked and woke with a start.

He struggled to sit up, fighting the effects of the sleep-inducing tonic that Dhanavantri had administered. He thought about his dream for a moment. And slowly, through the tunnel of disorientation, the realization touched him. It hadn't been a dream. Betaal had reached out to him. Borderworld was in danger. Veeshada's dagger was in danger. *He had been called to the rescue.*

The samrat sprang out of bed and took three long strides to the door when the horror of the situation came down on him like a bolt of lightning. He froze.

There was no Vetala Bhatta in Ujjayini.

And without the Acharya, he couldn't make the crossing into Borderworld.

Borderworld

Flicking a bead of sweat off his eyebrow, Amara Simha squinted at the small procession of figures advancing slowly in their direction. Behind the approaching party was the wooden stockade marking the village of Gaiz, the air around the stockade shimmering and distorting in the midday heat, playing tricks on the eye.

"How many?" the councilor asked, shading his eyes against the glare.

"Hard to say," said Angamitra, sitting astride a horse to Amara Simha's left. "A dozen?"

"So, they have agreed to our terms," said Amara Simha.

"Unless it is a ruse." Angamitra ran his eyes along the length of the stockade, searching for signs of men lying in wait for a signal to attack—a careless spear poking out here, a curious head bobbing up there.

"Then we will make them pay." Amara Simha gripped his shield tighter, hoisting it up as he flexed his neck and shoulders. Behind him, the *samsaptakas* straightened on their saddles and squared their shoulders.

The ride had taken half the day, and as soon as the village

had become distinguishable from a blot on the horizon, it was clear the place was large, well populated and probably adequately defended. The warriors from Avanti had concluded that while storming the village was an option, an outright attack in broad daylight was inadvisable and would likely cost them a few lives, which they could ill afford at this stage. With nightfall still many hours away, and his time to find Ghatakarpara running out quickly, Amara Simha had decided to fall back on a spot of muscular diplomacy.

One of the *shy'ors* they had brought along as their hostage had been sent to Gaiz with a message for its chief. The message was simple. They were looking for the prince and had no intention of raiding the village. If the prince was in Gaiz, he was to be handed over without question. If he wasn't, any information on him would be welcome. They also wanted food and water, then they would be on their way. The village had one hour to respond to Amara Simha's offer, failing which it would come under attack.

Amara Simha had also demanded that the village send ten of its own as a token of good faith. He had promised that the ten villagers would not be harmed as long as there was no breach of trust. If there was one, those ten would be the first to die.

The group was closer now. "No sign of weapons, unless they are cleverly concealed," said Angamitra. "They appear to be villagers."

"The *shy'or* we sent is with them," the interpreter said from the councilor's right. "He managed to get our message across."

The group drew to a halt some distance from where the riders from Avanti waited. One man made his way forward, accompanied by the *shy'or* who had taken the message to Gaiz. Amara Simha observed the man's approach, noting his measured gait, his grey beard and the weary wisdom in his slanting eyes. Once he was close enough to be heard, he stopped. The *shy'or* spoke a word into his ear. The man looked gravely from Amara Simha to the interpreter. Bowing a little, he finally addressed them in the Saka tongue.

"Your honour, this is Aab'za, *shy'or* of Gaiz," the interpreter spoke when the man had finished. "He says the prince is not in the village, but we are free to search the place and satisfy ourselves. He also says he is happy to share whatever food and water they have, and that he personally welcomes you to Gaiz. All he asks is that we honour our word and ensure that his village and his people are not harmed."

The councilor gazed at the forty-odd roofs huddling behind the stockade, squat in the middle of the desert. He cast a glance over the line of ragged villagers, standing patiently and listening to the exchange. Finally, he stared their chief straight in the eye.

"Tell him Amara Simha never goes back on his word," he said to the interpreter. "Thank him for his hospitality, but also let him know I do not tolerate treachery. If he tricks us, he will die, his people will die. Tell him we demolished Ki'barr for the prince, that we are roaming this miserable land *only* for the prince. The prince is all we want, and we will find him, even if it means going over a mountain of dead bodies."

It was a little while later that Amara Simha, Angamitra and the interpreter sat at a low table, partaking of a meal of steamed rice mixed with beet and lentils. Aab'za, the chief, sat across them, a child of about two—his grandson—on his lap. The child stared at Amara Simha in open-mouthed fascination. They were waited upon by Aab'za's wife and his two daughters, while his son, still in his teens, stood respectfully by the door. The rest of the party from Avanti was being catered to in an adjoining hall.

The village itself had no more than thirty men defending it, the rest having left to join the slow march eastward in answer to the call for war. The moment they had entered the village, it had become apparent to the councilor that there was no will to fight in the people of Gaiz; the villagers were willing to accommodate any demands as long as it assured their survival. The search for Ghatakarpara had been swift, full of everyone's cooperation and had turned up nothing.

Aab'za leaned across the table and spoke to the interpreter.

"The *shy'or* wishes us good luck in our search for the prince, your honour."

"Tell him I thank him," Amara Simha nodded. As he chewed his food, the councilor considered the chief thoughtfully. He turned back to the interpreter. "Tell me something… he offered himself as one of the ten villagers we asked for. He is the chief of this place. Why did he put himself in danger? Why did he trust us to keep our word?"

The interpreter and the *shy'or* exchanged words. Amara Simha saw the chief smile.

"He says it is the most he could do to earn our trust."

Seeing the councilor's surprise and disbelief, the interpreter nodded. "Also, the welfare of Gaiz rests on his shoulders. That is a responsibility he cannot pass on to anyone else. It seems the news of the destruction we wrought in Ki'barr has travelled all over the desert, and your exploits in particular are being spoken of extensively." The interpreter paused and grinned. "They even have a name for you here now—*kaaz'i Ki'barr*."

"What does that mean?"

"The Horror of Ki'barr, your honour." The interpreter smiled again. "The chief says he did not want his village to suffer the same fate as Ki'barr, which is why he came. So that we would trust him. He knows his life was at risk, but he did it for Gaiz and its people."

Amara Simha looked at the chief with respect. He smiled at the child on the man's knee. The boy shot a shy smile back and buried himself in his grandfather's chest. A man entered the room, knelt by the *shy'or* and spoke softly in his ear. Amara Simha saw the interpreter lean forward, a sudden spark in his eye.

"What is it?" the councilor whispered urgently.

"They have some news."

Aab'za and the interpreter conferred, with the newcomer adding a word or two. "They have a travelling salt trader visiting the village. It seems he met a young man in the desert yesterday morning. The man was starving, so the trader gave him some food. He asked the man where he was headed, but the man didn't say. But the trader is sure he was bound for Avanti."

"How is he so certain?"

"The man could speak only Avanti. He didn't understand a word of the Saka tongue."

Amara Simha stared at the interpreter.

"A young man roaming deep inside Saka territory, speaking Avanti," Angamitra's eyes shone with excitement. "Who else could it be, your honour?"

"Where did the trader meet this young man?" the councilor asked.

The interpreter consulted the *shy'or* once again. "A day's ride to the north-east."

"Get the men and the horses ready. We must leave immediately."

Aab'za stopped the interpreter from rising. He spoke in a measured tone, and the interpreter listened, nodding, posing questions now and then.

"Your honour, the chief says that the sighting occurred *yesterday* morning, a full day's ride from here. The prince would have moved on."

"So what? He is on foot. We are on horses."

"Yes, but the chief asks in which direction we intend searching for the prince once we get there. The prince could have gone whichever way it pleased him."

"Does the chief have a solution to the problems he is posing?" Amara Simha snapped.

"He suggests we use a tracker, your honour."

"We don't *have* a tracker," the councilor growled.

"But he does, your honour."

Amara Simha stared at Aab'za, then at the interpreter. "Who?"

"His son, Nor'han."

The councilor looked at the *shy'or*, who nodded his head at the teenager standing by the door.

"The chief says the boy is an expert tracker."

"They can track people in these shifting sands?" Amara Simha asked, mystified.

"Apparently they can, you honour."

"And the chief will lend him to us?" Amara Simha's voice trembled in expectation.

"The chief wants us to take good care of the boy. And the boy will lead us only up to the frontier, and no further. The chief wants a solemn promise from us."

"Yes, of course. Tell him we agree. And tell him I thank him for this." The councilor turned grateful eyes on the man sitting opposite. "Thank you." He reached out and took the man's hand, gripping it firmly. "Tell him I am in his debt, and I hope I can find a way of repaying him someday."

The interpreter translated. The *shy'or* smiled and replied, giving the councilor's hand a warm squeeze.

"Perhaps through friendship, he says," said the interpreter.

As Amara Simha stepped out into the sun and walked to where his horse had been hitched, he pondered the nature of brotherhood, where the oldest friends could become sworn enemies, and the worst enemies could somehow end up as friends.

***

"How am I to do this without the raj-guru's assistance?"

Vikramaditya ran a hand through his hair in frustration, trying hard to focus on a solution, but not being able to think of anything beyond the impossibility of the task.

"Did the Ghoulmaster say how bad the situation was?" asked Dhanavantri.

The king shrugged. "He just said to come now, that the tree is in danger." He walked to the window and gazed into the sky, filling his lungs with air. He turned to face his councilors. "I have to go, *somehow*."

"How?" asked Varahamihira.

Vikramaditya's shoulders sagged in defeat. He went to the council table and sat down, resting his elbows on the table, his chin on his hands, brooding at the elaborate sun-crest spread before him.

"We don't even know where the raj-guru is at the moment," said Kshapanaka. "He has been gone a long time, so he might be on his way back. Maybe he'll be here today or tomorrow." She looked at the men in hope.

"Or maybe he won't," said Varahamihira.

Kshapanaka's face fell.

"You are right," Dhanavantri nodded. "Waiting for the Acharya won't help."

"But we don't have a choice, either," Varahamihira said darkly, sweeping his long, white hair back from his forehead and knotting it into a small bun. "We can't wait, yet we have to wait."

Four figures, seated or standing like statues, rooted in inaction, the silence heavy on their stooped shoulders.

"We can't wait." Vikramaditya placed his hands flat on the council table and sat up. "We will *not* wait."

The samrat looked at his councilors slowly, one by one, and there was an unsettling clarity in his eyes—a firmness, a resolve—that told them something was coming. His gaze finally settled on Dhanavantri.

"You will help me cross over."

"*Me?*" The physician stared at the samrat, mouth open.

Kshapanaka and Varahamihira looked from one to the other.

"How?" Dhanavantri blinked in incomprehension.

Vikramaditya leaned back in his chair. "What is Borderworld?"

The councilors looked at one another, wondering where this was going.

"Borderworld is the place between the living world—our world—and the world of the dead," the king answered his own question. "And how does anyone usually go into Borderworld? By dying. That's how things pass from our world into the world of the dead."

"I don't like this, Vikrama," said Kshapanaka, catching on, shaking her head.

"I still don't understand." Dhanavantri's eyes went from Kshapanaka to the king.

Kshapanaka rose from the table and stalked to a window, full of disapproval.

"If I have to enter Borderworld, I have to die," the samrat said.

"This is too dangerous," Kshapanaka snapped from the window. "You can't do this."

"We don't have a choice," Vikramaditya said, appealing to his sister-in-law with his eyes.

"How will your dying help in any way, Vikrama?" the physician looked aghast. "Once you are dead, you are dead, and there is no coming back—"

"He wants you to help in the coming back," Kshapanaka said tightly.

"I want you to help me in the going into *and* in the coming back," the king nodded, looking keenly at Dhanavantri.

"You want me to assist you in dying… and then you want me to revive you… from death?" the physician stared, finally understanding.

Vikramaditya nodded again.

"How is this even possible, Vikrama? I am only a physician. I can *cure* people. I can't bring them back from the dead." It was Dhanavantri's turn to slouch in anger. "And you want me to help you die? How? I take a knife and—"

"I don't want you to help me die. I want you to keep me from dying."

"*How?*" the physician barked. "Tell me how. You kill yourself, and you are dead. And if you are not dead, you are still alive *in this world*. You are not in Borderworld."

"Poison."

The king and the other two councilors turned to Varahamihira sharply.

"Poison kills gradually," the old councilor pointed out. "Poison someone and the victim starts dying. You administer an antidote, the victim revives. Touch and go, in and out of death."

"Do you even know what you are talking about?" asked Dhanavantri, exasperated.

"You said you are a physician, you cure people. What would you do to cure someone who has been poisoned?" Varahamihira paused. "You just have to do that process over and over again. Poison, antidote, poison, antidote, so Vikrama is in Borderworld long enough to save the dagger."

"You make it sound as if I do this sort of thing every day," Dhanavantri said.

"But you *are* a physician," Vikramaditya said, leaning across the table. "Your work involves dealing with poison." He looked into the councilor's eyes. "Please. This is the only way."

Dhanavantri stared at the king. Then, with a small shake of his head, he heaved a huge sigh. "I don't know... I hope this works."

"If it doesn't, we are all doomed," said the samrat. "So, let us make it work."

"What will I tell Vishakha if she awakes?"

Vikramaditya looked at Kshapanaka. "Tell her I will be back."

Kshapanaka shook her head, fighting back her tears. Vikramaditya stood up and went to her. He took her by the shoulders and bent to see her face.

"I will come back."

"Let me come with you," the councilor offered. "You can't go in there all by yourself. You might need help in fighting the asuras. You might need help in saving Betaal's tree. You—"

"No, Kshapanaka, you can't come," the samrat said gently. "What if the city needs you, what if there is a crisis here? You will have to lead the men into battle. No, Kshapanaka. You must stay here and protect Ujjayini." Seeing her nod, Vikramaditya smiled. "Also, if you come with me and Vishakha awakes, who will reassure her that I will be back?"

The councilor nodded. Then in a spurt of impulse, she threw her arms around the king. "Take care of yourself," she whispered, holding him tight. "Vishakha and I will be waiting for you."

"Kshapanaka has a point," said Varahamihira. "You will probably need help in Borderworld. It would be good to have someone around."

"But who?" asked Vikramaditya, disengaging from the embrace. "It can be dangerous there, and I don't want to risk anyone's life—"

A soft knock on the door interrupted the samrat. As everyone turned to look, the door opened and a figure stepped in.

The chief of the Palace Guards.

"Yes, Vismaya?" Varahamihira asked.

The chief bowed. "My deepest apologies for intruding, your honour, but I couldn't help overhearing what was being said here about Borderworld—"

"You were eavesdropping," said Varahamihira.

"I was, your honour, but out of no ill intention. I heard you and the Samrat speak of someone accompanying the Samrat to Borderworld. I am here to place myself at the Samrat's service." He looked directly at Vikramaditya and bowed again. "I don't profess to be as proficient a fighter as Councilor Kshapanaka, but I will do my utmost to assist you in your mission, my king. All that I am, I owe to Avanti and its throne, so grant this old soldier the opportunity to repay his debt, Samrat."

The king and the councilors looked at one another.

"Do you even know what this entails, Vismaya?" asked Varahamihira.

"Whatever it entails, if the Samrat is willing to do it, so am I."

"Well, you are trustworthy enough, so I guess that settles it," said Varahamihira.

"You mean I will have to keep *two* people from dying on me?" Dhanavantri looked from the councilor to the king in horror.

"Get Kunjala to help you," Varahamihira grinned.

"You can do it, can't you?" Vikramaditya looked at Dhanavantri earnestly.

"I don't even know if I can keep *one* person alive," the physician replied. "But if I am taking a chance with one life, what's the harm in taking a chance with two?"

"I like your spirit," said the samrat with a smile. He turned to the chief of the Palace Guards. "Are you sure you're up to this?"

"I have never been more certain about anything, Samrat," the man answered, a small smile lurking at the corners of his lips.

***

His legs ached from having to yank his feet out of the deep, loose sand every time he took a step. His feet hurt from the blisters that had formed on his toes while ploughing through the grit. His nostrils and lungs were singed from breathing the hot, dry air as he exerted himself just to keep plodding along. His skin, red and peeling, baked in the heat of the sun, and his hair, which had been a matter of great pride to him until not long ago, was now dishevelled, rough and full of sand.

But Ghatakarpara was not thinking about any of this as he dropped to his knees, moaning and clutching at his stained tunic, his fingers digging into the cloth.

He wasn't thinking because his mental faculties had almost ceased functioning as hunger tore at him, radiating outward from his stomach in shards and spreading through his body, nibbling at his veins, chewing into the bone marrow and gnawing its way into the recesses of his skull. Hunger skewered each one of the prince's thoughts and consumed every ounce of his rapidly depleting energy. Hunger was eating Ghatakarpara raw from the inside.

When he had run from captivity—he didn't know how long ago that was, for he had lost all track of time—Ghatakarpara had made the mistake of not taking food along. Had he planned his escape better, he could have squirrelled away some of what his captors had been feeding him, or he could have tried raiding the kitchen before that last dash to freedom. But he had done neither, intent only on getting out, not thinking ahead enough to realize that without food, he was as good as dead in the wastes of the Marusthali.

To throw any pursuers off his tail, the prince had taken a zigzag route, at times even backtracking, and while this had seemed like a smart idea at first, it came back to haunt him when he lost his bearings early in his flight. With only the sun and the stars to guide him, and nothing in the flat landscape to use as landmarks, holding a straight line towards the east became a challenge. And all the while, the hunger kept growing in his belly, and the hungrier he got, the more disoriented he became and the further he blundered in his path.

Just once in his wanderings had the prince chanced upon a group of men, walking in the far distance. He hadn't been able to say if they were Saka warriors or peasants—or a hunting party looking for him—and he was loath to find out, so he just lay flat on the desert floor and waited for them to disappear from sight. Later, on two occasions, he had seen signs of habitation in the distance, and while he avoided the first settlement out of the fear of being captured, the second one he lost as night set in. And then the starvation had taken over, and Ghatakarpara had no recollection of how he had survived up to the point where a man with three mules had woken him up and shared three of his fire-baked *rotis* along with a piece of dried lemon pickle. The man, who said he was a salt trader, had been kind enough to part with two additional *rotis* for the prince to consume later, and these Ghatakarpara had stretched for as long as possible, taking tiny bites and saving the rest. But now the two *rotis* were finally gone, and the hunger, howling like a rabid dog inside his head, was back.

The prince doubled over on the sand, hands on his stomach, his forehead almost touching the ground, and he crouched that way for a long time. Then, grinding his teeth, he slowly raised his head, blinking, until he was upright again. He rocked and swayed uncertainly, then brushing his dirty locks away from his forehead, he gazed straight ahead—at the line of grey mountains rising steeply from the flat of the desert.

The Arbudas.

And beyond them, Sindhuvarta.

Another wave of hunger wrenched through Ghatakarpara, and he almost toppled over at its violence and fell back on the sand. But steadying himself with one hand, he propped himself back up.

He licked his lips. They were dry. They needed water.

Disregarding the pangs building in his stomach, the prince stretched out a hand, palm open and cupped, pointed at the sky. He moved his fingers slowly, and as if by a miracle, small beads of moisture glistened on his fingertips. As Ghatakarpara kept moving his fingers, more and more moisture distilled from the air until his fingers were wet and running with water. The prince channeled the water carefully into his palm—a small pool, less than a mouthful—and put it to his lips, tasting the water, letting it wet his tongue and throat. Once it was gone, he sucked his palm and fingers dry so that none of what he had procured with so much effort went to waste.

He performed the trick once again, managing to extract a little more water this time, satiating his thirst by forcing the desert air to yield whatever little moisture it retained.

Licking his lips, feeling the soreness in them, the prince looked at the mountain range. Slowly he pushed himself to his feet, staggering, finding his balance. At last he set off, keeping his mind off the hunger, keeping his eyes on the Arbudas.

***

The houses that lined Ujjayini's streets were all in ruins, empty shells with mossy, crumbling walls, and vacant windows that gaped like eye sockets. The streets were no better, the mortar cracking and coming loose underfoot, so Matali had to watch his step as he hurried after Vikramaditya. They reached an intersection in the street where a *peepal* had come crashing down in a storm from long ago; it barred their way, forcing them to clamber over it. On the other side was the city's central garrison, and Matali looked at it curiously as they passed by; the garrison had been charred by fire and was covered in thick, black soot. It was also quiet as a grave, so that their footsteps echoed as they jogged past. It struck the deva that the whole city was silent, and that they hadn't seen a single soul, not one living being, since they had left the palace and crossed the broken causeway.

"Something is wrong with the sun," the samrat called out as he shot a worried glance at the sky.

Everything was wrong with the sun, as far as Matali was concerned. For one, he was able to look at it without being blinded. For another, it was scarred with dark splotches, resembling a sinister moon. And of course, it gave no heat—in fact, Matali was certain this particular sun was shedding cold over the city.

"It shouldn't be so dark," Vikramaditya added, looking around anxiously.

Matali didn't have a clue, as this was the first time he was stepping into Borderworld. "Is it usually brighter, your honour?" he asked, catching up.

"Mm-hmm," the king replied. "There's always been more light, but today there are shadows everywhere." Again, he looked up at the sun, which was directly overhead. With an unhappy shake of his head, he increased his pace, suddenly putting distance between himself and the deva.

Matali looked at the samrat, marvelling at the man's cunning. No one in Devaloka or Patala had even suspected that the human king knew the Ghoulmaster, so it was no wonder that neither the devas nor the asuras had imagined Veeshada's dagger being in Borderworld. Indra had sent the Ashvins and the Maruts—and now him and Urvashi—to the palace to look for the Halahala, when all along it had been in the custody of the Ghoulmaster. The story had been no different for the asuras—only now they had somehow got wind of the dagger's whereabouts and were here to claim it.

Overhearing the conversation in the council chamber and learning about the dagger's location, the deva's first instinct had been to rush off and inform Indra about it. But Matali had been quick to realize that that wouldn't be of much help as the asuras were already in Borderworld—perhaps even close to laying their hands on the Halahala—whereas it would take Indra time to figure out a way of getting there. Then, on hearing Vikramaditya volunteer to enter Borderworld to save the dagger, Matali had taken no time to decide that he would somehow accompany the king and swipe the dagger at the first available opportunity.

As Ujjayini's western gate came into view, sagging at the hinges and in a state of disrepair like everything else, the deva plotted his moves, wondering when it would be opportune to rid the samrat of the Halahala and rid himself of the samrat. He looked at the two old iron swords swinging at the king's waist and chuckled to himself; he might be the Wielder of the Hellfires, but the samrat was in for a nasty surprise when he came face to face with the asuras. For whoever had given the king the swords—he remembered it was the demon, Laayushi—had obviously skipped telling him that they didn't work against Diti's children.

"Vismaya, hurry," the samrat called over his shoulder as he ducked into the shadow of the western gate.

"Yes, my king," Matali said, adding speed.

As he slipped out of the gate onto the broken steps of the bathing *ghat*, the deva saw Vikramaditya standing two steps down, gazing across the dark, stagnant waters of the Kshipra, looking over and beyond the twisted trees that bordered the river. Following the king's eyes, Matali saw a darkness falling over the distant countryside, curtains of shadow sweeping across the landscape, casting gloom everywhere.

"Come," the samrat snapped, rushing down the steps. "Let's hope we aren't already too late."

***

The black chariot sped across the tiles unhindered, sweeping along until it ran into the carved white elephant standing plumb in its path. The chariot easily knocked the elephant aside, and the hand guiding the chariot reached out and plucked the fallen elephant off the tile.

"I totally missed that," groaned Hiranyaksha, smacking his thigh in exasperation.

"Focus, brother," Holika grinned in triumph as she put the conquered elephant figurine into a little lacquer box. Rattling the box, she added, "I have taken nearly all your primary pieces, so not much longer before your king falls."

The asura lord heaved a sigh and knitted his brows, eyeing the *chaturanga* board that was spread between him and Holika. Her black pieces outnumbered his white ones, and most of his pieces comprised low-value infantrymen. With just a horse and the queen left to defend his king, the end was near, as Holika had predicted. "I'm never this bad," he scowled. "Must be because my mind is on the mahaguru and Borderworld."

"Excuses, excuses," said Holika in reply. "Go on, make your move."

Hiranyaksha hunkered down, chin in one hand, trying to plot his king out of trouble. Except for the low roar of the accursed Patala Ganga cascading in the distance, silence filled the gallery. The asura lord finally made a defensive move, but in the next instant, he lost another of his infantrymen to a flank attack from Holika's horse.

"Oh no!" Hiranyaksha said, rubbing his forehead ruefully.

"You can do better than that, brother."

Hiranyaksha and Holika looked up at one another, startled. As one, they turned to look in the direction of the door, their eyes bright with anticipation, their faces alight with smiles.

"Brother," they cried in unison at the sight of the figure standing by the door, smiling down at them with affection.

Abandoning their game, brother and sister rose as Hiranyakashipu stepped forward, sweeping his siblings into his arms.

"It is so nice to have you back," Holika exclaimed. "The mahaguru told us to expect you."

"Was your penance fruitful?" asked Hiranyaksha, looking up at his brother, who was half a hand taller than he was, and a little broader as well. His heavily muscled body was the colour of ebony, while his hair and beard were golden, the contrast so striking and incongruous that one could nearly overlook the big antlers growing on his head.

"The penance went well," Hiranyakashipu replied. He walked over to look at the *chaturanga* board. "Not having a good day, I can see," he said, turning and smiling at his brother.

"No," Hiranyaksha grimaced. Then, with a grin of his own, he added, "But even on a day like this one, I can beat you blindfolded."

"At *chaturanga*, yes. Not at *chausar*."

"*Chausar* is not a real game, brother," Hiranyaksha protested.

"Do you say that because you are so bad at it?" asked Hiranyakashipu, smiling.

"Come on, brother," Hiranyaksha said. "How can anything that involves rolling of the dice be called a game? Games are about strategy, about out-thinking one's opponent, about surviving by one's wits alone. That is what *chaturanga* offers players. The moment you bring a pair of dice into a game, you introduce chance into the equation, and games of chance like *chausar* can hardly be a fair test of a player's skill."

"In my opinion, games involving a roll of the dice are superior precisely because the element of chance is built into them," the eldest sibling chuckled. "An element over which the player can exercise no control."

"How does that make them superior?"

"Because they mirror life's reality, brother. We might plan and prepare for every eventuality, but life will always throw something at us that we haven't accounted for. You speak of a *fair* test of a player's skill, but life is unpredictable, life is *unfair*. Yet we play the game day after day, challenging and outwitting our fates, overcoming the odds to win. That is *chausar*. No matter how the dice roll, the player has to plot to beat destiny, our biggest opponent."

"Hmmm..." Hiranyaksha bit his lip, pondering.

"But let this be for now," said Hiranyakashipu, clapping his brother on the shoulder. Turning to Holika, he asked, "What's been happening in my absence? And where is the mahaguru?"

"There is so much to tell you, brother," Holika replied. "The mahaguru is in Borderworld."

"Borderworld?" Hiranyakashipu stared. "Why?"

"He has gone to get us Veeshada's dagger."

Hiranyakashipu's eyes bulged in their sockets. "The Halahala? In Borderworld?"

"Also, you are to go to Devaloka and get us the mantras to raise Ahi," Hiranyaksha grinned.

***

The second war mahisha fell within minutes of the first one. And the third dropped its axe and staggered away from the tree almost the very next moment.

Panic gripped Shukracharya as he watched the mahisha grab its throat, gasping and choking as it fought for breath, the air running out of its lungs as the effect of the *sanjivani-*

mantra began wearing off. The mahisha panted and let out a piteous grunt before its eyes rolled back in the sockets and it toppled over to join the other two dead mahishas, the ground shaking under the impact of its fall.

The high priest ran a quick eye over the remaining mahishas. They seemed alright and able, swinging hard at the banyan's trunk, driving their axes deep into the wood. Slightly relieved, Shukracharya then looked towards the asura army—and the worry came rushing back as he saw two asuras fall to the ground, wheezing and letting out strangled screams as they too died in Patala, the mantra losing its influence over them.

"Faster, faster," he exhorted the mahishas, assessing the damage they had done so far. From what he could see, they had whittled the trunk down to roughly half its original diameter, but there was still a lot of tree left to cut, with fewer mahishas to do the job. "Faster," he shouted again, egging the mahishas on.

Spinning on his heel, he strode over to one of the asuras. "How many asura warriors have we lost so far?"

"More than two dozen," she replied, and Shukracharya saw the uncertainty and fear in her eyes. "How much longer… urk… aah…" She grabbed the high priest's shoulder, her eyes glazing over, and then she was falling, dragging Shukracharya's *angavastram* down with her. She lay on the ground convulsing for a moment, and then she went still. The high priest stepped gently away, bent down and prised his *angavastram* from her dead fingers. Wrapping it over his shoulders, he gripped his *danda* and strode into the fog.

"Betaal, where are you?" he screamed, his one eye flashing in rage. He looked wildly one way then the other, seeking the Ghoulmaster in the fog. "Enough of this. Give me the dagger *now*."

He got only silence in response.

"The dagger is of no use to you, Ghoulmaster. Give it to me and I will go in peace."

He waited. Nothing.

"I will destroy you and Borderworld, I will destroy the human king and his kingdom, I will destroy everything for the dagger, you hear me?" Shukracharya shouted, flailing his arms and stomping through the fog. "Give me what I want, and everything can be saved, Ghoulmaster. Don't be stubborn. Do the human king a favour. Save him and his people."

The high priest waited for a response, but when none came, he rammed the *danda* into the moist earth in anger. "Very well, do as you wish," he roared. "I will not stop until I have torn your abode from its roots, Ghoulmaster. You will pay for your stupidity."

Shukracharya wheeled around and walked back to the tree. "Faster," he called. "Tear it down."

The mahishas redoubled their efforts, attacking the tree with increased fury, but at the same time, one more mahisha turned and stumbled into the fog, choking and groaning.

Four mahishas had died so far. Shukracharya ran his fingers through his beard nervously, wondering whether the remaining mahishas would survive long enough to bring the banyan down. He wasn't sure they would, so he stalked over to the asuras.

"Go and help the mahishas," he commanded. "Use your swords, use your javelins, use what you have, but bring that accursed tree down. Go, go..."

Corpse

"Are you sure you wouldn't want to enjoy our hospitality for a few more days, raj-guru?" Veerayanka enquired, as a palace hand set down three bowls of rice *ksheera* on the small teakwood table. Picking up one of the bowls and offering it to the Acharya, the king of Kalinga added with a smile, "We realize we were a little sparing in our hospitality earlier, so we would like to make amends."

"There was nothing lacking in your hospitality, good king," said Vetala Bhatta, accepting the *ksheera*. He tasted a spoonful and nodded in appreciation. "Your offer, like this delicious *ksheera*, is most tempting, and I would love to see more of this beautiful land. But I have already stayed away from Ujjayini for far too long, and I fear my king and his council may need me urgently. So, with a heart heavy with regret, I shall, indeed, be taking your leave."

Veerayanka inclined his head. The king and the queen, as well as their guests from Avanti and Vanga, were in a private terrace, partaking in a sumptuous lunch served under a bower of frangipani and *parijata*. Queen Abhirami was in conversation with Sudasan and the other Vanga chiefs, while

Veerayanka and the Acharya were together by a small pond where a pair of large catfish swam in sedate circles.

"I cannot tell you how glad we are that you came to us, raj-guru," the king said. "We owe you our thanks."

"We owe you a lot more than our thanks, raj-guru," said Abhirami, sailing up to them before the councilor could reply. She held out a scroll made of finely woven bamboo leaves. "Here is a little something that we hope can make good for what you have done for us."

"Thank you, my queen," Vetala Bhatta bowed, accepting the scroll.

"You may go through it at leisure, raj-guru, but in essence, it is a royal permission granting Avanti the rights to trade iron with Odra," Abhirami continued. "It also allows Avanti and its allies the freedom to use the ports of Tosali and Uttara Tosali to trade with the kingdoms of Sribhoja and Srivijaya."

"Thank you," the Acharya bowed again.

"In addition, I have already dispatched riders to our mines with instructions to have ten mules laden with iron ore ready to take back with you to Ujjayini. By the time you near the mines, the mules will be waiting for you, raj-guru."

"You are most kind, my queen," the councilor bowed for a third time. "This is much more than I expected, and Avanti is grateful for this."

"We realize that your need for ore may be pressing," Abhirami replied. "I hope what we are sending will suffice for now."

Vetala Bhatta nodded. Setting the empty bowl aside, he looked from brother to sister. "Are you certain you are equipped to deal with the threat from Magadha by yourself?"

"Odra has an army of some five thousand men," the queen said. "Kalinga has close to seven thousand more. That is twelve thousand men to defend this city."

"I have already sent my army the summons," said

Veerayanka. "My soldiers will be here in eight or nine days, so we will be ready when Shoorasena's army comes marching over the Riksha Mountains. Uttara Tosali will not fall to Magadha."

"This city might be safe, but what about Odra's countryside?" asked the Acharya. "What if the Magadhan army chooses to plunder and brutalize Odra's smaller towns and villages first, with the intention of drawing your army out into the open? How will your soldiers protect those not in this city?"

"Why would the Magadhan army waste time ravaging Odra's countryside instead of coming straight here, raj-guru?" Abhirami countered. "Magadha is under the impression that we are expecting an attack from the sea, so they would hurry to assault Uttara Tosali from the land. Raiding the countryside would only set off an alarm, warning us of a land-based attack and giving us time to mount a suitable defence."

A sly smile lit Vetala Bhatta's face. "You are obviously well acquainted with battle strategy," he said, looking keenly at Abhirami. "I am willing to wager that Odra and Kalinga's reluctance to go to war has much to do with an intimate knowledge of warfare."

Brother and sister glanced at one another but said nothing.

"I should be on my way," the Acharya said. "On behalf of my king, Vikramaditya, I again thank you for agreeing to ally with Avanti. And I do hope this is the beginning of a friendship that will last as long as the sun travels your sky and ours."

"We hope so as well," said Abhirami. "That scroll also has an invitation to the Samrat to visit our court. We would be honoured to host him."

"And you can accompany him as well, raj-guru," Veerayanka added with a smile. "To see the sights of this land, and those of my own, the ones you regret missing out on."

"Indeed," the councilor smiled back. "It is my assurance that the Samrat will pay Odra and Kalinga a visit at the earliest possible opportunity. And I can add that the Samrat will be more than pleased to reciprocate the gesture—you are most welcome to our kingdom, even though I believe it would be best to wait until we win the war that is coming to us."

"May we both win our wars, raj-guru," said Veerayanka, suddenly grim.

"And may we both help each other win our wars," added Vetala Bhatta with a bow.

***

The chamber was becoming uncomfortably stuffy from the combined heat of the large charcoal brazier and the two smaller ones that burned in the middle of the room. A bronze cauldron, steaming with hot water, was set atop the big brazier, while smaller basins sat on the small braziers, bubbling with boiling water. The first basin was filled with the roots of the toxic *vajranaga* plant, while the second contained an arcane mixture of roots and herbs to counter the effects of the *vajranaga*. The rest of the floor space was littered with mounds of roots and herbs, while in another brass vessel, more than a dozen leeches crawled in shallow water.

"Open one of the windows," Dhanavantri called out as he sidestepped a pile of herbs and scuttled to Vikramaditya, who was lying on the bed on his back, perfectly still. "Just one," the physician added, taking the king's hand by the wrist, feeling his pulse. "We don't want too much of a draught."

As one of the junior physicians carried out his instructions, Dhanavantri let go of the samrat's hand and went over to Kunjala, the court's assistant physician. Kunjala squatted next to Matali, who lay on a straw mat that had been spread on the floor.

"How is he doing?" Dhanavantri asked.

"His pulse is steady," Kunjala replied. He opened the deva's eye and peered. "The pupils are dilating, though."

"Give him a small dose of the antidote in a little while."

Dhanavantri turned and came up to Varahamihira and Kshapanaka, who stood by the door, anxiously watching the physicians move between the braziers and the two men who were being kept from death's door.

"Are they alright?" asked Varahamihira.

"For now, yes," the physician replied, wiping a sheen of sweat from his chubby face.

"And have they entered Borderworld?"

"I have no idea," Dhanavantri threw up his hands. "I don't know how this works. I don't even know if any of this will be of any use."

Varahamihira nodded, conscious of Kshapanaka's worried glance at him. "Vikrama was sure it would work. He's been there before, so he would know."

The physician heaved a sigh in response.

"Something is bothering you, my friend," Varahamihira eyed Dhanavantri keenly. "What is it?"

"It occurred to me... how would we know when the Samrat is ready to return? And if we don't know, we'll be keeping them both in this state, between poison and antidote, even when they want to come back to consciousness."

Varahamihira and Kshapanaka looked at one another with eyes widening in horror. "You think of this *now*?" Varahamihira turned to the physician in shock.

"I can't be expected to think of everything, can I?" Dhanavantri said defensively. "*You* were the one to come up with the idea of poison. *You* could have thought of this problem too, but you didn't."

It was Varahamihira's turn to heave a sigh.

"The raj-guru knows how to bring Vikrama back," said

Kshapanaka. "Perhaps there is a sign that Vikrama gives when he is ready to return."

"Perhaps, but if we don't know how to recognize it, it would hardly be of help," Dhanavantri looked away unhappily. "What wouldn't I give to see the Acharya walk in here right now—"

"The Samrat's breathing isn't normal, vaidyanath."

Everyone turned sharply to look at the junior physician who stood by the king's bed.

"Watch the chief of the guards," Dhanavantri said to Kunjala as he rushed to Vikramaditya's side, the other two councilors right behind him.

Dhanavantri bent over the samrat, who looked pale, and was drawing his breath in shallow, erratic gasps. Checking the king's pulse, he snapped, "Quick, get the antidote."

A junior physician ladled two measures of the distilled herbal concoction into a bowl. He had just brought the bowl to Dhanavantri when the king convulsed in the bed, opening his eyes wide for a moment and gasping for breath, before falling back on his pillow and sinking into a shaky stupor.

***

Vikramaditya felt his legs give way under him as his vision went black for a fleeting instant.

He fell to his hands and knees, the ground damp and cold under his palms. He stayed where he was for a moment, head down, taking deep breaths and fighting off the nausea and dizziness, while around him, giant banyan leaves dropped slowly from the murky fog above.

"My king, are you alright?"

The samrat could feel the deva crouching next to him. He nodded heavily.

"Take my hand, Samrat."

Vikramaditya blinked to clear his vision. Then, with Matali's support, he struggled back to his feet, still feeling the marsh sway a little, as if it was floating on water.

"Are you feeling better, your honour?"

The king nodded. The rocking motion had subsided, the nausea had receded. He let go of the deva's hand. "What about you?" he asked.

"I am alright, my king."

"Then let us not dally any more. Let's keep moving."

They resumed walking through the fog, which was no longer white, as it used to be. A smoky grey texture had infiltrated the fog, as if to match the dimming of the light in Borderworld, and the very air of the marsh appeared to have become heavier and coarser, so that walking felt a lot harder, as if they were pushing past invisible curtains strung in a line.

And the leaves had started falling. Not a heavy shedding, but a steady fall, one after another. Broad, green leaves, still fresh and in their prime, but falling. Like they never had before.

Borderworld was changing.

Vikramaditya picked up his pace, drawing the Hellfires from their sheaths at the same time. At once, the blades caught fire, small flames hugging the surfaces and flickering along the edges.

"Are we close, your honour?" the deva whispered from behind in anticipation.

"It's hard to tell. Everything is different this time." The samrat peered into the fog. "I know the way, but... but I can't seem to find it."

They walked a little way further before Vikramaditya drew to a halt, looking around him. He had lost his way, he realized, because the way itself was no longer there.

"This is bizarre," he said, more to himself, with a frustrated shake of his head.

Standing next to him, Matali said nothing.

Borderworld was changing, and he had to quickly do something about it, the king realized. *He* had to find a solution.

"There is only one thing to do," Vikramaditya shrugged. "It involves a risk, but it's a chance we have to take." Raising his voice, he called into the fog.

"I am here in answer to your call, Ghoulmaster. Are you there? Can you hear me?"

***

The boatman was in the eastern section of the lake, deep underwater. Along with the others, he had been going in and out of the water all morning and afternoon, and now he was tired. He wanted the sun to set quickly, so they could wind up the search and he could go home to his new bride. The thought of his comely wife and what they would do when he got home distracted the boatman, so he almost missed the thick clump of waterweeds growing near the perimeter of the lake.

Which meant that he almost missed seeing the thing that lay trapped and submerged in the weeds. *Almost.*

Observing the weeds out of the corner of his eye, the boatman swam over, pushing the long, slender stems aside to have a look—and immediately catching sight of the body. Turning around, he kicked away and broke surface. Wiping the water from his eyes, he put two fingers in his mouth and whistled loudly to catch the other boatmen's attention.

"What is it?" asked their leader.

"I've found it," the boatman replied, his voice swelling in triumph, as if he had just netted a great catch. "Down here."

Two more swimmers came down and helped him free the body from the weeds. It was lifted up to one of the boats, which was then punted to a spot where the body could be transferred ashore. Word had spread by then, and a sizeable crowd comprising guards and palace staff had gathered to watch the boat bring the corpse in, and everyone craned their necks as it was finally taken off the boat and put down on a landing near the palace causeway.

A couple of palace guards cleared their way to the body, which was bound tight by a thick vine, its head and face covered by a dark, stained cloth that had been knotted firmly around the neck with jute rope. The body was clad in a plain cotton dhoti, and it was pale from being in the water. Apart from the fact that it was undeniably a male corpse, there was nothing to help distinguish who it might be.

"Remove the vines and untie the cloth," one of the senior guards commanded.

The vines were fairly easy, but the jute rope had soaked water and tightened, making the knots harder to loosen. But finally, the boatman was able to get through the knots, releasing the cloth. He pulled the cloth from over the corpse's head—and lurched back in horror, dropping the cloth and propelling himself away from the body, gagging as the bile rose to his throat.

He was not the only one. From the palace guards to the other boatmen, everyone drew back from the body, widening their eyes first, then quickly averting their gaze in shock and horror. Onlookers everywhere gasped in revulsion, groaning and covering their mouths and noses, turning away in the hope that they could un-see what they had just seen.

The thing that had been pulled out of the water. The corpse.

***

Shukracharya paced the ground in front of the great banyan, switching his *danda* from hand to hand while throwing fretful glances at the tree, eyeing its whittled trunk. Though greatly reduced in girth, the trunk was still solid enough to hold the banyan up, and was, much to the high priest's dismay, nowhere close to being brought down by the mahishas.

Because the mahishas themselves had been brought down in number—from fifteen to five.

Even these five were growing weaker with every passing moment, the swings of their axes barely making a notch on the wood, their breathing laboured. The high priest knew that every swing they took could well be their last. And the fate of his asura army was no better, now numbering not more than thirty, a ragged bunch trying to make an impact on the tree with the swords and javelins and failing.

Suddenly, in the high priest's eye, the whole attack on Borderworld seemed to have been poorly planned—and he could blame no one for it but himself. Why hadn't he brought twice the number of war mahishas, he asked himself furiously, why had he thought just fifteen of them would suffice? And why had he allowed the mahishas to cease chopping the tree when he had been negotiating with Betaal? Those precious moments when the mahishas were still well under the force of the *sanjivani-mantra* could have made the difference between where he was and where he could have been.

He looked once more at the tree, and there went another mahisha, falling without as much as a groan, a cold slump to the ground as the light left it in a wink of an eye. Four mahishas left. Shukracharya sighed to himself, though it came out more like a whimper of frustration. He would have to return to Patala and marshal another force, plan another attack, but he would do it if it was the last thing he did. He would make Betaal pay for his insolence, he decided as anger seized him. He would take the Halahala *and* destroy Borderworld.

Casting one last glare at the tree, the high priest decided that it was best he abandon this lot to their fate—none of them would survive the journey out of here, anyway—and head back to Patala. The sooner he got back, the sooner he could return with the next army to finish what this lot had started.

With a scowl of resignation, he drew his *angavastram* over his shoulder and set off into the fog.

He hadn't taken more than ten steps, however, when he heard something and stopped.

He listened.

At first, there was nothing but the gentle sound of the banyan leaves landing on the ground.

Then the wind shifted direction, and he heard it again.

"...are you? I have come..."

He knew that voice.

"...answer me, Ghoulmaster..."

He remembered that voice. It had given him one night to leave Ujjayini and two days to get out of Avanti. And it had forbidden him from setting foot in Avanti ever again.

The human king was here to take back the dagger.

Shukracharya turned and dashed to the tree. "Stop," he shouted, waving his hands to get the attention of the asuras. "Stop."

The asuras and the mahishas ceased their assault on the tree.

"Forget the tree," the high priest hissed. "The human king is here to meet Betaal and take the Halahala back with him. He has to be stopped. Come with me."

The asuras and mahishas turned their backs to the tree and followed Shukracharya into the fog.

***

"A rider just got back from the garrison of Palavi, your honour."

"Mm-hmm?" Vararuchi nodded but didn't look up, instead continuing to darn the tear in his tunic.

"The news is not good," Sharamana reported. "The

commander there says they will not back our demand asking the Samrat to step down. This is the second garrison to go back on their word since this morning, your honour."

The councilor pushed the needle through the cloth, tightening the silk thread and drawing the rip together. "And they offer the same reason?" he asked, finally looking up at Sharamana.

"Yes," the commander replied.

Vararuchi nodded and went back to the stitching. "Let us see how Suhasa and Ajanya fare in winning the support of the garrisons of Lava and Ashwapuri."

"Lava is a very large garrison," Sharamana agreed. "Getting them on our side would be quite an achievement. Commander Ajanya has close contacts there; he sounded very confident."

"That was two days ago," Vararuchi studied the commander levelly, "when the Samrat hadn't addressed the troops at the city garrison. Everything has changed since this morning. All the old bets are suddenly off."

Sharamana nodded and opened his mouth to say something, but changed his mind at the last moment. The councilor saw the hesitation, though, and raised his eyebrows in enquiry.

"It's... I overheard some of the men talking outside." Sharamana paused. "They were saying the same things. The Samrat has sworn to fight the barbarians at the frontier, the Samrat has placed his trust in us... all the usual stuff."

"So?"

"So..." the commander hesitated, "...nothing, your honour. I was only saying even the men here are being swayed."

The men were bound to be swayed. Vikramaditya could have summoned the various captains and commanders to the palace for the address. But no. In a masterstroke, he had addressed them in the central garrison. *He had gone to the men. The palace had reached out to them.* And by all accounts, it had been a fantastic address, with Kalidasa having been named as the enemy, and the Hellfires playing a key role in boosting morale and mustering support. Vararuchi could tell that it hadn't been just an address; it had been a performance designed to sway opinion.

"So, the Samrat intends fighting the barbarians. That is good. But what about the fact that the Samrat is not the son of King Mahendraditya?" The councilor stared at Sharamana. "What about the Queen Mother—"

"The men don't care, your honour."

Vararuchi blinked at the commander, not believing that he had been interrupted, not believing what the man had just said.

"The men want leadership and a show of determination. The men want reassurance that they matter, that they will be looked after." Sharamana paused. "That the king may not be King Mahendraditya's son means nothing to them, your honour."

Setting the needle and the tunic aside, Vararuchi stared out of the window. The sun was on its way to the horizon, dissected by the branches of a *jamun* tree growing just outside.

"Let me know of any further developments," he said to Sharamana.

Once he was alone, Vararuchi rose and went to the window. Leaning out, he plucked two *jamuns* that were within hand's reach. He didn't particularly like the fruit, but he had pulled them on an impulse, so he popped one into his mouth, biting it and tasting the juice, tart on his tongue.

The men don't care, your honour.

Now that Sharamana had put it out there in no uncertain terms, Vararuchi saw the truth for what it was—and everything that had happened since that morning only served to reinforce the truth.

Vararuchi sucked on the *jamun* in dismay and disbelief. Not once had it occurred to him that Vikramaditya not being Mahendraditya's son might not be so much of a burning issue to the soldiers of Avanti, something that demanded redressal. But Vikramaditya had understood the men and what moved them, which had led to the address in the central garrison. He had been completely outsmarted by Vikramaditya, and what stung most was that having misread the men, he hadn't seen it coming. Vararuchi spat the seed out in frustration.

Looking at the second *jamun* and deciding against eating it, the councilor pondered his next course of action. If the soldiers were shifting towards the samrat's rhetoric, there was no way he could stop them. What could he say to them when Vikramaditya had allayed their deepest fears and there was no more discontentment left to stoke? And if the matter of the samrat's patriarchy didn't really bother them, there was very little left for him to play with. That meant he would now have to depend on whatever Pralupi was planning for Vikramaditya, and hope it was as big as she had promised it would be.

She had promised a scandal. She had promised humiliation. She had said one more councilor would abandon Vikramaditya's side. She had also said she wanted Ghatakarpara crowned as the king of Vatsa in exchange. That was the deal, those were her terms.

Vararuchi sighed, desperately wishing he did not have to take his sister's help. He couldn't even begin to get his head around how he would go about making Ghatakarpara king of Vatsa, how he would explain it to everyone, but he would have to do it if...

The councilor shook his head and flung the *jamun*, high and hard. Watching it sail past the trees and disappear into the undergrowth, he was left with a sinking feeling that whatever happened, this gamble was no longer his to win.

***

A guard slipped in through the door, nudged his way to Kshapanaka's side and offered her a stiff bow. "Your honour, there is a palace guard outside."

"Okay..." Kshapanaka looked at the guard in expectation.

"He has a message, your honour."

"For me?"

"Well, it was for the chief of the Palace Guards," said the soldier, stealing a glance at the mat where Matali lay in Kunjala's care. "But as he can't come—"

"I am busy here," said the councilor.

"Your honour, they have found the body in the lake."

Kshapanaka looked at the man and nodded.

Outside, a young guard stood waiting. Seeing the councilor, he bowed.

"Whose body is it?" asked Kshapanaka. After the heat of the braziers inside, it felt positively cool outside in the gallery.

"I don't know, your honour. I was only asked to deliver the message to the chief."

"That's alright. Do you know where the body is?"

"Near the causeway, your honour."

"I will see to it."

Finding the body didn't pose a problem. The councilor only had to follow the animated buzz of the palace staff, and in no time, she saw the throng near one of the causeway's landings. She approached the crowd, and her appearance subdued the chatter. A path cleared for her, and she was nearly at the landing when a senior guard stepped forward and bowed.

"My apologies, your honour, but I would recommend you don't see the body."

"Why?" Kshapanaka asked, eyes narrowing. "Whose is it?"

"We don't know."

"Let me see it."

"As you wish, your honour."

The man moved to one side and Kshapanaka walked to the edge of the causeway and looked down at the landing.

She recoiled at the sight that greeted her, her stomach heaving in protest.

She blinked and forced herself to breathe deeply, staying her nerves. With an effort, she gazed down at the corpse once again.

From the neck downward, it resembled any male cadaver that might be pulled out of water—rubbery white skin with small marks of fish bites, the belly slowly bloating in the sun. From the neck downward, it was just another dead body.

Neck upward, it was a nightmare come true.

The corpse's face and head had been stripped of all skin and tissue, so that only a thin layer of pink-white flesh remained, sticking so close to the skull that the underlying bone structure was visible. Even the eyelids were peeled off, leaving the corpse's eyes open and staring—even here, both the irises and pupils were missing, as if they had been pecked out, so only the empty whites could be seen. A macabre leer ravaged the bottom of the face, teeth and gums laid bare by missing lips, while the corpse's nose and ears were nothing more than stubby holes embedded in raw flesh. The ghastly spectacle was rounded off at the throat, which had been torn open and emptied of the larynx.

To Kshapanaka, it looked as if someone—*something?*—had ripped the face off whoever this unfortunate soul had been. But who was he?

With a face like the one staring up at her, there was no way of knowing.

It struck the councilor that after all the effort that had gone into fishing the body out of the lake, its mystery was far from solved.

Matali

It took Matali a few moments to realize that there was indeed a shape in the fog, and it was heading in their direction. Tightening his grip on his sword and bracing himself, the deva darted a glance at the samrat. The king had noticed it too, and his guard was up, although he was swaying a little, as if inebriated, and he kept blinking to clear his vision. Despite the chill sweeping across the marsh, the samrat's forehead was beaded with sweat, and Matali felt a trickle of perspiration run down the back of his own neck.

Diffused and smudged, the shape emerged from the fog, until the deva was able to discern a strange nimbus of fire around it. At almost the same instant, he sensed the king relax by his side.

"Betaal," Vikramaditya breathed in relief, lowering the Hellfires and stepping towards the approaching figure.

Retaining his hold on the sword, Matali followed, his eyes widening as the fog fell back and Betaal finally became distinct. He had only heard about the Ghoulmaster before, and that too always sketchily described, so he was totally unprepared for the flaming-haired apparition that now stood before them, viewing him with eyes that were deep black holes of infinity.

"Who is this, king?" the Ghoulmaster asked, the eyes now glowing with red dots.

"The chief of my Palace Guards," the king replied. "He can be trusted."

"That is good then," Betaal replied.

Without wasting time on niceties, the ghoul extended a hand towards the samrat... and Matali spied the blade of a dagger protruding from the bony fist. His eyes shone bright.

The dagger that had brought all three worlds colliding into the fourth—Borderworld.

"I am sorry I couldn't keep this for you longer, wise king," the Ghoulmaster said.

The deva kept his eye on the dagger, its invaluable obsidian hilt barely showing as the blade changed hands.

"And I am sorry I brought this on you and Borderworld," the king replied, looking at the darkening fog and the leaves that continued to fall lazily around them. "I should never have brought the dagger here. I am afraid the wisdom that you attribute to me failed me on this occasion, Ghoulmaster."

"This is how it is meant to be, how it turned out the last time as well," Betaal replied. "But go now, before the asuras find us."

Matali felt pain slice across his chest, so sharp that the sword loosened and fell from his hand, and he grabbed his ribs and bent over.

"Vismaya," the king was already at his side. He had sheathed one of the Hellfires and was holding the deva by the shoulder. "Are you alright?"

The pain eased. With a nod, Matali bent to retrieve the sword. As he righted himself, he wondered if he should make his move now. The samrat was standing right beside him, exposed and unsuspecting, and he could easily drive his sword into the king and kill him. But the Ghoulmaster was a problem—he had no idea what the lord of Borderworld was capable of doing to stop him. And even if he did give the ghoul the slip, there was no way he could figure a way out of the fog all by himself. He needed the king around a while longer, he realized.

"I am alright, your honour," he said, wondering where the dagger was. Then he saw it, tucked away in the king's belt.

"You should go," said Betaal. There was urgency in the voice.

"Thank you, friend," said Vikramaditya, nodding once at the Ghoulmaster.

Seeing Betaal begin to withdraw into the fog, Matali turned to follow Vikramaditya. They had barely taken four steps when a sharp voice hailed them.

"So, we meet again."

Matali looked to the right, where a short figure stood in a thin veil of fog.

Guru Shukracharya.

And two steps behind him were nine or ten shadowy outlines bearing javelins.

The deva's first reaction was to panic. If the high priest saw through his disguise and revealed his true identity to Vikramaditya, all the work he had put in would be undone—

"For the last time, hopefully," replied Vikramaditya, drawing the sheathed Hellfire and facing the high priest.

Shukracharya smirked at the two swords, the flames burning low along their surfaces. "Those will not be of any use to you here."

The king glared at the high priest, but before either of them could say anything, the samrat's legs suddenly wobbled and he staggered. A gleam of interest leaped to Shukracharya's eye, and he motioned to the figures standing behind him.

Seeing the asuras step forward, Matali sprang to

Vikramaditya's side, his sword up, its point marking a tight arc from Shukracharya to the asuras ranged behind. "Stand back," he barked, gritting his teeth against the pain that was crisscrossing his chest with even greater intensity. "*Back.*"

"Don't do this, please."

Matali cast a quick glance to find that the Ghoulmaster had returned and was hovering disconsolately in the fog. "Let the king depart in peace," Betaal continued in a pleading tone, but Shukracharya cut him off with a scowl.

"You had your chances, Ghoulmaster," he snapped, "but you blew them. I will deal with you later." The high priest looked back at Matali curiously. "Who are *you*? You are not one of the councilors."

"Stand back," the deva rasped, grateful that he hadn't been recognized.

Shukracharya's attention went back to the king. "You and I started on the right note in Avanti, remember?" he said. "We can end this on the same note. We can even carry on being friends. Give me the dagger, and this ends happily for everyone."

Vikramaditya was still gasping for breath, although he had managed straightening. He now looked at the high priest through the fog and the swirling rain of leaves. Taking a deep breath, he drew himself erect. "Do you remember my last words to you that evening in the palace, before you left Ujjayini?" He paused to let the high priest recollect what had been said. "I told you that if our paths crossed again, our meeting wouldn't be amicable." The samrat's voice hardened in anger. "You come to Borderworld, defile my friend's home and expect friendship from me? *Never*. We will *never* be friends, and you will *never* get the dagger from me."

The high priest's eye turned bleak. "We will fight as enemies then," he snarled, motioning with his hand to the asuras to attack.

Matali watched one of the asuras fall inexplicably to the ground, but before he could devote more thought to it, the remaining nine asuras charged at him and the human king. The deva raised his sword, and the asuras were ten steps away when another one stumbled and went crashing to the ground. And then Vikramaditya sprang in front of him, straight into the path of the onrushing asuras, the Hellfires drawn, burning and rock-steady in the samrat's hand.

The king parried the thrust of the foremost javelin, then spinning on his heel, he drove his elbow into its wielder's neck, crushing the windpipe. He slashed a second asura's chest open, then dodged a third one's javelin, skewering the asura in the neck as he overbalanced and floundered. Next, as two javelins came at him simultaneously, the samrat dropped low and got under them, cutting at his attackers' stomachs with the Hellfires, first in, then outward, so the asuras' entrails spilled out even as they stared at each other in surprise.

Overawed by the king's reflexes and the fluid brutality of his counterattack, Matali watched, distracted, so he nearly missed the asura charging his way. The asura was almost upon him, the javelin lunging at his chest, when he blocked the attack with his sword. Grabbing the javelin, Matali yanked it hard, and as the asura lost his footing, the deva slid his sword between the asura's ribs. Two more asuras came at him, and Matali dispatched the first by feigning a thrust, before spinning around and decapitating him. Turning to tackle the fourth one, he saw that she had already been impaled by one of the Hellfires.

Matali felt giddy again. Waiting for the spell to pass, he observed Vikramaditya walk into the fog, searching.

"Where are you?" the samrat called. "Show yourself instead of hiding like a coward."

Matali looked around to see that Shukracharya had disappeared. "Where did he go?" the deva asked Betaal as he stepped after Vikramaditya.

"One moment he was here, the next, he was gone," the Ghoulmaster replied.

"You are lucky most of the asura army was dead before I found you," the high priest's voice came from the fog, laced with undisguised hatred. "Otherwise, this would have ended very differently."

Matali picked his way to the samrat's side, and they both stood and considered the fog.

"What *could* have happened and what *has* happened are very different things," answered the samrat. "The former is where the defeated invariably find their solace."

"It is good that you count this as a victory, king," Shukracharya's voice sneered. "I recommend you return to Avanti and revel in this moment of triumph, savour it as deeply as you can—for it is the last victory you will have in this miserable life of yours."

"My victory is nowhere near complete until I have settled scores with those who have ravaged Borderworld and my kingdom. A price has to be paid, and a price will be extracted." Vikramaditya paused. Wincing in pain, he held his stomach. "Do you hear me? Or have you already fled back to wherever you came from?"

There was no reply from the fog. The silence was full of the murmur of falling leaves.

"I think he has gone," Matali whispered.

Sheathing the Hellfires, Vikramaditya turned to Betaal and nodded. The Ghoulmaster moved away into the fog.

"We must leave." Patting the dagger for reassurance, the samrat stepped over the dead asuras and began walking.

***

"The chief's heart is beating too fast," Kunjala called as he leaned over Matali. "The antidote seems to have stopped taking effect."

"Increase the *yashtimadhu* in the next dose," Dhanavantri passed on his instructions before turning back to Vikramaditya. He rose and went to the pile of herbs, from where he picked out five maroon-red leaves. Putting the leaves into a copper pestle, he ground them as he returned to the samrat's side.

"How is he?" asked Varahamihira.

"He is slipping too often," Dhanavantri replied with a frown. "His heartbeat keeps dropping."

Varahamihira watched as the physician dug the crushed leaves out of the pestle and mixed them into a bowl of turmeric water, which instantly turned blood red in colour.

"Don't you think they have both been gone for too long?" said Varahamihira, eyeing Dhanavantri. "I mean with the raj-guru it was never so—"

"I am not the raj-guru. Don't ask me these questions," the physician snapped. His face softened almost immediately, and he looked at his friend. "I know you are worried. So am I. But we just have to hang in there and hope that everything will turn out alright."

Varahamihira gave Dhanavantri's shoulder a friendly squeeze. "You are right. And you are doing your best, which is a lot more than what I am doing."

Dhanavantri soaked a small square of muslin in the concoction he had made. He then wrung the cloth carefully over Vikramaditya's lips, so the liquid went in slowly, drop by small drop.

***

By the time the boat was halfway across the oily, black-green waters of the Kshipra, the spasms in Matali's chest were so severe and so frequent that he had trouble focusing on the rowing. He also had trouble focusing on the other big task at hand—taking the Halahala from the man sitting behind him, struggling with the other oar.

The deva had witnessed Vikramaditya's speed and dexterity while battling the asuras, bringing them down with such swiftness that the fight had ended even before it had begun. Of course, as Shukracharya seemed to have implied, had there been a greater number of asuras, the outcome of the fight would have been very different. Skirmishing with a handful of asuras and fending off a horde of them singlehandedly were not the same thing, especially since the *churails* couldn't be called on to counter Diti's children. Still, there was no doubting the samrat as a warrior, quick to react to threats, so pinching the dagger would require care.

What he had was the element of surprise. And, of course, the king's complete trust.

"You don't look too good, Vismaya," the samrat said.

"I am okay, my king," the deva grunted.

"Good. Just hold on and don't let go. We'll be back in the palace in no time."

Flinching in pain, Matali looked up to see Ujjayini's ramparts draw close. Perhaps it was best he struck right after they had docked, he thought. He would be the first one off the boat and on firm land, so maybe he could use the oar—

Pain shot through his chest, cutting off his train of thought.

The pain subsided and his vision cleared in time for the boat to bump against the *ghat*. Holding the rotted oar, Matali stood up to step off the boat, but he was instantly struck by a bout of nausea and began retching heavily. He had no recollection of what happened thereafter, until he swam back into a degree of self-consciousness to find that the king was holding him by the shoulders, escorting him up the last few steps towards the city gate.

Realizing that this was his best chance at taking the Halahala, the deva tried to reach for his sword—but he was horrified to find that his hand was numb and completely immobile. He tried working his other hand, but it wouldn't move either. He looked at the samrat in shock.

"I can't move my hands."

As he spoke, Matali felt the sensation leave his legs. The next moment, his knees buckled and he sagged, with only Vikramaditya's hands stopping him from hitting the ground.

"I can't feel my hands and legs, Samrat," he said weakly.

Vikramaditya grimaced as his own body was racked with pain. He lowered the deva to the steps, and then doubled over, panting and staring emptily at the steps. The pain passed, and he looked at the deva.

"What shall we do now?" Matali asked.

"We continue," the king replied.

"I can't walk, king," the deva's voice quavered.

With a nod, Vikramaditya put his hands under the deva's arms and pulled him up. Once they were both erect, the samrat bent and hoisted Matali over his shoulders.

"Are you fine now?" he asked.

"Yes, your honour."

With the deva on his back, Vikramaditya mounted the final step and entered the city. The king retraced his steps, making slow progress, stopping every now and then to fight off pain or nausea. Matali had only a vague notion of their progress as he drifted in and out of a fugue. And then, they were at the fallen *peepal* tree that had blocked their path on the way out.

It was still blocking their path.

"I can't hold you and climb over that thing, so you will have to hold me tight," the samrat said to Matali. "Can you?"

"Mmmph," the deva nodded, hooking his arms around Vikramaditya's neck and shoulders.

The king began mounting the massive trunk, finding toeholds in the bark, using his fingers to pull himself up and over. Suddenly, he grunted in pain, and then, as the pain ratcheted up, he screamed in agony—and his hold on the groove in the tree trunk loosened.

He slipped and fell, taking Matali down with him.

Matali landed hard on his back, the samrat's weight on top of him. Pain jarred his body and engulfed his mind, and he screamed.

And blinked.

And saw the face of Kunjala, the other court physician, staring down at him.

"The chief is back," the physician called to someone in relief before returning his gaze. "We were worried... How are you?"

Matali brought his hands to his face and studied them, flexing his arms and wrists cautiously, and wriggling his fingers. He raised his head and observed his legs, lifting and bending one, then the other.

"What's happened?" Kunjala asked, watching him closely. Varahamihira and a pair of junior physicians had come over to look at him, crowding around eagerly.

"Back there, I had lost all sensation in my arms and legs," the deva explained. "But I seem to be alright." He tried to prop himself up, but Kunjala shook his head and pushed him back onto the mat.

"You are weak. Rest a little."

Dhanavantri appeared in Matali's line of vision, looking anxious. "Where is the Samrat?" he asked.

"Isn't he back?" the deva asked, looking to the bed where Vikramaditya lay inert. He turned to Dhanavantri in surprise. "We fell together, and then I was here."

"Fell where?"

"Near the *peepal* that was blocking our path. The one near the city garrison."

Dhanavantri shook his head, clearly not understanding. He hurried back to the king's bed. Almost everyone followed, so only Varahamihira was left standing by his side.

"And the dagger?" the councilor asked in an undertone.

"We got it. The Samrat has it."

With a nod, Varahamihira hobbled over to Vikramaditya's bed. Matali lay by himself for a moment.

"His pulse is extremely low," he heard Dhanavantri say.

Matali sat up, then pushed himself groggily to his feet. Walking over to the huddle around the samrat, he peeked over a shoulder and saw the king lying deathly pale in the light of a lamp. That was when it struck the deva that evening was here, though the sun hadn't quite set as yet.

"They got the dagger," Varahamihira said to Dhanavantri. "It is with the king."

Dhanavantri shook his head. "I can barely feel his pulse." He turned to Kunjala to say something, when Matali spoke.

"I can go back to get it. Them, I mean."

Everyone looked at him. "I can. I was *there*, I know where the Samrat is, where to find him." He looked from Varahamihira to Dhanavantri, pleading with them to let him go. He had been *that* close to the Halahala, and he couldn't leave it in Borderworld. All he had to do was go back, kill the king and bring the dagger back. Then, before anyone in this room realized it, he would be gone—

"It is too dangerous," said Dhanavantri. "I don't know how you came back—"

"He knows where Vikrama is," Varahamihira interrupted. "If anyone can bring the king back, he can—"

"I can't leave my king there. Please let me go." *Please let me go.*

"The Samrat has stopped breathing."

The junior physician's shout topped every other voice, the words ushering a horrified silence into the chamber. Everyone looked at the king. Dhanavantri bent and put a finger under Vikramaditya's nose, feeling for breath. The physician's eyes widened in distress as he looked at Varahamihira.

"I told him I can't do this, that it was too dangerous, but he wouldn't listen. *He just wouldn't listen.* And now? Now, I will have to live with this burden for the rest of my life."

Varahamihira just stared at the king in disbelief. To Matali, it felt as if everyone in the room had stopped breathing.

Dhanavantri knelt and took one of the samrat's hands into his own, grasping it tight. "You can't go like this, Vikrama," his voice quavered with grief. "What will I tell Kshapanaka? What will *she* tell Vishakha? You promised her you would come back. Is this how you keep your promise? Come back, Vikrama, come back."

The physician bowed his head and brought the king's hand to his forehead as the first tears flowed down his cheeks. Matali watched Dhanavantri squeeze Vikramaditya's hand in anguish—and he noticed a warm, incandescent glow slip between the clasped hands, flowing from the physician's fingers onto the samrat's hand, where it disappeared into the skin like water in parched mud.

Matali looked at Dhanavantri with interest, while the physician, for his part, suddenly became alert and attentive, watching the king's face expectantly, his eyes shining.

"What is it?" asked Varahamihira.

"Something is happening," said Kunjala, and glancing in his direction, Matali figured that the other physician had also seen the light pass from Dhanavantri to Vikramaditya.

"But what?" Varahamihira asked again, leaning forward to get a better view.

Vikramaditya coughed and opened his eyes.

As everyone gasped and heaved sighs of relief, Matali's eyes darted to the king's other hand, the one lying idle on the bed.

The hand was clenched into a fist, and the fist clutched a dagger.

***

The sky was still a brilliant blue in the spaces between the trees overhead, and sunshine dusted the very tops of the tallest trees, turning the leaves golden. But close to the floor of the forest, it was already darkening, twilight approaching the eight travellers on swift, murky wings. The travellers had begun pitching camp for the night, a small fire burning cheerfully in the middle of a space that had been cleared for the campsite.

Greeshma finished lighting a tiny earthenware lamp, which he then carried to a tree at the periphery of the clearing. Placing the lamp at the base of the tree, sheltered from the draught, he joined his palms and offered a long and silent prayer. The soldiers in the group eyed the old bandit now and then while exchanging unhappy glances, but Shanku kept her attention focused on whittling a short stake to a point at both ends. Four of the soldiers were planting these stakes all around the clearing so that they jutted up and outward haphazardly, creating a dense and prickly carpet against intruders. The remaining two men were getting a meal ready for the night.

Rising from his prayer, Greeshma shambled back and plunked down by the fire, rubbing his hands for warmth. The days were hot and sticky in the Dandaka, but the temperature dropped as soon as night approached.

"Give us a hand, old man," one of the soldiers working on the stakes called to the bandit. "You're not royalty to be excused from hard work."

A grimace passed Greeshma's lips, but he pretended not to have heard.

"But he *is* working very hard," said another soldier with a snigger. "Can't you see how diligently he lights that lamp for us, evening after evening?"

As a round of snorts and chuckles went around, the scowl on Greeshma's face deepened.

"The lamp is to appease the spirits of the forest, so that they grant us mercy," he bridled. "That lamp is what has kept us safe from harm all these days."

The soldiers shook their heads and chuckled some more.

"Don't laugh at things that you don't understand," Greeshma glared. "And my job is to show you the way to the city of the danavas. The Samrat didn't mention anything about helping you with your work."

A moment's silence followed as the men tensed and looked at one another.

"You aren't doing a particularly good job with that either," the soldier tending to their dinner said flatly from across the fire. "Today is the fourth day since we entered the Dandaka, and by your own admission, you are clueless which way to go next."

"And all you do is waste precious mustard oil on your lamp," piped in his partner.

"Instead of begging them for their mercy, why don't you convince your forest spirits to show us the way to Janasthana?" one of the men at the stakes suggested.

"You disrespect my gods," Greeshma growled angrily. "They will bring their wrath on you—"

"Enough," snapped Shanku, looking up from the stake she was sharpening. "Everyone, *enough*." She stared at the soldiers until they quietened obediently. Her gaze then came to rest on the bandit.

"They are right, you know," she said, pointing at the soldiers with the knife. "You have done little to justify your presence or your worth. Four days, and you still don't know which way to go..."

"I told you, the forest has changed," Greeshma mumbled defensively. "The old paths... they are no longer there. The trees have grown over everything, and I honestly can't—"

"Find the old paths. I don't care how. Just find them."

The bandit shrugged. "How can I find—"

"If you aren't able to uncover a path by this time tomorrow, I will take it as a sign from the forest spirits," said Shanku. "A sign that they demand a sacrifice from us. I don't need to tell you who will be sacrificed to obtain the spirits' blessings. A favourite devotee is always special, I've been told."

The councilor picked up her knife and went back to her whittling. Greeshma blinked at her over the fire, unsure about what to make of her threat. One of the soldiers preparing dinner looked across at him and grinned. "This way or that, you will be responsible for showing us the way to Janasthana," the man said under his breath, though Shanku heard him nonetheless.

Out of the corner of her eye, Shanku watched the old robber get up and go over to the men putting the stakes into the ground. As he squatted to help them, her mind clouded at the thought of how little they had achieved since crossing the Payoshni. By the end of their second day in the forest, it had become clear that there really were no paths left, that the jungle had claimed everything back. All the same, they had persevered, watching their backs as they had scouted around for a sign telling them in what direction Janasthana lay.

Greeshma was probably being truthful while claiming he couldn't find the paths, but Shanku needed results quickly. They were deep within the Dandaka, and their rations had begun depleting, though there was enough food available in the forest to keep them from starving. The forest itself was hopelessly humid, and they were constantly assailed by parasitic insects. Everyone was sore with bites and rashes, and there was an onset of fever in two men. What was most disquieting, though, was the constant sense they had of being watched—a tingling sensation on the back of their necks, impossible to pinpoint. None of them knew whether it was a predator, or if the eyes belonged to the very beings they had come in search of, but with every passing moment, the feeling of dread had grown on them.

"I told the Samrat coming here was madness," the bandit

muttered, driving a stake into the ground. "These stakes won't stop the things that are out there in the dark. They will come for us, and we will die, one by one, like my men died—"

"Shut your mouth and work quietly," one of the men snarled in irritation, swatting an insect that had alighted on his arm.

Greeshma fell back into a grumpy silence.

Raising her head, Shanku noticed the soldiers stare nervously into the surrounding darkness. They too had felt the sudden shiver on their napes, she realized. They too had felt the eyes on them again...

***

Palace hands were lighting the lamps along the galleries as Matali strode past them, a perceptible swagger in his step, a half-smirk playing on his lips. He had recovered swiftly from the trip into Borderworld, suffering no visible ill effects, and though he rued not being able to snatch the dagger when he'd been alone with the king, he now knew its whereabouts. All he needed to do was to send Indra the message, and then sit back and wait for the deva armies to begin attacking Ujjayini.

He intended sending that message as soon as the matter of that stupid dead body from the lake had been sorted.

Since he was the chief of the Palace Guards, a corpse in the palace lake was his problem, which was why he had been summoned as soon as they heard he had returned with the samrat. The message to Indra was a priority, but as he had to keep up appearances here for a while longer, the body came first. He would, of course, feign ignorance, pretending to be flummoxed and horrified at its gruesomeness. Then, once everyone had agreed that it was quite impossible to tell whose corpse it was, he would decree that it be taken away for a quiet, anonymous cremation.

And that would be the formal end of Vismaya. No one to miss him when he was alive. No one to miss him when he was dead.

That was one of the main reasons Matali had decided to impersonate Vismaya to infiltrate the palace. Yes, he and Vismaya had shared a similar physique, and the man was indeed well placed within the palace, his rank granting him almost unlimited access. But the fact that the old chief of the Palace Guards had no close relations meant there was no one to notice if he accidentally said or did something that could blow his cover.

Vismaya had died that night, his body disposed of in the lake, because he was a lonely man.

Under Kshapanaka's orders, the body had been moved to one of the palace's smaller hospices, out of the public gaze. It was into this hospice that Matali turned, brushing aside the door curtains and entering a room moderately full of people. He saw Kshapanaka talking to a junior physician, while seven or eight palace guards stood around exchanging notes.

The deva bowed to Kshapanaka, who responded with a nod. Matali walked up to the corpse, which lay on the floor on a straw mat, its face and head covered with a cotton cloth. The deva looked at the palace guards in enquiry, but they simply shrugged back. Matali squatted next to the corpse and reached for the cloth when Kshapanaka spoke.

"It's not a pretty sight," she warned.

Matali knew that. He was the one responsible for what was under that cloth. He knew exactly what to expect.

"Who is it, your honour?" he asked, looking at her, his hand hovering over the cloth.

"There is no way of telling."

Of course, there wasn't. Matali had made certain of that. Not out of any love for brutality, but out of sheer necessity; he had needed the man's face and features—*and* his vocal cords—for his disguise.

The deva lifted the cloth. As the guards grunted in distaste at the mangled visage, Matali too pretended to be offended, dropping the cloth back and covering his nose and mouth.

"This is horrible, your honour. How can we ever know who this was?"

"That is our problem," Kshapanaka replied. "Also, who did this to him?"

While the deva pretended to stare at the corpse in bewilderment, the door curtains were swept aside and Kunjala entered, trailed by a pair of guards. As the physician came to Matali's side, the guards sidled up as well to stare curiously at the body.

"We must try to get an identification," said Kshapanaka. "If we learn who this is, we might be able to find out who did this."

"It will be difficult, but we must try," Matali agreed, rising. It wouldn't be difficult; it would be impossible. And that was why, even after the oracle had brought the body to everyone's notice, not once had he worried about being found out.

"We were trying to figure out a way of preserving the body, vaidyanath," Kshapanaka said to Kunjala, gesturing at the junior physician.

"It depends on the state the body is in," the physician replied. Taking a nearby lamp, he bent to examine the corpse.

Everyone crowded around, and Matali took the opportunity to study the effect of his work more closely. He watched the physicians consult each other, and he listened with satisfaction as Kunjala told Kshapanaka that the body was already decaying, and that it couldn't be preserved for more than a couple of days. After that it would have to be disposed of—

"Your honour... *your honour...*"

The words had been spoken loud enough for everyone to hear, so everyone stopped to look.

Matali saw that the speaker was one of the two palace guards who had accompanied Kunjala. "Yes?" he raised his eyebrows. "What is it?"

"Your honour," the guard avoided the deva's gaze and looked at Kshapanaka instead.

"Speak up," the councilor egged the man on with a wave of her hand.

"Your honour... my friend here thinks he knows who that is."

Everyone stared at the second guard, a young man, junior in rank to most of the other guards in the room.

"Who is it?" asked Kshapanaka.

The man hesitated, looking nervously around the room, but the older one prodded him with his elbow.

"Your honour," the young man said, licking his lips and gathering his resolve, "I think the body is that of Vismaya, the chief of the Palace Guards."

There was a moment of stunned silence. Matali tensed and took a careful step back.

"You mean *him*, your chief Vismaya?" Pointing at the deva, Kshapanaka stared incredulously at the guard. "You are saying this is *his* body?"

The other guards had started snickering and nudging one another, but the older guard cleared his throat.

"Everyone, let us please listen to him." He nodded encouragingly to his younger companion.

"Your honour," the guard said, disregarding the derisive glances he was getting. "If we look carefully, we can see that the corpse is missing the tip of its little finger... not this hand, the other one, *there*."

Everyone craned or bent to look.

Matali cursed and clenched his left fist tight. He had carelessly overlooked the finger, and it had given him away. He realized that he shouldn't have stopped at the man's head and face. He should have stripped and worn the whole body. He took another step back.

"Vismaya doesn't have a part of his little finger," the young guard said. "He told me he had lost it in the war against the savages. We were chatting about the barbarians one night a few weeks ago, and that's when he told me. That is why it is still so vivid in my memory."

"I remember," Kunjala nodded slowly. "The wound had become infected, and if I am correct, Dhanavantri vaidyanath had treated and cured it." The room was suddenly serious. Lifting the corpse's hand, Kunjala examined the stumpy finger. He then looked sharply across at Matali. "Show us your left hand."

"He has five full fingers, your honour," the deva heard the young guard say. "I saw, and *that* is what made me sure about the body."

"Would you care explaining this?" Kshapanaka faced Matali, her hand going to her sword.

Matali smiled at the councilor thinly, before directing a venomous glance at the young guard. All the while, he kept backing towards the wall.

"There is no way of escaping from here." Kshapanaka drew her sword, and the guards all followed suit, three of them swiftly blocking the way to the exit.

The deva retreated until his back was pressed against the wall. He smiled again. Then he started slipping and oozing through the wall.

"What is this...?" one of the guards yelped.

No one responded. Everyone remained frozen, their soles stuck to the floor.

Matali grinned, relishing the expressions of bafflement

on everybody's faces. Then, passing right through the wall, he found himself in a large, airy chamber where the palace's washing had been hung out to dry.

"He is in the laundry next door," he heard Kshapanaka shout. "Get him."

There was a rush of feet, but the deva was already moving, weaving in and out of the hanging clothes, running to the other end of the chamber. A couple of maids watched him as he floundered by, and from their expressions, he could tell they were convinced that the chief of the Palace Guards had lost his mind.

"Inform the guards," Kshapanaka yelled from somewhere behind. "Close all exits and seal the causeway."

Matali chuckled at the absurdity of the instructions. The humans had seen enough to know that doors, gates and walls couldn't keep him from going where he wanted, yet... He heard feet pounding after him. Reaching the end of the laundry, he oozed out, and into a storeroom stacked with sacks of grain. He turned and went through the wall to his left into an empty terrace, which he crossed before turning right through a closed door, into a curtained room full of musical instruments. Listening to the sounds of the chase grow distant, he traversed the room before slipping into another, dark and musty from disuse.

Confident of having shaken off his pursuers for the moment, the deva paused to catch his breath and take stock, using the opportunity to revert to his own identity. Right now, being a stranger in the palace wasn't as risky as being Vismaya's double.

There was nothing to be gained by simply dodging around the palace like this, Matali saw. The search could last forever, and he didn't have time—there was a message waiting to be delivered to Indra. It was best he left quietly. Of course, he could try hunting for the Halahala first, but with the alarm having been sounded, the guard would be up, and Vikramaditya would have been warned. It wasn't a risk worth taking.

Still, there was one last thing that needed doing.

Matali slipped out of the dark room into a gallery. Checking to make sure that he wasn't being observed, he turned and set off in the direction of the samrat's chambers.

The palace was in a state of tumult, swarming with guards, so it took the deva a detour—slipping in and out of many walls and doors—before he made it to the king's bedchamber. The room was empty, and Matali didn't spare it a glance, going straight to the adjoining anteroom instead. Stepping right through the door, he sought out the table that was pushed against the wall. The room was indirectly lit by the lamp burning in the bedchamber, but the light was sufficient to see what lay on the table.

An unlit brass lamp. An inkwell and a pair of quills.

And something long, concealed within the folds of a length of satin.

The deva crossed over to the table and brushed his fingers lightly against the fine satin. Peeling the soft cloth back, he exposed a pair of curving swords nesting in their scabbards. Heavy hilts protruded from both sheaths, which were crafted out of old animal hide.

Yes.

Smiling to himself, Matali lifted one of the scabbards, surprised at its weight. Running his fingers along the plain, iron hilt, he glanced at the second sword, ascertaining that it was, indeed, a twin of the one he was holding.

On an impulse, the deva drew the sword from its sheath. Maybe, he thought to himself at the back of his head, just *maybe*, he was also worthy enough to... He peered at the blade, turning it one way and the other, hoping to see a flame catch and come alive. But nothing happened. Cold metal gleamed back at him in the dull light. With a sigh, he slid the weapon back into its scabbard. In his hands, this was just another common iron sword. Only in Vikramaditya's hands would it transform into a Hellfire.

Which was why it was so vital he took these swords away from Vikramaditya. Without them, Diti's *churails* couldn't materialize to stop Indra's armies from devastating Ujjayini. Without them, the samrat would cease being the Wielder of the Hellfires—powerless to protect his city and his promise made to the Omniscient One.

Swaddling the swords quickly in the length of satin and holding the bundle close to his chest, Matali left the samrat's chambers. He didn't regret not getting hold of Veeshada's dagger as much now—he had the Hellfires, which would make the task of finding the dagger that much easier.

He knew Indra would be pleased with him.

Brother

They are saying the Samrat nearly died, your honour."

Queen Upashruti stared at her maid in horror, unable to find words to express how she felt. At last, getting up from the seat in front of the large bronze and tin alloy mirror, still holding the rosewood comb in her hand, she moved in the direction of the door. "I have to see him," she announced to no one in particular.

She took a few steps and stopped abruptly, as if remembering something. Her face fell, and she turned towards the large bed that stood in the middle of her bedchamber. Flinging herself down onto layers of soft cotton quilts, she buried her face in the crook of one arm and let out a sob.

"Are you alright, Queen Mother?" the maid asked.

Upashruti nodded tightly without raising her head.

"I can get you something if you are—"

"I am *fine*," the Queen Mother shout-wailed, glaring at the maid with tearful eyes, the kohl already beginning to run. "Just... just leave me alone."

The maid withdrew with a hasty bow, leaving Upashruti in the company of a moth that had flown in through the open window and was now circling the single lamp furiously, flying dangerously close to the flame as if it were on a death wish. The queen stayed on the bed with her head down, so still that she gave the impression she was asleep, but her thoughts were a frantic flutter that could rival the wingbeats of the suicidal moth.

They are saying the Samrat nearly died.

Upashruti's mind went back to the night her son had died for the first time. The brain fever had set in one afternoon, and by the evening of the next day, all the palace physicians were struggling to keep the young Vikramaditya from slipping into coma. And then, just like that, they had told her that the boy was no more. The Queen Mother remembered wailing at the half-moon that hung outside her window as King Mahendraditya took her into his big arms, comforting her even as fat tears rolled down his cheeks. She recalled the despair and loneliness that had set in, taking her in its cold, relentless grip.

Even after Kunjala had hurried in to inform them that their son had miraculously returned to life, that despair and loneliness had never really left Upashruti, taking the shape of a fear and lurking in some faraway recess like a ghost. And now, after so many years, fear had given way to certainty as she grappled despair and loneliness in this bedchamber of hers, alone and abandoned by her son—who, they said, had nearly died while undertaking a trip to Borderworld to keep a promise made to Shiva.

I will shield you, mother. Because you are my mother, and nothing can ever change that. And also, because father would have wanted it no other way. It is a promise I made him when he gave me his sword—to uphold your dignity to my last breath. He loved you very much, mother. I will not break my promise to him.

Vikramaditya would never break a promise, she knew. He

had promised to uphold her dignity, and he would.

She wished he had instead promised Mahendraditya that he would love her, no matter what happened. Then he would have had to talk to her, laugh at her jokes like he used to, or play her the *rudra veena* when she felt like listening to him play. Then he wouldn't have been able to scratch her out of his life the way he had, avoiding her whenever he could, and scarcely speaking beyond what was necessary when a meeting was inevitable. He had been the centre of her life, all her life. Everything that she had done, she had done for him. Upashruti couldn't bear to think that nowadays, she wasn't even allowed into the fringes of his.

Yet, her son was not to blame, she knew. On the contrary, he was the victim, bearing the consequences of her actions, while trying to keep her dignity intact—and keep his paternity from being called into question. She knew about Vararuchi's rebellion, and understood its impact on not only her son, but also on the authority of the throne. Her past was casting a long shadow on the unblemished rule of the Adityas, and it was her son who was shouldering that burden—

"...a guest, your honour."

Upashruti thought the maid's voice seemed to come from afar, until she realized that she had her pillow over her head.

"What?" She looked at the maid irritably. "Didn't I say I wanted to be left alone?"

"My apologies, Queen Mother, but you have a guest."

"Who is it?" asked Upashruti, getting up and leaning forward to look at the door.

Her face went pale and she froze.

The figure at the doorstep was in shadow, yet the Queen Mother knew who it was. She hadn't seen the figure in over a decade, yet she knew.

I should have seen this coming, Upashruti thought to herself, as she rose and went to the door slowly, not knowing what to expect. The woman standing there had not set foot in the palace since the day Mahendraditya had returned to Ujjayini with Upashruti as his young bride. She had refused to move into the palace even when the barbarians were laying Avanti to waste. She had been resolute in her decision to keep away from the palace—and from her husband's second wife.

Yet, here she stood now, inside the palace, at the entrance to her bedchamber.

Ushantha. Mahendraditya's first wife. Vararuchi's mother.

Here at last to demand explanations, to rub her rival's nose in the dirt, to exact her revenge.

***

The maid's large, almond-shaped eyes stared back at him and Kshapanaka, their depth and beauty marred by the slightest ripple of doubt and apprehension, probably revealing more than they intended to, Vikramaditya thought to himself.

"Can you tell me once again how Vismaya is related to you?" asked Kshapanaka.

"He is my uncle, your honour."

"We got that. But in what way? I mean—"

"My mother was his sister… his cousin, actually." Urvashi paused. "Why do you ask, your honour? What is this about?"

Vikramaditya turned casually to see Pralupi glowering by the door to the balcony, watching the conversation with uneasy eyes. He fleetingly wondered about the expression on his sister's face.

"You are not from Ujjayini," Kshapanaka persisted, ignoring the apsara's questions.

"No, I was born and brought up in Viswapuri. My mother had married there."

"Into which family did she marry?"

Vikramaditya thought he saw the woman tense.

"I don't want to talk about them, your honour. They were unkind to mother and me."

"Why do you suddenly want to know all this?" Pralupi interrupted petulantly.

Kshapanaka looked at the king, who motioned to his sister, seeking patience. He then nodded at the councilor to continue.

"Where is your mother now?"

"She died owing to failing health, your honour. That's why I came here to *mama*."

"And your father?"

"He too is no more. He went before mother did." Urvashi paused again. "Is something the matter? Why are you asking me all this?" Her eyes went to Vikramaditya's and held for a fraction of a second. Again, the samrat sensed a hint of panic in them. "Is... is *mama* alright?"

Kshapanaka glanced at the samrat again. This was the crucial bit, and the crux of their problem: who was this woman who was serving as Pralupi's maid? Was she really the niece of the dead chief of the Palace Guards, as she claimed to be, or was she another component of the grand deceit that had been playing out in the palace? *Which* Vismaya had been instrumental in bringing her to the palace and introducing her into Pralupi's service—the one they had fished out of the water, or the one who had volunteered to accompany the samrat into Borderworld? Kshapanaka and Vikramaditya were here to try and determine the truth, but they knew getting to it would be far from easy; one false step could put the potential mischief-maker on her guard. They needed answers, but these had to be unearthed cleverly.

"Mithyamayi," said Kshapanaka, taking a deep breath, "You must have heard about the body at the bottom of the palace lake by now. Perhaps you also know that the body was brought out of the lake this afternoon, horribly mutilated and almost unrecognizable." The councilor paused. There was no reaction from the maid. "Well, the body has been identified. It belongs to your uncle, Vismaya."

Urvashi's eyes widened in shock and her fingers flew to her mouth. "No... oh, no."

It struck the samrat that the woman's expression was wrong—it was too soon for shock. Considering the copycat Vismaya had been around in the palace until a little while ago, fooling everyone, surprise or puzzlement should have come first to Mithyamayi. *Unless she knew the truth beforehand...*

"How can it be Vismaya?" Pralupi asked. "I saw him just this morning—"

"We are certain it is him, sister," Vikramaditya replied, glad to note Pralupi's reaction. Hers was the right one, not the maid's reaction.

"I know this must be very distressing," Kshapanaka continued, "but there's more. In all these days that Vismaya's body was in the lake, we had *another* Vismaya here, walking around the palace, dispensing his duties. Which means that for some time, we have had *two* Vismayas—one dead in the water, the other alive here. The dead one, the real Vismaya. The living one, an impersonator."

Urvashi's eyes stayed round in wonder. "Where is he?"

"Who?" the samrat asked, suddenly alert.

"He... the imposter?"

Vikramaditya looked at the apsara closely. "When confronted, he managed giving us the slip, and now he appears to have vanished from the palace."

"Oh..."

The king was certain the woman's shoulders had sagged in relief.

"Oh..." she said again, burying her face in her hands and sobbing. "*Mama...*"

"That's enough." Pralupi sailed up to put her arms protectively around the apsara. "She has lost an uncle. Leave her be and stop bothering her."

Urvashi turned gratefully to the princess, her doe-like eyes brimming with tears.

Vikramaditya cleared his throat. "As Vismaya has no family of his own in Ujjayini, the duty of conducting his last rites falls on you," he said gently. "We will get someone to help you. You can count on the sympathy and support of the palace."

"Thank you, your honour," the apsara replied, joining her palms.

Kshapanaka and Vikramaditya were almost at the door when the king stopped and looked back.

"What was your mother's name?"

"Karunya, your honour," Urvashi said, blinking through her tears.

"And your father's?"

The apsara hesitated for just a moment. "Ayyan."

"Ayyan..." the samrat paused, as if in thought. "Father knew an Ayyan from Viswapuri. One of the best horseshoe makers of his time. Could they be the same?"

Urvashi shook her head.

"What did your father do?"

"He was... a fruit seller."

"Mmm... definitely not the same." With that, Vikramaditya left Pralupi's chambers.

Kshapanaka was silent by his side for a dozen paces. "What did you think of her?" she asked finally. "It's hard to say—"

"She is lying."

The councilor stared at her king. "Really? Are you certain?"

"Almost."

"Would you care to explain?"

"Her discomfort with talking about her father's family is odd, to begin with. I understand it can be traumatic if there has been discord in the family, but I'll come back to that later. Then, when she learned about the body being that of

Vismaya, she registered shock, whereas she should have been surprised at the absurdity of it being Vismaya's body. Her reaction suggests she knew it was Vismaya beforehand. And when told about the imposter, she was more interested in *him* than in her own dead uncle. Strange, right? Also, she was eager to know *where* the imposter was, and not *why* he had been masquerading as her uncle—*because she already knows why*. Lastly, when asked her mother's name, the answer came easily, but she struggled to give her father's name. Why? The first had been rehearsed, but she had to invent the second. To test this, I asked about Ayyan, the horseshoe maker."

"The one the old king knew," Kshapanaka nodded.

"I doubt whether father knew any horseshoe makers in Viswapuri," Vikramaditya shrugged. "Definitely none by the name of Ayyan. But Mithyamayi doesn't know this. She obviously can't say it was the same Ayyan, and as expected, she denies it. But now, when I offhandedly ask what her father did, she is cornered. She is compelled to provide us with an answer. So, she cooks up his trade."

"Fruit trader," the councilor smiled thinly.

"Send a message to Viswapuri, asking them to look for a fruit trader by the name of Ayyan. He would have been alive in the last twenty-five years. Someone who was married to a woman named Karunya and had at least one daughter. Let us also find out what we can about Vismaya's family, particularly about this cousin, Karunya." They had reached the turning to the council chamber. "It's my guess we won't find anyone to match either Ayyan or his wife Karunya. They are both made up."

"Why not have the maid arrested and questioned then?" asked Kshapanaka.

"Because we have nothing against her. Everything I just said is conjecture, based entirely on my observations. There is no evidence that she's been up to something, that she has lied to us." The samrat paused. "Though I am certain she *has* an agenda." He nodded at Kshapanaka. "I have to tell you something. Come."

Once they were inside the council chamber, Vikramaditya leaned forward in his chair. "Keep this to yourself, but last night, Mithyamayi tried to seduce me."

Kshapanaka stared at the samrat, her outrage growing steadily as he summarized what had transpired in Pralupi's chambers. By the time he was through, the councilor's face was red with rage, her hands clenched into fists on the council table.

"What nerve!" she burst forth. "How dare she even think of pulling such a stunt? Why didn't you say anything sooner?"

"I didn't know what to make of it," said Vikramaditya. "I didn't know whether it was just a palace maid's foolish fancy, or whether she had a deeper motive. As no harm had been done, I decided to let the matter rest. But now, I wonder..."

The king and councilor sat quietly in the flickering lamplight, deep in thought.

"I say we arrest and interrogate her," said Kshapanaka at last.

"Without concrete proof, that is of no use," the samrat insisted, shaking his head. "We must give her an opportunity to incriminate herself. It is best that she imagines she has fooled us; then chances are she will slip up and give herself away. But make sure she is put under tight surveillance. I want to know everything that she is up to."

***

The clatter and roll of the bones on the cold marble floor reached Hiranyaksha's ears, over and over again, as he stood gazing at the mist rising up from the Patala Ganga. His brawny arms were folded tight against his chest, and his brow under the curling ram horns was knotted and quivering, as if he was struggling to contain a mighty rage—which had been the case ever since Shukracharya had returned from Borderworld.

Hearing the bones being swept up and thrown down once again, the asura lord looked over his shoulder at Shukracharya, who was sitting on his haunches, a mandala drawn on the floor in front of him. The high priest was focused on reading the bones, frowning hard as he delved into every little detail pertaining to the Halahala and endeavoured to decipher each cryptic answer correctly. He had hardly spoken a word since his return; frazzled and fretful, he had stormed straight to the bones, leaving Hiranyaksha and Holika waiting impatiently for him.

"The devas have stolen a lead on us," the high priest broke the silence with a grimace.

"They haven't got the dagger, have they?" Holika's voice had an edge of panic as she turned from the other window to consider the mahaguru.

"No, the dagger is still with Vikramaditya," Shukracharya replied, gathering the bones and getting to his feet. "But the devas are closer to it than ever before."

"How did they manage that, mahaguru?" Hiranyaksha frowned in displeasure.

"Indra got the crafty Matali and Urvashi to infiltrate the king's palace. Their cover was so good, Vikramaditya suspected nothing—he even brought Matali unwittingly to Borderworld to help him retrieve the dagger." Shukracharya combed his beard with his fingers in disbelief. "The Halahala was within a hand's reach of the deva, but not for a moment did the king or I realize it."

"Is it possible that the king has allied with the devas against us?" the asura lord's golden eyes narrowed in apprehension.

"The bones tell me the humans have seen through Matali's disguise, and that the deva has fled the palace. That overrules the possibility of any alliance between them."

"What about the apsara?" asked Holika.

"She is still in the palace. Presumably, her disguise is still intact."

"That is worrying," Hiranyaksha grimaced.

Shukracharya nodded. "What also bothers me is that an army of nagas and kinnaras led by Takshaka and Tribhanu is all set to attack Avanti. They are close to the kingdom and could unleash an assault at short notice."

"The humans should be able to resist the nagas and kinnaras," Hiranyaksha looked at the high priest hopefully. "The king wields the Hellfires, and his council comprises the Nine Pearls…"

"True. But remember that the power exerted by the Nine Pearls has diminished considerably, and the humans have been greatly weakened. It is also possible that the nagas and kinnaras are there only to distract the king, so Urvashi will be free to hunt for the dagger."

Hiranyaksha and Holika looked at each other, aghast. "We can't let the devas win," said the Witch Queen.

"We are too far away to do anything other than hope that the humans prevail," said the high priest. With a scowl and a rueful shake of his head, he added, "Had I taken a larger army into Borderworld, this would never have come to pass. I estimated the potency of the *sanjivani-mantra* wrongly, and Vikramaditya reached there in the nick of time…"

"Let us not agonize over bygones, mahaguru," said Holika. "Let us instead devote our energy to doing whatever needs to be done next."

"You are right," said Shukracharya, squaring his shoulders. "We cannot let one setback drag us down."

"We must strike at Ujjayini as swiftly as possible," said Hiranyaksha. "If the devas tarry for some reason, or if their plans get thwarted, we can still recover the dagger."

"Yes," said the high priest, thoughtfully. "It would have

been ideal if Hiranyakashipu had been with us, but as he is well on his way to Devaloka, we will do this ourselves." He looked at the asura lord. "Order the vyalas to be harnessed and readied for battle. I will ask Amarka and Chandasura to make preparations for departure."

***

Standing ten paces apart, and separated by close to four decades of simmering rivalry and mistrust, Queen Upashruti and Ushantha stared at one another. The wavering light of the lamp illuminated a small portion of the bedchamber, leaving the remainder of the room in unfathomable shadow. The palace appeared to have gone still, all sounds suddenly muted, as if in deference to the moment that had brought the dead king's two wives together.

"At last," sighed Upashruti.

"I would have come earlier had I known," Ushantha replied. "Where I live, news takes its own time to arrive."

Upashruti let silence briefly take over as she assessed Ushantha. "I expect you want to know what the truth is, whether the charges levelled by Indra have any substance?" She turned her back to the king's first wife wearily.

"That is not why I have come. I am here for Vikrama."

A wrinkle formed on the queen's forehead. She blinked at Ushantha in confusion.

"I feel terrible about what Vikrama has had to undergo," Ushantha continued. Stepping closer to the light, she peered at the Queen Mother. "You do realize that it is *your* actions that have brought this crisis upon your son and this kingdom, don't you?"

Upashruti assessed Ushantha suspiciously. "Why do you care about Vikrama? He's not even your son..."

Ushantha gave the queen a pitying look. "I don't expect you to ever understand this, Upashruti," she said with a shake of her head.

The Queen Mother turned and went to her bed. Sitting down heavily, she picked up the rosewood comb and began running it through her hair absentmindedly, her eyes on the lamp. The moth had burned its wings and now lay half-submerged in the oil, dying slowly, draining out in minute gasps and pants.

"If only we could see into the future and know the consequences of our actions," she said whimsically, almost speaking to herself. "We would be so much the wiser, more prudent." Upashruti looked up at Ushantha. There were unshed tears in her eyes, and now when she spoke, her voice was smaller. "I can only say that I am sorry. Had I known that one day, this is how the kingdom would tear itself apart, I would never have given in to the deva's charms, *never*. I did King Mahendraditya wrong, and this is how my misdeeds have come back to haunt Vikrama and me."

Upashruti dropped her gaze to her hands, which lay on her lap, inert and defeated. Ushantha's eyes crinkled at the corners, and she took another step in the queen's direction. But stopping herself, she drew herself erect, and her eyes hardened.

"While you did grave injustice to Mahendra, the actions that I refer to pertain not to the deva, but to your treatment of Vararuchi." Seeing the queen look up sharply, she added, "Had he not suffered the way he did, he would never have rebelled the way he now has."

Upashruti stared at the older woman in shock. "How…?" her voice trembled and cracked.

"He told me everything." Ushantha paused and stared coldly. "You pushed him too far, and now poor Vikrama is bearing the backlash."

The Queen Mother's lip quivered, and one tear broke its

shackles and ran down her cheek. A second followed, swift and hot with pain. Upashruti buried her face in her hands, her shoulders convulsing as shame and sadness racked her body.

Ushantha looked down at the queen, her own face tortured with grief and anger. "Why did you do it, Upashruti, *why*? Tell me why Vararuchi deserved the treatment you meted out to him. What had my boy done to you that you hated him *so* much?"

Upashruti wept into her hands. "I am... sorry," she gasped between sobs.

"But I want to know *why*," said Ushantha, relentless.

"*I too want to know what you did and why.*"

Upashruti gave a start. Ushantha turned at the same time. Both women looked towards the door—where Vikramaditya stepped across the threshold into the ring of lamplight.

The samrat put his hands together in a *pranaam* to Ushantha. "They told me you had come to the palace, *badi-maa*," he said. "I came by to see you. I couldn't help overhearing you, so..."

Without waiting for an answer, he considered Upashruti's stunned, upturned face. "Tell me, mother. I'm listening."

***

There were seven sentries posted at the city's eastern gate. All seven of them sat or leaned on the stone platform adjoining the gate, which formed the base of the stairwell that gave access to the walkway on the walls above. The soldiers had been whiling away their time in a game of *ashtapada*—the grid crudely drawn on stone using charcoal, pebbles to substitute for the playing pieces—but the game had been abandoned, and they were all now in the midst of heated discussion, their weapons lying about them unattended.

"I am telling you, the barbarians stand no chance against us," said the one who looked to be the most senior of the lot, a thickset man with a bushy grey beard, his eyes combative in the flickering torchlight. "Have any of you seen the Hellfires in the Samrat's hands? I have," he thumped his chest in pride. "The barbarians will all be burned, you'll see. *Burned alive*." He snapped his fingers rapidly to demonstrate how the barbarians would have their lives snuffed out.

"Yes, but this time, they have Councilor Kalidasa—" one of the guards began arguing, but the senior man waved a hand to silence him.

"Humph… that makes no difference," he said. "You heard what the Samrat said in the city garrison this morning, didn't you? No Kalidasa can stand up to the Hellfires."

"Councilor Kalidasa wrestled and threw one of those rakshasas into the palace lake," a third sentry reminded. "That is how strong he is."

"Ehh…" the old guard of the City Watch grunted with a dismissive shrug.

"What about Councilor Vararuchi?" a fourth voice chipped in, wondering. "Will he be with us or against us when the barbarians come?"

"He is against Councilor Kalidasa."

"But he is also against the Samrat—"

"Yes, but I have heard he has started losing support…"

The men were so caught up in their debate over the imminent war with the Hunas that they failed to notice the ground begin to shift and heave at a few places inside the city gate. It had to be said in the guards' favour that the movements were subtle and inconspicuous, the soil moving so softly it would have been impossible for them to tell in the dark, unless they had been staring straight at the ground, which they had no reason to do. So, the upheavals continued, a burrowing up from underneath that gained momentum as more and more mud was pushed aside for something to rise to the earth's surface.

"From what I know, the garrison of Musili is the only one that is holding out against the Samrat."

"You are right. Some of the others had agreed initially—"

A hand thrust into the air from underground, the fingers hooked and clawing for purchase.

"The Samrat's speech made the difference—"

A horned head with a snake's snout emerged from below at another spot. A third head broke into the open elsewhere.

The heads had small eyes, perfectly round and coppery in the reflected torchlight. The eyes watched the sentries, intently and without blinking.

Two more heads pushed their way out of the topsoil.

"I am inclined to agree with you. With the Samrat's Hellfires, we are invincible—"

At an unseen signal, the five sets of eyes widened. The next instant, the ground near the gate erupted as five naga warriors rose out of the earth like spectres, showering mud everywhere, wicked knives gleaming in their long, sinewy hands.

"I would think the councilor—" the guard who was speaking stopped, his eyes popping out of his head as he saw the grotesque nagas emerge from the dark.

"*What is this?*" he yelped in panic.

The rest of the sentries took too long to react. They were still turning to look when the nagas were upon them, slashing and hacking. The guards were cut down even as they scrambled for their weapons, the nagas' knives curving and slicing expertly so the soldiers of the Watch were choking on their own screams and dying before they could raise an alarm. Blood scattered in the torchlight, spraying on the walls, splattering on the stone floor, smudging the charcoal lines of the half-completed game of *ashtapada*. The sentries fell quickly, one after another.

It was over in a few moments.

The nagas sheathed their bloodied knives.

As four of them began the task of hiding the sentries' corpses—hoisting the bodies onto the platform, dragging them into the stairwell, and stowing them out of sight—the fifth naga pushed open the small door built into the larger gate. Stepping out, he stood in the dark, his tail twitching in the dirt behind him. Then, lifting his head to the air, he spoke in a whisper that had no words, and was all the rustling of dry leaves and the melancholic sighing of the wind.

And it was the wind that possibly bore the whisper from Ujjayini's eastern gate all the way across the broken countryside to a copse of trees, where Takshaka waited in the company of Matali, Tribhanu and a few other kinnaras. The naga lord listened with a cocked head before turning to Tribhanu.

"My nagas have seized control of the city's gates," Takshaka's own words came out in half-whispers. "There is nothing to stop your army from riding into Ujjayini."

"Thank you, my friend," Tribhanu replied, looking towards the splash of radiance midway to the horizon. Addressing Matali, who sat astride a white horse, he added, "We must go."

The deva glanced down at the naga. "I will meet you at the palace shortly."

Takshaka nodded as Matali turned his horse around.

Tribhanu and his generals followed Matali, the bells on the kinnara lord's feet jingling softly in the dark. Once the group had melted into the darkness, the naga turned to gaze upon the patch of light that was Ujjayini. He was the sole member of his tribe out here now—the rest of the naga army was already buried deep, waiting for his sign to... A rumble emerged from Takshaka's left, sweeping up to him all the way from the south, interrupting his thoughts. He turned to observe the army of centaurs ride out of the forest and pick up speed, thundering towards Ujjayini.

It took a while for the sound of the hooves to ease into silence. When all that was left of the kinnaras was a thrum in the earth underfoot, Takshaka crouched and dug the ground furiously with his feet and bare hands. He kicked at the dirt, scooping it aside with his strong fingers, shovelling mud swiftly, tunnelling deeper and deeper, until in no time he was gone, lost from sight.

***

The Queen Mother sat with her head bowed, her eyes on the rosewood comb that was still in her hands.

Vikramaditya looked at Ushantha briefly, his face pained. Turning back to Upashruti, he asked, "But why, mother? Why?"

"For you." The queen's voice shook. "I was afraid for you."

"I don't understand."

Upashruti was silent for a moment. Then, with a visible effort, she raised her head to look at Ushantha. "The king always loved her more," she said, blinking, forcing herself to face what she had silently dreaded all her life in the palace. "Nothing I did could change that, so I was afraid he would love her son more than mine. That her son would become king."

The samrat and Ushantha stared at one another in shock.

Ushantha slowly sat beside the queen. She placed a hand on Upashruti's shoulder. "Mahendra loved you very much," she said gently. "And there was nothing dearer to Mahendra than your Vikrama. Yes, he loved Vararuchi too. But like a king would love his general, not as a father would love his son. In Mahendra's eyes, there was only one future king of Avanti. And that was not my son."

"Even if it had been Vararuchi, *so what*, mother?" Vikramaditya stood with his hands on his hips, shaking his head. "He is just, and he loves Avanti with all his heart. He would have been a good king to his people. Why was it so important to you that *your son* became king?" He paused. "At least now I know where Pralupi gets *her* obsession from."

He turned to Ushantha. "And you, *badi-maa*... you knew of this all along? What brother was going through?"

"I have known for some time now—"

"Why didn't you tell anyone? Why, *badi-maa*?" The king turned to face the shadows. "And not once did brother share this with anyone but you. Why? Why did he suffer in silence?"

All three figures remained in their places, not moving, steeped in thought. The lamp's flame wavered in a mild draught, so that shadows moved and waned around the chamber.

"The reason behind brother's anger and resentment is now plain," Vikramaditya said at last. "Grave injustice was done to him; he has been wronged for too long. The palace owes him an apology. I owe him an apology." He turned to the women. "I will bring Vararuchi back to the palace, *badi-maa*. I will make things right."

The samrat headed for the door, but Ushantha's words stopped him.

"Before you go, Vikrama, you should know that I am not here to seek justice for Vararuchi. I am here to make things right for *everyone*. I understand Vararuchi's anger. But I disapprove of his actions, which have brought disrepute to this palace and divided the kingdom that his father fought so hard to protect from the barbarians. While he is my son, you too are like a son to me, Vikrama. And as a mother, I must be fair to both my sons. Now go and bring him back."

With a nod, the king strode away, so he did not see Upashruti place her head on Ushantha's shoulder and dissolve into tears. He also missed Ushantha putting her arms around the Queen Mother and holding her in a tight, forgiving embrace.

The samrat was crossing the gallery when he drew to a sudden halt. His face grew tense and he listened.

A bell had started tolling somewhere. *One of the city's alarm bells.*

He broke into a run. Turning a corner, he came upon a pair of palace guards looking anxious and undecided as the bell sounded into the night.

"Do you know what this is about?" Vikramaditya asked.

"We don't, your honour," one of them replied.

"Never mind," said the samrat, "Listen, you know the drill, don't you? Take everyone who is in the palace into the Labyrinth. Understand?"

The guards nodded.

"I am banking on the two of you to do this. Go."

The men went off at a brisk jog as the king continued down a flight of steps. On the landing below, he met Kshapanaka.

"What's happening?" he asked, noting an increase in the number of bells now ringing.

"No idea."

They leaned over the railing to look into the hallway below. At precisely that instant, a palace guard entered the hallway with a captain of the City Watch.

"What is going on?" Vikramaditya shouted to make himself heard over the noise of the bells.

"Horsemen at the eastern gate, your honour," the captain replied.

"What horsemen?" asked Kshapanaka, shooting a glance at the king. "The ones that came the last time? The ones that split into two...?"

The captain shook his head. "These are apparently half-horse, half-human—and much bigger than either."

Kshapanaka turned mystified eyes to Vikramaditya.

"We mustn't let them past the gates," the samrat nodded to the councilor.

"Your honour, they..." the captain hesitated. "The horsemen are already *in* the city."

The king's gaze pierced the captain. "How?" The question was shot like an arrow.

"Through the gates," the captain said. "The eastern gate was open... somehow."

Vikramaditya looked at Kshapanaka and nodded again. The councilor went rushing down the stairs, yelling instructions at the captain and the palace guard. The king, meanwhile, crossed the palace to his own chambers, telling himself that Vararuchi would have to wait a little longer. Striding into his chambers, he went to the anteroom and flung open its door.

His eyes went to the table, and he stopped.

He stared.

On the table was a brass lamp, an inkwell and a pair of quills.

That was it. There was nothing else on the table.

No swords, carefully swaddled in folds of satin cloth, where he had left them.

Listening to the rising clamour of the bells, the samrat's eyes hardened as he realized what had happened to the two swords.

Attack

The spear took the soldier in the chest with such force that he was lifted off the ground and hurled back four yards, falling and dislocating his right shoulder on impact. Before he could even scream out in agony, the spear descended again, its blade finding his exposed throat and going in, a lightning-quick stab that snuffed him and his scream out in the same stroke. Reversing the spear in mid-leap so it again pointed ahead, Tribhanu vaulted over the man he had just killed and lunged at the next soldier of the Watch, pinning him under the clavicle and forcing him to let go of his sword. With a deft flick of the wrist, Tribhanu dug into the soldier's chest, opening a wound that spurted blood and dropped the man screaming to his knees. As he went past, the kinnara delivered a kick to the back of the soldier's head, sending him sprawling, dazed and mumbling, face-first into the mud.

This was way too easy, Matali said to himself as he observed the handsome centaur tackle a third soldier, swiping at the man's face with the edge of the spear-head, opening up his cheek from ear to mouth. As the soldier reeled away, Tribhanu shielded an incoming blow from the left, delivered with neither strength nor precision. Switching his grip on the spear, the kinnara skewered his assailant in the stomach, then struck another, then a sixth soldier, leaving them all torn and moaning in the dust.

Way too easy, the deva decided as he brandished his own sword and brought it down hard on the head of a soldier of the City Watch who was trying to block his path. The sword bounced off the soldier's helmet, the impact of the blow running up Matali's arm in a shiver, even as he heard the satisfying crack of the man's skull imploding under the helmet. The soldier collapsed, blood rushing out of both nostrils.

Around him, behind him, everywhere, there were similar scenes of carnage, the kinnara army's progress into Ujjayini marked by a trail of mutilated human bodies. The centaurs were uncheckable, and the soldiers of Avanti showed up in ragged little groups only to die, like offerings at a ritual sacrifice. Matali had known that Ujjayini was not at its strongest, but looking at the way the city's defence was caving in, it was plain that Avanti had been badly prepared for a strike of this sort.

Between one lot of Avanti's soldiers dying and the next lot still to make an appearance, there was a brief lull in the fighting, and Matali took the opportunity to spur his horse—which he had nicked while making his escape from the city—and draw level with the kinnara lord.

Noticing the deva ride up beside him, Tribhanu dropped his pace. "What a grand fuss the Ashvins and the Maruts made of this place after their botched efforts to claim the Halahala," the kinnara snorted, the words shouted out so they could be heard over the pealing of the city's bells and the pounding of the hooves. He slowed to a steady trot, and Matali and the kinnaras coming behind them did likewise. "On and on they went about how well this city was defended, how fiercely the humans fought... Where is all that gutsy ferocity? The king's troops are buckling without a semblance of a fight. I could have brought just a *third* of my army and still taken this city." With a rush of confidence, he added. "You and I can storm the palace by ourselves. While you secure the dagger, I will take the king prisoner. Where's the need for the nagas?"

"Maybe, but we should stick to what we had agreed upon with Takshaka," Matali cautioned. "Let us not change plans at this stage."

"Mmm," the kinnara replied tersely, not pleased with the deva's lack of enthusiasm at his proposal.

"And comparing this to the attacks led by the Ashvins and the Maruts is incorrect," Matali added. "The resistance they faced was far, far stronger. We should count ourselves lucky that six of the Samrat's nine councilors are not in Ujjayini—and the stories I've heard about some of them are remarkable. There's one who apparently turns into a raging half-lion. Another just disappears and appears wherever she wishes. She's just a girl, and a piece of hell with the knife, I've gathered. Then there is the giant who has crossed to the side of the savages from the desert; they say there is no warrior on earth like him. We should be thankful none of them are here today."

"Six human beings could have altered the course of this kinnara attack?" Tribhanu sneered at Matali. "Is that what you're saying?"

"Actually, *one* human would have been enough to stop us—the king himself, if he had the Hellfires with him now. Fortunately, the two swords are far from here and are getting further away with every stroke of the garuda's wing. To answer your question, these humans have fought and repelled the devas and the asuras before. They are tough, and it would be foolish to underestimate them."

The kinnara lord turned away with a shake of his head, the jeering smile not leaving his lips.

"Which way, lord?"

Tribhanu swivelled around to see one of his generals point to a fork in the road ahead.

"Whichever way we wish," he replied, "as long as we don't stray too far into the city's centre, and stay away from the palace. Our task is to draw Ujjayini's defenders away from the palace and towards the city's walls so that the nagas and the deva here," he waved a hand casually at Matali, "can enter the palace for the dagger."

"No one is living in these," another of the kinnara generals remarked, peering at the houses in the light of the torches that lit the fork in the road. "They're all empty. No wonder the streets are also deserted."

"The residents have all been moved to safety," Matali informed. "Many parts of the city have been under evacuation for a while now."

"How do we get the human king and his soldiers to leave the palace and come here if there is no one left in the town to kill or maim?" the general grumbled.

Matali thought that was a problem too, but Tribhanu had an easy solution. "Let us look some more. If nothing else, we will surely find more soldiers to kill." He paused and pointed at the torches lighting the city's streets. "Otherwise, we can always set the houses on fire. That will bring the humans running."

The general nodded. Without warning, Tribhanu kicked into a gallop, randomly turning into the street to the right. Matali followed Tribhanu, while the two generals kept going straight. The kinnaras coming behind them divided into two groups, one going after the generals, the others tailing Matali and their king.

They had covered less than a hundred yards when, out of a side-street up ahead, a small force of cavalrymen of Avanti's Imperial Army emerged, some of them bearing torches. Matali guessed there were about fifteen of them, and the horsemen caught sight of the advancing kinnaras at the same time. For a moment, the cavalry was rooted to the spot, undecided whether to attack or to retreat, and the kinnara lord took advantage of that hesitation. Setting his spear firmly so its point didn't waver, his shield up, Tribhanu charged down the road, and a second later, the kinnara force followed him, swords and spears poised to kill.

Matali raised his sword and kicked his mount, but he was already lagging behind. He knew he needn't have bothered.

Avanti's cavalrymen broke into two groups—one set of ten or eleven horsemen who charged at the kinnaras out of desperation, the other set hanging back in awe and terror, already abandoning their fellow riders and turning to flee. The first set of horsemen met the kinnaras in a suicidal crash, impaled and killed in their saddles by the kinnaras' spears. The second set tried escaping into the night but went much further into the dark with daggers and arrows buried deep in their backs.

Way too easy.

Matali rode up as Tribhanu worked the tip of his spear free of a dead cavalryman, the old soldier's body unbalancing and toppling off the horse's back to hit the ground with a bone-jarring thump. The kinnara turned to the deva, a challenge in his smile.

"You still think there's fight left in the humans, deva?" he asked, cocking an eyebrow.

Matali shrugged, even though he knew the answer. This would end up as a perfect rout, with nothing to save the human king and his army. No doughty displays of defiance from his troops, no great acts of heroism, no pluck, no derring-do.

No sign of the king or his council either. It looked as if they had already given up the will to resist.

Matali understood what Vikramaditya must be going through. With no Hellfires to help him stop the attacking kinnaras and the nagas, this battle was as good as lost, the Halahala as good as taken—the promise to the Omniscient One as good as broken.

A capitulation was imminent; Indra would get to see his grandson in chains.

Stepping over the dead horsemen, the kinnara lord grinned at Matali in triumph.

Way too easy.

***

With hooves pounding the ground hard, Vikramaditya's horse barrelled out of the stable and charged headlong to the palace grounds, where Kshapanaka waited with a band of soldiers. The company was roughly eighty strong, divided equally into two groups, cobbled together from units of the Imperial Army and the City Watch, in addition to a dozen *samsaptakas* and a handful of the civil militia. The night was resonant with the bells, which were ringing with a frenzy that didn't bode well for Ujjayini.

"Any updates?" the samrat asked, reining his horse in with a sharp yank that caused the beast to dig its heels in and rear up on its hind legs in surprise. Stroking the horse's neck to soothe it, he looked at Kshapanaka. "Anything that we can act on?"

"All we know for certain is that the attackers are half-horse and half-human," the councilor replied dolefully. "And that they are big."

"How many?"

"Hundreds," Kshapanaka shrugged. "It is impossible to make an estimate in the dark. And there are hardly any survivors who could fill in the details..."

The councilor trailed off ominously, her words hanging in the air like a dismal warning.

"How many have we lost?" the king asked darkly.

"Many. Some say fifty, some say more."

The king winced. "Civilians?"

"None that we know of, thankfully."

"The attacks have been limited to the east and the south, your honour," a captain of the City Watch chipped in.

It was a relief that there were no civilian casualties so far. The timely evacuation of the city had helped. "Good, though that doesn't mean the attacks won't spread," Vikramaditya said. Raising his voice, he addressed the soldiers. "Those of you coming with me, head to the east gate. Those going with Councilor Kshapanaka, wait for her at the city garrison. Go now!"

The men dispersed, the horsemen riding off at a gallop, while infantrymen and archers jogged after them at a steady pace, melting into the darkness.

"How did they get into the city?" The samrat spurred his mount forward. Kshapanaka fell in step beside him.

"Through the south and east gates," the councilor answered, "though no one knows how they got in. Before anyone knew of it, they were inside."

"They must have broken the gates and forced their way in."

The councilor shook her head doubtfully. "Breaking those gates open calls for a lot of hard work. *Noisy* work. The guards would have had ample time to raise an alarm."

Vikramaditya mulled this over for a moment. "Then someone or something opened the gates for the half-horses *from within*."

"There were guards manning those gates."

"Perhaps they didn't have time to respond."

"Could the imposter have opened the gates?" Kshapanaka eyed the samrat shrewdly.

The samrat's mind flashed to the two missing swords. He shrugged. "It's possible. What I am really getting at is that besides these half-horses, we have at least one more devious enemy to keep an eye out for." With a nod, Vikramaditya flicked the reins. As his horse responded with a burst of speed, he called out to the councilor, "Fight well."

The two parted, the councilor heading for the city garrison as the king went after the men he had ordered to the east gate, overtaking a dozen of the infantrymen and archers in a matter of minutes. He thundered along the winding streets, his thoughts on fending off the attackers, so coming around a sharp bend, he nearly crashed into the three horsemen of the Imperial Army who stood huddled in the middle of the street. Vikramaditya drew on his reins hard to avert a collision.

"What's the matter?" he demanded, frowning in anger. "Why aren't you on your way?"

On recognizing him, the startled horsemen bowed. "Fire, your honour," one said, pointing.

The samrat followed the man's finger.

The fire was easy to spot—a bright blaze in the middle distance, northeast of the palace, its glow scattering in the night sky. He wouldn't have missed it had he not been so immersed in his own thoughts, the king realized. It wasn't possible for the alarm bells to ring any louder, but even as he listened, Vikramaditya thought they did go up a notch in volume and intensity.

"There's no one there," said one of the horsemen. "That part of the city has been evacuated."

"The attackers must have started the fire then," said another.

Vikramaditya stared at the blaze. "Isn't that in the vicinity of the old cattle market?" he asked sharply.

"It is, your honour."

There are these two households in the eastern section. Both refuse to vacate... insisting they won't obey the orders of someone who is not worthy of being the king of Avanti.

Kshapanaka's words, uttered as they had stood watching the boatmen search the palace lake.

I made enquiries. Both houses belong to families related to the garrison chief of Musili. Commander Sharamana. Vararuchi's right-hand man.

Vikramaditya faced his men. Pointing to one, he said, "Proceed to the eastern gate and inform the commanders of the City Watch and the Imperial Army that I have stopped to complete an important errand. Tell them I will join them as soon as I can. Go."

The man nodded, turned his horse around and rode off.

The samrat addressed the remaining horsemen. "Come with me," he ordered. "That part of the city has not been entirely evacuated. There are two households still living there, and their lives are now in mortal danger. It's up to us to rescue them."

Vikramaditya dug his heels into his horse and the beast sprang into action, cannoning past the two horsemen. Reaching the end of the street, the king veered into a by-lane, vanishing from sight as the horsemen spurred their mounts in a bid to catch up.

***

They came out of the earth less than a hundred yards from the palace, the whole brood of them, tearing and clawing their way to the top, emerging from underground, clutching barbed swords and spears.

The palace guards milling on the causeway had no inkling of their existence. Holding their swords and shields tight, the guards strained to see in the dark, watching out for the half-horses that had broken into the city, mumbling and drawing anxious conjectures about the attackers. The poor souls did not know what to expect, so they ended up fearing the worst.

Yet, the worst—when it came at them, bounding out of the darkness on short, powerful legs—was worse than anything the guards had been preparing themselves for.

The nagas came out of the earth and assailed the palace from all four sides, throwing themselves at the palace guards, hacking at them with swords, spears and claws. The melee at the end of the causeway was a grisly affair, although those watching from the safety of the palace were spared the worst of it, thanks to the darkness and the ringing of the bells, which muted out the screams of the dying. When it was over, it was far from a pretty sight, corpses strewn everywhere, dark shapes lying on the ground, lifeless—and the nagas clambering obscenely over the dead bodies, slipping on spilled blood before leaping onto the causeway.

"Come with me, *quick*," a senior soldier ordered, assuming charge. "We must block the causeway."

"These don't look anything like horses," someone else yelled. "What *are* these things?"

"Whatever they are, we have to fight them. Hurry up."

Ignoring the questions and injunctions being flung around, Varahamihira hobbled to Dhanavantri's side. The physician stood by one of the gallery windows that overlooked the causeway, his feet set apart, fingers curled tightly around his ironwood quarterstaff, his eyes on the bloodbath that had just unfolded at the tip of the causeway.

"What do you make of it?" asked Varahamihira, peering out of the window.

"It's not good."

Varahamihira was mum for a moment. Then, "It's on us defend the palace from these... *creatures*, my friend."

The physician shot a sidelong glance at the lame councilor before returning his attention to the causeway, where a dozen palace guards had assembled near the midway point, swords and spears poised, creating a crude and prickly barricade.

The nagas, numbering in excess of twenty, came slinking down the causeway, their own swords and spears up. Seven or eight soldiers rushed out of the palace to reinforce the defence, but just at that moment, the nagas began bizarrely slicing open their own shoulders, arms and torsos with their own swords and talons. This outlandish act of self-mutilation was ominously riveting, and both councilors watched as if hypnotized, even as the nagas drew steadily closer to the palace guards. Unnerved by this strange behaviour, and unsure what to make of it, the guards appeared to have frozen into a state of panicked inactivity.

"What are they doing?" Varahamihira hissed.

Dhanavantri snapped out of the spell he had sunk into. The question his friend had posed was a rhetorical one, so the physician didn't bother answering. Instead, he looked back at the causeway, his chubby shoulders tense. "The men must withdraw," he said with a note of urgency, "or they'll all get butchered."

Even as he spoke, more nagas spilled out of the darkness and joined the concourse on the causeway.

"Oh, no..." Dhanavantri said under his breath. Turning around, he yelled into the atrium below, "Order the men to retreat... I repeat, order the men to *pull back*."

"Yes, your honour," a guard shouted from below.

However, before the command could be relayed, the nagas threw themselves at the barricade. Loping and leaping, they assailed the palace guards, heedless of the swords and spears that drove into them. Their lifeblood streaming out of them, the nagas grappled with the guards, holding them tight and close, restricting their movements, and serving as a cushion between the guards and the nagas advancing from behind. As the palace guards started screaming in agony, more and more nagas charged down the causeway and pushed at the human barricade. Outnumbered, the guards were shoved sideways and back so that they lost their balance and fell screaming—in a moment, the barricade collapsed entirely, crashing down on itself. While one group of nagas broke through and came rushing towards the palace, their brothers who came after attacked the fallen palace guards mercilessly, slaughtering them before they could regain their feet, and kicking their bodies into the lake.

"No," Dhanavantri groaned in anguish and horror. "*No.*"

"Close the palace gates," somewhere a guard screamed. "Hurry, don't let them inside."

"*The gates, yes,*" Varahamihira shouted, hobbling to the stairway that led into atrium. "They shouldn't come in."

Fortunately, the newly installed iron gate was already closed, which meant that only the smaller door built into the gate needed shutting. The door swung smoothly on its hinges and sealed with a resounding clang, the bolts shooting into their hoops and the latches slipping into place in the nick of time, so that the nagas flung themselves at the gate in vain.

Listening to the futile banging and rattling at the gate, Dhanavantri drew a huge sigh of relief, his grip on the quarterstaff easing. He eyed Varahamihira, standing ten paces away, leaning on his crutch, and said, "That was close. Whatever these things are, we have to make sure—"

The physician saw Varahamihira's attention shift from his face to a spot over his shoulder. Simultaneously, the older councilor's eyes grew wide in alarm, and his lips began to form words, but Dhanavantri was already ducking instinctively, dropping his head low and going down on his haunches. Even as he did so, the physician felt something whip over his head, and he was certain he heard the singing of metal as it cut through air.

And then Varahamihira was holding his right hand up in the air, palm facing outward, as if stopping someone, his eyes glued to the same spot. Dhanavantri wheeled around to see one of the nagas from the causeway pushing against a thin film of energy that buzzed and crackled. The physician stared at the grotesque creature, which had the head of a snake and a body that was partially human. It had crawled partway in through the window that he and Varahamihira had been looking out of, its entry arrested by Varahamihira's energy shield. The creature was striving hard to rip its way through the diaphanous curtain, attacking it with its talons, but to no avail.

The naga's sword, with which it had tried to decapitate Dhanavantri, had fallen from its hand and lay on the floor.

"Will the thing hold?" the physician asked, slowly rising to his feet.

"Mmm-hmm."

"And can you control... the creature?" Dhanavantri stared from the naga to his friend's hand in wonder.

"I don't know. Don't ask so many questions."

"Try."

Varahamihira grimaced, brows furrowed in concentration. For a moment, nothing happened. Then the councilor jerked his hand in a short, repelling motion, and as Dhanavantri watched, the energy curtain heaved and the creature was pushed out of the window, into the night. The curtain dissipated immediately, as if it had never existed. The physician darted to the window and looked out, and a moment later, he heard a heavy splash as the creature fell into the lake.

"That was wonderful..." he began, grinning in satisfaction, when he glimpsed movement to his left. He turned to see another of the creatures come crawling through the window. *Where were they coming from?*

But Varahamihira was ready for this one. Before the creature could gain a proper foothold, he had flung his hand out and cast the energy shield against the window. The creature strained against the curtain with all its might, but it too failed to tear its way in. Again, Varahamihira pushed with his hand,

and it was this creature's turn to sail out of the window, into the night, into the lake.

"Where are they coming—" The physician was cut short once again by a voice calling out in warning.

"They are everywhere in the water. They are swimming towards the palace."

That explained how the creature had reached the window. Exchanging an ominous glance with Varahamihira, Dhanavantri rushed to the end of the gallery and peered out of a window that afforded an unobstructed view of the lake. Even though he sensed a peculiar disturbance in the water, the physician saw nothing at first. But as his eyes adjusted to the darkness, he discerned four or five vague shapes bobbing along the lake's surface, heading for the palace. On reaching the bottom of the palace wall, the first of these figures hauled itself deftly out of the water and started scaling the wall, using the slightest of toeholds for purchase. Moments later, another two had commenced the climb.

Dhanavantri spun around to face Varahamihira. "Those things are climbing up the walls."

"The windows." Worry flashed in Varahamihira's eyes. "The palace has too many windows."

"And too many balconies and terraces," Dhanavantri added. "Shutting one gate will make no difference if these things can get in—" he stopped in mid-sentence and stepped to the railing. Leaning over, he shouted into the atrium, "We need archers. Get them here. *Fast*."

"*Aaaaaa....*"

The scream came from somewhere above, and startled by its intensity, the councilors looked up to see a palace guard come tearing along one of the upper galleries, his eyes crazed, his face ashen with terror. He flailed down the stairs, nearly tripping over, but somehow saving himself from a nasty fall.

He came running towards Dhanavantri, who blocked his way with his bulk.

"What is the matter?" the physician asked, peering at the man, trying to make eye contact.

The soldier's gaze flicked frantically from side to side as he sought a way past the physician. Finally, his eyes settled on Dhanavantri, and a look of recognition dawned. He shivered and a low moan escaped his lips.

"What is it, soldier?"

The man drew a breath and pulled himself together, even though the fear didn't quite leave his eyes. "Your honour... their blood. It is their blood."

"What blood?" Varahamihira asked.

"The creatures... their blood." The guard looked up, in the direction from where he had come, and Dhanavantri felt his skin crawl. *The creatures were already inside.*

"What about their blood?" he demanded.

"Their blood makes our flesh rot."

The physician stared.

"When their blood touches us, our skin and flesh rots." Again, the man looked back and up nervously. "I saw some guards near the council chamber rot and fall. I escaped by hiding."

That was why the creatures cut themselves, Dhanavantri realized. *To bleed.*

And that was why the guards on the causeway had screamed so horribly before dying. The blood had touched them.

"The creatures were near the council chamber?" the physician asked unnecessarily.

The man nodded and shivered. "Two of them, your honour."

Dhanavantri looked at Varahamihira, aghast. It was probably much too late, but they still had to do something.

"We need the archers," he yelled. "Why aren't they here yet? *Somebody... fetch them.*"

What he really wished was that Kshapanaka were here...

***

Matali emerged softly from underwater, a shadow hugging the palace wall, right under the overhang of a low terrace so that he was hidden from view. He suspected there were eyes scanning the lake from above, watching out for nagas scaling the walls, but this didn't bother him; he didn't intend crawling up the wall to get into the palace.

Stopping to catch his breath, he wiped the water from his eyes and looked about him. He was on the western side of the palace, directly opposite from the causeway and the east wing, where much of the fighting was underway. The royal kitchens were directly above him, and from what he remembered of the palace drill, the cooks and their attendants would have abandoned their stations by now, leaving the kitchens empty—and ideally suited for him to steal back into the palace. The palace blocked his view of Ujjayini's eastern quarter, but a tinge of orange reflected in the lake's waters told him the kinnaras had started setting the city on fire. Faraway yells and screams came to his ears from the palace.

The deva grabbed the bottom edge of the terrace and pulled himself clear of the water. Getting to his feet, he stepped through the nearest wall, so that all that was left of him on the terrace was a splash of water and half a dozen wet footprints that ended mysteriously at the wall.

Matali found himself in a dark room that smelled strongly of spices. He detected turmeric and dried chilli, and his nose wrinkled reflexively, a sneeze building rapidly to the point of expulsion. Burying his nose in the crook of his arm, trying his best to suppress the sneeze, the deva turned and stepped through the wall to the left, which brought him to what he presumed was the cooks' quarters. The room was large, with five quilts laid out on the floor. A pair of old but clean dhotis hung from a jute rope, and Matali quickly removed his wet dhoti and wound one of the washed, dry ones around him. He was still mopping the water off with the second dhoti when, without warning, the sneeze he had fought to curb burst through, the roar disconcertingly loud in the silence of the room, ringing and echoing in the deva's ears.

Matali held his breath, listening for approaching voices or footsteps.

Nothing. Slowly, he tiptoed to the door and poked his head outside.

The passage was empty, and as far as he could tell, so was the entire wing. Which was to be expected—everyone would have been herded to the Labyrinth.

Sighing in relief, the deva stepped into the corridor to begin his search for the Halahala.

Rescue

Kshapanaka had had an arrow nocked and ready in her bow for a while now, but for a variety of reasons, she hadn't been able to get even one clean shot at a kinnara so far.

For one, she and the kinnaras were now in the densely populated south-western section of Ujjayini, an old part where the streets were treacherously narrow, winding and uneven, and the houses and shops so tightly bunched together that there was hardly any room for an arrow to fly unimpeded. Then, as compared to Kshapanaka's mount, the centaurs were stronger, quicker and much nimbler, accelerating and changing direction with enviable ease. It made the councilor realize that no matter how strong and reliable one's horse was, there was a distinction between riding a horse and *being the horse*—an advantage that these half-horses were exploiting to the hilt.

Still, she could easily have loosed off an arrow or two in the hope that they would find their mark, and under normal circumstances, she would have taken her chances without a second thought. But she had a very limited number of arrows in her quiver, and there wasn't a garrison, watchtower or foundry in the vicinity from where she might replenish her stock. Knowing she had to make every arrow count, she held herself back, conserving her arrows as she chased after the kinnaras, wondering how she could steer them away from the areas that had still to be evacuated.

The one edge she had over the half-horses, it occurred to her, was that *she* knew the lay of the land.

Reaching the end of one side-street, Kshapanaka turned away from the centaurs, rather than follow them. She cut across a market and skirted a temple with a large pond, going up a hill before coming out onto a road that curved away to the left. Crossing the road and taking position behind a cluster of *gulmohar* trees, she drew the bowstring back slowly, listening to the wood creak as the bow bent, feeling the strain spread through her arms and shoulders...

In four skips of the heartbeat, the first kinnara swerved into view.

Kshapanaka drew the bowstring as far back as possible before releasing the arrow.

The councilor's aim was true, and the arrow took the kinnara in the throat with such force that it bored right through the thick neck to come out from the back, snapping the vertebra in two. The kinnara was dead before it had even fully turned the corner.

Carried along by momentum and muscle memory, the centaur kept galloping down the road, which suited Kshapanaka perfectly—the kinnaras coming behind didn't suspect a thing and came charging around the corner, one, two, three, four, five...

One. Two. Three. Four. Five.

In quick successions, the councilor drew and shot five arrows, all five fired with such skill and precision that the targets lay dead in the middle of the road, sprawled one on top of another, a mess of tangled bodies and limbs.

Six half-horses down in almost no time, Kshapanaka nodded to herself with satisfaction. That was the good bit. The not-so-good bit was that, alerted by the sight of their dead brothers, the kinnaras coming behind had drawn to a halt, keeping well out of her line of sight. She had to do something to bait them into showing themselves.

Stepping from the cover of the *gulmohars*, the councilor rode to where the dead centaurs lay. She pretended to look at the bodies, examining them, while revealing glimpses of herself to anyone watching from further down the road. She knew she risked attracting an arrow, but it was a chance—

"There!"

The voice came from down the road. A second later, Kshapanaka heard the sound of hooves kicking into a gallop.

Wheeling her mount around, the councilor took off in the opposite direction, hoping the half-horses would come after her.

They did, all ten of them, charging around the bend, devouring the road, narrowing the gap between them and her.

Even though Kshapanaka was certain the centaurs chasing her did not have bows and arrows, she rode hard to keep them from getting within striking distance, dodging right and left to evade any spears that might be hurled at her. Changing direction suddenly, she would slip into unexpected alleyways, yet would always pick paths that the centaurs could follow her into. The councilor's tactics were glaring, one that any intelligent soldier could see through, yet the half-horses came after her—which made them incredibly fearless or terribly dumb.

Turning another corner and seeing the roof of a house overhang the road, Kshapanaka reined in her horse just a little—this was what she had chosen this route for. Slinging her bow over her shoulder, she hoisted herself onto the saddle and crouched on the horse's back, her eyes judging the distance between her and the roof. As the horse rode under the overhang, Kshapanaka slowed the beast just enough so she could grab the roof with both hands. The same instant, she kicked the horse on the rump.

"Tchk, tchk," she clicked her tongue, urging the beast on.

The horse picked up speed, and the councilor swung her legs free and pulled herself onto the roof. Crouching low, she clawed and clambered up the incline until she was right at the top. Planting her feet square and balancing herself, Kshapanaka turned to face the way she had come.

The kinnaras came riding around the corner, hot on her heels.

Kshapanaka watched the centaurs slip under the overhang, their eyes on her horse, which was already halfway down the poorly lit street, an indefinite shadow, more heard than seen. The kinnaras had no way of telling that the horse they were chasing had no one on its saddle. Not just yet, at least.

Unslinging her bow, the councilor fitted an arrow and pulled the string back. She waited for the last kinnara in the group, the tenth one, to pass below the roof, and when she had it clear in her sight, she released the arrow.

The arrow smacked into the target's neck, burrowing just under the skull. The centaur's legs crumpled, and it fell.

Kshapanaka ran along the length of the roof shooting at the kinnaras, picking them from behind, each shot bringing one down. Nine, eight, seven, six, five... The centaurs in front were so focused on the chase that they didn't realize their brothers at the back were being taken down systematically.

They were nearing a cleft in the street that was illuminated by a pair of torches. Knowing that the four remaining half-horses were bound to see that her mount was riderless, Kshapanaka nocked another arrow in place and upped her pace, eager to finish what she had started before the kinnaras were alerted. However, in her hurry, the councilor lost her footing, and before she knew it, the bow had been knocked out of her hand, and she was slipping down the roof, scrabbling desperately for a handhold in the old, mossy tiles. Gravity exerted its influence, however, and her descent was rapid, the fall checked momentarily as she swung by the edge of the roof with one hand.

Her hold loosened and she fell.

Landing on her feet and unbalancing, she dropped to a crouch and rolled to soften the impact on her knees. Finding her feet once again, she was halfway up when she noticed the heads of four spears pointing at her. Her hand sped to the sword at her hip, but before her fingertips grazed its hilt, the spears thrust forward, warning her against the idea. Dropping her hand, she looked up—straight into the hard eyes of the four centaurs she had been chasing.

The centaurs looked back in the direction they had come from. Kshapanaka couldn't be sure, but she guessed they could see the bodies of the dead kinnaras lying on the road. Seeing their faces turn cold, she knew she had guessed right. The four kinnaras exchanged glances, then one of them spoke.

"You should have killed us too when you had the chance. Miss that chance and—"

The kinnara's big mistake was that it did not follow its own advice.

The shape came lunging out of the dark and down a roof, a blur that landed on the back of the centaur. The shape held something in its hand, and as Kshapanaka watched, the hand flashed across the kinnara's throat and blood spurted from a deep slash. Before the half-horses could even register that they were under attack, the shape—Kshapanaka now saw that it was a man—leaped sideways onto the next kinnara, quickly cutting its throat as well. The two remaining kinnaras turned to tackle this new threat, spears arcing, but the man had already anticipated this. He ducked under one of the spears and came up fast, driving his *katari* hard into one centaur's belly, disembowelling it. Meanwhile, taking advantage of the distraction, Kshapanaka pulled her sword free and sprang at the last kinnara, the blade sliding flat and fast under the kinnara's armpit. As blood sprayed on her fingers, she pushed away, dealing a hard death blow to the side of the centaur's head. The beast staggered and fell.

Kshapanaka turned to see that all the half-horses were down. The man stood in the middle of the carnage, gripping his *katari* and catching his breath, his face averted.

Kshapanaka did not need to see his face to recognize him.

The man turned, and the torchlight finally illuminated his features.

Vararuchi.

***

The locality around the old cattle market was up in flames, marked by a wall of stifling heat and smoke. The heat radiated outward, pushing Vikramaditya back bodily, and the samrat's fine beard and eyebrows were already singed as punishment for trying to get too close. Black smoke boiled up from the heart of the fire and rose giddily above the burning roofs, lit orange from below before blending with the night and vanishing. With no one around to tame it, the fire went where it pleased, encroaching upon new neighbourhoods, sweeping up more and more of the city into its destructive embrace.

"It doesn't look as if there's anyone here, your honour," called one of the horsemen. The man looked tired, his face streaked with soot and sweat, and from his tone, it was clear that he was prepared to abandon the search.

"Perhaps they managed to escape," the other horseman offered. For all the hope in his words, his eyes flitted dubiously across the fire-engulfed landscape, betraying what he imagined had *really* happened.

Vikramaditya nodded grimly, staring at the smoke pouring down a street. There was no way in past all that smoke. *And there was no point finding a way in either*, he thought to himself. Perhaps they were too late. Perhaps the two families were already dead—burned or asphyxiated or both—and this was a complete waste of time; perhaps they should turn back and make themselves useful where they were really needed…

"Have we looked everywhere?" he asked.

"I think so, your honour."

"Mmm-hmm." Vikramaditya returned his gaze to the burning district. "What about that section over there?" he asked, pointing over the roofs. "Close to where the goldsmiths had their guild during father's time? Did we check that out?"

"I… haven't, your honour. But it is surrounded by the fire on three sides, so they would have come out if…"

Vikramaditya looked at the second horseman. Seeing him shake his head as well, the king turned his horse around. "Let's go and see."

The horsemen tailed the samrat, and they rode hard, keeping the blaze to their right, working around the inferno, coming in as close to the fire as they possibly dared. The alarm bells had been ringing ceaselessly from the moment Ujjayini had come under attack, so their din was no longer conspicuous, their pitch down by a few decibels and sounding cowed and weary. Under different circumstances, it would have been easy not to pay attention to them.

Turning into a side-street that led towards the old goldsmiths' guild, Vikramaditya and the horsemen were half the way in when a great bank of smoke barred their way. The smoke was thick with the heat of the fire, and telltale orange-red tongues of flame leaped and danced in its murky folds, acting as a warning against trespassing. Wheeling their mounts around, the three riders retreated to a safe distance, from where they observed the smoke saturate the street and roll slowly towards them.

"Is there no other way in?" the samrat asked, even though he knew the answer. As a curious young boy, there wasn't an inch of the city he hadn't explored, there wasn't an alleyway that he couldn't figure his way out of. There was nothing about Ujjayini that Vikramaditya did not know.

The horsemen knew this too, so they didn't say anything.

"I guess that is it then," the king said with heavy finality, his brows knitting in vexation. "At least we tried our utmost—"

The scream came out of the dark, high-pitched and full of terror, clipping the samrat's words. A short shriek in a woman's voice.

The king and the two horsemen looked around them, struggling to place its source amidst the ringing of the bells. They cocked their ears, waiting to hear something.

There. Again. This time, accompanied by a short, panicked command. "Amya... *Run!*"

"That way." One of the horsemen flung his arm out, pointing to his right.

Before the man's hand returned to his side, the samrat had turned his horse north. Digging his heels into the animal's belly, he was off like an arrow, the horsemen taking a few moments to hit their stride and go galloping after him.

Vikramaditya saw them the moment he turned right at the intersection.

Two women and a girl of about eight, the women on either side of the girl, holding her hands, literally dragging the child along so her feet skimmed the road.

They came around the far bend in the road, so they were partially silhouetted against the glare of the fire, running towards him, but not noticing him in their desperation to escape whatever had terrified them.

The girl's foot snagged on the uneven path and she stumbled, then sprawled, breaking the sprint and pulling the women back.

"Amya... child... *hurry*."

The women hauled the girl up as the younger of the two sneaked a look over her shoulder. "Hurry, *mama*..." she yelled to someone, slowing down marginally, still looking behind her.

"Let's go, let's go..." the other woman insisted, tugging the little girl's hand, her voice rising hysterically. "*Let's just go... please...*"

"Mother..." the child whimpered, looking up at the younger woman, afraid their hands would break contact.

The woman turned to her daughter. "Yes, child. Come, come..."

Taking a firmer hold on the girl's hand, their fingers interlinking, the woman upped her pace, and the three of them set off again, feet pounding on the hard mud.

Coming up behind Vikramaditya, the horsemen noticed that their king had slowed his mount to a measured walk. They saw the samrat's hands cross in front of him and go to the swords at his hips. As the king's fingers wrapped around the hilts and he drew the swords free of their scabbards, the horsemen did likewise, peering uncertainly at the women and the child on the road.

The horsemen had their eyes trained on the three fleeing women when two more figures appeared at the far end of the road—a man and a woman, both frail and advanced in age, hobbling on weak legs, supporting each other as they tried their best to outrun whatever was coming after them. Another moment or two, and what was chasing the five terrified citizens came into view from around the curve in the road.

Seven big, broad-shouldered half-horses, bearing spears and swords.

Vikramaditya's horse kept up its sedate walk, the swords rigid in the king's hands.

The kinnaras came at a steady canter, all seven of them crudely lined up across the width of the road, full of the lazy bravado of predators confident of making a kill.

It was the older woman in front who first sighted the samrat and the horsemen, letting out a small shriek and pulling up abruptly. The mother and daughter noticed them the next instant, and all three women froze in their tracks, eyes widening in horror.

"It is me, your Samrat," Vikramaditya called to them, understanding the cause for their fear. In the half-light of the inferno, he and the horsemen behind could easily be mistaken for the half-horses. "You have nothing to fear from us."

The king rode slowly towards the women, the horsemen following. The women stared, relief slowly draining back into their faces as the light from the fire fell on the samrat. Up ahead, the old man and woman kept up their stumbling run, alert only to the half-horses that came roaring and laughing after them, their spears and swords thrust out, their hooves drumming on the road, their rich manes flying in the light of the fire raging behind them. All seven of them, picking up speed, riding faster, closing the gap...

The swords hung from Vikramaditya's hands, one on either side, the sharp tips pointed at the ground.

The sharp tips reflecting the firelight.

The tips suddenly on fire, orange flames catching and coming alive on smooth metal.

"Samrat," the older of the women whispered, her voice trembling as Vikramaditya rode past them, her eyes going from the swords to the king in wonder and disbelief.

"Get behind us," the king motioned to the women, his eyes pinned on the half-horses.

The kinnaras were nearly upon the elderly couple, spears and swords primed for the kill. The couple themselves seemed resigned to their fate; they were tiring, their shoulders slumped in defeat, surrendering their will to survive...

The samrat raised his arms high and brought them down hard—and the flames on the swords' surfaces snapped and flared, lengthening and tapering off the tips of the blades, acquiring a whip-like suppleness. At the same time, the flames turned a bright shade of green, trailing off the swords and spilling to the ground. His eyes narrowing in anger, Vikramaditya slashed the air in front of him, both swords crisscrossing in a fast, cutting motion—and the belts of flame detached from the tips of the swords and sailed towards the centaurs, curling and spinning in the air, hissing and spitting maliciously as they grew in length.

The horsemen of the Imperial Army stared, awestruck by the whips of green flame.

The three women whimpered in fear and sidled behind the horsemen.

The old couple watched in dread and astonishment as the belts of flame flew low over their heads.

At the first sight of the looping strips of flame, the kinnaras had drawn to a clumsy, crashing halt, bumping and barrelling into one another in surprise. Stomping and shying in the middle of the road, they now stared at the cords of flame twisting towards them, not knowing what to make of the blazing belts, their ominousness beyond doubt. Rooted to the spot, the kinnaras watched in dread and fascination as death approached them on that narrow road in Ujjayini.

Two elongated whips of wicked green flame smacked into the centaurs, striking them across their torsos and curling around them, cleaving their bodies wide open, combusting flesh and bone, cauterizing their wounds while setting their bodies ablaze. The kinnaras' weapons fell from their nerveless hands, landing on the road in a dull clatter, and the next instant the street exploded with their agonized screams that tore through the fire-swept neighbourhood, all but drowning out the clamour of the bells. At the same time, a hideous smell of burned flesh and hair blew down the road, foul and nauseous.

"For Ujjayini," Vikramaditya said to himself through teeth gritted in rage.

Watching the centaurs drop to the ground one after another, the elderly couple stared, not believing how fortunate they had been to escape death. As the last of the kinnaras collapsed into a burning wreck, the couple turned slowly in the direction of the samrat, the man's hands joining in a grateful *pranaam*, his knees sagging in relief. The women emerged from behind the two horsemen and ran to the couple, calling out to them, giving and seeking assurance.

All the seven half-horses lay writhing and kicking in pain, wrapped in relentless green flames that scorched the life out of them, slowly and quickly.

They died quickly because they had all ceased moving by the time Vikramaditya rode over to ascertain they were dead; they died slowly because they burned for a long, long time after the light had left their eyes and their hearts had melted in their chests—a prolonged and painful burning, the way Diti had intended the victims of the Hellfires to burn.

***

Reaching the head of the palace causeway, Kshapanaka reined in her mount and swung off the saddle, landing on her toes before the horse came to a nervy halt, whinnying and stamping its hooves at the torch that came bobbing out of the darkness. The torchlight revealed the faces of three palace guards, flustered and out of breath as they pulled up next to the councilor.

"What is it like inside?" Kshapanaka asked, eyeing the palace. She held the frightened beast by the bridle, stroking its neck to calm it. The horse wasn't hers—her own mount had run away while she had tumbled from the roof and tangled with the centaurs. She had borrowed this one from the rider who had come looking for her on Dhanavantri's orders. "How many men have we lost?"

"Quite a few, your honour," one of the men answered with an uncertain shrug.

"The archers are doing what they can to stop the creatures from getting into the palace," said another. "But the palace has too many windows, and the creatures are way too many..."

"I was told they emerge from underground," the councilor peered suspiciously into the dark.

"They do, your honour."

"And they are good swimmers. That is how they were able to breach the palace."

Kshapanaka nodded briskly. Handing the reins to one of the guards, she said, "Arrows."

The men blinked at her, not comprehending.

"I need arrows," the councilor said. "I have run out of them."

"Um... we don't have any, your honour," one guard replied. "We didn't know—"

"It's okay," Kshapanaka said. She pointed at one of them. "Your spear and your shield."

Slipping her hand into the old shield's hoops, she weighed the spear with her other hand. It felt solid and well balanced. She started walking towards the causeway.

"What is special about the blood of these creatures?" she asked. "The messenger who came for me wasn't coherent at all..."

That Dhanavantri's messenger had found her in the dark—and in all the confusion of the attacks—was in itself a miracle.

He had appeared almost immediately after Vararuchi and she had disposed of the quartet of kinnaras, his eyes widening at the sight of Vararuchi standing in the middle of the street, blood dripping from his *katari*, the centaurs lying sprawled at his feet. The rider had given them a bare-bones account of the attack on the palace, informing Kshapanaka that Dhanavantri had summoned her to the palace.

"Go," Vararuchi had told her, "but tell me if there is a plan to counter the rest of these." He had pointed to the dead kinnaras.

Kshapanaka had explained the plan in three simple steps, and they had parted.

"...and all I understood was that their blood is unique." She stepped onto the causeway.

"It is venomous, your honour." The guards had stopped following her, hanging back warily instead. The horse also neighed and rolled its eyes, probably smelling the blood that had been spilled on the causeway.

"If it touches a human body, the body decomposes. It is horrible."

"That's why they cut themselves..."

Kshapanaka stopped and turned. "Cut themselves?"

"So that the blood can flow and fall on us, your honour."

Now, at last, the councilor understood why Dhanavantri had wanted her here. He was hoping she could somehow neutralize the venom that these creatures secreted with their blood. She had, after all, her own newly discovered gift, as the Mother Oracle liked to put it...

"Okay." Hefting the spear, she glanced up at the palace.

"There is blood on the causeway, your honour," one of the guards warned her. "Some that even belongs to the creatures. Please be careful."

Kshapanaka was halfway across the causeway when she planted a foot in a shallow pool of congealing blood, her toes squelching in its cold, slick viscosity. The knowledge that the blood belonged to some of Avanti's bravest almost made the councilor gag, but she fought the urge and stepped gingerly through the pool, pressing towards the gate.

She was also secretly relieved that the blood from the creatures had done nothing to her. It was possible their blood hadn't touched her yet, but perhaps Dhanavantri had been right, and she was immune to whatever venom...

"Open the gate," she called as she neared the palace, her voice loud so she could make herself heard over the din inside the palace.

The naga attacked the councilor from above, dropping with such speed and stealth that it very nearly got her. Instinct kicked in at the last moment, and Kshapanaka looked up, raising the shield over her head to ward off the shape swooping down from between the torches that lit the palace gate. Her defence was limp and came in too late, though, and the naga smashed into her hard, its talons scraping the shield, causing sparks to fly. The impact of its landing was like a hammer blow, sending the councilor staggering to the ground. Leaping on top of her, the naga slashed open its torso to draw blood, even as it tried to trample the councilor under its powerful legs.

Kshapanaka bunched herself tight under the shield, fighting to keep the creature's feet from landing square on her body and crushing her bones. At the same time, she kicked back at it while attempting to pry out her spear, which had slipped from her grasp and now lay pinned awkwardly under her body. Blood from the naga's wound sprayed on her, but Kshapanaka didn't feel the worse for it. Snarling in frustration, the creature bent to strike her, and the councilor seized the opportunity to drive a foot into its stomach and pitch it over her, onto the causeway. The creature sprawled, struggling to regain its balance, and Kshapanaka quickly rolled over and jumped to her feet, the spear ready in her hand, lunging...

The naga whipped around to confront the councilor, but it went immobile in mid-turn, a painful hiss issuing from its yawning, serpentine mouth. Its eyes dropped to its midriff—where a spear was buried deep, the head almost all the way inside. Blood gushed and gurgled from around the wound, black in the light of the torches by the gate.

Kshapanaka held the other end of the spear, and as the naga looked at her, she gave the shaft a violent twist that drove the spearhead deeper into the creature's body. The naga howled in agony and slumped against the spear, its green-black body bleaching, the skin cracking and peeling off. The councilor yanked the spear free, and the naga collapsed on the causeway in a shower of scales and ashes, crumbling right before her eyes.

"Open the gate," Kshapanaka yelled at the windows above the gate.

"It's Councilor Kshapanaka," a lookout shouted from inside. "Open the gate."

Stepping through the small door, the councilor sensed the panic inside. The palace was in a state of chaos, guards running everywhere, but singularly lacking focus. Even as she crossed the atrium, the body of a guard came crashing down from one of the galleries above, the flesh of his chest disintegrating and bursting open the moment the body hit the floor of the atrium. Chunks of decaying flesh and pieces of bone sprayed and splattered everywhere, forcing Kshapanaka to bury her nose and mouth in the crook of her arm to keep herself from retching.

"I need arrows," she yelled at a guard who had made eye contact. She cast the spear and shield aside and unslung her bow, which she had retrieved after her fall. "Lots of arrows. Get as many quivers as you can and come with me. Hurry."

In almost no time, two guards bearing over a dozen loaded quivers joined Kshapanaka. Slipping a quiver over her shoulder and fitting an arrow into her bow, she looked at the guards. "Where is Councilor Dhanavantri?"

"Somewhere upstairs, your honour."

Kshapanaka and the guards ascended two flights of stairs—the councilor bringing down five nagas along the way, each felled by an arrow to the head or through the neck.

"Ah, there you are."

The councilor turned to see Dhanavantri approaching. "You don't know how relieved I am to see you, Kshapanaka."

Kshapanaka inclined her head. "It's good your rider found me then." She looked around. "How many are inside the palace in your estimation?"

"I would think close to a hundred, if not more," the royal physician replied. "But that's only counting *this* wing. Who knows how many have infiltrated the other wings of the palace? Hundreds, maybe."

"All the better for target practice," said Kshapanaka, limbering her shoulders and flexing the fingers of her right hand. Pulling a fresh arrow and fitting it in the bow, she paused. "Where is Councilor Varahamihira?"

"He's using his energy net... *curtain*... to prevent the creatures from getting in." Dhanavantri looked at Kshapanaka hopefully. "Does *your* power work against them?"

Kshapanaka nodded. "Their blood doesn't affect me." She started down the gallery and the physician heaved a huge sigh of relief as he followed her.

"And when the councilor shoots them, they die *weirdly*," one of the guards piped in.

"Really?" Dhanavantri asked, his eyes shining. "In what way?"

In reply, Kshapanaka levelled her bow and shot the arrow at the gallery straight across, where two nagas had put in an appearance. The arrow took one naga just above the eye. Even before it keeled over, a second arrow followed, swift and smack into the second naga's cheek, shattering its jaw and tearing its snout to shreds. Dhanavantri watched the two creatures turn pale and unravel as the venom in Kshapanaka's arrows contaminated their blood and spread through their bodies.

"Something tells me the palace can now be saved," said Dhanavantri, grinning. Then his face abruptly turned serious. "What about the half-horses outside? Are they still holding the city to ransom?"

"I believe they have met their match," Kshapanaka said over her shoulder.

"In Vikrama?"

"And in someone else." Kshapanaka nocked another arrow and drew the string back.

"Who?"

She smiled. "You would never guess."

***

"The half-horses are everywhere, Samrat."

The riders had met him as he had swerved into the street leading to the city's eastern gate, all five of them young and nervous as hell.

"Have we got them against the wall yet?" Vikramaditya asked. One Hellfire smouldered in his right hand, the other back in its sheath for the moment.

"We have been trying to, your honour," a captain of the Watch, replied. "But they are too fast and too strong..."

The samrat looked to his right, where a group of soldiers comprising swordsmen and archers stood in a huddle, clearly at a loss. He beckoned them with a wave of his hand. Turning to the five horsemen, he said, "Do you know where the bulk of the half-horses are?"

"There... and over there," one of the riders pointed, his arm moving in a wide arc.

"Alright. Listen closely now..." When he had the attention of all the men, Vikramaditya said, "If I drive the half-horses this way, can I count on all of you to push them towards the wall, making sure they don't slip off in any other direction?"

The men murmured and exchanged hesitant looks.

"They will be running from me," the samrat said helpfully. "All you have to do is attack them such that they keep fleeing—" he motioned with his sword, "—towards the wall. Will you do that?"

"Yes," came a chorus of voices, sounding more confident.

"Kill as many as you can and send those that survive to the wall." The king raised the burning sword high. "Glory to Avanti."

"Glory to Avanti," the soldiers roared back as Vikramaditya spurred his horse forward.

He galloped through the streets, hoping he could locate the centaurs quickly. The detour to rescue Commander Sharamana's kin had been both unexpected and unavoidable, costing the samrat time. If Kshapanaka had managed turning the half-horses in the south around and bringing them back to the eastern wall—and Vikramaditya knew it was a big *if*—he would need to move swiftly and get the centaurs in *this* part of the city to the wall as well, so that all the centaurs would be in one place and he could...

Turning a sharp corner, he saw close to three dozen of them clustered in a square, laughing and calling out to each other as they torched the shops and houses nearby.

The sight of them setting his beloved city afire with such casualness made the samrat's blood boil. The next instant, he was off, seated low on his saddle, charging at them, eyes blazing, the Hellfires burning in his hands.

They spied him and turned, squaring their shoulders and raising their weapons. One of them barked an order, and ten to twelve of them set off down the street to meet the challenge head-on.

Vikramaditya raised the Hellfires and whipped them, the flames looping into belts.

Watching the lone rider come galloping towards them, belts of fire suddenly sprouting from his swords, the kinnaras dropped pace—and then drew to a complete halt. They stared as the fiery belts detached from the rider's swords and came whirling at them. Sensing danger, the cannier among them turned to beat a quick retreat, but the centaurs coming from behind were in their way; the kinnaras rammed into one another, kicking and shoving in panic, desperate to get away. But there was no escape.

The belts slapped into them, cutting them open, burning them mercilessly.

The centaurs screamed and died. And those that didn't die took to their heels, trying to put as much distance between themselves and the man with the burning swords.

Vikramaditya chased the kinnaras, sending whips of fire after them to encourage them to flee towards the south-eastern section of Ujjayini. And where that failed, he worked the centaurs around to where his soldiers waited, so that *they* could drive the kinnaras to the wall. Along the way, he met a contingent of the City Watch, to whom he entrusted the task of pursuing the kinnaras, so he could go hunting for the second band of centaurs.

The kinnaras that had laid siege to the southern quarter were far greater in number; and to compound the crisis, unlike in the city's east, the district had yet to be fully evacuated. Riding into the streets, the samrat was greeted by the sight of a few soldiers of the Watch escorting a flock of citizens to the relative safety of the City Watch command centre.

Hailing one of the men, Vikramaditya asked, "Where are the half-horses?"

"That way," the soldier replied, pointing behind with his thumb.

"Have you seen Councilor Kshapanaka around?"

The soldier shook his head. He looked rattled.

The king was about to ride on when the man spoke.

"There are people still stuck in houses, your honour."

"Where?"

"Near the flour mills next to the bridge."

"How many houses?"

"I don't know, your honour. But there are half-horses everywhere."

"Get them to safety quickly," the samrat barked, inclining his head at the citizens, "then come back to fetch the others. Hurry up."

Vikramaditya took off in the direction of the bridge that had once spanned a narrow stream that filled with water every monsoon. With the building of the city wall, the water had been diverted and the stream had dried, but the bridge remained, the horse's hooves hard and loud on the old, weather-beaten wood as the king crossed it.

Straightaway, the samrat ran into approximately a dozen kinnaras.

The half-horses were milling around the street, setting fire to houses at random. Wails of terror could be heard issuing from one of the buildings. Vikramaditya was still sizing up the situation when, all of a sudden, two boys of around twelve darted out of a house and ran onto the road, not very far behind the centaurs. The boys were in plain sight—all it would take was a turn of the head for the half-horses to see them.

"Get back inside," the king shouted in distress, rising up in his saddle.

Distracted for a moment, his eyes off the kinnaras, the samrat glared at the boys, willing them to return to the shelter of their home. And in that fraction of a moment, drawn by his shout, a kinnara aimed and shot an arrow at Vikramaditya.

The shot was powerful but poorly directed, fired too low.

Still, it managed striking the king's mount in the neck, burying deep.

The horse neighed and stumbled. Its front legs folded, and it went face down on the road.

Vikramaditya, who was balanced in the saddle, Hellfire in each hand, pitched forward. Borne by momentum, and with nothing to arrest his fall, he cartwheeled over the horse's head and crashed to the ground hard, but twisted around so that his shoulder took the brunt. Falling and rolling, his shoulder flaming with pain, he came up on one knee, his arms outstretched, the Hellfires blazing.

In the wink of an eye, he slashed two fresh belts of fire into existence and sent them sailing at the kinnaras in front of him.

The belts had still to reach their targets when the king spun around to confront the remaining centaurs, his eyes narrowing against the pain in his shoulder, a dull throb blossoming in his right hip. The kinnaras were too many though, and Vikramaditya's movements were slowed by injury, his reflexes dulled with pain. Seeing the samrat struggle to his feet, the half-horses lined up their weapons to put him back down when a volley of arrows whistled in from both ends of the street, taking the kinnaras by surprise and felling them.

At the same time, a horseman thundered out of the dark, a flexible band of steel trailing from his hand.

Nearing the first kinnara, the rider swung the *urumi* expertly, slicing the centaur's back open. Next, he took off a kinnara's arm from just above the elbow, before splitting another's face in two. The *urumi* snaked and flashed in the firelight, red with centaur blood as Avanti's archers kept nailing the kinnaras under a relentless rain of arrows. In a matter of moments, the street was full of dead and dying half-horses.

Vikramaditya blinked at the fallen centaurs before turning to look back down the road, where the two boys still stood, staring wide-eyed at the carnage.

"I said get back inside."

The boys stared at the dishevelled and battle-scarred king, the Hellfires burning in his hands, fire reflected in his deep, black, angry eyes. Turning around, they fled indoors.

Drawing his breath, the samrat winced and looked at the horseman, who sat on his horse. The *urumi* dangled from the man's hand, slowly dripping blood.

"You came," Vikramaditya said with a tired, lopsided smile.

"I came for Avanti, which is bigger than the throne."

The smile widened on the samrat's face, the pain in his shoulder already beginning to fade. "Which is why the throne needs you, brother."

Vararuchi did not reply.

"I can't fight all these battles by myself," Vikramaditya looked at the burning houses by way of explanation. "I need you by my side."

Vararuchi thought about this for a moment. "Kshapanaka told me about your plan," he said at last. "Most of the half-horses have been pushed back against the eastern wall." He looked at Vikramaditya. "Burn them, brother. Make them pay for what they have done to our city."

The samrat's grip on the Hellfires tightened. "For Avanti."

"For Avanti," Vararuchi replied.

***

The three *churails* mowed through the night sky, shrieking and monstrous and horrific, disgorging green flames from their mouths, trailing green fire in their wake, the hollows of their eyes eerily crazed with bloodlust.

Matali stared at them, his eyebrows arched in disbelief, struggling to make sense of the disastrous turn this raid had taken.

You made a mistake.

But where and how, the deva asked himself, as he observed the *churails* from a high roof of the palace. He was clearly visible to anyone from below, silhouetted against the nimbus of green that saturated the sky, but he knew no one would be looking in his direction; everyone in Ujjayini had their eyes firmly trained on the sky above the south-east corner of the city, where the *churails* held sway.

He had been slinking around the palace, searching for Veeshada's dagger—and slowly losing patience as it became obvious that the samrat had hidden it well—when he heard the terrible wailing in the wind. Looking out of a window, his breath caught at the sight of two *churails* sweeping along the sky, breathing fire; and as he had watched, belts of green flame rose and fused to take the form of a third banshee.

It had taken the deva all of one moment to figure out from where these screaming apparitions had materialized.

And as if to corroborate him, Takshaka had appeared at his elbow, frowning at the *churails*. "I thought you said you had stolen the human king's swords," the naga king had said.

"I did. I… I showed them to you and Tribhanu, remember?" Matali stared in bewilderment. "You saw them before the garuda took them away… right?"

The naga gave his head a dubious shake.

"What?" Matali glared in exasperation. "Now you deny seeing those swords?"

"All I know is that those things appear from those two swords," Takshaka had pointed at the *churails*. "And my guess is those things are decimating Tribhanu's kinnara army as we stand here watching. If I were Tribhanu, I would be very unhappy with the way things have turned out," he added drily.

Matali looked at Takshaka sharply. "And I am to blame for that?"

The naga pinned the deva in a cold gaze. "We trusted you to neutralize the Hellfires. We have a right to feel let down."

Takshaka turned to leave the room. Matali shot a worried glance at the *churails* draped across the sky, then looked back at the naga. "Maybe the king somehow took them back from the garuda."

Takshaka gave the deva an even stare. "You know that is not possible. The garuda left with the swords long back."

Matali threw his hands open in defeat. "What happened then?"

"You made a mistake."

The naga was at the door when Matali called to him again. "What do we do now?"

Pointing past Matali, Takshaka replied, "With the *churails* unleashed upon them, the kinnaras are down to two options—die or die fleeing. I doubt whether many of them will make it back alive, but I don't intend to stay and find out, only to have the *churails* come after us next. Anyway, too many of my nagas have fallen to the woman who is immune to our venom—and is one hell of an archer. I'm getting out of here while I can, and unless you have a very good idea of where to look for the Halahala, I recommend you do likewise."

That had been a little while back, and now, standing on the high roof, Matali sensed the battle below him easing, as the nagas abandoned the fight and left the palace by way of the lake, burrowing down and coming out in the safety of Avanti's countryside. In the east, Ujjayini was in flames, but the eye was naturally drawn upward to where the *churails* patrolled the sky. He was too far away to see what was happening by the city wall, but the deva harboured no illusions about the kinnaras' fate.

You made a mistake.

As a freshening wind tore at him, Matali cast his mind back to the antechamber where he had picked up the Hellfires, swathed in satin. He saw the table in his mind's eye, the unlit brass lamp, the inkwell with the quills… and the swords.

He remembered picking one of them up, drawing it out of its scabbard. He was certain he had wrapped them both back in the satin cloth and left the samrat's chamber, holding the bundle close to his chest. Not once had the swords left his hands until he had surrendered them to the garuda, to be taken to Devaloka.

There was no question of him having made a mistake, yet the demonic *churails* were circling above Ujjayini…

We trusted you to neutralize the Hellfires. We have a right to feel let down.

If I were Tribhanu, I would be very unhappy with the way things have turned out.

Takshaka's admonitions notwithstanding, Matali cared nothing about having failed the nagas and the kinnaras, nor was he particularly intimidated by Tribhanu's unhappiness; what really worried the deva was incurring Indra's displeasure. No Halahala, no human king in chains—the repercussions of returning to Amaravati empty-handed would be severe, he knew. If only he could find the Halahala, everything would be forgiven, and he would be given a hero's welcome. But try as he might, he couldn't think of one place where he hadn't already looked for the dagger. The council chamber, the king's rooms, the councilors' quarters, the Throne Room, the assembly, the treasury, the royal weapon room…

Watching the banshees loop and swoop down to earth, Matali weighed the prospect of hiding in the palace and waiting for the battle to blow over. Then maybe, believing that the threat had passed, the humans would drop their guard. Then maybe he could sneak out again, and perhaps kill a palace hand and take his place to resume the hunt for…

One of the *churails* suddenly whirled to face the palace. Matali got the creepy sensation that the *churail's* empty eyes had settled on him, picking him out from thousands of Ujjayini's inhabitants, singling him out as the enemy, the one deserving punishment... Panic reared in the deva's mind.

I don't intend to stay, only to have the churails *come after us next.*

Matali imagined the *churail* had begun moving along the sky, heading towards the palace—towards him. A strange dread seized him, blotting out even the fear of facing Indra's anger.

I'm getting out of here while I can, and unless you have a very good idea of where to look for the Halahala, I recommend you do likewise.

The *churail* appeared to gather momentum, skimming over the city, its mouth opening wide to spill flames...

Matali's heart turned cold in terror. He had no desire to die the way the kinnaras were dying, chased and charred to the bone by the banshees.

He didn't want to die at all.

He didn't want to stay in the palace. He didn't want to look for the dagger.

All he wanted was to get away from the infernal *churails*.

He turned and bolted from the roof.

Frontier

Thin daylight, low on warmth and colour even though the sun had been up for a couple of hours, seeped through the blanket of smoke drifting over Ujjayini. Closer to the ground, darkness still huddled, mixing with the dense smoke that rolled up from the gutted remains of the city. The fires had been fought through the night and brought under control, but pockets still remained where soldiers of the City Watch worked with the populace to douse stubborn flames. Hospices had sprung up around the city's southern quarter, where *vaidyas* rushed about treating lines of soldiers and civilians for burns and other injuries. There was an overpowering sense of fatigue all around, the silence of the bells a relief as well as strangely burdensome, adding to the doleful atmosphere.

The good news for Ujjayini was that just five civilians had lost their lives in the attack, though a dozen or so were reported missing. The bad news was that military casualties were in excess of three hundred, and they weren't done counting. The dead were almost evenly divided between the palace and the city, the ones in the palace harder to count and identify as the bodies were mangled and rotted beyond recognition. The fire itself had claimed some twenty lives, all in the populated southern quarter.

"Nearly half the city has turned to ash. It will take us forever to rebuild it."

"We've done it before. We'll do it again."

The smoke parted a little to let the two riders amble through.

"After the barbarians were driven away... you're right." Vararuchi waved at the curtain of grey in front of him and nodded. "We'll do it again."

Vikramaditya stared through the smoke, grim and unblinking. "It's the men we lost last night... *that* won't be so easy. A city can be rebuilt in a few years, but it can take decades to build brave men who are ready to lay down their lives for their kingdom. Sometimes, such men are impossible to replace."

"I know what you mean," said Vararuchi. "But sometimes, it is through their deaths that the brave and the fearless spawn a new generation of brave and fearless men."

"True. It is our good fortune to be blessed with such men, that too in such abundance." The samrat's face hardened. "Still, the dead cannot go unavenged. Ujjayini owes those who have died defending her a fitting retribution."

Before Vararuchi could add anything to that, the outlines of the palace emerged through the pale sunlight. The councilor immediately reined his horse back.

"What?" Vikramaditya asked, tugging at his own reins and turning.

Vararuchi drew a deep breath and shrugged uncertainly. "I don't know... I..."

"*Badi-maa* is waiting for you. I promised her I would bring you back."

Vararuchi gave this some thought, then nudged his horse forward, and the brothers resumed riding. They were both stained in soot, their hair, beard and moustaches thickly matted with ash and mud. Their faces were drawn, eyes red and bleary from a long night spent saving the city from the attackers and the fire.

"Had it not been for mother, I would never have reached here in time."

"What do you mean?" Vikramaditya turned to his brother, perplexed.

"It has been a while since I have met mother. So, last night, on a whim, I decided to pay her a visit," said Vararuchi. "I had no idea she had come here, of course. It was sheer chance that I was passing through the countryside, heading for the old mansion, when a shift in the wind brought the sound of the bells. I would never have heard the alarm in Musili."

The samrat nodded thoughtfully. "One more reason to thank *badi-maa*," he smiled.

"It's hard to believe she is here," Vararuchi said. "She had promised never to set foot in the palace, you know. Which is why she never came..."

A bitter smile passed Vikramaditya's lips. "All of you, keeping secrets from me, pretending as if everything was normal. Why?"

Vararuchi didn't reply.

"Why?" the samrat asked, twisting around in his saddle to look at his brother. "Why did you keep silent all these years and not tell me anything?"

"What was I supposed to tell you?" Vararuchi asked, his tone suddenly hurt. "What could I have possibly said to my younger brother—that his mother reviled me from the bottom of her heart, and that she would have liked me to disappear from the face of the earth? Do you know how absurd that sounds even now? And what difference would it have made—"

"I would have confronted her," the king interrupted forcefully.

"What good would that have achieved? She was clever at concealing her hatred for me from everyone—remember, in all these years, you didn't have the slightest inkling that something was broken between her and me. She would have denied disliking me, saying I was just being silly and paranoid. Her word against mine, what would you have done?"

"I would have strived to learn the truth," Vikramaditya replied dourly.

"And in the process, you would probably have lost some respect for your mother, you might even have ended up loving her less, making me an *even* bigger villain in her eyes. Telling you would only have alienated me even more, and all of us would have ended up being unhappy, that's all."

"So, you suffered in silence, letting the pain and anger build inside you. And look where that has brought us. All of us are unhappy. You and I were scheming against one another, full of resentment born out of ignorance and misunderstanding, squaring off when Avanti needed us to be together..." Vikramaditya trailed off, his voice trembling.

A prickly silence stretched between them. Vararuchi shot a sideways glance at his brother. "I am sorry," he said shortly.

The king stared firmly ahead, ignoring the apology. They rode in silence for a few moments, before Vararuchi took a deep breath.

"When councilors Varahamihira and Dhanavantri came to meet me at Musili, Dhanavantri reminded me about how father and I used to hold your hands when you were learning to walk, and how we would make sure you never fell. Dhanavantri does not remember this, but one day, I was distracted and was not watching you closely. You fell, rolled down a couple of steps and bumped your head against a bench. Father was so furious that he didn't talk to me for two days." Vararuchi paused to look at his half-brother. "That day, I promised myself that I wouldn't ever let you fall again, Vikrama. I'm sorry I almost forgot my promise."

"You didn't forget, brother. You came when you heard the bells, and you saved me from dying at the hands of the half-horses." Tears glistened in the samrat's eyes. "You couldn't let me fall even if you wanted to. I of all people should have known that, instead of believing the worst about you."

They were almost at the causeway, within earshot of the palace hands who were ridding the causeway's stones of the bloodstains from the night's gruesome battle.

"How is the shoulder?" Vararuchi asked, deftly switching topics.

The king grimaced. Stretching his right arm, he moved his shoulder gingerly back and forth. The shoulder had been trussed in a crude bandage at one of the hospices.

"Hurts enough to make me cry," he laughed, swallowing the lump that had suddenly formed in his throat. "It's sore with all the swinging and cutting, but it'll heal."

"We'll get Dhanavantri to look at it."

In the palace, they were told that both their mothers had returned from the Labyrinth, and that they were in the Queen Mother's chamber. Vararuchi held himself back once again, reluctant to meet Upashruti, afraid of facing the past and opening forgotten wounds. But persuaded by Vikramaditya, he finally climbed to the gallery which housed the Queen Mother's chamber. The samrat knocked on the door, and a maid promptly opened it to let him and Vararuchi in.

"*Badi-maa*, look who I have with me," he said.

Ushantha rose from Upashruti's side and swept Vararuchi into an embrace, not caring about the ash and grime, holding him to herself for a long moment. Finally, letting go, she stepped back and looked into his face.

"First things first; you are my son, and my love for you

will never recede as long as the sun rides the sky," she said. "But your decision to go against your brother was wrong. You broke the promise to your father that you would stand by Vikrama's side to preserve Avanti's glory. It wasn't Vikrama who disrespected your father by defending the queen mother from Indra's allegations; it was *you* who disrespected your father by going against what he had asked of you."

"I am sorry, mother. I made a mistake—"

"*Badi-maa*, please let brother be—" the samrat remonstrated at the same time.

"Wait…" Ushantha interrupted, raising a finger to silence both men.

Taking Vararuchi's hand, she led him to Upashruti, who stood by the bed, twisting the corner of the bedspread nervously between her fingers.

"Bless my son, sister," Ushantha said, "and pardon what mistakes he might have made. He is *my* son, but he is as much *yours*, as Vikrama is yours and mine."

It was a struggle to look Upashruti in the face, but when their gazes finally met, the councilor was surprised to see regret in the Queen Mother's eyes. Without knowing it, he put his hands together in a *pranaam*. "I apologize for any mistakes—" he began, but before he could finish, Upashruti took his hands between hers.

"You have nothing at all to apologize for," she looked at Vararuchi through a sparkle of tears. "I am the one who needs to make amends for mistreating you. Forgive me for what I was and what I did, son. I was…" Upashruti bowed her head over Vararuchi's hands. Clutching his fingers tight and raising them to her forehead, she broke down, her shoulders heaving in grief and shame.

"*Rani-maa*… please…" Vararuchi looked from Upashruti to Ushantha, distraught. The latter stepped to his rescue, taking the Queen Mother by the shoulders and seating her on the bed. Settling down beside her, Ushantha pulled the queen's head to her shoulder to comfort her.

"Much of this could have been averted had the rider just delivered Shanku's message to the maid that day," Ushantha sighed.

"What rider, what message?" Vararuchi looked at his mother in puzzlement.

"That afternoon when you last left home, a rider came with a message for you from Shanku. I was asleep when he arrived, so the maid received him and told him you had left. The rider went away without sharing the message, which I now realize was meant to inform you about Ghatakarpara's kidnapping. Why the fellow didn't tell the maid beats me, for if I had known about the kidnapping then, I would have come here sooner, and all this would probably never have happened..."

Upashruti's soft sobbing permeated the silence that unfolded in the room. With a tilt of her head, Ushantha beckoned Vikramaditya to her and the Queen Mother's side.

The samrat had taken two steps in their direction when there was a rap on the door.

"Yes?" Vikramaditya said, turning.

The door wedged open to reveal the face of the maid. "A messenger for you, your honour."

The king nodded, and the door opened wide. A palace guard stood outside.

"What is it?" Vikramaditya demanded.

"I have a message from the Mother Oracle, your honour. She has some pressing news for you from the Great Desert."

***

It was cold.

Miserably, mind-numbingly cold.

So cold that even the hunger chewing away at his innards had become a lesser source of discomfort.

Shivering uncontrollably, the chattering of his teeth loud in his ears, he burrowed into the shallow depression on the side of the mountain, seeking warmth and comfort and finding neither. The cold wouldn't let him sleep in peace, pressing down on his hunched shoulders and slipping easily under the thin cottons that covered him, clothes suited for the desert, but painfully inadequate in the wind-blown ridges of the northern Arbudas. Every bone in his body ached, his toes and fingers tingling and slowly losing sensation. Yet, every time he resolved to awaken, a part of him rebelled, snuggling into itself against the draught blowing down the mountains, refusing to follow instructions, just wanting to lie there in the hope that sleep would eventually overtake him.

Ghatakarpara had had no inkling of how cold the night would get when he had shuffled into the shadows of the Arbudas late the previous afternoon. Although the gullies were filled with a whistling wind that didn't bode well, he had hardly noticed, relieved to put the blazing hot desert behind him. It was only well after the sun had set—and after he had made a fair bit of progress into the mountains—that the bite had got into the wind. Thereafter, he had stumbled about in the dark until, somehow, he had chanced upon the spot where he now lay, dead tired, sleeping fretfully because of the cold and the hunger.

The prince knew that he should force himself to rise, that if he didn't get his body moving and his heart pumping, there was a danger of slipping into a stupor from which he might never awaken, freezing to death in his sleep. But the notion of waking up was hard to comprehend, the effort it demanded not in proportion to whatever benefits there were to be had. So, he ignored the woozy voice of reason and let himself drift...

He didn't remember the mountains being so cold around Udaypuri. Even the far-flung outposts dotting the frontier were warmer. Bedar, Balipura, Kaanja…

Ghatakarpara stirred in his half-sleep, the thought of Balipura triggering a memory that he fought to hold on to, a face forming behind his eyelids. Round and light brown, with lustrous eyes that he could sink into, and luscious lips that had tasted of nectar as twilight had settled around the countryside.

If father doesn't accept you, I am willing to leave everything and come with you.

Throwing off the lethargy and numbness that gripped him, the prince pried his eyes open a crack, surprised to see that the new day had broken. The light was grey where he was huddled, softly illuminating the dour mountains, the sun not high enough yet to reach this flank of the mountainside. Ghatakarpara tried turning over, but the cold grabbed and pinned him back with a vengeance, compelling him to roll into a tight ball.

It was cold. Unbearably cold. Too cold to move, to rise. It was better he slept…

Memories of Aparupa came washing back to him, bringing with them a realization that she was waiting for his return, heartbroken and sick with worry. He had to get back to her.

It took all the effort he could muster for Ghatakarpara to roll onto his back. He unfolded his body in arthritic fits and jerks, stretching out stiff limbs and flexing joints to remove the kinks in them. The cold redoubled its assault on his unprotected body, but the prince willed himself to a seated position, before struggling to all fours. With a dose of supreme determination, he finally got to his feet, teetering dangerously before finding his balance.

Aparupa.

He had to tell her he was willing to leave everything to be with her.

Hunger squeezed from within and the cold from without, as Ghatakarpara resumed the trudge up the mountain on slow, shaky legs.

***

"Takshaka and Tribhanu were neither stupid nor reckless; they were merely under the wrong impression that the human king did not have the Hellfires."

Perplexed, Hiranyaksha and Holika stared at Shukracharya.

"And why would the Hellfires not be in the king's possession?" the asura lord grunted.

"Because Matali thought he had stolen them," the high priest's eye twinkled with gaiety. "He even sent the swords he had nicked to Devaloka through a garuda. As gifts for his master."

"But the swords he took were not the Hellfires?"

Shukracharya shook his head. "He was tricked into believing they were, and the kinnara army paid for his mistake with their lives. Less than a quarter of them survived the attack; the rest simply burned to death."

"And the nagas?"

"They didn't fare much better, even though they didn't encounter the Hellfires."

"What did them in then, mahaguru?" Holika asked curiously.

"The nagas tangled with the councilor who has the ability to harness venom, the one embodying the cobra pearl. She was immune to the nagas, and was also able to get their venom to work against them." Shukracharya paused, his brow darkening. "It's worrying, the way she got the better of the nagas… Even the other one has returned, the king's brother, the embodiment of the bamboo pearl. He set his differences with the king aside, and came back to fight against the kinnaras."

Holika and Hiranyaksha looked at one another doubtfully. "You had said that the Nine Pearls had weakened, mahaguru. That the force binding them had been broken—"

"It had," the high priest glared back at the asura lords. "Which is why I said this is worrying. The humans shouldn't have been able to fight back so well... though looking at it from our point of view, it is great the humans triumphed. The devas have been sent packing, and Indra will soon discover that all he has are two useless swords. This is a happy situation for us."

"More so because it was so unexpected," Hiranyaksha agreed. "And the dagger...?"

"The king had it with him all along," Shukracharya said, adding with a chuckle, "Poor Matali spent half the night searching the palace for it. He filched the wrong swords, failed to find the Halahala, was responsible for the death of a few thousand kinnaras... Indra won't be terribly pleased with his pet soldier this time."

"Indra won't be pleased with a lot of things in the time to come," Holika grinned. "How far is brother from Devaloka?"

"He still has some distance to go."

"And the mantras to raise Ahi—"

"Are with the devas, the bones assure me," said Shukracharya.

As silence settled over the chamber, Hiranyaksha drew himself erect.

"The humans may have fought well, but they have been battered. The devas are in no better shape, routed and demoralized. This is a golden opportunity to take the Halahala, mahaguru."

"Absolutely," Shukracharya agreed. "It is fortunate that the humans have already lost half of their city to fire. I don't suppose it will take my sons and an army of vyalas long to convince them that they risk losing the other half as well—if they don't surrender the dagger to us."

***

"The Mother Oracle says the clouds speak of a dust storm moving east over the Marusthali."

"Maybe that's all it is—a dust storm," shrugged Kshapanaka.

"A dust storm with thousands of legs," Vikramaditya clarified.

"Oh," Kshapanaka replied. "An army on the march."

"More like an army at a gallop," Dhanavantri said, peeling off the bandage that covered the samrat's shoulder to inspect the bruise, swollen and purple-red under the smear of an oily unction. "Raise your arm." He assisted in lifting the king's hand, prodding around the wound, ignoring the king as he winced.

Vikramaditya had summoned everyone to the palace infirmary so that they could make plans while Dhanavantri attended to his injury. Varahamihira leaned back where he was sitting next to an array of jars filled with *kashayams* and peered out of the window.

"I can barely see anything past all this smoke," he muttered. "I wonder how the oracle saw all the way up to the clouds."

"She didn't seem to have any doubts about the signs she had read," said the samrat.

"After the body in the lake, I'll believe anything she says," said Dhanavantri.

"Right," Varahamihira nodded. He looked at Vikramaditya. "Nothing about Kalidasa?"

"No, but we have to assume he is riding with the Huna army, probably even leading it."

"Does she know how far this dust storm is from the frontier?"

"No, but we can be sure it is only a matter of time before they attempt crossing the Arbudas." The king flinched as Dhanavantri applied a compress of hot mustard seeds over the bruise. "We must do whatever it takes to stop them, and that means leading the men from the front."

Vararuchi, leaning against the door with his arms across his chest, straightened. "I will go."

Vikramaditya shook his head. "I let Kalidasa leave Avanti. I must stop him from returning." There was a resolve in his voice that brooked no argument.

The councilors exchanged glances.

"You'll have to be careful with this arm," Dhanavantri warned.

"I thought you could find a quick remedy for it," the samrat's lips turned at the corners.

"I am a man of medicine, not a magician."

"That's not what they are saying in the city," Varahamihira countered. "I've heard reports of you having brought instant relief to many of last night's wounded. People are comparing you to the Healer, I'm told."

"Not him, please," the physician frowned.

"And the way you pulled Vikrama back from Borderworld was nothing short of miraculous."

The king looked at Dhanavantri. "I didn't thank you for that—"

"Please," the physician waved the samrat away, looking embarrassed. "About your arm," he changed the subject, "there's no dislocation, thankfully, but you've torn a ligament, so I will have to put you on a sling. You mustn't strain the shoulder for some days."

The king smiled. "I will try not to, if the Hunas allow it."

"What about the Halahala?"

Everyone turned and stared at Varahamihira.

"Are you taking it with you?" the old councilor persisted.

"It's too dangerous," the samrat said with a shake of his head. "The frontier is far away, and the dagger could get lost in the midst of battle..."

"So where will you leave it?"

"Here."

All four councilors went silent, stealing furtive glances as the enormity of what Vikramaditya had proposed dawned on them.

"You believe we can protect the dagger?" Varahamihira eyed the king doubtfully.

"Yes."

Varahamihira looked far from convinced. The silence in the chamber was absolute.

"All of you can protect the dagger, but most definitely you," the king said to Varahamihira.

"I don't understand—"

"Dhanavantri told me about your energy shield... that thing that you do. He says you were able to keep the creatures that attacked the palace out by casting the shield. You also told us how you blocked that serpent's venom when you were on your chariot with Shukracharya." Seeing the old councilor nod, the samrat continued, "It's powerful, what you do. Things can't easily get through that shield of yours, and that is how you will protect the dagger."

"I don't know how strong that shield really is," Varahamihira protested. "I don't know what it can or can't stop. What if it can't stop a threat that is too powerful—"

"You will discover the limits of your power only when you use it to its full extent," the king replied. "Have faith in your power. Moreover, you are not alone. Kshapanaka, Vararuchi and Dhanavantri are here, and with luck, the others will return very soon."

For a long moment, Varahamihira studied the wrinkles on the back of his hands. Finally, he transferred his gaze to Vikramaditya, and then to the other councilors.

"Do you think Vikrama is right?" he asked them.

"There's only one way of knowing," Kshapanaka smiled. Vararuchi shucked his shoulders in agreement.

"When do you propose to leave?" Kshapanaka asked Vikramaditya.

"Immediately." The samrat turned to Vararuchi. "Assemble a company of fifty sturdy riders. Also have signals sent to Udaypuri and Gosringa, informing them to double the patrols in the mountains, and have the patrols report back to the garrisons and command centres every three hours. Any sighting of movements in the desert must be reported immediately. And have the garrison commander at Udaypuri—what's his name? Atulyateja?—well, have him know that I will reach there in a day or so."

Vararuchi left the room. Varahamihira watched him go before turning to look at the others.

"It's good to have him back," he said, smiling.

The other three nodded back vigorously.

"I can't tell you how relieved I am," the king added, cradling his arm. "His return has lifted a weight from my shoulders—and my chest."

"I will put the ligature on once you have bathed and changed," the physician said.

Seeing Vikramaditya rise from his seat, Varahamihira said, "Before you go, tell us about the Hellfires. It's not like you suspected Vismaya—or whoever was impersonating him—so what exactly happened? If he stole the swords, where did these two come from?" he pointed at the Hellfires at the king's hip.

"I suspected no one in particular, but I did realize that there was a genuine threat of someone trying to steal the Hellfires," said the samrat. "So, two days ago, I asked Barisa, our palace blacksmith, to make replicas of the two swords. In fact, Barisa was here that morning, before you and Dhanavantri came to meet me, right after the storm. I made him promise not to tell anyone what I had asked of him. Anyway, he made the counterfeit swords, and not a moment too soon. I left the copies in the place where I kept the Hellfires and hid the original swords. Vismaya's double took the copies, thinking they were the Hellfires."

"Clever of you," Varahamihira marvelled.

"Perhaps you should get Barisa to make a dozen more replicas," Kshapanaka grinned.

"I doubt whether he would agree," Vikramaditya answered with a smile of his own. "He was already complaining about the iron shortage; he would hate to indulge in its wastage." Walking to the door, he added, "Besides, here onwards, the Hellfires will always be with me, until we have put an end to the threats facing Avanti."

***

Maybe there was something to what the townsfolk were saying about Dhanavantri, the samrat thought to himself as he lowered himself onto the vacant seat next to Vishakha. His body still felt stiff and sore, and his hip hurt from the fall off the horse, but the pain in his shoulder had begun receding within minutes of Dhanavantri's ministrations and was nearly negligible now. Perhaps the physician had discovered a touch, a power comparable to what Varahamihira and Kshapanaka and the rest of them had acquired, which allowed him to heal better…

A pity Dhanavantri couldn't do anything to ease the pain in his chest, Vikramaditya sighed, taking the queen's hand in his own. That pain was hardest to deal with, a constant, dull ache that flared and wrenched at his heart every morning and evening, when he came to this room. And knowing that he wouldn't come here for some time now, the pain seemed to redouble, as if accounting and compensating for his absence.

"I must go, my beloved, I don't have a choice," he whispered, raising her hands to his lips and kissing her fingers lightly. "But I promise to be back before you miss me."

She will not miss you, a voice inside his head reminded him cruelly, and the king felt a pall of despair wrap itself tight around him. It was possible that she would never miss him again, not knowing what she had lost and what he kept losing day after day, every single day she did not recognize him...

"Ah, you're here already."

Vikramaditya looked to see Dhanavantri enter the queen's chamber. "I came to say goodbye before leaving," the king said.

The physician nodded as he drew up to the bed. "How's the shoulder?"

"The people are right about you. There's hardly any pain." The samrat wiggled his shoulder, which was in a sling.

"Easy," Dhanavantri warned. "Don't get too taken in by what others say. Injuries take time to heal. Keep the sling on and avoid straining the shoulder."

Vikramaditya placed Vishakha's hand back on the bed. "Please take good care of her," he said, looking at the queen while speaking to the physician. He reached out a hand and stroked Vishakha's forehead, as if smoothening a frown.

"I will."

The samrat looked up at the physician. "I know you don't care much for it, but I desperately want to believe it when they compare you to the Healer. If he brought her back... maybe you can too."

Dhanavantri's head bobbed, but he avoided Vikramaditya's gaze. Seeing this, the king's face fell, and he rose to his feet. He looked down again at Vishakha with sad eyes.

Dhanavantri placed a comforting hand on the king's arm. "Maybe I can," he said. "As you told Varahamihira, we will know the limits of our powers only when we use them."

The samrat smiled and covered the physician's hand with

his own. "Thank you, friend." With a final, backward glance at Vishakha, he left the room.

He walked down the gallery and climbed the stairway to his own chambers, his mind already on the journey and the frontier, chalking out strategies to keep the Hunas from crossing the mountains and devising plans to counter an onslaught if the first line of defence fell.

Vikramaditya turned into his chambers, but he was so caught up in his thoughts that he did not realize there was someone already in the room. It took him a moment to orient himself to this other person, who stood by the door that led to the terrace outside.

The light was behind the figure, so the samrat didn't immediately recognize who it was.

He blinked and his eyes opened wide in astonishment... and anger.

He knew the face from a crowded street in Ujjayini, a face that he had seen recently for the first time.

A face he was never likely to forget.

The deva Gandharvasena.

"What are you doing here?" the samrat roared, eyes blazing.

"I come in peace, son—" the visitor began, but Vikramaditya stepped forward, his fists rolled into tight balls of fury.

"*Don't...*" the word shot out in warning. "Don't... I am *not* your son. *Never.*"

The deva stepped back in alarm, hands raised, palms facing forward. "I have come in peace; I don't mean any harm to you or your mother."

"What do you want then? How did you get in here?" The king's eyes darted around the room, while his left hand went to the Hellfire hanging on his right hip.

"I swear I come in peace... not like father, who came only for his own gain."

Vikramaditya locked eyes with Gandharvasena.

"You came with Indra. You knew what harm you were about to cause me."

"Father only told me that I was to tell you who I was to you," the deva shook his head. "I did not know that the outcome would be so terrible."

"Had you known, would you have refused to come with him?" the samrat challenged.

The king and the deva stared at one another before the latter dropped his eyes.

"The blood in my veins is the blood of a lion, not of a lamb," Vikramaditya sneered. "I cannot be your son."

A broken sigh escaped Gandharvasena's lips. "Mahendraditya must have been a great father to have reared a bold lion like you," he said. "Few have had the courage to stand up to Indra the way you did. Your defiance put me to shame, which is why I am here to make amends."

"Amends? In what way?"

"You have suffered enough on account of father, so I have come to help you."

"I don't want your help," Vikramaditya snapped. "Leave, and never come back again."

Gandharvasena looked at the samrat with a pained expression. "You may not want my help, but trust me, you *need* it. Your kingdom needs it." He cast a glance towards Ujjayini, covered in smoke. "I should have come sooner. Please, for heaven's sake, show some sense and listen to what I have to tell you..."

***

"Does he know what he's doing?"

"His father said he was an expert tracker, your honour."

"Hmm," Amara Simha grunted as he squinted at the young man squatting on his haunches, studying the desert floor. "We don't have much choice anyway," he admitted. Reaching for the sheepskin flask, he took a mouthful of water, tasting it, letting his lips and tongue soak moisture.

"Where in the Marusthali are we?" asked Angamitra, looking around.

The councilor followed the *samsaptaka*'s gaze. Like the day before, and the days before that, the land was more or less flat, the soil either hard and dusty, or brittle and sandy. The sky overhead was pale blue, unbroken from horizon to horizon, except for the glaring sun on its lonely vigil. The men looked tired, their spirits sapped by the heat and the looming futility of this chase.

"The kid said this is the northern part of the desert," the interpreter said.

"That's pretty obvious," said Amara Simha. "What I'd like to know is exactly where."

"Are those mountains over there?" Angamitra suddenly peered and pointed.

Everyone stared with sudden interest, hoping to see the contours of the Arbuda Range resolve out of the haze that blotted the eastern horizon. But none of them could tell for sure.

"It's too far to see clearly," said the councilor. "But we've been keeping an easterly course."

The interpreter spoke to the boy, who was investigating a pinch of dust by rubbing it between his thumb and forefinger. The boy glanced to the east and nodded. "*Ghe'yar*," he said.

"It is the mountains," the interpreter translated.

The men smiled in relief.

"And Ghatakarpara?"

The interpreter studied the boy as he rose to his feet. He had a slender build and shy smile, and he spoke only when spoken to, or when he saw a sign and wanted to stop to take a closer look. Seeing the enquiring look on everyone's faces, he spoke, pointing to the north-east. The interpreter listened.

"He says the trail leads that way," he said.

"Is he sure?" Amara Simha looked sceptical. "We've been heading north-east for a long time. If this is the route the prince picked, he'll end up in Matsya, not in Avanti."

"The boy is certain."

"Let's move on then."

Once the boy was back in his saddle, they resumed riding.

"I just hope this will not be a hopeless exercise," the councilor grumbled.

"The kid's name is Nor'han, which is the Saka name for the pole star," the interpreter said. "I believe that is a very good omen. He will guide us to the prince."

Shashivardhan

"I am Mithyamayi —"

"No, you are not," said Vikramaditya.

The apsara stared, biting her lower lip to stop it from quivering.

"You are not Vismaya's niece either. Your mother's name is not Karunya, and your father never traded fruits in Viswapuri."

"I don't understand…" the apsara fluttered her eyelids.

"You came to Ujjayini with Indra—"

Vikramaditya had the pleasure of watching the woman's eyes widen in shock, but just then, Pralupi's voice rang out from the doorway.

"What is all this?"

The king's sister shouldered past the guards, her gaze switching between Urvashi and Vikramaditya. "Why can't you leave her alone? She is just a maid. Stop harassing her."

"She is not a maid—"

"Of course, she is," the princess insisted. Her eyes flitted back to Urvashi, and the samrat was surprised to glimpse a flicker of anxiety in them. "Come, child," she took the apsara by the hand, "Don't you worry. I will take care of this—"

"Enough." Vikramaditya's tone was so severe that a chorus of startled squawks and chirrups issued from the birdcages hanging overhead. Pralupi's hand flew back as though it had been scalded, and she shrank away from her brother.

"This is *not* your maid Mithyamayi. This is the apsara Urvashi, and she is in Ujjayini at her master Indra's bidding. She is here to ascertain the whereabouts of the dagger that the Omniscient One has left in my safekeeping, and she has been conspiring to steal the dagger in collusion with the deva who impersonated Vismaya. It is reasonable to assume she had a hand in the killing of the loyal Vismaya—"

"No," Urvashi cut in, vehemently. "I had no role in the man's death."

The king appraised the apsara keenly. "So, you accept everything else I just said."

Urvashi didn't offer a reply. Pralupi glowered at the apsara.

Vikramaditya stepped towards Urvashi, holding her gaze. "The stealing of my swords... whose idea was that? Or your visit the night before..."

The king was watching the apsara closely, so he did not notice Pralupi's eyes dart to Urvashi in alarm.

"I don't know anything about the swords." The apsara hesitated, as if she meant to finish articulating what she had in mind, but she decided against it and dropped her eyes.

The samrat considered Urvashi for a moment. "There is no way of telling how much of what you say is the truth. And even if you are being truthful, I cannot afford to let you leave Avanti and return to Devaloka, only to have you spill any secrets you may have unearthed here to Indra."

"You intend keeping me here as your prisoner?" Urvashi stared, taken aback.

"You are a threat to Avanti, to this city and to its people. You surely didn't think I would summon a palanquin to send you back to Devaloka, did you?"

Shedding the mild sarcasm from his voice, Vikramaditya said, "The kingdom's enemies are held in the dungeons, but that is no place for women. You will remain in the palace as a prisoner of Avanti, but you will be accorded the dignity a woman deserves."

The samrat nodded to one of the guards.

"How long do you intend keeping me here?"

"I cannot say," the king answered. "But you will be returned to Devaloka once we are sure that you no longer pose a risk to Avanti."

The guards had escorted her to the door when the apsara paused to look at the samrat.

"How did you find out?" she asked. "What gave me away... or *who*?"

"Try working the answer out while you are in confinement," Vikramaditya offered her a thin smile.

***

Shashivardhan's fingers were numb around the reins, the stiffness in his joints spreading insidiously to his hips and back as his horse plodded through a carpet of thin, wet snow. The prince's eyes watered from the cold, so he had to keep blinking to clear his vision, if only to take in the broken hills of southwestern Matsya, dotted with clumps of patchy *devadarus*. Whichever way he looked, Shashivardhan was greeted by the sight of a cold and desolate land with no signs of human habitation.

"Did we really need to come out this far?" the prince enquired, his thoughts on the small wood brazier in his room at the outpost, where he kept his hands warm against the chill wind blowing from the north. "There's not a soul around to take note of us here."

"It is good you have come, your honour," his bodyguard,

Piyusha, insisted. "The men at the outpost will now be convinced that the soon-to-be king of Vatsa is made of steel."

Shashivardhan didn't feel as if he was made of steel—in all honesty, he wasn't sure if he cared either. All he wanted was to be back at the outpost with a jar of firewater and a warm fire to expel the cold from his bones. It would be even nicer to be back in Kausambi, where the sun shone all year round... but then it occurred to him that he had volunteered to be at the frontier, defending Matsya from Saka incursions. Despite his father's reservations, he was *here*, *out in this freezing vastness*, instead of being comfortable indoors, or being in sunny Kausambi. It showed he cared.

Maybe there was steel in him, after all.

He thought back to his conversation with Piyusha two nights ago, which had led to this expedition. Piyusha had approached him right after dinner, as he lay in bed, drowsy from a pleasant evening spent in the company of firewater and song. The bulky soldier had waited patiently for Shashivardhan to finish humming an ancient oarsmen's song, and when the prince looked happily up at him, he had spoken the most unexpected words.

"The soldiers of Matsya think you are weak."

It took Shashivardhan a moment to process that. "Why?" he blinked in surprise.

"They talk about how you never leave the outpost and always keep indoors. They see that as a weakness, your honour."

"I can show them my strength if they want to fight me," Shashivardhan said irrationally, the colour mounting in his cheeks.

"A fight with the soldiers of the outpost won't serve any purpose other than ruining an excellent relationship between Matsya and Vatsa. Moreover, it is not your skill with the sword that they doubt, but your ability to lead a fight in these conditions, in a place that you are not at all familiar with."

Shashivardhan considered this carefully before asking, "What should I do to show them I am not weak?"

"Leave the comfort of the outpost, go for inspections along the frontier, get to know the lay of the land. When you get back in the evenings, talk to the men about what you saw, what conclusions you drew... Show them that you can think like a soldier with the same ease as you sing the boatman's tune, your honour."

So, yesterday, they had left the outpost and ridden north, returning only at sundown, cold and exhausted. Shashivardhan couldn't be certain he had learned anything of significance on the trip, but Piyusha had pointed out that half-a-dozen Matsya patrols had seen him riding along the frontier, which was all that mattered.

Today, they had left the outpost and taken a southward trail. Today was also a lot colder than yesterday, and the expanse to the south was much wilder and emptier.

"How is it that we haven't encountered a single patrol unit so far?" Shashivardhan wondered. "And I haven't seen a single watchtower for miles."

"Mmm-hmm," Piyusha grunted in agreement. "Not good at all."

"The Sakas could easily ride in from here." Encouraged by his bodyguard's words, the prince continued speaking. "What is the point in shoring up defences to the north if we're going to leave the backdoor wide open to the barbarians?"

This time, Piyusha didn't offer a reply.

"How many patrols would it take to secure this area? Three? Four? That's what—fifty men? I am sure the garrison of Kasavati can spare that many. I must have an immediate word with Commander Adri..."

The prince glanced to his right, expecting to see Piyusha riding at his elbow. The bodyguard was not beside him, though.

Surprised, Shashivardhan turned on his saddle to see that his escort had drawn to a halt some twenty paces behind him. All ten men sat on their mounts, watching him with shuttered expressions.

"Are we done?" the prince asked, hope kindling in his eyes. But there was confusion as well. They hadn't ridden long enough or far enough yet to turn back… "Are we returning?"

None of the men spoke.

Seeing them sitting there, eyeing him levelly, Shashivardhan was overcome by a sudden sense of foreboding.

"Yes, we are done," Piyusha said at last. "We are returning."

Something in the bodyguard's tone caused the prince's heart to lurch in his chest. He realized that his lips had gone dry, and it wasn't because of the cold. Trying to read the man's face, he turned his horse around. "Good. Then let's go—"

"Not you."

Shashivardhan stared at his bodyguard. "What?"

Piyusha shook his head. "You are not going back with us."

Time appeared to wind down and accelerate at the same time, so that everything slowed to a crawl and simultaneously leaped and shuffled forward before the prince's eyes. He saw Piyusha turn to one of the men and say something, the words taking ages to come out of his mouth… and then suddenly the man had his bow out and was already nocking an arrow in place… and then the man started drawing the bowstring back and back and back forever…

"…what have I done to you?" Shashivardhan heard himself shout in a quavering voice that came to his ears as if from far away.

Piyusha turned to look at him but said nothing.

"Tell me why," Shashivardhan's voice pleaded.

The prince saw his bodyguard turn away and look at the man drawing the bow.

"Is this why you brought me here? So that Matsya's soldiers wouldn't witness my killing?"

Piyusha nodded at the bowman.

Shashivardhan felt giddy as his gaze went from the bodyguard to the bowman to the head of the arrow pointing at him. Fixated, he watched the arrowhead draw back another impossible inch.

His gaze switched back to the bowman's face behind the arrow.

Dark. Bearded. A scar over the left eyebrow.

The face contorting all of a sudden in a rictus of pain, lips peeling back to show uneven teeth clenched in agony. The lips and teeth parting involuntarily, and blood spilling from the man's mouth, drenching his beard.

Shashivardhan watched in wonder as the bow snapped loose and slipped from the bowman's nerveless fingers, the arrow whizzing past, missing him and his mount by a hand's breadth. Meanwhile, the bowman pitched forward onto his horse's neck, lost his balance and crashed to the ground in a heap.

He lay motionless as his horse stamped the ground next to his head nervously.

"What is this?" Piyusha shouted, drawing his sword as he stared at his fallen mate.

The men all drew their swords in quick succession. They were still gathering their wits and looking around wildly to pinpoint the origin of the attack when a second man screamed on his saddle. Looking at him, Shashivardhan spotted the cause behind his agony straightaway.

Something had pierced the soldier's neck, entering from the right side, driven with such force that it had skewered right through and emerged onto the other side. The projectile resembled a dart, its head dripping blood, but from where Shashivardhan sat astride his steed, the blunt end of the dart appeared to be made of ice, melting and dripping water...

A dart made of ice.

***

"I want my son back."

Vikramaditya gave Pralupi a blank-faced stare. Then, accepting the belt for his swords from the palace hand, the samrat nodded at the man, indicating he wanted the princess and himself to be left alone. Only after the man had had left the chamber did Vikramaditya address his sister.

"Amara Simha is looking for him. Give him time."

"It has been a week since Amara Simha left for the frontier, and we haven't heard from him *once*. Why hasn't he sent us any news? How much more time should we give him?"

"Searching for anything takes time, sister. And we're talking about the Marusthali here, a place we know practically nothing about." The king paused, and his face softened. He took a step towards Pralupi. "I know how helpless this feels but have faith in Amara Simha. He will find the boy."

"Faith." The princess spat the word back as if it had tasted vile in her mouth. "Everyone in whom I placed my faith has let me down, so faith is not a boat I will ride easily. And why should I put my faith in Amara Simha to find Ghatakarpara? Ghatakarpara is not his nephew; why would *he* care what happens to the boy?"

Horrified at his sister's words, the samrat opened his mouth in protest, but Pralupi was not done. "We don't even know if he is looking for the boy anymore. For all we know, Amara Simha has called off the search. Which is why *you* should go, brother. You owe it to me."

"I would trust Amara Simha to turn the Great Desert upside down if that's what it takes to find Ghatakarpara," Vikramaditya said vehemently. "He made me a promise before leaving Ujjayini, which he will keep at all costs. Amara Simha *will* bring Ghatakarpara back."

"You can go and help him," Pralupi mumbled adamantly.

"I am leaving for the frontier, but for other reasons, sister," the king sighed, slipping the sword belt around his waist. "The Hunas are coming, and I have to stop them."

The princess flashed a glance at Vikramaditya. "Considering Vararuchi is back in your good books, he can go then. Send him to stop the Hunas or to find Ghata—"

"Vararuchi has to stay here to protect Ujjayini and the dagger," the samrat's face was a picture of long-suffering patience. He picked up the Hellfires, which lay on a low table, oiled and polished. "You only need to look out of the window to see the destruction that has been wrought for the dagger—"

"*That stupid dagger*," Pralupi lashed out angrily. "I wish the devas or asuras would just take it when they come next."

Vikramaditya blinked at the princess in disbelief.

"You care for the dagger, you care about your promise to the Omniscient One, you care about this city... The only thing you don't care the least bit about is my son. But then, why would you..." The princess glared at the king viciously. "You are not an Aditya. There's no Aditya blood in you, so of course, Aditya blood means nothing to you."

The samrat stood straight, his eyes narrowed at his sister, his hold tightening on the Hellfires. There was the faintest hint of a tremor running through his taut, finely muscled arms, and for a fraction of a second, the metal of the swords glowed with heat.

The next moment, Vikramaditya quietly slid the Hellfires into their scabbards swinging from his waist. Without uttering a word, he crossed the chamber, brushed past Pralupi, and walked out of the door.

Watching her brother's departure, the princess was overcome by a sense of despair. She gazed at the empty doorway and realized that her last, desperate move to incite the king into action had failed. Vikramaditya had not risen to the bait.

She drifted aimlessly through the room, running her fingers over the furnishings, till she came to the terrace. She walked to the parapet and leaned on it, looking at the city across the lake. Helped by a northerly breeze, the smoke had lifted a little, but the air still felt heavy on the lungs. Pralupi's eyes were naturally drawn to the dark shape of a vulture that sat hunched on the crest of a *gulmohar* growing by the lake's edge.

She had failed, she thought to herself as she watched the bird ruffle its feathers. Failed again.

Vararuchi was back on Vikramaditya's side, cowed and spineless. She had guessed he'd be back the moment she had seen *badi-maa* with her mother in the Labyrinth, the two women inseparable all of a sudden. She had no idea what had taken hold of her mother, or why Ushantha was in the palace after all these years, but she knew she couldn't bank on Vararuchi's support any longer.

That was a setback, but Pralupi had consoled herself that she still had Mithyamayi. The woman was a charmer, and with her uncle dead, she had nowhere to go. She would be in the palace, and another opportunity to seduce Vikramaditya would present itself; all Pralupi had to do was make sure Kshapanaka was a witness to it— But no! The maid had turned out to be an apsara sent by Indra, and now she was in confinement, and the samrat was going to the frontier...

Failed. Again.

Pralupi felt her eyes prickle with tears of frustration, and her breath caught in her throat as anger and sorrow welled up inside her. She hated the world for its blatant unfairness. She wanted her son back. She wanted her son to become king of Vatsa. What was wrong in that? Why wouldn't the fates comply with her wishes? Why?

Why, she screamed silently at the smoky sky. *What would it take to make Ghatakarpara king?*

Three birds circled high over Ujjayini, wheeling in and out of patches of smoke. Their wings were spread wide, their flight patient and majestic. More vultures, the princess made a mental note, remembering that vultures also presaged death.

Was this an omen?

Pralupi bit her lip, dearly hoping it was. If Shashivardhan were to unexpectedly die...

***

He peered at the horsemen through a narrowing tunnel of darkness, suddenly wondering which of them was his brother—and feeling a stab of panic at the thought that he might have killed him by mistake, instead of saving him from the killers. Blinking and shaking his head to clear the shadows that were gathering around the edges of his vision, he looked again. This time, he sighted the prince some distance away from the pack of riders; the prince was staring back at him in open-mouthed astonishment.

Ghatakarpara was familiar with that look of doltish disbelief, an expression he had seen many times when they had duelled as young boys and he had knocked the sword from Shashivardhan's hand—with increasing frequency as time went by. Yet, despite being bested by a cousin who was many years his younger, Shashivardhan had never displayed rancour towards Ghatakarpara, treating the boy with affection whenever he visited Kausambi. Ghatakarpara remembered those visits with great fondness, raiding the orchards for juicy raw mangoes and bathing in the Yamuna, where Shashivardhan had first taught him to swim against the currents. In those growing years, the crown prince of Vatsa had been the closest Ghatakarpara had had to a kindly older brother.

But what have I done to you?

It was that gentle, lilting voice from many summers ago that had reached Ghatakarpara as he had stumbled about the tree line, struggling to escape a waking nightmare in which he was fleeing shadows across sand dunes, but sinking deeper and deeper into the sand every minute. He had blinked through the trees, fighting cold-induced disorientation, trying to discern whether the voice was part of the nightmare, when he had noticed the cluster of horsemen, one of who had his bow drawn, the arrow trained at another rider who was saying...

Tell me why.

Staring at Shashivardhan and at the arrow pointing at him, it took a moment for Ghatakarpara to realize that this was happening for real.

Though every joint in his body hurt from his trek over the mountains and into the valley, though his mind was playing tricks on him and he could hardly keep the darkness out of his eyes, though the cold had robbed him of sensation, Ghatakarpara propelled himself forward, his fingers already extracting water and ice from the atmosphere, and packing them together to fashion a crude ice missile...

Is this why you brought me here? So that Matsya's soldiers wouldn't witness my killing?

The bowman was drawing the bow all the way back. If he did not do something quickly, he wouldn't be able to save... Ghatakarpara moulded the ice dart swiftly, sharpening its tip to a point between his numb fingers. Raising his hand, he sent the dart flying into the back of the bowman's head. The man fell.

Having manufactured a second dart with similar efficiency to dispatch one more of the horsemen, Ghatakarpara had a third missile in his grasp and was choosing his next target—when the shadows came rushing in from all sides, and the earth pitched beneath his feet and he staggered.

Shashivardhan's would-be assassins spurred their horses and charged at Ghatakarpara.

"Watch out, brother!"

Heeding his cousin's warning, Ghatakarpara raised his head, and the shadows lifted like curtains from his eyes. The ground too stabilized, but hearing the hoof beats and looking up, instead of observing individual riders, the prince saw a nebulous mass approaching. The snow underfoot also changed to sand once again, and Ghatakarpara could no longer be sure whether or not he was back in his nightmare.

"*Brother...*"

Shashivardhan's desperate cry breached the fugue, snapping Ghatakarpara back to his senses in time to see that the riders were ten paces away, rapidly narrowing the distance. Focusing on the man straight ahead, he launched the ice dart.

The missile whipped across and buried itself at the base of the man's throat.

As Ghatakarpara crafted a pair of darts simultaneously using both hands, Shashivardhan drew his sword and tailed the horsemen, awkward in his saddle, but assured in his intent, yelling at the top of his voice to divert their attention from his cousin.

The seven horsemen were drawing closer to Ghatakarpara...

The prince let fly one of the darts, but in his haste, his aim faltered, and the missile went wide of its target. He was about to launch the second dart when the darkness came down on him again, pulling him bodily to his knees. The dart slid from Ghatakarpara's fingers and fell.

Two horsemen had turned to meet the challenge from Shashivardhan, but the other five were almost upon Ghatakarpara, who was reeling on his knees. The two riders in front were on the verge of striking the prince down when a pair of long lances came flying at them, taking them in their chests and knocking them clean off their mounts, straight into the path of their mates coming behind.

His vision clearing, Ghatakarpara blinked in surprise, watching the horses tangle and trip and bring everyone down. The riderless horses rushed past him, the thunder of their hooves in his ears, the earth trembling under his knees. Then, over the noise of the hooves, he heard a shout from behind him.

"*For Avanti...*"

Glancing back, he saw a force of riders galloping out of a cleft in the mountainside. In the lead were two faces he recognized.

Amara Simha and Angamitra.

Ghatakarpara's shoulders sagged with relief and exhaustion. The darkness returned, and on this occasion, he submitted to it, falling forward, his face buried in the thin snow.

Amara Simha leaped off his horse, landing next to Ghatakarpara. In three strides, he put himself between the samrat's nephew and his attackers, who were still extricating themselves from a jumble of limbs. Angamitra and the troops spread out, disarming the two men fighting Shashivardhan, surrounding everyone and blocking all escape routes. Two *samsaptakas* came running to attend to Ghatakarpara.

"Is he alright?" Amara Simha asked tersely over his shoulder.

"He is breathing, your honour, but his pulse..." one of the *samsaptakas* shrugged. "That is all I can tell."

Angamitra and the interpreter hurried over to help lift Ghatakarpara and carry him away.

Amara Simha glared at the guards, who stared back at him in awe, recognizing his fierce red beard and heavy mane. "I see all of you fancy ganging up against one... so come," he hoisted his broad battle-axe with his brawny arms. "Fight me. Come."

The men stared wide-eyed, refusing to move a muscle.

Amara Simha's eyes flashed from one face to the next. "Where is your courage, your fighting spirit?" he goaded. "Show me you have blood running in your veins, not *milk*. I promise you that my men will not interfere. It will be just you and me. *Come on...*"

One by one, Shashivardhan's guards dropped their swords in response.

"We yield to you, your honour," said one of them timidly.

Amara Simha shook his head, though from his expression it wasn't clear whether it was disgust or plain disappointment. "Who are you and who is your leader?"

"They were my guards, respected councilor," said Shashivardhan. "They were attempting to take my life when Ghatakarpara intervened and saved me. That one," he pointed, "is the chief of the detail. His name is Piyusha."

The head bodyguard lay on the ground with a lance buried deep in his stomach, right under the breastbone. The man's breathing was uneven, colour draining rapidly from his face.

"Why did they want to kill you, prince?"

"I don't know."

Amara Simha looked expectantly at the men who had surrendered. One of them quickly said, "The captain offered us ten gold coins each and promised us promotions."

"But why?"

"We don't know. He said not to ask questions."

Squatting beside Piyusha, the councilor gripped the shaft of the lance. "Does it hurt?"

Piyusha sighed and winced.

"It will hurt a lot more if I move the lance around, you know that."

The bodyguard nodded to show he understood.

"We can do this the easy way or the hard way. The choice is yours."

Piyusha nodded a second time.

"Good. Why did you want to kill Prince Shashivardhan?"

Piyusha shook his head.

Amara Simha leaned closer. "What?"

"Not me," the bodyguard managed through clenched teeth.

"I see. Then who wanted him killed? Who paid you to do the dirty work?"

Piyusha was silent for a moment. Then, as Amara Simha tightened his grip on the lance, the man hurriedly nodded, signalling his willingness to cooperate.

"It was… mmmph," he groaned, "…it was Councilor Yashobhavi."

***

Lengths of finely woven linen, freshly dyed in shades of deep blue and red, hung from tall bamboo poles, billowing in the afternoon breeze, as workers mixed *manjishtha* and indigo compounds into large vats simmering over open fires. The men called out orders to one another or joked lewdly among themselves, scarcely paying attention to the two old men who stood conversing softly in a private corner of the dyeing ground, concealed by the lengths of fabric hanging like draperies around them.

"I too have heard rumours about this witness," the one sporting a scruffy moustache the colour and texture of flax said under his breath, looking about him uneasily.

"He is not a rumour," Asmabindu insisted, leaning over the other man.

The shorter man looked up at Magadha's legal adviser. Scratching his expansive belly, he asked, "How do you know that?"

Asmabindu gave a small, noncommittal shrug, but didn't break eye contact.

The two men assessed each other. "It seems he is hiding in Kosala," the other man said, his eyes searching Asmabindu's face for clues to help him navigate the conversation.

The legal adviser didn't reply. Instead, he watched Councilor Ashrava wrestle with what he had just been told. Ashrava was one of the richest men in Magadha, enjoying a near monopoly in the lucrative fabric dyeing business in the region; and by virtue of all that amassed wealth, he was also one of the most powerful councilors in Girivraja. He could sway opinions in the council. And the best part was that he had benefitted commercially from his proximity to King Siddhasena—Asmabindu hoped there was some gratitude for the old king that could still be leveraged.

"But is it the truth?" Ashrava grunted unhappily. "Did this musician really witness what he says he did, or is this Kosala's elaborate ploy to discredit Shoorasena and strike back at us for having exposed Councilor Pallavan as a spy? How do we believe this witness, especially when his claims seem backed by Kosala?"

Asmabindu drew a deep breath and shook his head. He had anticipated this.

"I believe this musician is why Pallavan and our erstwhile colleagues, Uttama, Diganta and Bhaskara are dead in the first place."

As Ashrava narrowed his eyes shrewdly, Asmabindu nodded.

"A couple of days before Uttama, Diganta and Bhaskara were arrested along with Pallavan, Uttama had reached out to me, saying something important had come up that he needed to discuss. He didn't say what it was about; all he said was I should come to his mansion in the hills, where we could talk freely. But he did mention it had to do with Siddhasena's death."

"He asked you to come the same evening he and the others were arrested?"

Asmabindu nodded. "I'm guessing he asked all of us."

"But you didn't know Bhaskara and Diganta had been called as well? Or that Pallavan would be there?"

"No," the lie slipped out, nice and easy. "Not a clue."

"Then how come you—"

"I couldn't go as my wife was very unwell that day," Asmabindu shuddered theatrically.

Ashrava was lost in thought for a moment. "Pallavan and the others were arrested on charges of aiding the Kikatas," he said.

"Trumped-up charges," Asmabindu replied. "None of them had anything to do with the Kikatas. I mean, I have nothing to do with the Kikatas. Then why would Uttama invite me if they were meeting to help the Kikatas?"

Seeing the dubious expression on the other man's face, Asmabindu continued, "Look at this logically. The morning Siddhasena died, a travelling musician was in the palace; he had performed for the king the night before. The same morning, Pallavan had been in Girivraja... remember, we were all in court when Shoorasena refused to honour Pallavan's reminder that we send more troops for the defence of Sindhuvarta? Put two and two together. A musician is in the palace when the king dies. Pallavan is also here, visiting from Kosala. Later, Pallavan comes to Uttama with information pertaining to Siddhasena's death. Uttama, Bhaskara and Diganta are arrested, charged with treason and executed publicly. Pallavan, who is also under arrest, isn't executed though; instead, he is killed somewhere at the border with Kosala, while purportedly trying to escape—though there is no explanation about how he got that far from Girivraja in the first place. Now, rumours of the musician hiding in Kosala have surfaced... Think... What can all this mean?"

Watching Ashrava ponder over this, Asmabindu smirked inwardly. They had gone back on their word; they had reneged on their promise, appointing some idiot from Vanga as governor instead of him. He had been smarting ever since, angry but powerless, but after last night's visit from the two Kikata tribesmen, he now had a way of hitting back—

"Shoorasena did this just to become the king?"

Asmabindu shrugged. "He certainly wasn't getting his way on attacking Vanga. Siddhasena was vehemently against the idea, remember? Kapila and Daipayana were the only ones who were enthusiastic about invading Vanga."

"You think they are also involved in the killing of Siddhasena?"

The legal adviser shrugged again.

"Why didn't you tell anyone about Uttama's invitation to you?"

"What could I have said? That I had been invited to a meeting where everyone present had been charged with conspiring against the crown? You think I wanted to end up the way the other three had?" Asmabindu shook his head. "I didn't know what to make of it all, and... it is only now that the musician has come into the picture. Even now, it is because I trust *you* that I am here."

"Who do you think gave Uttama and the rest of them away?"

The legal adviser blinked. It hadn't occurred to him that this question could also come up. "I don't know."

"That means someone out there knows what Pallavan and Uttama were up to, someone who betrayed them to Shoorasena." Ashrava fell silent. The linen flapped in the freshening breeze. "Why bring all of this to me now?"

"Siddhasena was a fair and kind king to us. He deserves justice, and we owe it to him."

Ashrava stroked the frizzled ends of his moustache. "A travelling musician claims he saw a son kill his father and frame the father's bodyguard for the murder. The son, who is now a king, refutes this allegation, calling it a plot hatched by his kingdom's enemies to defame him. A common musician's word against that of a powerful and popular king. Who would the people of Magadha believe, my friend?"

"I admit that mere allegations would be impossible to prove, but..." Asmabindu leaned into Ashrava conspiratorially, "...I have a plan to trap Shoorasena into incriminating himself and admitting his guilt."

The shorter councilor's eyebrows crept up his forehead. "Let's hear it then."

***

The wind speaks of death coming on many wings.

Looking over his shoulder, Vararuchi observed that the oracle had already shut her eyes and had gone back to rocking gently back and forth, seated exactly the way he had found her minutes earlier, when he had shown up at her door.

"You are the king's brother," she had said, opening her eyes and appraising him wearily from the mat upon which she sat.

"I am, mother," Vararuchi replied, wondering how she had figured out he was here when her eyes had been closed. He stepped silently into the room. "You wished to see me?"

"The king told me to ask for you should anything come up while he is not here."

The councilor nodded.

"I presume the king has left for the frontier?"

"He has, mother," Vararuchi inclined his head, standing patiently before her.

The oracle had stayed silent for a while, making up her mind.

"The wind speaks of death coming on many wings," she said finally.

"Death on many wings," Vararuchi repeated, not liking the sound of it at all.

The old woman nodded.

"And?"

"And?" the Mother Oracle looked puzzled.

"I mean, what else did the wind tell you?"

"Lots of things. It keeps telling me things, most of which are not worth knowing."

"Nothing else about this approaching death? Where it is coming from, who is—"

"No. That was all."

"Our gratitude, mother," the councilor said with a bow as he withdrew.

Walking away from the oracle's room, turning the woman's prediction over in his mind, Vararuchi wondered what he should do next. Death coming on many wings could only mean an attack from the sky, which was so much harder to counter. It would call for a large number of archers, and probably Varahamihira's heavier ballistas. But did it mean birds or something altogether different with wings? Many wings, the oracle had said. But how many, and when could this attack be expected—and how bad was it likely to be?

The oracle had used 'death' to describe whatever was coming. It had to be bad.

Vararuchi broke into a jog. He had to share the forecast with the others in the council. The city's defences needed fortification. Nightfall was due in under an hour, and if something was coming from above, fires would need to be lit for illumination. Varahamihira would have to take full charge of guarding the dagger...

Hurrying along a trellised verandah, his mind making plans for contingencies, the councilor's gaze went to the palace roofs—and his eyes widened. Arresting his stride, he approached the trellis, peering through its gaps at the sky over Ujjayini, before venturing onto a terrace that offered an unhindered view of the cityscape... and the vultures circling overhead.

Hundreds and hundreds of them, flying in broad, sedate arcs before dropping slowly to settle on the trees that lined Ujjayini's streets and filled its many beautiful parks.

Vararuchi turned a full circle where he stood, taking in the sweep of the entire sky. He had been wrong, he realized.

Not hundreds, but thousands and thousands of vultures in every direction.

Never before had he witnessed such an amassing of the birds, Vararuchi thought uneasily as the Mother Oracle's warning came back to him.

The wind speaks of death coming on many wings.

Was *this* the death that the oracle had hinted at, or were the vultures arriving in anticipation of the death that was to come? The people of the Southern Kingdoms believed vultures could tell when death was near...

Shivering at the thought, the councilor turned and strode back inside. He had to summon the council quickly, so they could decide what—

"Whoa... *watch it*."

Vararuchi pulled up sharply to prevent colliding with the guard who was coming around the door in a great rush.

"My apologies, councilor," the guard said, bowing and stepping back hurriedly. Catching his breath, he added, "I was looking for you. Councilor Dhanavantri sent me."

"What's happened?" Vararuchi's jaw tensed and his hand went reflexively to his sword.

"It is Queen Vishakha, your honour. She is awake."

Vararuchi stared.

"The vaidyanath told me to inform you, your honour," the guard said.

With a nod, Vararuchi pushed past the guard, trying to estimate how far Vikramaditya would have ridden, and determining the quickest way of getting the news to him. Riders could be dispatched, or the message could be relayed using *suryayantras* while there was still adequate sunlight... Vararuchi crossed a gallery, evaluating his options. The samrat would want to be by Vishakha's side, so *he* would have to lead Sindhuvarta's defence against the savages from the desert. If he left Ujjayini before sundown and rode through the night, he could catch up with Vikramaditya's escort, so they didn't lose time getting to the frontier... but there could be unforeseen delays in the delivery of the news to Vikramaditya, so there was no guarantee the king would turn back.

Also, there was the oracle's warning to consider.

The councilor took the stairs two at a time and turned into the passage that led to the queen's chamber. There was no way he could leave Ujjayini at the mercy of whatever was coming in the hope that Vikramaditya would be back in time... He would have to wait for his brother's return, though that meant leaving the allied forces of Sindhuvarta leaderless in the event of a barbarian attack led by Kalidasa...

The door to Vishakha's bedchamber was open, allowing voices to spill into the passageway. Nearing the door, Vararuchi was about to poke his head in when he ran into Dhanavantri on his way out. Their eyes met, and Vararuchi raised his eyebrows in enquiry.

"How is she?" Vararuchi asked.

"She has awoken," the royal physician's reply held no intonations.

Vararuchi craned his neck to peer past the physician's girth. Other than the four palace maids, Kunjala and three junior *vaidyas*, there was Kshapanaka, seated beside Vishakha, holding her sister's hands. Vishakha sat propped against soft cushions, her face deathly white. Vararuchi noticed that the queen's eyes were alive but conflicted, filled with mistrust and confusion, her gaze darting about the room as if seeking escape.

Vararuchi considered Dhanavantri. "Not alright?" he asked with a troubled shake of his head.

The physician shrugged and turned to glance back at the sisters.

"She doesn't recognize anyone," Dhanavantri said. "She doesn't know where she is."

"Oh..." said Vararuchi grimly, wondering what the message to Vikramaditya should say. *She doesn't recognize anyone.*

"But she is asking for Vikrama by name."

Vararuchi stared at the physician before turning to the queen in bewilderment. "You just said she doesn't recognize anyone," he whispered.

"Well, except for Vikrama." Dhanavantri drew a deep breath. "*She clearly remembers him.*"

Janasthana

Darkness that was not so much black as it was bleak, not so much a colour as it was a mood; a depressing miasma that manifested in spilled blotches and crude brushstrokes, as if dealt on canvas by clumsy, inartistic hands.

And trapped between the folds of darkness, there was the fog.

White and tightly packed in some places, standing up to the encircling darkness. Straggly and attenuated in others, interlaced with the darkness and unable to resist its invasive squeeze.

Tatters of darkness and fog, drifting along on a wind he couldn't feel.

And through the fog and the darkness, a voice, borne and snatched away by the wind.

...over... it is the last... gone...

The voice was familiar. He had heard it recently.

...is how it passes... our home... to a memory...

Betaal.

There was a strain in the old voice that managed to worm into the king's consciousness. The Ghoulmaster was trying to tell him something, Vikramaditya realized.

...hear me anymore... is the end... but we are helpless... tree is dying...

The neighing of a horse. The clinking of bridle. Men talking.

The samrat tried to shut out all sounds so he could listen to Betaal.

...tell you, good king... too late for us...

The veils of darkness parted, the fog brightened and Vikramaditya blinked his eyes open to a clear dawn framed in a window right next to the rough wooden bed where he lay.

More neighing of horses and men laughing. The smell of horse manure and hay.

It took a moment for the king to orient himself. He was at the horse station, he remembered.

In the interest of time, he and his escort had picked the shortest possible route to Udaypuri, which meant bypassing the garrisons of Lava and Biddhira, located to the north and south of the direct route. Arriving at this old horse station, which lay square on their path and catered mostly to trade convoys, they had elected to break briefly for a night's rest.

Getting up on one elbow, the samrat manoeuvred his injured shoulder gingerly, waiting for a stab of pain. Nothing happened. Emboldened, he wiggled his arm around, experimenting, and though it hurt mildly at some angles, the rawness from yesterday was gone. Dhanavantri was proving to be quite a healer, the king thought, swinging his feet off the bed. They had to get going before the sun got higher—

He stopped as his mind served up a reminder of his dream about Borderworld.

Betaal had sounded sad, but incoherent. What had he been trying to say? Vikramaditya tried to recollect the Ghoulmaster's words. Something about the tree dying and it being too late... But wasn't that from the last time Betaal had called out to him, when the asuras had attacked Borderworld?

When the Ghoulmaster had wanted him to come and rescue the Halahala and the tree before it was too late. Then what about now? Had Betaal reached out to him again? Or had he just dreamed the old dream again, a trick his mind had played?

The only way of finding out was to go back to sleep and wait for Betaal to come to him, but the samrat knew he couldn't afford to lose more time sleeping. Getting to his feet, he strode out of the station warden's room and made for the well that stood in the compound outside. He had no inkling where the Huna army had reached, but he had to get to the frontier before those fierce warriors of the desert spilled over the Arbudas into Sindhuvarta.

***

"*Eb'a, zuh'i ghel'la...*"

The Huna commander's deputies acknowledged their superior's order by raising small triangular flags over their heads and dropping both hands sharply, so that the flags traced red downward arcs in the clear light of daybreak. At the same time, the two deputies repeated their commander's injunctions loudly, so they would carry to the other Huna captains coming behind.

"*Eb'a, zuh'i ghel'la...*"

'Rein in your horses.'

Eb'a, zuh'i ghel'la... Eb'a, zuh'i ghel'la... Eb'a, zuh'i ghel'la...

Relayed over the heads of the warriors, the order swept backwards like a tide, weaving past the pointed spears and fluttering banners, sifting through the rising dust, until even the men at the very back had heard and understood what was expected of them. Slowly, the great army drew to a shuffling, stuttering halt, the weary horses stamping the desert floor in relief after a long night's march.

"*Yer goho't,*" the commander called again. 'Pitch tent.'

Getting off his saddle, Kalidasa stretched his back, filling his lungs with the cool morning air. Then, massaging his lower back with his knuckles, he walked some distance into the desert, his sights set on the distant mountain ridges starkly outlined against the lightening sky.

"We will be there tomorrow."

Kalidasa turned to see Khash'i Dur by his side. The chieftain's scarred face was caked with dust, and his eyes crinkled with fatigue as he stared at the dark, craggy range.

Kalidasa nodded but said nothing.

"You are certain you want all the *shy'ors* to be there and not just the two of us?"

Kalidasa glanced at the other three chiefs of this vast Huna army. "Unless they are afraid and don't want to come," he said.

Khash'i Dur's face darkened. "A Huna fears nothing, Thra'akha."

"That is not what I meant," Kalidasa replied. "Maybe they still think I might betray them. Maybe they don't trust me enough—"

"If everyone didn't trust you, your bones would have bleached and turned brittle in the desert sun by now, Thra'akha," the *shy'or* glowered.

Kalidasa inclined his head. "In which case, all the *shy'ors* must come along."

It was Khash'i Dur's turn to nod. Both men turned to observe the sun hoist itself slowly over the Arbudas and flood the desert with sunlight.

"Are you looking forward to meeting your old friend?" the chieftain eventually asked.

The giant stared into the rising sun with narrowed eyes. "I want to see the Samrat's reaction when our *droiba* conjures up the *yah'bre*."

***

Raking a finger through the char from last night's fire, Shanku scooped a pinch of the fine, black soot and smeared it over her gums and teeth, scrubbing vigorously. Rinsing her mouth and splashing her face with water, she glanced around the little clearing at the base of the outcrop, where they had set up camp.

Everyone was up, she noticed in the semi-light of Dandaka's daybreak.

Correction. Everyone was on their feet.

Everyone had been up through much of the night—as they had on the night of the day before as well—sleeping fitfully, often waking with a start to peer uneasily all around before trying to fall back to sleep. And upon failing, lying quietly and pretending to be brave while sneaking furtive glances at the night that concealed the forest besieging them from all sides, an oil-black darkness edging into the firelight, smothering it.

And within the folds of the dark, that faceless, formless entity also edging in... a notion, an unnerving sensation of being watched, *being marked...*

"One more night over and we're all here, old man."

Shanku assessed the speaker; one of the soldiers, standing by Greeshma's side, staring down at the bandit sitting cross-legged on the ground, shoulders slouched, a grumpy-sleepy scowl on his face.

"We won again," the soldier grinned, more relief than triumph in his voice.

"You owe each of us three coins now," a second soldier chipped in. "A good thing you have the Samrat's reward to fall back upon."

Greeshma scratched a cheek and looked away, seeming not to care about losing another six gold coins in a morbid wager that he and the men had got into. Each evening, the men bet against the bandit on the group's chances of seeing the night through safely. If they survived, the soldiers won; if there were casualties—as Greeshma had predicted there would be—the bandit would. Greeshma had lost three nights in a row, but as he liked reminding the soldiers, were he to win, they would collectively stand to lose a lot more than a few gold coins.

Greeshma, Shanku realized, wasn't bothered about losing another handful of coins because he was sure the odds were impossibly stacked against any of them escaping the Dandaka and making it back to Ujjayini. The question of settling gambling dues simply did not figure in his scheme of things.

"Let us get going," she said, applying a salve of *tulsi* and turmeric on her arms and neck to soothe the flaring insect bites.

Observing the men dismantle camp, Greeshma rose too, and made a show of assisting with the work, but he was stopped by Shanku.

"How much further?" she asked, pointing with her chin.

Greeshma didn't have to turn to see what the girl meant. He knew she was referring to the thin trail that skirted the clearing, pale in the diffused morning light. They had come upon it quite by chance, and the bandit had quickly insisted that he recognized it as one of the paths leading to Janasthana. Shanku had had no way of telling if he was lying to stop her from carrying out her threat of offering him as a sacrifice to the forest spirits, but as it was the closest thing to finding a way through the Dandaka, they had followed it... here.

"We've been on the path for two days," Shanku added coldly. "You said you were sure this would take us where we want to go."

"It will," Greeshma shifted from one foot to the other.

"When?"

"I don't remember. It was such a long time ago that I have no..."

Something about the clearing changed. It could have been a subtle shifting of the light or a change in the flow of air currents. Perhaps it was the clearing itself; to Shanku it looked smaller, it *felt* as if it was folding in upon itself, shrinking from something...

The councilor's eyes travelled around the perimeter of the clearing. The tree line was still in deep shadow, wreathed in ribbons of mist, but as her gaze rose, the morning sunlight alighted on the treetops, from where a pair of roosting birds took startled flight. It had to be the light, Shanku told herself, watching the birds fly—*flee?*

She couldn't be certain, but she thought she heard a twig snap somewhere in the forest... not far from the clearing. Her arms broke out in gooseflesh. She shivered.

Greeshma had ceased talking, his mouth half-open, his grizzled head cocked, listening.

The soldiers had paused too, drawn by whatever it was.

"Let's go," the girl clapped her hands, urging speed while trying to keep the nervousness out of her tone, and failing. Turning to the bandit, she snapped, "Hurry up." She grabbed one of the iron pots, hoisting it off the stones laid around the cold fire. "Get the other one."

In a matter of minutes, the group had exited the clearing and was on the crude path built of uneven stones. The forest quickly pressed in from both sides, causing shoulders to tense. Shanku sensed that everyone had their ears perked, listening for approaching sounds. The thought of being the one bringing up the rear of the small convoy sent an involuntary shudder through the girl, making her look back the way they had come, but other than the trail curving away into the trees and the mist, there was nothing in their wake.

The path assumed a natural gradient, twisting past trees with heavy, exposed roots. The sun climbed higher, brightening the trail but staying hidden behind the dense foliage over their heads. The anxiety that had taken hold of them seemed to melt with the ascending sun, and Shanku settled into a steady march, keeping her head down and watching her step as she grappled with whether or not to trust Greeshma anymore—and if yes, for how much longer. She was yet to arrive at a decision when her thoughts were interrupted by a sudden exclamation from ahead.

Looking up, the councilor saw that the path had crested a hillock, and the two men in the lead were already at the top of the rise, gazing down at whatever lay beyond. From their postures, it was plain that the soldiers did not feel threatened, and the group immediately picked up pace. Moments later, Shanku had joined the soldiers at the top of the knoll.

She stared wide-eyed at the sight that greeted her.

The tree line and the trail ended where they stood, the hill falling away sharply at Shanku's feet, sloping into a thickly wooded valley that stretched towards a faraway fold of hills, dark in the morning sunlight. The valley was blanketed in mist, but Shanku discerned the ramparts of a wall jutting through here and there, showing between the treetops. From behind the wall rose a single brooding tower, thrusting up through the trees like a sentinel, an admonition, a dire warning.

"Janasthana." Greeshma's voice was part-gasp, part-whisper, shivery with awe, surprise and sudden, unrestrained dread.

Janasthana.

Despite her grandmother's insistence of its existence, her father's tale about Greeshma, the highwayman's own accounts of the Dandaka, and her volunteering for this perilous journey and their march so deep into the Forest of the Exiles... Despite all this, Shanku realized that one part of her had never really believed in the fabled capital of the danavas. Yet, here she was, looking at Janasthana.

And Janasthana was staring right back at her, its tower silent and forbidding.

"What is that?" a soldier interjected.

Shanku turned to observe a swathe of trees swaying violently at the bottom of the valley, as if caught in a gust of wind that was snaking its way along the valley's floor.

"It's just the wind—" one of the men began, only to be interrupted by his mates.

"There... one more."

Another section of the forest below them was in a similar state of tumult, the treetops rippling as a draught ripped through the branches.

They watched the currents of wind zigzagging along the valley floor, heading in each other's direction, as if with the intent to converge. Shanku struggled to make sense of what she was seeing, mesmerized by the synchrony of the sinuous movements, while dimly conscious of a mounting sense of menace inside her.

"Something is not right," the soldier standing next to her mumbled.

The words had barely left the man's mouth when the two channels of wind changed course in unison and ploughed towards the hill where the group stood, gaining force and momentum with every passing second.

"It... *they* are coming this way," one of the men called out in alarm.

Shanku watched, transfixed, as the dual streams suddenly acquired colour and texture, soot-black and velvety like oil-smoke, dipping and flowing swiftly through the forest, mimicking the murmuration of birds. The sound of branches straining and snapping under pressure rose from the valley floor, and trees bent under the force of the shadow-wind, which now howled in a mighty rage and came rushing like a pestilence, sweeping up the valley, hurtling towards Avanti's small diplomatic detail in a breathless crush.

"Turn back," Greeshma shouted. "Run."

Shanku observed the bandit turn to head back the way they had come. She saw her men turn as well, spurred into obeying their instincts of self-preservation. And she watched all of them stop in their tracks and stare, their faces going pale in the morning sunlight.

Following their line of sight, the councilor saw a third stream of the shadow-wind coming at them along the path they had taken to reach this point. A fast-flowing current of oil-black malevolence, tearing through the trees, screaming-howling towards them.

Shanku cast a glance into the valley, at the two streams chasing up the slope, closing in on them. She looked at the third stream coming up the trail.

She looked at Greeshma and her men, frozen in fear at the vortex of three converging streams of something horrible, something unworldly, something inescapable, the horrors of which she could not even begin to comprehend.

***

Running a finger and thumb over the contours of his freshly trimmed beard, Shoorasena leaned forward to examine his reflection in the flat, tin alloy mirror the servant was holding. It was a handsome face that stared back at the king, though marred by thin, cruel lips and an unmasked arrogance in the eyes. Spotting a solitary strand of grey hair in his beard, he drew the court barber's attention to the offending strand, and it was only after he was satisfied with his appearance that he acknowledged the tall man who had entered the bath and stood quietly to one side.

"Yes, Commander Shirsa?" he enquired.

"There is news, my king." The commander was a large-boned man with a rugged face that had seen over fifty summers. His head was covered with a shock of iron-grey hair.

"What is it?"

Shirsa hesitated, his eyes straying to the barber and the two servants puttering around. "The news pertains to Kosala, my king," he said delicately. "And to King Siddhasena."

Shoorasena's eyes hardened. He dismissed the barber and the servants with a nod.

"It is about the musician, my king," Shirsa said once they were alone.

"What musician?" the king snapped in annoyance. "There is no musician. It is a lie concocted by Kosala."

The commander bowed. "It is, without a doubt, my king. But the lie is spreading."

Shoorasena rose from the stool. He had yet to bathe, and his broad torso and back gleamed with sweat and oil. He clenched his fists and flexed his shoulders. "Bhoomipala will pay a heavy price for sowing doubt and suspicion in my kingdom to malign me. We will march to Sravasti once Daipayana is back from Odra."

"Yes, my king," Shirsa paused. "The news I bring pertains to Kosala's plans, information we picked up in the city's taverns. A pair of boatmen were overheard talking about how Kosala intends to smuggle the musician into Magadha."

Shoorasena glared at the commander.

"We took the boatmen in for questioning. It seems one of them was approached to bring the musician downriver by boat to Pandara. Probably the plan is to bring him to Girivraja, where Kosala hopes he will start spreading the rumour—"

"They're bringing him *here*?" Shoorasena exploded, a panicked edge in his voice. "Have they gone insane?" Drawing a deep breath and composing himself, he began pacing the length of the bath, hands locked behind him.

"Do we know when they are scheduled to arrive at Pandara?"

"In the next couple of days, according to the boatman."

"Where is this boatman?" Shoorasena asked, stopping suddenly.

"We let him go, my king. He had nothing to add, and he hadn't done anything."

"Find him. We need to know exactly when and where they intend landing in Pandara."

"We will try, my king, but the boatman was not from hereabouts. He might even have left the city." Seeing Shoorasena's brow darken, the commander hurriedly added, "We can dispatch a company of soldiers to Pandara straightaway and have lookouts posted along the river. I can increase the deployment of guards at each of the city's entry points—if the musician is being brought to Girivraja, the task of nabbing him becomes all the easier. Wc only have to keep our eyes and ears open and catch them when they show up."

"Find out everything you can about the landing in Pandara. Get more informants to visit the taverns, have them talk to boatmen, traders... Get more information as quickly as possible."

"Yes, my king. And... what about sending soldiers to Pandara and increasing patrols—"

"No," the king commanded. "Just concentrate on what I've asked for."

Shoorasena turned and stepped into the bath. He walked down the steps, then dived into the water with a small splash, going underwater immediately and drawing away from Shirsa.

The commander turned and made for the door. He had done what was expected of him.

***

High in the folds of the Riksha Mountains, the early morning air was cool and scented with wildflowers, and wherever he looked, Vetala Bhatta saw brown and green dragonflies flitting about in the slender, dew-laden grass that reached almost up to the horses' knees. The trail wound along the range's southern flank, the sun dazzling behind the Acharya and his escort, who were now accompanied by ten mules laden with ore from Odra's iron mines.

The journey had hitherto been uneventful, the small convoy keeping away from the Aanupa's insidious influence by picking a steeper, more circuitous route about which they had learned from Odra's miners. Even so, they had made good progress and were already approaching the passes between the Vindhya and Riksha ranges that served as an access to the northern plains of Sindhuvarta; the raj-guru estimated that if they could keep up the pace, they would be back in Ujjayini in three to four days.

They were riding single file, with Kedara, the chief of the escort, in front. The Acharya was in the centre, the mules plodding behind him, and two guards bringing up the rear. The raj-guru's thoughts were on Avanti's many problems, so he didn't immediately see Kedara raise a hand, signalling the convoy to draw to a halt. Once the horses and mules had bumped into one another's behinds and stopped, the Acharya craned his neck and looked at the captain.

"What is the matter?" he asked, keeping his voice down, instinctively sensing trouble.

Kedara pointed away to the right in reply.

At first, Vetala Bhatta saw nothing, but just when he was about to turn back, he spotted the faint patch of smoke drifting lazily above the treetops. Lifting his head, the raj-guru sniffed delicately, smelling cooking oil interlaced with firewood smoke, distinctive and alien among all the other fragrances of the wilderness.

He nudged his way around to Kedara's side.

"Could be bandits, your honour," the captain cautioned.

"Could be innocent hill folk," the Acharya murmured back. "Let us take a look."

With a nod, the captain turned to his men. "You come with us," he said, pointing to two of the guards, "while you two take the mules off the trail and into that thicket of trees. Wait for us to come back before showing yourselves."

"And if we don't," Vetala Bhatta added drily, "it is up to you to take the ore to Ujjayini."

As the two men started herding the mules up the slope, the Acharya, the captain and the other two guards dismounted and tied their steeds in the shade of a nearby tree. They moved in the direction of the fire, drawing their swords and spreading out so they could view what was happening from different perspectives, while staying in sight of one another.

The land dipped before dropping steeply into a wooded ravine, and as they crept along, the Acharya's ears registered the growing rush of a swift mountain stream. It took a while for the stream to come into view—and as soon as it did, the raj-guru spied men on both banks, sprawled on the ground and chatting idly or splashing in the cold water. From his vantage point, Vetala Bhatta saw that the men were roughly a hundred strong, well-armed and in uniform.

The uniform of the royal army of Magadha.

And planted on the ground next to the men were a couple of banners bearing Magadha's flaming-hawk ensign, painted bright orange and red on white.

The chief councilor backed away silently and climbed up the ravine, ducking between clumps of vegetation until he was beyond the Magadhan soldiers' line of sight. One of the two guards climbed back onto the trail at almost the same time, but they had to wait a couple of tense minutes before Kedara and the second guard joined them.

"Magadhan troops, your honour," the captain said.

The Acharya nodded. "How many, do you think? I saw about a hundred, but they're bound to be a lot more than that."

"At least a thousand of them, your honour," said the guard who had been the last to return. "I was on the other side of the ravine, so I could see all the way downstream. Both banks are full of soldiers. Maybe more than a thousand."

"Logical," said Vetala Bhatta, realizing that this was the vanguard of Shoorasena's army that was bound for Odra.

"Should we hide the horses?" asked the other guard. "They might send scouts this way."

"That's unlikely," the councilor said. "This trail is too narrow for a marching army... and I doubt they know of its existence at all. They will stick to the broader path down in the valley, the one we took to Odra."

Right then, one of the guards who had taken the mules to the thicket at the top of the hill came scrambling down, accompanied by a minor avalanche of mud clods and pebbles. Those below watched the man's descent with alarm and astonishment.

"An army on the march, captain," the guard panted as he drew to a sliding halt. Catching his breath, he pointed up at the thicket. "That way, in the valley over the hill."

Vetala Bhatta and Kedara exchanged glances.

"Stay here," Kedara ordered, turning to accompany the Acharya and the guard up the hill.

Cresting the hill, the guard took the chief councilor and the captain through the thicket that concealed the mules and brought them to a high promontory overlooking the valley on the other side. The view was panoramic, the land sprawling to the distant fold of mountains, the lush valley cradling a lake that sparkled in the sunlight.

But this was not what drew Vetala Bhatta and the captain's eye.

Their gazes were pinned on a column of soldiers marching along the trough of the valley by the lake's edge, white banners with the flaming-hawk ensign fluttering in the breeze. A line of *mahashilakantakas* trundled at the end of the column, each drawn by teams of four elephants, and behind the gigantic catapults came the elephant-drawn carts bearing the boulders and tree trunks that the *mahashilakantakas* would hurl at a fortified city.

"How many men?" the Acharya asked.

"A couple of thousand," Kedara replied unhappily. "And a dozen *mahashilakantakas*."

"Are you sure—"

"*There*," the guard exclaimed, interrupting. "More men."

It took the raj-guru a few moments to figure what the man was pointing at. Then he saw—across the valley, a stream of soldiers, almost impossible to mark from this distance, except for the white banners flying in the wind.

"They are advancing in waves," Kedara muttered, sighting the third set of soldiers. "Probably another two thousand men, half a day's march behind."

More or less a thousand men already in the ravine. Two thousand marching by the lake, in addition to a dozen or so heavy catapults. Two thousand soldiers across the valley. Not near, but not far either. Five thousand soldiers, marching towards Uttara Tosali.

And just two days away from their destination.

I have already sent my army the summons. My soldiers will be here in eight or nine days, so we will be ready when Shoorasena's army comes marching...

Abhirami and Veerayanka would *not* be adequately prepared to defend Uttara Tosali when this Magadhan army assailed the city in the next few days, the realization flashed through Vetala Bhatta's mind. Without reinforcements from

Kalinga, Uttara Tosali would be overrun by the Magadhan troops, and Odra would fall to Shoorasena.

"We must do something to stop them," the raj-guru exclaimed.

He turned to see astonishment on the young captain's face... and the absurdity of what he'd just said struck him. Five thousand fully armed Magadhan soldiers were marching to capture Uttara Tosali. And they were just the six of them.

The odds were truly staggering.

***

"What else do you remember about the Samrat?"

Vishakha stared vacantly across the palace lake, appearing not to have heard the question. Then, turning her head, she considered Kshapanaka thoughtfully.

"Why do people address him as Samrat?"

"Because he is the Samrat of Sindhuvarta."

Vishakha nodded slowly, but Kshapanaka wasn't sure if she had understood.

"We can just call him Vikramaditya," she said. "So... what else do you remember?"

The queen gazed up at the sky, where vultures were still wheeling by the dozens, drifting down in silent, sweeping arcs. Reports of the vulture invasion had come in from all over the city, and wherever she looked, Kshapanaka encountered the birds' hunched forms—on the palace's roofs and ledges, on the trees across the lake, on the buildings in the city beyond... The bizarre influx had set everyone on edge, and despite repeated efforts by palace guards and soldiers of the Watch to shoo them away, the vultures had shown no inclination to budge, merely shuffling in their roosts on their scrawny, scaled feet.

"As if they are waiting for something that they know is coming," Varahamihira had remarked ominously the previous night during dinner, after Dhanavantri had administered Vishakha a dose of a soporific *kashayam*. The lame councilor's words had sounded especially menacing, coming in the wake of Vararuchi's revelation of what the Mother Oracle had said about death arriving on many wings.

"He is incredibly kind," Vishakha said with a faraway expression in her eyes. "He would do things to make me happy after—" she stopped, blinking and frowning, as if struggling to call up a memory and failing.

"After…?" Kshapanaka prompted.

"I can't remember." Vishakha stared down at her palm unhappily, running a thumb along the crisscross of lines that, according to the astrologers, determined one's fate.

"It is alright." Kshapanaka placed a hand on her sister's arm and smiled in reassurance. "You were saying he makes you happy."

Vishakha nodded, her fingers going to the middle finger of her right hand. "I had a ring with my name on it," she said, rubbing the spot where the ring would have rested. "I lost it in the palace bath, but Vikrama searched the water's depths to find it for me. He knew the ring was dear to me."

"Why was it dear to you?" Kshapanaka asked, hoping this would open a door.

"Because it…" Again, the queen stopped, groping for an answer. She looked pained. "I don't know… it has to do with something sad, but I have no idea what it could be." She stared at her sister uncertainly.

"It doesn't matter," Kshapanaka said hastily. "What's important is Vikramaditya found it for you. You're right, he is incredibly kind."

"But I seem to have lost it again." Vishakha showed Kshapanaka her right hand, fingers splayed, all five digits unadorned. Her eyes went to her sister's, and suddenly there were tears in them. "He found it, but I still couldn't take care of it... Where is he? Why isn't he here yet?" The queen snatched Kshapanaka's hand up between hers, holding it tight. "Please... take me to my Vikrama... *please*..."

"You can't go because it is too dangerous, but we have sent word to him," the councilor said, giving her sister's hand a squeeze. "He will be here in no time."

Kshapanaka realized she was smiling a little too broadly and hoped that her insincerity would not show. In truth, while the news of Vishakha's revival had been relayed by *suryayantra* to the garrisons of Lava and Biddhira, both of which lay on the main routes to Udaypuri, neither garrison had confirmed the delivery of the message to the samrat. In fact, a communique from Biddhira's garrison commander had arrived an hour before, stating that Vikramaditya had not showed up at *his* garrison, which could only mean the king had spent the night in Lava, but there was nothing from Lava yet—

"Where is the frontier?" Vishakha asked, interrupting her sister's thoughts.

"Mmm... far away."

"Far?" The queen's face turned anxious.

"Not *very* far," Kshapanaka corrected herself. "Vikrama wouldn't have got there anyway, so it doesn't matter."

The sisters sat for a moment, looking over the finely landscaped terrace with its potted ferns and ornamental creepers swaying in the breeze, which was losing its battle to the day's heat. The sun was climbing; soon, there would be no shade left and they would have to adjourn indoors...

"Why has he gone there?"

"To stop the barbarians from returning."

Vishakha's face was blank. "Are they bad that they have to be stopped?"

"The Hunas and the Sakas..." Kshapanaka felt a sudden weight constrict her chest, and her breath caught in her throat awkwardly. She wondered if she should pursue this line of conversation to see if it triggered her sister's memory, but she was also aware that this could be a deeply traumatic re-entry for Vishakha. And it wasn't a topic that she wanted to get into at the moment. "Yes, they are bad," she let the matter rest for now.

"What will happen if they are not stopped?"

Before the councilor could answer, a shrill, grating screech tore through the morning's silence. It came from a considerable distance, but there was a terrifying quality to it that made the two sisters glance at each other in alarm, before turning their heads to try and identify its source.

"What was that?" Vishakha asked.

Instead of replying, Kshapanaka rose, went to the end of the terrace and leaned out to look in all directions. The sound had been sharp enough to trouble the vultures, and all along the palace roofs, the birds were hopping about and flapping their wings nervously. A couple of palace guards had emerged onto the causeway to investigate the sound, while maids had appeared at windows, craning their necks to see what was happening. Up in the sky, the flight of the few vultures that were still airborne seemed disturbed, and from what Kshapanaka could tell, they seemed to be scattering... scattering *away* from the southern section of the sky—

It came again, a blaring, scratchy squawk like that of a rooster, only filled with loathing, quivering with rage and bloodlust. And before the scream had even subsided, a second one followed, like an echo, but louder and even more crazed than the previous one.

"What is it?" asked Vishakha. She had come to stand at her sister's side, looking around wide-eyed, and now she gripped Kshapanaka's arm in fright and huddled close. Kshapanaka instinctively put a protective arm around the queen.

"I don't know," the councilor began, her eyes scanning the southern sky. "It could be—"

She stopped.

Something was in the sky, approaching Ujjayini rapidly. Something large...

No, not just something. *Many things*. On wings.

The air was suddenly full of the ragged, infernal shrieks that tore at the eardrums and caused the blood to curdle in the veins. Vishakha burrowed her head into Kshapanaka's shoulder, as if trying to seek refuge in her sister's tresses to shut out the noise, while the councilor gritted her teeth and stared at the things that were flying in... flying overhead...

They were the most grotesque and outrageous creatures she had ever laid eyes on. They were birds in essence, of this there was no doubt; they had broad, powerful wings that they used to propel themselves with incredible speed. They had large bodies and long legs, and as one swept over the palace, screeching in defiance and sending ripples along the lake's surface, Kshapanaka saw the hooked talons at the end of its feet, razor-sharp and vicious.

But what really had the councilor's attention was the five heads that sprouted from the beasts' bodies, each scaly, bulbous head bobbing on a long, twisting, wattled neck, each neck and head pulling in a different direction, so the five screaming heads appeared to be working at cross-purposes. What seemed to keep the beasts from going completely out of control were the horned figures who sat on the creatures' backs, guiding them...

One of the creatures suddenly spun around in mid-flight and swooped in the direction of the palace—and came straight at the terrace where the sisters stood, totally exposed and without any place to hide. Rooted to the spot and unable to move for some reason, Kshapanaka watched as the beast honed in on her and Vishakha, diving, the sun beating off the heavy, black armour of scales that covered its body, all five heads poised and looking straight at her through ten beady eyes brimming with malice.

The rider of the beast was hidden behind the five heads, but what wasn't concealed from the councilor's view were the beast's legs—which extended and thrust forward as the creature neared the sisters, its massive talons snapping wide and arcing to grab its targets… or to slice them into pieces. At the same moment, one of the beast's heads opened its beak and shrieked in anger.

The scream broke the spell and galvanized Kshapanaka into action. Holding Vishakha's hand tight, she whirled and made a desperate dash for the door, pulling her sister along. She had taken three steps when the thought flashed through her mind—they would never outrun this creature, whatever it was. Vishakha and she would be dead before they were halfway to the door. The councilor instinctively threw herself onto the terrace floor, yanking the queen hard as she crashed, dragging her down as well, but cushioning Vishakha's fall with her own body. They landed in a heap, but Kshapanaka was up in an instant, rolling over her sister, protecting her from the beast's talons which were reaching for them… closing in… lacerating her skin… gouging open her back and left shoulder…

white blinding pain

…Kshapanaka shut her eyes and pressed as low as possible with Vishakha under her…

pain

…and then the creature was pulling away, soaring back into the sky, its talons empty…

Kshapanaka shook her hair out of her eyes and glanced up, making sure that the threat had passed. She then looked down at Vishakha, who was staring at her in fright. Feeling the blood run from the wounds that the beast had inflicted, Kshapanaka pushed herself off her sister and sprang to her feet.

"We need to get inside," she hissed, ignoring the pain and offering the queen her hand. "Get up."

Vishakha grabbed the hand and stood. "What are these?" she asked, sounding stunned as she looked at the beasts flying over the city.

"Don't know," the councilor snapped. "Hurry."

Turning Vishakha around, Kshapanaka half-pushed, half-dragged her towards the safety of the palace. Upon reaching the door, the councilor shoved Vishakha through it before turning to make sure that they were indeed safe.

They were. For the moment, at least. The nearest beast was across the lake, flying low over Ujjayini.

Then, without warning, the creature she was looking at opened all five of its beaks and spat great balls of fire over the city.

Hiranyakashipu

The screaming-howling was everywhere.

Manic screaming-howling, blotting out every other sound, setting the teeth agonizingly on edge and causing the eardrums to throb in pain. Yet, Shanku's mind was not as much on the screaming-howling as on what was—or *were*—causing it.

The group from Avanti stood rooted at the head of the valley, watching with wide-eyed apprehension as the streams of shadow-wind swooped up and spun around them in ever-tightening circles, tendrils from the oil-black mass reaching out towards them, probing, prodding. The men had their weapons out and were swatting and stabbing haphazardly at the coils of oil-black, and Shanku could hear snatches of Greeshma's voice, scared and desperate, pleading…

"—want a sword—"

"—defend myself, please—"

…but no one acknowledged the bandit, and the oil-black drew in, round and round.

And then a puff of oil-black detached and lunged, grabbing a soldier by the wrist.

"Help me," the man yelled in terror over the screaming-howling as another skein of oil-black wrapped around his neck and yanked him into the air. "Hel— *urk*," he gurgled, strangulated, his legs kicking wildly, eyes bulging obscenely out of their sockets.

The sight of their mate being lifted over their heads caused the others in the group to stare, the blood draining out of their faces as an oil-black void opened in the larger oil-black and the soldier disappeared into it, swallowed out of existence in one gluttonous gulp, his sword useless and sliding out of the lip of the oil-black mouth and landing on the ground with a dull, metallic thud.

"What *is* this thing?" someone screamed.

"Run, run," Greeshma shouted, but no one moved. There was nowhere to run. Oil-black screaming-howling surrounded them from all sides.

Seeing the men distracted, the oil-black moved in again, snatching another of them by the neck and arms, hauling him high.

The soldier mouthed something that was lost in the screaming-howling. He flailed at the oil-black, cleaving it with his sword while his eyes sought Shanku, imploring her to come to his rescue, somehow. Higher and higher he was lifted, and again the oil-black mouth opened, greedy to gobble him whole as well.

And then there was a screaming over the screaming-howling. Shanku saw that it came from the men around her. It came from her as well, she realized, spilling from her open mouth, a manifestation of the terror that had seized her and was squeezing her.

The oil-black mouth was wide open, the soldier dangling over it, also screaming.

Screaming and screaming-howling.

Oil-black pressing in on them, like from the night before in the clearing. Pressing in like a nightmare, except without the hope of a waking-up at the end. *Like a nightmare that was the end...*

"Throw your weapons down," Shanku shouted, forcing the words past the scream that wouldn't stop escaping from her mouth.

Somehow, the men heard her over their own screams and the screaming-howling. They stared at her as if they had misheard her.

"Throw down your weapons," she repeated.

They stared as if she had suddenly gone mad, gripping their swords and spears tighter, afraid they would be subliminally influenced into letting their weapons drop.

"We are not here to fight," the councilor yelled at them. She flung her sword to the ground, far enough so it couldn't be reached, before switching her gaze to the oil-black that was all around them. "We are *not* here to fight," she announced to the oil-black in a paradoxically challenging tone.

The spinning of the oil-black slackened. The screaming-howling dropped in intensity.

Shanku looked at the men and nodded. The men exchanged glances, unsure.

"No, *no*... what are you doing—" Greeshma began, but the soldiers had begun laying down their arms, one by one.

"No, this is madness," the bandit protested. "We will be killed—"

He stopped and stared as the soldier who was suspended over the oil-black mouth was lowered clumsily to the ground. The mouth itself melted back into the mass of oil-black.

Shanku put her palms together. "We come in peace," she said, addressing the swirling mass of oil-black. "We come from the court of Samrat Vikramaditya of Avanti, and we seek audience with Shalivahana, lord of the danavas."

For a long time, nothing happened.

Oil-black continued to churn and circle the group. The noise generated by the shadow-winds dropped to a low, petulant keening.

Then, at last, oil-black began fusing and forming powdery ash, and particles of ash fused to form bits and pieces of burning charcoal, and slowly, the swirling mass stabilized and rebuilt itself, embers turning into charred wood, wooden stumps reintegrating into bigger chunks of branches and tree trunks... Abruptly, before anyone in the group could register the fact, the air cleared, and around them stood three hulking, four-armed figures fashioned out of trees and vines, their horned heads nearly touching the treetops, all four of their muscular arms trailing vines, like tentacles, on the floor of the Dandaka.

***

For the second time in three days, Ujjayini was on fire.

The heat and smoke rose from burning buildings, eddied through the streets and spiralled into the sky, where the things that were assailing the city spun and swooped among the rising vultures in arbitrary patterns, beating the air with their large wings and spewing fireballs by the dozens, their screeches drowning out the peal of the alarm bells that no longer served any purpose. The city couldn't be in a greater state of alertness and panic, with soldiers of the City Watch and the Imperial Army doing their best to shepherd the citizens of Ujjayini from one burning shelter to the next while trying to keep themselves out of harm's way. If there was hardly any display of resistance, it was because getting the people to safety was the priority, and the creatures were anyway airborne, far beyond range and too swift to serve as targets for a counterattack. For the moment, at least, the best recourse was to keep heads down and stay alive.

Also, as Kshapanaka had learned on the three occasions when the creatures had flown low enough for her arrows to hit them, her missiles had simply glanced off their black, scaly hides.

"The archer units must be informed that their armour is hard to penetrate," she called to Vararuchi over the pounding of their horses' hooves. "Best not to waste any iron."

"It will be hard getting the word out in all this mayhem, but we should try." Vararuchi glanced up at the creature they were chasing, its large shadow skimming ahead of them, over the street and the rooftops. "I hope the ballistas work, though. It's our only hope."

"Did Varahamihira say how many?"

"Five at the central garrison."

"Do they have enough arrows for the ballistas?"

"No idea. We'll know when we get there."

Kshapanaka nodded, covering the lower half of her face with a corner of her headdress to keep the smoke and ash out of her nose and mouth.

Both councilors thundered after the marauding creature. The beast itself seemed to tease them, holding a straight line and forcing the last few vultures to sway and dodge out of its destructive path. The vultures had taken wing the instant the first fireballs had struck Ujjayini, abandoning their perches and soaring to escape the flames. Even though some had inevitably burned, the attacking beasts had ignored the scavengers for the most part.

"Vile things," the king's brother cursed under his breath, looking up.

Kshapanaka raised an eyebrow at him.

"The vultures. They knew death was in the air. That's why they came." Vararuchi eyed the retreating birds balefully. "They flee now, but they will be back when everything is over. They always do, to feast on the remains of death. *Vile things*."

As if to underscore the futility of their pursuit, the creature they were chasing abruptly banked and lifted into the sky, disgorging a barrage of fire over a locality half a mile to the east. Reining in their mounts, the councilors stared in anger and frustration at the carnage being wrought everywhere. To their right, a house and an attached granary were ablaze; straight ahead, the vacant residences of Kunjala and two other courtiers were smouldering; and from where they sat astride their horses, Kshapanaka and Vararuchi could see smoke and flames spreading along the taverns that lined the riverfront.

"We put the fires out in these parts just yesterday," Vararuchi shook his head in dismay.

Kshapanaka stayed silent, gritting her teeth as the pain from the wound inflicted by the beast's talon flared suddenly.

A clamour arose behind them. Turning, the councilors observed a straggly bunch of civilians being herded along a street by a posse of soldiers. The citizens were terror-stricken, a young mother among them holding her baby close to her chest and sobbing as she shuffled along.

"Stay to the side, but keep moving," the soldiers ordered, hurrying the pack along.

"If things go on like this, nothing will be left of this city," Vararuchi murmured, a note of helplessness creeping into his voice. Then, gathering himself, he said, "Let's go."

Kshapanaka said nothing, though one could tell from her expression that she too wasn't far from losing hope. They spurred their horses and rode hard, crossing three more burning streets before arriving at the central garrison, where men were rushing to execute orders.

Swinging off his saddle, Vararuchi grabbed a passing captain of the Watch by the arm. "Get a message out to all archers that they are not to squander their arrows shooting at these things," the councilor said. "Clear?"

"Yes, your honour."

"Good. Where is the commander of the Royal Engineers?"

"On the roof, your honour."

Vararuchi made for the door that led to the stairway. Kshapanaka followed.

"What news, commander?" the samrat's brother asked as he ducked out of the door and strode onto the roof. "Any success with the ballistas?"

The chief of the Royal Engineers, a heavyset man with a big moustache and curly hair, turned from one of the ballistas mounted on the edge of the roof. Three men crouched by the big machine, which had a heavy arrow already slotted in place, ready to be fired. To the right and left side of the roof were two more ballistas, similarly mounted, manned and fitted with arrows.

"Not really, your honour," the engineer shrugged.

"Why is that?" Vararuchi came over to the ballista.

"The damned beasts are just too fast," the man shrugged again. "The ballistas are heavy and take time to turn and point. By the time my men train their sights, the creatures have changed course and are away."

"How many attempts have been made?"

"We've fired six arrows so far, all way off the mark."

Vararuchi grimaced. "How many arrows do you have left?"

The engineer looked around the roof. "Another twenty or so."

A frown creased the *tilaka* on Vararuchi's forehead. "Not good." He glanced at Kshapanaka unhappily.

Just then, one of the creatures swooped over a section of the city close by, all five heads screeching simultaneously so the air reverberated with the noise. Those on the roof watched its flight, and at a gesture from their commander, the men operating the ballista began swivelling the machine around to point at the beast. However, the creature swerved again and spat fire. Yet another portion of Ujjayini erupted in flames.

"No, not again," Vararuchi exclaimed in exasperation.

Seeing the beast soar upward, Kshapanaka glared at the horned figure riding it, who, at that moment, turned to look towards the roof. The creature changed its path in mid-flight to face the roof, and an instant later, it was being guided straight at the garrison.

"It's coming this way," the commander shouted, and the men began to rise from the ballistas and scatter.

Kshapanaka didn't budge. Overcome with rage, she locked eyes with the horned rider. These things were laying her precious city to waste, and she was being able to do nothing but watch the destruction... Biting her lip against the pain searing her back, not thinking, letting her heart rule her mind, Kshapanaka unslung her bow. In one smooth action, she nocked an arrow in place and pulled the string back, all the way... lifting the bow... aiming...

The arrow sped towards its target, swift and lethal. It struck the rider in the mouth, split his lips and shattered his teeth. It drove in all the way, drilling into the back of his head, killing him before his mind even registered the pain. He rolled off the creature's back and cartwheeled headlong into one of the buildings burning below.

Kshapanaka didn't see any of this. She had a second arrow out and fitted, which she let fly at one of the creature's five bobbing heads. The arrow broke the top of the skull, and the head lolled stupidly at the end of the long neck, drooping down, discolouring...

Kshapanaka was reaching for a third arrow when the rest of the four heads unfurled fire.

"Get away."

Grabbing her elbow, Vararuchi pulled Kshapanaka from the exposed roof. They dashed to the door and hurled themselves through it just as the fireballs landed behind them and exploded, raining flames everywhere. Fire leaped through the door as the councilors ducked and scrambled for cover behind the walls.

With nothing combustible anywhere to fuel the fire, the flames withdrew.

Catching his breath, Vararuchi stared around the stairway where the men were huddled. "Did everyone make it?"

"I think so," said the commander of the Royal Engineers, conducting a quick headcount.

Vararuchi peeked around the door. There was no sign of the the creature. It had flown past. Getting up, he dusted himself as he stepped back onto the roof.

Built of red sandstone, the roof itself was unaffected, but two of the ballistas had caught fire and were burning slowly, the wood already smoking and turning black.

"Fetch some water," the engineer roared to his men. "Fast."

Kshapanaka came up to Vararuchi, flexing the muscles in her back and wincing in pain. She appraised the damage.

"I couldn't stop the thing," she pulled a rueful face.

"You got the rider," the older councilor replied. "That was some shooting."

"I had to make it count." Kshapanaka looked towards the palace, over which five of the beasts were circling. "At least we now know these things' heads are vulnerable. There's hope there… *if* they come within range."

Vararuchi followed Kshapanaka's line of sight. "The question is how much longer the palace can hold up to the attack," he said.

Kshapanaka offered a grim nod. "We should get back there. That's where the dagger is, and Varahamihira and Dhanavantri could use some help." With a pause, she added, "It's not like we can do much here anyway. The men are doing what they can…"

Vararuchi glanced at the sky, which was again patchy with smoke and crisscrossed with the flight of the murderous beasts.

The last of the vultures were disappearing through the vents in the smoke clouds.

"It's not like we can do much *anywhere*," he muttered under his breath, but loud enough for Kshapanaka to hear. "But you're right. Let's go."

They strode out of the garrison building and headed for their horses.

Mounting her steed, Kshapanaka looked to see where the creatures were, to take stock. The vultures were all gone. She tracked two of the beasts, black and threatening against the sky. A sky that was growing dark and ominous, the clouds smearing like paint, every splotch and swirl heavy with undulating shadows, as if they concealed some deep, bitter secret. The light had changed too, dimming, and despite the heat from all the fires, the air appeared to have turned colder, a wind picking up out of nowhere.

Kshapanaka shivered. There was something in the air, she could tell. Something strange, a hint of something else to come...

***

No one in the palace saw the meteor falling from the sky.

Later, some devas and apsaras in the city claimed to have observed a fireball plummet towards the rising spires of the palace from afar. But for those inside, it was the shivering impact of the meteor smashing down upon the palace's main courtyard that announced the arrival of large-scale death.

A yard or two in diameter and trailing smoke, the meteor struck the courtyard and broke open in a shower of black rocks, sending debris flying everywhere and spilling golden flames and embers over the courtyard's old, cracked stones. As the crash echoed off the surrounding cliffs like a clap of thunder, and the palace juddered on its foundations, a figure rose out of the crumbling ball of fire. Antlers crowning a head full of golden hair and a golden beard to match; a powerful, muscular body, shiny and ebony-black; a face with hard eyes; the hand gripping a heavy mace studded with spikes.

As the meteor collapsed around him, Hiranyakashipu gazed at the palace of Amaravati and the cliffs all around. Then, stepping clear of the flames, he made for the entrance.

The asura wasn't yet at the door when the first of the devas rushed out to investigate the source of the upheaval. Two more devas appeared close on his heels, and all three sighted Hiranyakashipu simultaneously, their eyes widening and their hands going to their swords. They hurried down the steps to intercept the intruder, but the asura lord surprised them with a burst of speed not anticipated from someone of his size, swatting one, then a second deva out of his way with perfectly timed flicks of his mace. He drove his fist, which was wrapped in a bristly gauntlet of hooks and barbs, into the third deva's face, putting him down before he had a chance to free his sword from its sheath.

Hiranyakashipu crossed over from the sunlit courtyard into the shade of the palace, and in that threshold between light and shadow, his body glimmered vaguely for a moment. As he strode inside, a shadowy form peeled and separated from him. In the blink of an eye, the form gained substance to become a replica of the asura, identical from the tips of the antlers to the toes. The original Hiranyakashipu blurred and vanished briefly, and the double turned to face the onrush of a new lot of devas at the mouth of a stairway.

The devas charged towards Hiranyakashipu's double, fanning out and circling the asura, who stood in their midst, appraising them. The devas made a couple of feints before a pair of them sprang forward and slashed at the asura's exposed back—staring open-mouthed as their swords sliced through air that felt strangely thick and heavy, like water or molasses.

The asura's body rippled where the blades passed through, though neither sword made contact with skin, flesh or bone, nor did they appear to inflict an injury on their target. Turning casually, the asura assessed the two attackers, and immediately the other devas closed in with their swords and spears, hacking and poking.

The devas' weapons went right through the asura, hacking and poking at weighted air.

Then, in an explosion of violence, Hiranyakashipu's double swung its mace and barbed fist at the devas, who had stepped in close and were well within striking distance. Blood from ripped faces and torsos flew in the sunlight slanting down from the high windows, and screams rose to the vaulted ceiling where the lamps shuddered and went out in fits of panic. Within moments, seven dead devas lay at the feet of Hiranyakashipu's replica, who calmly stepped over the mauled bodies and headed for the stairway, drops of blood raining from its mace onto the white marble floor.

Meanwhile, the asura lord made his way into the palace undetected, his body flickering back into sight. Another shadow detached from his body, assuming mass and structure to become yet another replica of him. This facsimile turned and went in a different direction, leaving Hiranyakashipu to continue straight on, blurring in and out of view as he spawned a string of duplicates in his wake.

The doubles wandered about the palace seeking out devas, and the devas obliged, coming to do battle with the expectation of killing or capturing the trespasser, but dying savage deaths instead. And all the while, Hiranyakashipu pressed deeper in his search for the mantras to raise Ahi...

***

"What are we to do, raj-guru?"

Kedara and Vetala Bhatta crouched behind a set of boulders conveniently located at the top of the ravine where the vanguard of the Magadhan army was encamped. The spot offered concealment while affording a decent view of the riverbank, where the soldiers were still relaxing, waiting for the rest of the Magadhan force to catch up and whiling away the time in laughter and song as flagons of firewater were passed around. Kedara and one of his men had reconnoitred the place more thoroughly and reported back, confirming that the contingent was indeed a thousand strong in number.

"I haven't the slightest idea what to do," the Acharya replied. Shuffling and shifting, he once again peered from between the boulders, taking in the merriment by the stream.

"We won't be able to take the road leading to the passes until the entire army has crossed over," said the captain. "As long as we stay up here, we should be fine."

"Hmmm," the councilor nodded absentmindedly. Then, narrowing his eyes, he said, "Is that who I think it is?"

His curiosity piqued, Kedara leaned over to look.

"That man there by the flag, holding a sword and talking to the other four men," the raj-guru pointed. "The one with the big moustache."

The captain peered harder. "He does look familiar, your honour."

They stared some more. Then, as the captain began to tire, the man they were observing turned in their direction and laughed at someone's joke. Vetala Bhatta's face brightened instantly.

"There's no doubt it is him," he whispered fiercely, holding the captain's wrist. "Those teeth stained with *tambulam* and that moustache. I would recognize General Daipayana anywhere, even though it's been a few years since we met." The Acharya's face darkened. "No great desire to meet, of course."

"He has a reputation for being heartless, doesn't he?" asked Kedara, catching on.

"Cruel as they come. And a complete sycophant. I think King Siddhasena tolerated him only because he is a clever strategist. I can see how Shoorasena must have taken to him, birds of the same feather."

"Daipayana can't be good news for the people of Odra, then."

Vetala Bhatta looked troubled. "Not at all. We must find a way to stop this army. Or at the very least, delay it."

"How, your honour?"

"If only I knew."

The councilor stared into the ravine, his eyes trained sharply on the Magadhan general. The only sounds were the rush of water, a few bird calls and the discordant singing from further downstream. Then Vetala Bhatta spoke.

"Even an army with ten thousand feet marches to *one* man's orders."

Kedara stared at the Acharya, mystified, struggling to understand. "What does that mean, raj-guru?"

"It means I might have found a way to stop this army's march to Odra," the chief councilor's face lit up with a cryptic smile. "Get me my spear, will you?"

***

"He is everywhere."

Narada stared at the face in front of him, raked and tattered, the eyes wide open in fear.

"Everywhere meaning...?" he asked.

"He is at multiple places at the same time," the deva replied with a shiver in his voice.

"That cannot be," said Narada, pushing past the deva to see for himself. He rushed down a flight of stairs, his hold tightening on the hilt of his sword as he emerged into a passage that gave access to the arcades where young apsaras received training in the arts of song, dance and seduction. He looked both ways, debating where to go, before following his ear, which had picked up the sounds of battle.

Reaching a broad gallery, the first thing the diplomat noticed was a cluster of devas trying to fight Hiranyakashipu down a stairway to the left. Narada recognized the asura easily from his locks of golden hair and his haughty antlers; he also saw how despite being outnumbered, the asura lord had the better of the devas, felling one, then two of them in no time. The rest of the devas fell back, and the asura immediately gained a foothold on the gallery.

Narada was about to head over to offer the devas reinforcement when he heard a commotion in the hallway below. Taking three strides, he leaned over the railing—and was stunned to see Hiranyakashipu down below as well, in the thick of another fight. He watched in disbelief as this Hiranyakashipu swung his mace at a deva's head, shattering it open... Narada returned his gaze to the top of the stairway, where the first Hiranyakashipu was battering another deva to death.

He is everywhere.

But this cannot be, Narada repeated to himself as he gaped at the two versions of the asura lord, trying to tell them apart and realizing that he couldn't. What trickery was this, and how was Hiranyakashipu pulling this off? Where had he mastered—

A white-hot bolt of lightning jagged across the hallway, crackling and sparking with energy and dazzling Narada's vision. It struck the Hiranyakashipu who was down in the hall, sinking and burrowing into his body and disappearing from view. The asura's body pulsed and waned unevenly for a moment, before recovering its form.

The diplomat looked towards the end of the hall, from where the bolt had originated, to see Indra standing with his feet planted apart, his ice-blue eyes flashing, nostrils flared in anger. The lord of the devas held the *vajrayudha*, a massive bone-sword with blue electric currents running lazily along its length. Indra switched his attention to the Hiranyakashipu who was on the gallery. Raising the *vajrayudha*, he brought it down with a slash, and another sizzling burst of lightning sprang from the sword and struck the asura. But as with the version in the hallway below, this Hiranyakashipu too appeared to be immune to the *vajrayudha's* effects. Disposing of the last of the devas to have challenged him, this Hiranyakashipu stalked along the gallery, his back to Narada.

Blood rushed to the diplomat's head, and he took two steps in the departing asura's direction when a restraining hand on his shoulder pulled him back. He whirled around to see a giant of a deva with a huge, brown beard. The deva's face was bloodied, and he bore the iron shield of the Keeper of the Palace, in addition to an iron mace fashioned like a horned demon skull.

"It's of no use," Manyu, the Keeper of the Palace, said with a shake of his head.

"What do you mean?" Narada asked, his voice rising in consternation.

"Hiranyakashipu has created replicas of himself, mirages that are all over the palace," the big deva explained. "While killing them is impossible, they are lethal. Fighting them is futile, and the cost of figuring this out has been very high."

Bewildered, Narada stared at the dead devas at the head of the stairs. "How many versions of himself has he made?"

"Too many," the Keeper of the Palace answered tersely.

"And where is Hiranyakashipu himself?"

"We don't know because there is no way of telling him apart from his mirages."

As a wave of tiredness hit him, Narada looked into the hallway, where the other version of the asura lord was finishing off the last of the devas. Indra kept unleashing lightning from his *vajra*, but the bolts had no impact on the asura.

"How does he do it?" the diplomat whispered to himself. They had never known of the asura lord possessing such powers before...

"That one's a mirage too," Manyu muttered, peering into the hallway. Raising his voice, he yelled at the two remaining devas still battling the asura. "Back away. That thing is not real. It cannot be killed in combat."

The palace keeper's voice carried to Indra, who frowned at Narada and Manyu before letting another set of lightning bolts loose on the asura. Absorbing the zigzagging currents without the least bit of discomfort, the mirage clobbered the last deva, the gauntlet smashing the side of his head open. The deva crumpled and fell.

The mirage turned to face Indra square. The deva glowered back, gripping the *vajra* hard and breathing in deep. The mirage lowered its antlered head, preparing to charge.

"No," Manyu growled. "No..."

Before the mirage could launch into an attack, the Keeper of the Palace had vaulted over the railing and flung himself into the hallway. Narada tracked Manyu's plunge with bated breath, the Keeper falling directly on top of the mirage, his shield up to save himself from the spiny antlers. But instead of colliding with the mirage, he sailed right through and hit the floor with a deafening crash as the shield took the full force of the fall. Still, the deva was hurt, and for a moment, he lay curled at the mirage's feet, winded, before pushing himself up painfully and rolling onto his back.

Manyu stared up at the mirage of Hiranyakashipu. The mirage stared back at the Keeper.

Indra watched from the end of the hall, while Narada looked down from the gallery above.

The mirage raised its mace, swinging it high to make sure that the impact of the blow would be crushing. Manyu flinched, but he suddenly seemed reconciled to the inevitable, much too tired to defend himself. Narada felt his mouth go dry and his throat constrict in dreadful anticipation...

Lightning streaked and struck the mirage, to no effect.

The mirage brought the mace down, the blood-spattered spikes arcing towards Manyu.

And then, as if it had never been there, the mirage was gone.

Narada blinked, his eyes darting around the hallway. Manyu blinked as well, looking dazed before shutting his eyes and letting his head fall back wearily. Indra advanced down the hall, peering into corners and up at the gallery, the *vajra* poised to strike.

There was no sign of the mirage.

Sidestepping the slain devas, Narada descended the stairs. He had just set foot in the hallway when more devas spilled in through the doors, looking both shaken and relieved. They were all talking at the same time, exchanging notes furiously.

"...disappeared suddenly..."

"...just went away..."

"...couldn't see where he went..."

Narada joined Indra, who took Manyu by the arm and helped him to his feet. "What you did was extremely brave," the lord of the devas said to the Keeper.

The giant bowed, but instead of dwelling on his act of daring, he glanced around. "Did we get the asura lord?" he asked hopefully. "Is that why his doubles vanished?"

A troubled frown creased Indra's brow. "Did we get him, or did Hiranyakashipu get whatever it was that brought him to Amaravati?"

He turned and roared at the devas. "Search every corner of the palace. Open every door, look inside every hiding place. Get the garudas to search the city. Set up lookouts on Mount Meru. Look everywhere. Wherever he is, find him—and stop him from getting away."

Vultures

Urvashi stared at the soldier lying at her feet.

The soldier stared at the wall behind her, mouth half-open in surprise, and quite plainly dead.

Away from the stillness of the gallery, the vyalas screeched and squabbled over the city. Somewhere overhead, fire spat and crackled.

Stealing a quick glance around her, the apsara knelt and shook the man by the shoulder. She got no response. She leaned forward and waved a hand in front of his face. His eyes registered nothing. She put a finger under his nose. He wasn't breathing either. He just sprawled there on his stomach, legs splayed out, his right cheek pressed to the floor of the gallery. One hand was under him, the other flung to the side, still holding a spear. His neck was oddly twisted, and from this close, Urvashi observed the trickle of blood on the man's chin.

She got back up on shaky legs, scarcely believing how lucky she'd been not ending up dead herself. She eyed the clay tiles that lay broken around the guard's head, then looked up at the ceiling from where they had dropped, probably weakened by the fire spreading through the roof. Smoke emptied through the hole left by the fallen tiles, while more leaked through the cracks between tiles and crossbeams. Heat radiated into the gallery, but for the moment, Urvashi seemed oblivious to the danger of the entire ceiling caving in on her. That the falling tiles had missed her completely, leaving her without a scratch, was a miracle; that they had knocked down and killed the guard who had been escorting her to the Labyrinth was an unexpected stroke of good fortune, she thought.

She was without supervision, and the humans were too busy dodging the vyalas to notice that she'd gone missing. She had ample opportunity to escape and return to Devaloka, the apsara realized with a rush of exhilaration. All she had to do was stay out of everyone's sight and not get caught… or killed.

Common sense said the best way out of the palace was a swim across the lake. Keeping her eagerness in check, heart pounding in fear and anticipation, Urvashi sidestepped the dead guard and hurried to the window at the end of the gallery. Leaning out, she realized the lake wasn't close enough; she needed to descend a couple of levels before she could risk a leap into the dark water. Looking up, the apsara glimpsed a pair of vyalas tearing across a darkening sky, kindling memories of the devastation of Amaravati and sending shivers down her spine; and below, the horrifying vision of Ujjayini, wrapped in smoke and flames in every direction she looked, made her turn pale.

The prospect of being trapped in a burning city caused Urvashi to ponder if it was safer inside the palace or out on the streets. Coming to the conclusion that the city afforded more places to hide, and that fewer people were likely to identify her there, she ran back down the gallery, looking for a way to the level below, only to discover that the hallway ahead was filled with soldiers rushing about in a state of disorder. Urvashi retraced her steps, this time taking a turn that led to a flight of stairs to another hall below, but here too, she encountered panicked palace guards shutting and barring all points of entry.

With fires raging along two wings, the palace was in upheaval, and overhearing the soldiers relay orders and instructions, the apsara gathered that Ujjayini was under a terrible siege. The screeching of the vyalas was relentless, the rare interludes of silence marked by the frenzied shouting of palace guards, and the crackle and roar of fire.

Urvashi traced her way doggedly around the palace, slipping through passages, ducking into anterooms and scurrying across galleries in search of an unguarded door or stairway that would give her access to the lake. But as each attempt met with failure, the apsara was seized with desperation, making her reckless so that she nearly gave herself away twice to the palace guards.

Running low on hope and luck, no longer confident she could make it out of the palace, she was halfway down yet another winding passage, mentally preparing to backtrack if she ran into another set of soldiers, when a door she hadn't noticed suddenly opened ahead of her and a figure stepped into view.

The apsara tensed, cursing herself for not being more careful. She had nowhere to hide.

It was a woman, and she was looking the other way, away from Urvashi.

If it was one of the palace maids, she would probably be recognized, the apsara thought—

The woman turned in Urvashi's direction. She stared.

Urvashi stared back, her eyes widening. She had seen that face only once before, propped up against pillows, gazing away at nothing, dead to everything that was happening around her.

This is Vishakha, queen of Avanti. That's how the samrat had introduced her that night he had taken her to this woman's bedside. *The only woman I have ever loved—*

"Who is it?"

Urvashi blinked. The queen was approaching.

"Who are you? Are you lost?"

Was it the queen or was she mistaken? If it was, when had she recovered from the state she had been in? And why was she here when the palace was under attack, and not in the safety of the Labyrinth like the rest of the palace household—

"I am... I'm a palace maid, your honour."

"Oh... are you also looking for someone?"

"No, your honour."

"Oh..." she said again, looking around her, confused. "What place is this?"

"This is the palace of Avanti, your honour," the apsara said slowly.

Vishakha thought about this. "But *this* place. What is this place?"

Urvashi looked around her. She had no idea where they were, and she didn't know what the queen was trying to get at.

"I... don't know, your honour. I am new here."

"Oh."

Urvashi observed the queen's face, beautiful, but drawn and anxious. She knew there was nothing to be gained by hanging around; she should excuse herself and get out of here as soon as possible, lest someone came along... She pointed to the door from where the queen had exited, "Is somebody here with you, your honour?"

Vishakha shook her head.

"Why are you here then, your honour?"

"I don't know." The queen stared at Urvashi vaguely. "I was looking."

"For what, your honour?"

"Vikrama. My husband. Have you seen him?"

Urvashi considered the question.

"I did, your honour. Yesterday morning, very briefly," she answered truthfully.

"That must be before he left for the frontier."

The king was not here?

"If you know he is not in the palace, why are you looking for him here, your honour?"

Vishakha stared, thrown by the question. "I thought…" she looked away, nonplussed.

Despite staging a recovery, the queen's faculties were still rusty, the apsara gauged. So how much of what she was saying should she believe? Had the king really gone away, or was it entirely in the queen's imagination?

"Do you know why the Samrat has gone to the frontier, your honour?"

"To fight the barbarians. That's what they said to me."

"Who said, your honour?"

"All of them. The fat man with the smiling face who gives me medicines, the other one with the crutch… the tall, dark woman with large eyes… the one they say is my sister…"

Urvashi had stopped listening. Vikramaditya was not in Ujjayini. *But where was the dagger?*

It struck the apsara that they were in plain sight of anyone coming along the passage. Taking the queen by the elbow, she steered her gently towards the door.

"You should go back inside, your honour. It is not safe to be out here."

"Yes, those… *things* attacked us on the terrace. The woman… my sister… she protected me and told me to stay inside. She said she had to go and stop those things."

The tall, dark woman with large eyes… the one they say is my sister. It had to be Kshapanaka, who had accompanied Vikramaditya when he had come to inform her about the death of her 'uncle', Vismaya. The queen doesn't recognize her sister, Urvashi thought to herself…

Stepping through the door, they found themselves in a room lined with shelves holding stacks of palm-leaf manuscripts bound together with thin jute rope.

"Did they say when the Samrat would be back, your honour?" Urvashi asked, shutting the door behind them.

"The... my sister said they have sent him word, but they didn't say when I can see him." The queen looked suddenly dispirited.

"Did your sister or any of the others mention a dagger, the one that the Samrat is protecting?"

"Dagger?" the queen frowned distractedly. She shook her head after a moment's thought.

Urvashi could taste the disappointment, but she realized that it had always been a long shot. Figuring it was best that she left before someone came looking for the queen, the apsara was still thinking up an excuse when the latter spoke.

"It is so lonely here," the words tumbled out in a plaintive sigh. "I don't know anyone. I wish I was with Vikrama. If only I knew the way to the frontier..."

"The frontier is far, and the city is under attack, your honour. It is impossible to get out of the city, for it is too dangerous outside—"

"I know of a way. A secret route."

Urvashi stared at the queen.

"A secret route? Out of the city?"

"Vikrama showed it to me years ago," Vishakha nodded. "A passage from the Labyrinth to a stone well out in the countryside."

The room was silent, the screeching of the vyalas suddenly dulled. Through the window, Urvashi saw the rain coming down on Ujjayini. She couldn't believe her luck. Just when she had almost given up on the idea of escaping this place, a naïve and trusting woman eager to meet her husband had thrown her a lifeline. But could the woman be making it all up, or was she telling the truth?

The apsara drew a deep breath. Her choices were limited. She had to take whatever chances came her way.

"You can be with the Samrat, your honour," Urvashi's eyes were calculative behind her smile. "Show me this secret passage out of the city, and I will take you to your husband."

***

Seen through sheets of falling rain, Ujjayini was a hazy outline of buildings far below, now increasingly obscured by rising stacks of steam clouds.

Amarka cursed as the vyala he was riding banked and rose, ploughing against the rain that was driving down hard, the fat little drops striking his bare arms and splattering off the vyala's scaly back and wings. Water streamed down the half-blooded asura's face, dripping off his beard and getting into his eyes, so that he was forced to keep his head down and blink every few seconds to clear his vision. Visibility was poor wherever he looked, the air saturated with a dense, white mist through which he caught fleeting glimpses of other vyalas struggling in the rain. Amarka had no idea where his brother was, and it was futile to search.

Steering his vyala clear of the other beasts to avoid accidents, the asura coasted along, peering at the city they had come to ravage and wondering how swiftly circumstances had changed. The attack couldn't have started on a brighter note. The air above Ujjayini had been warm—with traces of smoke pointing to a recent instance of fire—and the city was still exuding heat when they had arrived. With conditions tailored to suit them, the vyalas had launched a scorching assault, sending the city reeling. There was a modicum of resistance, of course, and a couple of overenthusiastic asuras had paid the price, but for the most part, the humans were scared witless. Seeing them so utterly overwhelmed, Amarka was anticipating a surrender when clouds had formed rapidly out of nowhere, the skies had gone dark, and it had started pouring.

Never had Amarka encountered rain of such intensity. It doused the flames even as they left the vyalas' beaks, vaporizing the fireballs in their trajectories and bringing the attack to an abrupt halt. It extinguished the fires below in a sizzling rush, causing steam clouds to erupt, and where the fire was hard to reach, the rain choked its spread, containing it.

What struck Amarka as most peculiar was the speed at which the rainwater was turning cold, the temperature dropping so quickly that his teeth were already clenched, his shoulders hunched and braced against the chill. And though he thought he was imagining it, Amarka saw drops of rainwater *rising* into the air—*falling back into the sky*, it crossed his mind absurdly—squeezing past the falling drops to return to the sky and come back down all over again, which was all quite impossible because that wasn't how rain worked...

Amarka felt his vyala droop in mid-flight, as if it had suddenly lost energy. He assessed the beast's five heads bobbing in front of him. They appeared cowed, their habitual belligerence missing. He looked around him, trying to see how the other beasts and their riders were faring, but all he saw was the rain coming down—and *going up*, as he told himself. For a moment, he imagined he was alone in the sky, that somehow all the others had been swallowed by the hungry rain and it was finally his turn, but before the idea could give rise to panic, he sighted a vyala flapping its wings away to his right.

He was still wheeling around to head that way when the rain seemed to let up. However, the next instant, something soft alighted on his shoulder. He saw that the rain was quickly turning into icy splashes of water that were frozen at their core, landing on his forearms and clinging to his beard.

His vyala lurched, dipping sideways and dropping before correcting itself with some effort.

His teeth now chattering, Amarka saw that the vyala's wings were coated with a fine layer of powdery ice. The asura swore under his breath; the weather couldn't change so drastically, so fast, unless there was wizardry at play. He had to find out what was happening. Yanking hard on the reins, he guided his beast towards the vyala to the right. They couldn't let it slide; they had to take stock and pick a course of action, wrest the initiative right back…

"Have you seen Chandasura?" Amarka demanded when he was within earshot.

The asura riding the other vyala turned and opened his mouth to answer, but before he could get a word out, his vyala gave a sudden drunken spin and slumped. It appeared to get a hold on itself, but its ice-encrusted wings flopped in exhaustion and it plummeted to earth, its five heads corkscrewing ridiculously, the beaks open and croaking in terror.

Amarka watched the beast go down, its rider striving hard to regain control. Halfway down, the asura realized it was of no use. He shot Amarka a wide-eyed glance just as he toppled off the vyala's back.

Beast and rider crashed to their deaths in an ungainly tangle of broken limbs and wings.

"We are losing vyalas, commander."

Shivering uncontrollably, Amarka turned to stare at the rider on the vyala that had appeared on his left.

"They are falling," the rider continued, sounding anxious. His own vyala rocked and swayed uncertainly, not looking very capable of staying airborne for long. "It's the cold."

"How many are down?" Amarka asked, feeling his fingers going numb around the reins.

"Seven or eight of them already."

Amarka looked down at the fallen vyala and its rider in shock. Icy rain fell on their battered, slowly bleeding bodies.

***

I wonder if the women of Odra are any good in bed.

Hunched behind a pair of trees at the top of the ravine, Vetala Bhatta flinched. What sort of man would think—he wondered before checking himself. He knew precisely the sort of man who would not just entertain such coarse thoughts, but revel in them; the kind of man he was looking at.

You need to concentrate, the councilor told himself. Focus.

Maybe I can start with their queen... teach her a thing or two about opening up *to the royal court of Magadha...*

A lewd snicker wormed its way through the Acharya's mind, accompanied by the vision of a woman lying naked on a bed, behind a lace curtain that left nothing to the imagination. The chief councilor didn't recognize the woman; she was dusky and plump.

...maybe the queen and her handmaidens, all together...

Two more women appeared next to the bed, naked, bearing peacock fans. Both bore a strong resemblance to the woman on the bed. A giddy rush of lust surged through the Acharya.

He grimaced. He also reckoned that all the three women looked similar because they were all projections of the kind of woman Daipayana found attractive. The Magadhan general had no idea what the queen of Odra looked like, so he was imagining her to fit his lurid fantasies...

Focus, focus, the raj-guru admonished himself, shaking his head to clear his thoughts.

...good our men are already in place...

What was that? Vetala Bhatta concentrated on the general's thoughts; the skulls at the head of the spear glowed a deeper shade of red.

...clever of Shoorasena to have got men into the city early to open the gates...

It would be a complete rout, the raj-guru thought to himself, unless this army was stopped. And it was on him to stop it. He needed to slip in...

...two days and we will be there...

Vetala Bhatta saw the little ravine, only now he was *in* it, standing next to the stream and the Magadhan flag driven deep into the damp earth. Soldiers idled or sat playing *chausar* nearby. He was seeing through Daipayana's eyes, the raj-guru realized, and the general was gazing in the direction of the road that led south and past the Aanupa...

...Odra will be ours ...and by holding it hostage, we will force Kalinga to surrender...

The Acharya shifted behind the trees and gripped his spear. He drew a deep breath. *Two days*, he thought, pushing the words out, propelling them into the ether like feelers, *but can we get there even sooner?*

...can we get there even sooner? Why? The question reared in Daipayana's mind, spiked with surprise and suspicion.

It had worked, even at this distance. The chief councilor sighed with relief.

To take Odra by surprise, he sent the words into the ravine, planting the thought.

Hmm... I'm not sure... Still mistrusting, still wary.

If we shorten the journey, the men will get more time to rest before battle. It has been a long march...

Hmm... true. The general's field of vision swung to take in the ravine where the men sat and chatted. *But... how do we get there quicker?*

The Acharya paused. This was the critical moment.

You know the answer, he formed the words in Daipayana's head. At the same time, he cast an image of the Aanupa, spread along the base of the Riksha Mountains, into the general's mind.

The Ghost Marsh? Vetala Bhatta could feel the awe course through Daipayana. *But...*

See? You know the answer. You always knew it. That is why you are so good at what you do, that is why you are the master of men's destinies...

Yes... but... the general's gaze swung wildly. *But what of the Ghost Marsh—?*

You know the answer and you still ask? Vetala Bhatta pitched the words at the general with mild contempt. *Okay... How do we tackle the marsh?*

We go around it...

...wasting time. But if we cut right through it...

The Acharya cast another image of the Aanupa drawn from his memory—a path through the mist, surrounded by moss-covered trees and reed pools.

There is a path running through... Daipayana said in mild surprise.

Isn't it obvious there has to be a path running through it?

We can take it and hide in the Ghost Marsh... Daipayana's excitement rippled through the raj-guru.

Yes, we could hide in there and surprise Odra; they wouldn't expect us to come from inside *the marsh.*

But the marsh may not be safe... there are stories about how dangerous...

Who spreads these stories? Shifty little traders. Of course, they would say that the marsh is dangerous; that is how they keep their monopoly going... by scaring everyone else away. And the stories also help Odra stay safe...

Right, right...

There is nothing in the Ghost Marsh. Again, the councilor projected a harmless image of the Aanupa. *The path runs straight to Odra. Do the men a favour. Go through the marsh...*

...we can launch an early attack...

Absolutely.

...Odra won't be ready... the general was grinning and the Acharya felt the man's enthusiasm wash over him. *And I can be in the queen's bed even earlier...*

The plump woman in bed once again filled Vetala Bhatta's mind. He squirmed.

Yes, we will march right through the Ghost Marsh... Daipayana's elation was a warm glow.

You always get such clever ideas, the raj-guru encouraged him, feeding the man's sense of self-importance and feeling it swell in the general's head. In his own head.

I am clever, I am. I must let the men know... Daipayana scanned the banks of the stream, and Vetala Bhatta saw his vision settle on two soldiers leaning against a tree.

"Karti... Atiksha..." he called.

The soldiers came running over.

"I have had an idea, and there is a change in plan," the Acharya heard Daipayana speak. "We will wait for the rest of the army to catch up. Then, instead of marching all around the Ghost Marsh and wasting our time, we will march right through it... straight to Odra."

"*Through* the Ghost Marsh, general?" The men looked at each other, troubled.

"It is nothing," the general waved his hands dismissively. "I know of a path that will..."

Sensing the cocky self-assuredness coursing through Daipayana, Vetala Bhatta pulled himself away from the ravine, extracting himself from the general's mind. When he was sure that he was safe from detection, he relaxed behind the tree, slumping back and taking a deep breath. The glow in the skulls on his spear dimmed.

"Did it work, raj-guru?" Kedara whispered.

"I think it did," the chief councilor replied.

"They *are* going to march into the Ghost Marsh? The whole lot of them?"

Vetala Bhatta gave a tired nod.

Kedara's gaze swept from the councilor to the ravine,

where the two soldiers were nodding in agreement at the Magadhan general.

"You sent an entire army to its death without them knowing it, raj-guru," the captain spoke in wonder. "And without baring a single sword from its sheath."

***

"I have no idea what to make of it," said Vararuchi as he strode the length of the gallery. He blew on the fingers of his left hand—his right hand held the coiled *urumi*—rubbing fingers and thumb together to get some warmth in them, but to no effect; it was just too cold. "But whatever is happening has affected the beasts as well. They've ceased attacking the city, and it looks like they're having problems staying in the air."

Dhanavantri trotted beside Vararuchi, looking distracted and miserable. His podgy shoulders were hunched against the cold so his neck had virtually disappeared, and he kept away from the windows, shivering each time he came in the line of the draught that was blowing across the lake.

"The f-fires are also going out," he muttered between clenched teeth. He meant this as good news, of course, but it was impossible to tell from his expression. Huddling into himself with a grimace, he drew his *angavastram* tighter around his shoulders, tucking his arms under one another. "Th-thank god for the rain, but this c-cold is impossible."

Reaching the end of the gallery, Vararuchi leaned out of a window. He scanned the sky, observing the freakish ice-rain coming down over Ujjayini, the drops striking the parapets and walls and disintegrating into water and ice. It was still heavily overcast, but there was no sign of the beasts, at least none in this patch of the sky. The physician ducked behind a wall and poked his head out, meaning to get a glimpse of the sky, but he pulled back double-quick as the draught caught him square. "Brr," he shuddered.

"What is happening?" Kshapanaka asked from the other end of the gallery. Her bow was in her hands, arrow fitted and ready to be fired, but her arms were pressed to her sides, braced against the chill. There were goosebumps on her arms and shoulders. She joined the men at the window. "Where did all this rain... ice... suddenly come from?"

Vararuchi shrugged. "Never seen anything like this in Avanti before."

"Never so cold anywhere in S-Sindhuvarta," Dhanavantri cursed. "It's freezing."

"Not in this season," Kshapanaka agreed.

"Reminds me of the wilderness to the north of Matsya," the king's brother remarked.

"Do you think it will s-snow next?" the physician shot Vararuchi a look of alarm.

Vararuchi pulled a face to say he had no clue. Then, with eyes widening in excitement, he pointed skyward. "There, *there*... another one goes down."

Despite the cold, Dhanavantri and Kshapanaka stepped to the window, and straightaway they sighted one of the beasts in freefall, careening towards the ground, wings windmilling, necks flailing, beaks squawking in fright... The councilors followed the creature's clumsy descent all the way till it crashed out of sight somewhere in Ujjayini's southern quarter.

"It has to be the rain that is affecting these things," said Vararuchi.

"Could be the cold too," Kshapanaka added.

"Any idea h-how many m-might have fallen?" the words rattled out of the physician's teeth. "Those things..."

"Hard to say," Vararuchi said vaguely. "A dozen, maybe?"

"That's all?"

"Perhaps the rest will fall if the cold stays longer," said Kshapanaka.

Dhanavantri looked at her unhappily, but Kshapanaka didn't notice. Her gaze was fixed on the spot where the creature had fallen.

"We should check on the ones that fell," she said. "We don't know what threat they may still present."

"You're right," Vararuchi nodded. "One of us should—"

Something large whooshed past the window, cutting the councilor short and casting an immense shadow into the gallery as it went down. All three councilors lunged for the window, leaning out in time to see one of the creatures hit the lake with a mighty splash that sent plumes of water high into the air, drenching the causeway and the palace walls. The beast gave a tired heave before settling into the lake, offering no resistance, sinking noiselessly as water rained down all around it. Lower and lower the creature went, water lapping over its heavy body, first drawing its wings, then its twisting necks, and finally, the five bobbing heads into its grey depths.

The councilors watched, bewitched, as the beast was submerged, and all that remained on the lake's gently rocking surface were a few bubbles from the beast's last sigh, rising from below, and the pinpricks of the ice-rain falling from above.

"That settles it," Vararuchi exclaimed. "These things just die once they fall."

"We should still be careful," Kshapanaka insisted. "This one could be an exception."

"I agree," Vararuchi said. "I'll get some men to ride with me—" He stopped to consider the palace guard who had put in an appearance. "What is it, soldier?"

"The creatures are leaving, your honour. From everywhere."

The three councilors emerged onto one of the palace's main terraces, eyes sweeping the wet sky from horizon to horizon. They weren't the only ones looking. Word had spread rapidly, and disregarding the cold, soldiers and palace officials were thronging the terraces, while below, maids and palace attendants were stepping timidly onto balconies and even onto the causeway to verify the news with their own eyes. To Vararuchi's great relief, the skies were indeed rid of the ghastly creatures and their horned riders, the last of the beasts disappearing the same way they had come, their wings lethargic, struggling to cope with whatever had compelled them to beat such an undignified retreat.

Vararuchi also got a distinct sense that the clouds were chasing the beasts away, hustling them along; the sky definitely seemed to have lightened, except to the south, where the beasts were headed. The stinging ice-rain continued to fall on his upturned face, though.

A spontaneous cheer went up around the palace, born out of relief and a feeling of triumph of having survived an ordeal. From somewhere, a chant began—*Avanti... Avanti... Avanti...*—and voices joined in, swelling in volume to a full-blooded chorus that leaped across the lake and engulfed the city.

Avanti... Avanti... Avanti... Avanti...

As if in solidarity with the voice of the people, the ice-rain started letting up, the drops no longer as cold, now more water than ice. The air seemed to warm up as well. Looking at Dhanavantri, Vararuchi saw that the physician had his *angavastram* wrapped lightly around him, the cotton billowing in the breeze that had taken the place of the draught.

Avanti... Avanti... Avanti... Avanti...

"We must be watchful," Vararuchi said. "Their departure could be a decoy."

Neither Kshapanaka nor Dhanavantri replied.

"We should look for the fallen beasts," Vararuchi said.

Still nothing from either councilor. Vararuchi glanced at Kshapanaka.

She was frowning at the sky.

Avanti... Avanti...

Vararuchi heard the voices around him dwindle and falter. Even the roar in the city ebbed abruptly, the patter of rain rushing in to fill the vacuum in his ears.

Everyone was gaping at the sky, he realized.

Following Kshapanaka's gaze, Vararuchi saw that the clouds were once again collecting directly overhead, scudding in from all directions. With mounting anxiety, he observed the amassed clouds begin moving in a circular motion, a whirlpool in the sky, rotating on an invisible axis while it lowered itself over Ujjayini. A groan of terror escaped someone's lips, but Vararuchi ignored it. Transfixed, he watched the circling clouds form outlandish patterns that fused with one another, assuming the form of wings—*many* wings, many *hundred* wings, spreading and flapping. And from these wings, the forms of vultures emerged. Hundreds and hundreds of vultures growing out of the wings and not the other way round; hundreds and hundreds of vultures circling the city in great arcs while lowering themselves, dropping from the skies and growing larger...

They are back, Vararuchi thought to himself.

"These are no ordinary vultures," Dhanavantri exclaimed.

Vararuchi sensed panic renew its hold over the soldiers on the nearby terraces. They shuffled backwards awkwardly, wanting to be inside the palace whenever the next attack began.

It wasn't over, Vararuchi thought to himself. It had been a decoy all along. The vultures and the beasts were working in tandem to—

Two vultures suddenly separated from the rest of the gaggle and came plummeting towards the palace, making straight for the terrace—where Kshapanaka had her bow drawn and ready, the arrowhead tracing a tight arc between the inbound birds, deciding on its first target.

Beside her, Vararuchi had his *urumi* out and extended, the supple length of steel flashing idly as it swung from his hand.

The vultures headed for the terrace, undeterred.

"Should I shoot?" Kshapanaka asked through gritted teeth.

"Wait." Vararuchi braced himself. "Let's see what this is."

The vultures alighted softly at the edge of the terrace, by the parapet, folding their wings and tucking them in with practised ease. They hopped and hobbled so they were directly opposite Vararuchi and Kshapanaka, the latter's bow rock-steady, the arrow oscillating between one bald, black head and the other.

"You have nothing to fear from the vyalas."

Vararuchi blinked and shot a glance at Kshapanaka. Was he imagining it, or had one of the birds spoken?

"Fear what?" Kshapanaka's bow didn't waver. The arrow pointed at the talking vulture.

"The vyalas... the things that attacked you. I have made sure they won't return."

"And who are you?" Vararuchi kept his voice level.

"We come in peace, and as friends, Samrat Vikramaditya."

"I am not Vikram—"

The vultures erupted. In the blink of an eye, they altered form, feathers going up in grey smoke that in turn burgeoned into a dense, black cloud that dissipated before Vararuchi could register what was happening.

Where a moment ago there had been a tight black cloud—and before that, ashen smoke, and before that, two vultures—there now stood two figures. The one in front, the one who had spoken, was fat and hairy, his ample chest wreathed in gold chains. Rings glistened on his tubby fingers and toes, bracelets and armbands adorned his arms, and he even wore gold ornaments on his ears, on his nose, and in his braided hair and thick, black beard. He put his hands together in a *pranaam* to Vararuchi, Kshapanaka and Dhanavantri. When he spoke, the words emerged with a slight lilt from between his thick, puffed lips.

"Greetings, king of Avanti. I am Kubera, lord of the yakshas. We are here to help you."

Vararuchi stared in bewilderment at the extraordinary figure, too surprised for words. And in the prevailing silence, a flurry of footsteps issued from inside the palace. Turning around, he observed a pair of palace guards spill onto the terrace, falling over each other as they came to a halt.

"What is it?" Vararuchi demanded.

The guards fumbled. Then, gathering his courage, one of them spoke.

"Your honour, Queen Vishakha is missing from the palace and cannot be found."

***

"How far is it to the frontier?"

Urvashi hesitated. "Mmm... approximately a day's journey," she hazarded a guess, peering into the darkness ahead, trying to see more than what the torchlight allowed, and failing.

"Is that all? Why didn't they take me there then? They... *she* told me it was far." The queen paused, reflecting. "Maybe Vikrama is somewhere else, far from the frontier..."

Urvashi was wary of the doubt creeping into the queen's tone. "The Samrat is at the frontier, your honour. Everyone in the palace knows where to find him," she interjected. "They lied to you because they didn't want to take you to him."

"Why not?" Vishakha stopped and stared at Urvashi in apprehension.

"Because... they don't want you being with him?" the apsara suggested, conjuring answers.

"Why wouldn't they want me to be with Vikrama?" Vishakha's voice, charged with dismay and outrage, echoed along the winding passage, hollow and disjointed.

"I don't know, your honour," the apsara sighed inwardly, tiring of the questions. "As I said, I am new to the palace."

How did it matter why those who were in the palace weren't taking her to her husband? *She* was taking her—*well, not really, but anyway*—so the queen should be happy and shut up instead of going on and on... The apsara wanted her to focus on the path instead; she feared the queen would make a wrong turn and they would end up lost. The queen had seemed certain of which path to take at the junction they had left behind, but...

"Are you sure we've come the right way, your honour?" Urvashi asked.

"Vikrama loves me, he dotes on me," Vishakha turned to continue down the passage, which was narrowing and dropping at a steep angle. She gave no hint of having heard the apsara's question. "He would want to be with me."

He would. Urvashi had little doubt of that. She had seen the man's love for this woman. It had intrigued her then. It intrigued her now. It was an itch that had to be scratched.

"Why does the Samrat love you, your honour?"

"Why?" The question seemed to surprise the queen, making her stop and think.

"We must keep going, your honour."

Vishakha resumed walking, stepping carefully along the path. The low roar of running water came from somewhere ahead.

"Is it because you love him as well, your honour?"

"No. I mean, yes... I love him, but that is not why he loves me. I know, because he once said that he would love me even if I stopped loving him back. That he would not know how *not* to love me. He called his love a weed."

"A weed?" Urvashi stared at the back of the queen's head in puzzlement.

"Yes," Vishakha laughed fondly at the memory. "He said his love was neither a splendid lotus in full bloom on a moonlit night, nor a radiant *rudrapushpa*, nor a heady *champaka* in blossom. He termed his love for me a weed, which would flourish anywhere, thriving on as little as the sunlight of my smile." The queen shook her head, and Urvashi could tell that she was smiling to herself. "Vikrama could be quite a romantic when he wished to be."

A weed thriving on the sunlight of someone's smile. This too was a new idea to Urvashi. But then she thought back to what the king had said that night by this woman's bedside: this *is who I love*... this *is who I want to hold in my arms, who I want to sing to sleep, night after night*. For two years, the king had sat by this woman's bedside in the hope that she would awaken, thriving on less than the sunlight of her smile, stubborn, sinking his roots deep in the soil of his faith that she would return to him... his love, a weed...

Was it possible to love someone like this, so unconditionally, knowing that your love might never be reciprocated?

"Careful," Vishakha's voice brought Urvashi back to the passage. The rush of water was now loud. "We are nearing a narrow ledge," the queen said over her shoulder. "I need the torch to see better."

The apsara passed her the light.

"Come after me, but watch where you tread," Vishakha instructed. "One single misstep, and you could fall into the chasm and get washed away." She paused, thinking. "I can't remember who it was, but Vikrama once saved someone from falling into the river..."

Urvashi was no longer listening. Her thoughts had moved

on to the next problem: how to get rid of the queen once they were out of this passage and out of the city. She could take the opportunity and shove the queen off the ledge, into the river, the apsara thought as she negotiated the uneven ledge on tiptoe, her heels dangling over the chasm, hands gripping the rusted iron rail that had been driven into the face of the rock. A grab at the woman's shoulder, a wrench and a heave, and she'd be gone. But Urvashi needed her up to the point where the passage opened into the countryside...

"...as much as possible, and Vikrama would insist that..."

"How far are we from the well?" Urvashi interrupted, no longer bothered about keeping up the pretence. She'd had enough.

Vishakha stopped in confusion, then her face cleared. "Oh, we are close now."

"Good." Urvashi got off the ledge. The path widened and ran to the right. "Let's go."

Urvashi didn't know whether it was because of her brusqueness, or because Vishakha was tired, but the queen's talk petered out, and only their footsteps sounded off the walls as they trudged upward, the path now steep and twisting into itself. The walls dripped water, and here and there, the apsara saw the torchlight shine off the eyes of nesting bats hanging from the roof.

The climb seemed to last forever. Urvashi was beginning to fear that they had missed a turn or picked the wrong tunnel, when she noticed a faint blush of deflected daylight far ahead.

"Almost there," Vishakha announced, and the apsara felt relief coursing through her.

"Let me lead the way, your honour," Urvashi said, once again all courtesy and formality. "I will make sure the way is clear, and there's no danger lying in wait for you." Without waiting for an answer, she took the torch from the queen and edged ahead.

The opening at the end of the passage came into sight. Nearing it, the apsara saw that it faced a curved stone wall lined with green moss. Thrusting her head through the opening, Urvashi looked down into the still, green waters of a well, the surface speckled with dead leaves, a couple of lily pads, and some water insects that scuttled about idly. Glancing up, she saw the round mouth of the well high above, from where a few weak shafts of sunlight were shooting down through gaps in the canopy of trees outside.

"We will have to use the chain to get to the top," Vishakha's voice came from behind.

That was when the apsara noticed the chain hanging by the side of the opening, its sturdy links splotched with rust.

She knew what to do. She turned to the queen.

"Let me get to the top while you wait here, your honour," she said, her expression grim and filled with foreboding. "Remember, they don't want you meet the Samrat, so they might have stationed guards up there." She was happy to see the alarm on Vishakha's face. "Stay here, your honour, and wait for me. I will check for danger. If everything is alright, I will return, and then you can come out. Until then, stay here. Don't come after me, okay?"

"Okay," Vishakha nodded hurriedly, her face suddenly pale. "Be careful."

Urvashi slipped out of the opening and grabbed the chain. Then, using the toeholds that had been cleverly etched into the well's side, she began hoisting herself up, hand over hand, one toehold to the next. She did not look down, her eyes fixed on the mouth of the well, which grew wider the closer she got.

Gasping for breath, her palms raw from grasping the chain, her arms and shoulders hurting from the exertion, Urvashi climbed out of the well.

She looked all around and grinned to herself.

She was in the middle of open countryside, just as the queen had said. There were fields in all four directions, irrigated by a small canal. A crude bridge made of bamboo spanned the canal to her left. There wasn't a soul in sight, though there were a few hutments in the far distance. The ground beneath her feet was wet, dark mud squelching between her toes, and the apsara enjoyed the sensation, loving the fact that she was outside the confines of the palace, feeling the wind and the sun on her face, breathing in the fresh air of wide, open spaces.

She was free, all thanks to the woman waiting for her in the passage down below.

Urvashi turned and poked her head into the well to see Vishakha peering up at her from the opening.

"Is it clear?" the queen's voice came to the top, amplified by the architecture of the well.

The apsara said nothing. Instead, she took hold of the chain she had used to haul herself out of the well.

Vishakha continued looking at her. "Can I come up now?" she asked.

In reply, Urvashi started pulling the chain up.

The queen's eyes grew large in the semi-darkness of the well. There was surprise there. Also fear, as her mind told her something was seriously not right with the situation.

"What are you doing?" Born somewhere between a scream and a whisper, the queen's words trembled up the stony shaft.

Urvashi quietly tugged at the chain, reeling it up and up, drawing it further and further away from Vishakha's reach...

Decisions

These are what the garuda brought me..."

Indra thrust the two swords at Matali, his hands clenched so hard around the hilts that both blades quivered when he shook his arms to convey his point. "*These* are what you took from the human king?"

Matali shot a glance at the old swords with their plain iron hilts before bowing his head to avoid Indra's eye. Tribhanu, standing behind Matali, looked on in stone-faced silence.

"*These* are the Hellfires, I was told. If *these* are the Hellfires, where did the *churails* that destroyed the kinnara army come from?" When there was no response, the scowl on Indra's face deepened. "Answer me, fool."

"I made a mistake somewhere, my lord."

"Not *somewhere*," Indra growled. "I can tell you precisely where you made a mistake. You were foolish enough to underestimate the cunning of the human king. He led you to believe the Hellfires could be easily stolen, he probably even created an opportunity for you to take them—and all the while, he kept the real Hellfires carefully hidden. And *these*?" The lord of the devas flung the swords at Matali's feet; they fell with resounding clangs that rang up and down the broad hallway. "These are worthless counterfeits that I should gift back to you... *buried deep in your back*."

Indra stared at Matali ominously, and the latter quailed.

"I am sorry, my lord. I did not know these were not the Hellfires—"

"You did not know because you did not care to ascertain if these were indeed the Hellfires. And because of your carelessness, the kinnara army has been reduced to a quarter of what it was. You do realize you owe Tribhanu a very big explanation, don't you?"

Matali nodded. Tribhanu opened his mouth to speak, but Indra raised a hand, demanding his silence.

"But answer me first—what of the dagger? Why haven't you found it?"

"I searched the palace, but it was nowhere, my lord," Matali said, the words stumbling out. "If I had had more time—"

"Which you would have had if the *churails* had not arrived to interrupt our attack. Your fault again."

"I am sorry, my lord." Matali bowed his head deeply. "I will—"

"Count it as your good fortune that I have too much to distract me at the moment," said Indra, not allowing Matali to complete anything he was saying. "Otherwise, I would have decided what to do with you right now. Get out of here. But remember, this matter is far from settled, and in no way forgotten. Off with you, and..." he pointed to the swords, "...take these with you, so they can remind you of your uselessness, and that you still have a penalty to pay for letting Devaloka down."

Matali picked up the swords, the blades clanging loudly against one another in the hush of the hall. He offered a clumsy *pranaam*, before turning and leaving without a word. It wasn't until he was out of sight that Indra turned and began pacing the floor.

Narada, Tribhanu and Takshaka watched the lord of Devaloka brood, hands clasped behind him, deep furrows on his brow. Finally, ceasing his pacing, Indra turned to face the hall.

"Why am I surrounded with such incompetence?" he exploded, throwing his hands open in appeal to Narada, Tribhanu and Takshaka. "First the Ashvins, then the Maruts, now this… And of course, no one has the slightest idea what happened to Hiranyakashipu. What did he want, where did he go, nothing…" he snapped his fingers, "…just vanished into thin air? And what were the garudas doing?" The deva's voice grew angrier. "Why didn't they warn us of his coming? They could have, had they been keeping better watch on Patala. But of course, *no*… incompetence."

He paused for breath. Calming himself, he looked at the naga, the kinnara and the diplomat. "Is it just a run of bad luck, or is the human king really so hard to defeat?"

For a moment, no one spoke.

"He is the Wielder of the Hellfires, lord," Tribhanu said at last.

"And he was picked by none less than the Omniscient One to protect the dagger."

Indra looked at Takshaka sourly. "Is there a warning in your words?"

"Like Tribhanu here, I too just stated a fact, my friend," the naga replied stoically.

"Good. Because I refuse to be intimidated by the human king or be discouraged by a couple of setbacks. And I will not give up my quest for the Halahala."

"What do you propose to do, my lord?" Narada asked cautiously.

Indra gave the diplomat a shrewd glance before looking out of a window at Meru rising in the distance, grey in the early afternoon light.

"Perhaps it is a route that I should have picked earlier, instead of banking on Matali and all the other fools." The lord of the devas turned back to Narada. "But it's not too late."

"For what, my lord?"

"To command Ahi to do my bidding."

Takshaka, Tribhanu and Narada stood perfectly still.

"We will summon Ahi." Indra's eyes shone with malicious anticipation. "Ahi is an elemental being that cannot be killed. The Hellfires can do it no harm. Once Ahi begins destroying his kingdom, Vikramaditya will be compelled to yield to me."

Narada was about to speak when a low voice cut in from behind him.

"There is a small problem with raising Ahi."

The diplomat turned to see Brihaspati at the doorway, smoothening his hair nervously.

"What's the problem?" Indra's voice rang sharp.

The chamberlain plodded into the hall on his bowlegs, looking distinctly uncomfortable. He came to a halt by Takshaka's side and cleared his throat, still searching for words.

"What problem, gurudev?" Indra asked again, softer, yet somehow more menacing.

"The mantras... they were the reason behind Hiranyakashipu's attack on the palace."

As the implications of the words came crashing down on him, the deva lord's face darkened with impotent rage...

***

"Kubera." The name came out in a rasping, venomous snarl. "Kubera, Kubera, *Kubera*."

The bones bounced and skittered and scattered over smooth marble, spraying away from the mandala, as though they were fleeing the hand that had flung them so rudely to the floor. Two pieces slipped and disappeared under a writing table arranged in a far corner, three pieces found refuge under an ironwood bed, while the sixth vertebra rolled along the floor until, orphaned and with nowhere to hide, it surrendered to a stop at Hiranyaksha's feet.

"Kubera, that meddlesome lump of rotting yaksha flesh," Shukracharya cursed, glaring at the mandala drawn in front of him, his hands balled into fists, fists on his thighs, back hunched, his whole body taut and quivering with rage. "It's all his fault."

Hiranyaksha observed the high priest with narrowed eyes, still not understanding what had happened. The attack on the human city had been going so well...

"What did Kubera do, mahaguru?" Holika asked from the other end of the room.

"He brought his yakshas to rescue the humans," Shukracharya grunted.

The asura lord stared, taken aback. "Rescue? Why?"

"Because, in a moment of righteousness, he has chosen to ally with Vikramaditya." The high priest looked up from where he sat on the floor, his good eye going from sibling to sibling. "It seems he has decided to throw his lot behind the humans in the fight for Veeshada's dagger."

"Ally with the humans?" Holika looked perplexed. "That doesn't make any sense. What is in it for him and the yakshas?"

"I don't know either, but that is what the bones tell me."

"Could it be that Kubera wants to claim the Halahala, and this was a ploy to win the trust of the humans?" asked Hiranyaksha, bending to retrieve the bone that lay at his feet.

The Witch Queen and the high priest exchanged anxious glances.

"The humans are wary of friendship and offers of assistance," said Shukracharya. "Let's not forget that they spurned Narada's overtures, and they also turned down my proposal to cure their queen in lieu of Veeshada's dagger. I believe they will be careful of Kubera too."

"But he just saved their city," Hiranyaksha pointed out.

"And he helped them keep the dagger safe," Holika added.

"I know," the high priest frowned in frustration. "Kubera may be playing for the dagger. It's equally possible that he is not. Either way, the presence of the magical yakshas in Ujjayini is worrying."

"I still don't get how he thwarted us," said Hiranyaksha.

"When Amarka and Chandasura stormed Ujjayini, Kubera and his yakshas were already in the city disguised as vultures—" Shukracharya stopped Holika with a raised hand, "—don't ask me why. I am telling you what I learned from the bones. The point is they were in Ujjayini and the humans knew nothing of it. Anyway, our attack set the city on flames, and we were this close," he raised his hand to show a minute gap between thumb and forefinger "*this close* to forcing a surrender, when Kubera made his move."

"What did he do?"

"He knew the vyalas draw their energy from fire, that heat keeps them going. So, he got his yakshas to take the form of moisture particles and rain down on the vyalas and Ujjayini. The yakshas neutralized all available heat sources in and over the city, before transforming from water molecules into frost and ice. The air over Ujjayini became so frigid that the fire in the vyalas' veins went cold and they stopped generating fireballs. By the end of it, they barely managed to stay in the air and fly out to safety."

"Did we lose many vyalas?" the asura lord asked darkly.

"Fourteen of them."

"Most of them made it out then and can be put back into combat," Holika let out a sigh of relief.

"Yes, but the vyalas are of little use now as the yakshas know how to exploit their weakness," the high priest said. "Until the yakshas are in Ujjayini, we can't employ the vyalas to attack the humans."

"We don't have to," Hiranyaksha countered. "Now that we know the yakshas are aiding the humans, we can be prepared for them. If we attack Ujjayini with everything we've got, even with Kubera's help, it will be impossible for the humans to stop Holika and me. We can get the—"

"I'm done playing these silly war games where the humans end up having the upper hand," Shukracharya butted in with a shake of his head. "You're right, Hiranyaksha, when you say we attack them with all we've got. We must. An attack that annihilates the humans. But we must wait a little to launch that attack."

Holika and Hiranyaksha looked at one another. "Wait for what, mahaguru?"

"For Hiranyakashipu's return," Shukracharya's eye lit up with a hateful gleam. "Chandasura and Amarka will also be back by then."

"What do you have in mind, mahaguru?" Hiranyaksha asked, rolling the bone between his fingers, his golden eyes probing Shukracharya's face.

"There is something I have begun to want almost as much as I want the Halahala," the high priest announced, as he rose from the floor and went to the window that overlooked the seething waters of the Patala Ganga. "I want the human city destroyed. Destroyed. Razed to the ground, removed from the face of the earth, obliterated from memory."

He turned to face the asuras, lips curved in a cruel smile. "Once Hiranyakashipu is back with the mantras, Amarka and Chandasura can raise Ahi and send it to Avanti. At the same time, you two can help your brother break the human council's resistance and take possession of the Halahala. Between the three of you and Ahi, there is nothing that the humans and their allies can do to stop the devastation of Ujjayini."

***

"How do we know they can be trusted?"

"We don't even know if they are who they claim to be."

"Who knows, they might even have a hand in Vishakha's disappearance."

Vararuchi, Dhanavantri and Varahamihira exchanged uncertain looks, their opinions of the yakshas sparring in the stillness of the council chamber. Outside, the bright sun was slowly warming the city, the sky having been washed clean of the smoke from the fires that had reduced half of Ujjayini to coal and ash.

"They said they *transformed into water* and *rained down*... to *drive away the vyalas*?" Varahamihira stressed on the alternate phrases so the question came out in a singsong. He had posed the question before in the same dubious tone, the same look of incredulity plastered on his face.

Vararuchi nodded. Seeing the frown deepen on Varahamihira's face, he added, "Look, we *saw* them take the shape of vultures out of plain cloud, and we *saw* Kubera and the other yaksha turn into... well, what we now see, right before our eyes. Kshapanaka and I were not the only ones—there were guards, courtiers, palace officials, palace hands... Half the palace was on the terraces and witnessed it."

"Alright, but did they *really* drive the vyalas away?" Varahamihira scratched one of the pock scars on his cheek.

"You saw the rain. Okay, we've seen rain before, but you saw it was *freezing* everywhere—you *experienced* it. There is no explanation for that."

A theatrical shiver ran through Dhanavantri at the mention of the cold.

"We saw how the creatures started falling once the rain and the cold set in," Vararuchi continued. "So far, we have counted thirteen beasts fallen all over the city—fourteen, if we include the one under the lake's waters. All dead. The men have also found nine bodies of the horned riders. Kubera tells us they are asuras. The yakshas must have played some role in bringing those things down."

Varahamihira nodded. "So, do we trust them?"

"I didn't say that," said Vararuchi.

"What are you saying then?"

"I believe the yakshas helped get rid of the vyalas and saved Ujjayini from catastrophe. But I don't know why they did it, and if their motives are honourable."

"Yes, remember the Healer?" Dhanavantri warned.

"Exactly."

"I find the timing of Vishakha's disappearance worrying," said Varahamihira. "It's too much of a coincidence that these yakshas arrive and—"

"It's possible that she got lost during the attack on the palace," the physician said. "There was complete chaos..."

"How could she simply get lost?" Varahamihira argued. "Where could she be if she's not in the palace? There is no way she could have gone out in the middle of the attack—" Seeing the chamber door swing open, he stopped.

The other two councilors turned to see Kshapanaka framed in the doorway.

"She's been found," Kshapanaka announced.

"Vishakha? Where was she?"

"Is she alright?"

The questions shot out together.

"She is alright." Kshapanaka walked in, relief and fatigue showing in her stooped shoulders. "She was in the secret passage that leads to the well."

The men looked at one another. "What was she doing there?" Varahamihira asked.

Kshapanaka shook her head. "She was going to the frontier." She nodded at the astonishment on the men's faces. "To be with the Samrat. She remembered the route through the Labyrinth to the well."

"I must see her," said Dhanavantri.

"That's why I came," Kshapanaka replied.

"Where is she?"

"In her chamber."

The physician nodded and hurried out of the room.

"So, the yakshas didn't have anything to do with her disappearance," Varahamihira surmised.

"No. It was the other way round, in fact. It was a yaksha who helped find her."

Varahamihira and Vararuchi stared in surprise.

"Kubera was on the terrace when the men gave us the news about Vishakha," Kshapanaka sank into a chair, sounding exhausted. "He must have overheard what was said, and he got the yakshas to organize a search. I don't know how they were supposed to recognize Vishakha, but anyway, one of the yakshas saw a woman at the bottom of the stone well and reported it to Kubera. Kubera convinced the palace guards, and so they went looking... Sheer chance the yaksha saw her."

"Phew," Varahamihira blew his cheeks out. "Resourceful fellow, this Kubera."

"Does this mean Vishakha remembers the way to the frontier?" Vararuchi wondered.

"She doesn't," Kshapanaka replied.

"No? Then what was her plan once she was out of the well?"

"She didn't have a plan," Kshapanaka said heavily. "She says the palace maid who was with her had promised to take her to the frontier. They left the palace together, it seems."

"Which palace maid was this?" Vararuchi stared in consternation. "Where is she?"

"She abandoned Vishakha at the bottom of the well and walked away."

"What?" Vararuchi gaped. "Who is this maid?"

"We can only guess, but Vishakha says she was extremely beautiful," said Kshapanaka. "It just so happens that the apsara, Urvashi, is not to be found anywhere in the palace, and until recently, *she* did a good job of passing herself off as Princess Pralupi's maid. How Urvashi found Vishakha and talked her into going to the frontier is something we will probably never learn."

"She tricked Vishakha into helping her get away from Ujjayini," Varahamihira scowled.

"We should look for her," said Vararuchi hotly. "She couldn't have gone far."

"She could have gone in any direction, and we don't have enough men to spare for a search," Kshapanaka replied. "The city needs all the resources it can muster. There are still fires to be put out, defences to be strengthened... Let her go."

"We could ask the yakshas to search for her..." Vararuchi offered doubtfully. "But we would be in their debt."

"That we already are." Looking out of the window, Kshapanaka observed the sunlight sparkle on the rainwater dripping off leaves.

Vararuchi sat down opposite the queen's sister. Planting his elbows on the council table, he looked up at Varahamihira. "The yakshas got rid of the vyalas, and they also helped to find Vishakha. Kubera has offered us a hand of friendship and is waiting for us to reciprocate. We can't keep him waiting. We have to tell him *something*."

"It could all still be a ploy," the other councilor said, his hand going to his belt. The top of a dagger's obsidian hilt could be seen sticking out from a small sheath that was thrust through the belt.

"It could be," Vararuchi agreed. "But let's not forget that the vultures have been in Ujjayini since yesterday afternoon. If Kubera wanted the Halahala, he had plenty of opportunity to try and take it—without trying to befriend us or win our trust."

Kshapanaka placed her hands on the table and nodded. "The yakshas have demonstrated that they can be whoever... *whatever*, they want to be. That they have chosen to be our friends is something we must be mindful of."

"I see what you both mean," said Varahamihira, "and you might be right. But we should still be on our guard. So, until we are sure about Kubera's agenda, let the yakshas know nothing about me and the dagger's whereabouts."

***

...she has been gone for too long... she is not coming back... she is... *learn to be half the man your father is*... she... and what if she does come back... *else return to your mother's lap*... she doesn't love you... (*knock knock knock*)... but she does... he told you she does... *she knows your love for each other will incur Indra's anger*... he even said he would help... *I will help you—on one condition*... he promised... (*knock knock knock*)... *you are not to meet Shukracharya*... but he went away (*knock knock knock*)...

Knock, knock, knock.

Jayanta stirred and looked about him, brushing at the cobwebs that had knitted through his thoughts and hung in front of his face in dense, white curtains.

He waved his hand back and forth... before realizing that the white before his eyes was smoke. He coughed in reflex, wondering if something had caught fire, but as he inhaled delicately, the scent of stale cannabis infused his nostrils.

Remembering where he was, the prince peered to see better.

Despite two of the three tall windows being open, the room was so thick with *ganjika* smoke that it was hard to discern the details of the painting that rested on the easel, less than ten metres from where he sat on a straw mat, his back to the wall. Not that Jayanta cared about the painting, the latest in the line of Shachi's monotonous iterations of the two craggy cliffs visible from the room. These days, the prince cared about little beyond climbing the steep stairway to this room so he could smoke *chillum* after *chillum* with his mother, the two then whiling away time in a tolerable daze that neither remembered later. Which was quite alright, as every day was pretty much the same as the one before and the one coming after, reminders of not just what had been, but what would be.

Jayanta had made it a habit of coming here since he had returned from his misadventure with Ahi in the human kingdom, seeking refuge from his father's barbs in his mother's embrace, and slowly taking to the *ganjika* that was so abundantly available in the room. The cannabis had come in handy when Urvashi had gone away with Indra; it distracted him and kept the longing out of his heart and his loins. But he had still retained contact with the outside world, even running into Shukracharya briefly—the mahaguru leaving him buoyant with hope with his promise to come up with a way of getting Urvashi to acknowledge her love for him and submit herself into his arms.

But then, out of the blue, Brihaspati had forbidden him from leaving the palace and meeting Shukracharya, the guards strictly enforcing the chamberlain's orders in complete disregard to his own threats and entreaties to let him leave the palace. It was from one of the guards that he later learned about the high priest's departure from Devaloka under cover of night.

...he promised to help you... but she doesn't love you...

If despair had driven Jayanta to this room, it was a sense of abandonment that kept him here longer and longer, to the extent that he risked emulating his mother by becoming yet another hideaway, another of the room's permanent relics, slowly wasting away in a cannabis haze.

A haze that had anyway begun failing to keep thoughts of Urvashi in check.

...but she doesn't love you...

Knock, knock, knock.

It took the prince another moment to realize there was someone at the door. He glanced at his mother, hoping she would answer and save him the bother. But Shachi lay on her bed in her own stupor and displayed no signs of awakening. Jayanta turned away indifferently, wishing that whoever was outside would just go away...

Knock, knock, knock.

"Who?" he croaked, barely audible, his tongue heavy in his mouth.

Still, they must have heard. "There is a guard to see you, my prince." It was one of Shachi's maids who answered.

Me?

"I have been sent to fetch you, your honour."

Jayanta got to his feet and went to the door on stiff joints. Slipping the bolts, he opened it to find a tall deva standing beside the maid.

"Who sent you?"

"Your father, your honour," the guard bowed. If he had smelled the cannabis, he did a good job of concealing the fact.

Jayanta flinched, his mind suddenly alert and looking for reasons why Indra was likely to be displeased with him and would want to see him—

"The lord says the matter is of utmost urgency, and that you should come quickly," the guard stressed.

The prince was overcome by a fierce urge to disobey his father's wishes. Why should he hurry when there was nothing to be gained from it? Let him wait—

"Close the door when you leave, or it will get cold here," Shachi called from inside, her voice sounding hollow and haunted, as if it came from a great distance.

He turned to look at his mother, but she was already on her side, facing away, a wrap pulled up to her shoulders, her hair an untidy tangle on the pillow.

Unwanted here too.

Jayanta heaved a deep sigh and stepped outside, pulling the door shut after him.

By the time he was ushered into Indra, Brihaspati and Narada's beaming presence, the effects of the *ganjika* had worn off. The prince was clearheaded enough to sense the cloying spirit of goodwill that was being projected his way, something entirely unexpected from this trio.

"Son," said Indra, standing stiffly, hands locked behind him, his face frozen in a painful half-smile that was more a grimace to Jayanta's mind. "You are well, I presume."

"I... yes, father," the prince replied, immediately on his guard, shooting suspicious glances at the other two devas. Affection had never been one of Indra's strong suits, so this attempt at bonding jarred, scarier and more unnerving than everything Jayanta had prepared himself for.

Not knowing what to say next, Indra nodded. Awkward silence filled the chamber as Jayanta waited...

"How is Queen Shachi?" Brihaspati asked, his benign smile a little too affected.

"She is... asleep." Jayanta turned to Indra. "You asked for me, father."

"Yes." Indra drew himself erect, looking diffident. He glanced uncomfortably at Narada.

"We were wondering," the diplomat said, picking up the cue with a suave smile, "if you still remember how you raised Ahi."

That explained this sudden, excessive show of courtesy. A warm flush of satisfaction suffused Jayanta. *They wanted a favour of him.*

"I do."

Narada, Indra and Brihaspati looked quickly at one another, relieved.

"In which case, we would like you to help us raise Ahi again," the diplomat's smile widened with genuine pleasure.

"Alright."

"Alright," Indra echoed. "Let us do it."

The prince looked at his father, who was already turning away, the matter settled as far as he was concerned.

What have I done to deserve this for a son, gurudev?

Jayanta remembered his father's words to Brihaspati after he had returned defeated from the human kingdom, having raised Ahi, but having failed to get the Halahala. *What have I done to deserve this for a son…* Yet, now when he needed that same son to raise Ahi for his own benefit, Indra was showing a remarkable lack of grace, refusing to look his son in the eye and seek his help. Even a customary show of thankfulness was missing…

Jayanta felt a surge of resentment towards his father. *Tell me you need my help. Tell me you are proud to have me as a son. That is all I want to hear, father, but your pride is so great, even admitting to that is beneath you…*

"…to send Ahi to destroy the human kingdom," said Narada, and the prince understood, even though he had missed most of what the diplomat had said.

"Okay."

"Excellent," Narada was positively grinning at this stage. "We would prefer to move at the earliest. How long will it take to do the summoning?"

Jayanta shrugged. "I can start as soon as I have the mantras from gurudev."

Indra, Narada and Brihaspati stared back at him, all three silent all of a sudden.

"What?" the prince looked from face to face, puzzled.

"You need the mantras?" asked Narada grimly, the smile gone like it had never been there.

Jayanta didn't reply, wondering what was happening. He glimpsed Indra cast a harsh look at Brihaspati.

"The mantras are..." Narada stopped uncertainly. "They have... been stolen."

The prince stared at Narada before transferring his gaze to Brihaspati, struggling not to grin as a savage sense of elation thrummed through his veins. The old chamberlain had forced him to part with the mantras, insisting that he couldn't be trusted with them. He had barred him from leaving the palace and meeting Shukracharya, due to which he had never found out the way to win Urvashi. Brihaspati had been an impediment every step of the way, but now the self-important fool had gone and lost the mantras...

"Stolen by whom?" he asked.

"The asura lord, Hiranyakashipu," said Narada.

"Didn't you hear the battle being fought?" Irked by the thought of the loss, the habitual sneer was back on Indra's face.

That's more like it, father... that look suits you better. Jayanta shook his head.

"Where are you these days anyway?" Indra scowled. "Do you even *know* what is happening in the palace? Do you even *care*?" Taking a short pause, scowl still in place, he continued, "These mantras... don't you have them memorized? You've raised Ahi once already, so why is it so difficult remembering the mantras?"

Why is it so difficult remembering the mantras? Jayanta let the words grate against his skin, feeling the abrasions they made and absorbing the pain they inflicted. Even now, in this hour of need, his father was making it sound as if it was *his* fault that Ahi could not be raised. That was how ungrateful he was... *Why is it so difficult remembering the mantras... What have I done to deserve this for a son...*

"If the mantras had been left with me, I would have had the opportunity to memorize them," the prince lashed out. "But all of you insisted on taking them away, because I couldn't be trusted with them. *I* couldn't be trusted, *I* am the fool, *I* do stupid things... But now they are gone, *and not because of any fault of mine.*" He stared from his father to Brihaspati, furious at their arrogance, gloating at their humiliation, ecstatic to find it was finally in his power to rub their noses into the ground, to punish them, *to feel superior to all of them for once*. "I can help you..." he announced.

"...but not without those mantras."

His chest swelled with satisfaction watching the three powerful devas wilt in disappointment. "Bring them to me, and I will raise Ahi for you."

***

The room was cramped and damp from the stone walls that seeped moisture, the hard floor pitted with depressions where water had accumulated in small, shallow puddles. It was dark, but there was no light to see by; in fact, there were none in Janasthana, Shanku had realized. The danavas did not appear to need lamps or torches to find their way, even in pitch darkness. The crude, black holes that passed for eyes on their gnarled, knotty faces could see perfectly well in the dark. The only source of illumination she had was the faint starlight that filtered in from a barred window set into the ceiling.

"I warned you against laying down arms. I knew it was a bad idea."

Shanku could see the vague outline of the figure huddled up into the opposite corner, a shadow against the shadows. She didn't reply.

"*We come in peace... we come as friends*," Greeshma scoffed, mimicking her address to the three danavas earlier that morning. "Look where your peace and friendship has got you." His voice quavered, though Shanku couldn't say whether it stemmed from fear, the cold or both. He tried mimicking her again. "*We mean no harm.*"

Shanku still didn't utter a word.

What could she say in her defence? That her idea of surrendering to the danavas had been a masterstroke? That it had earned them the goodwill that she had hoped for?

It hadn't.

Without offering a word of acknowledgement, without a sign of having understood her, the three danavas giants had quickly confiscated the weapons that Shanku and her men had laid down. Then, before they knew it, the danavas had lashed them tight with vines, their protests and entreaties to no avail. All seven of them—there was no miraculous restoration of the eighth soldier who had been swallowed by the oil-black were then summarily marched into the valley and herded through the towering gates of Janasthana. Here, she and Greeshma had been separated from her men—presumably because a young girl and an old man presented no threat, whereas the soldiers did—and they had been brought to the cell where they now found themselves.

Despite all evidence to the contrary, Shanku had been hopeful of being granted an audience with Shalivahana, but as the day wore on and not one danava put in an appearance, it became clear that they were facing an extended stint of imprisonment, the prospect of making an easy getaway rapidly dwindling...

"Oiii," Greeshma suddenly hollered at the window in the ceiling. "Oiii, anybody there? Give us food. Hey, you idiots... give us some food..." They had eaten nothing since morning, and hunger was making the bandit reckless and brave.

Shanku didn't know if the danavas could hear Greeshma or understand him. She didn't know if they had understood a word of what she had said before their group had been taken captive. If they had, they obviously didn't care.

She tried to concentrate on the window. There was a tree above it, she knew; the shadow of leaves had dappled the shaft of sunlight that had lit the room earlier in the afternoon. And if a tree was there, there had to be branches—

"Do you still think surrendering was a good idea?" Greeshma was back to badgering her. She was a readymade target for his anger, hunger and despair, she realized. "Still think so, huh?"

"We've been through this before," Shanku mumbled, hoping he would shut up so she could focus—

"Right, of course," the bandit's head nodded in the corner, his voice steeped in sarcasm. "We are here to seek help, so if we fight or run, we will be seen as enemies. Except that we did not fight or run, and we are still being treated as one would treat one's enemy. No one listened to me..."

She said nothing to that. He was right. Was that the shadow of the branch she had seen in the afternoon? It had looked sturdy enough...

"I was right to refuse the Samrat," the bandit was ranting to himself. "We should never have come here. But the Samrat tricked me, bullied me... he *arm-twisted* me. Now, we will perish here, and our blood will be on the Samrat's hands."

Shanku got to her feet and took three steps, so she was almost directly under the window. She looked up through the bars.

"What are you doing?" Greeshma asked. "There is nothing to see up there. No one is coming to our rescue. We will die here and no one... *hey*... what are you doing? Wha—"

The bandit blinked and shook his head. His eyes darted to the left and right. He stared.

He realized he was talking to an empty room.

***

Flipping the pillow so its cooler underside faced up, Vikramaditya laid his head back down, shifting and nudging around, trying to find a comfortable position. He inhaled deeply to get his breathing into a rhythmic cycle, relaxing his body and bringing it to a state of stasis...

That felt better. Now all he had to do—

...other than you, the queen remembers nothing. She is asking for you, Samrat.

Vikramaditya turned on his side, Commander Atulyateja's words running through his mind.

The young garrison commander had met him just outside Udaypuri, a little before midnight. The provincial town was fast asleep, but Atulyateja had stayed up to await his king's arrival.

"A message came in for you from Lava this evening, your honour," he had said, bowing. "It says that Queen Vishakha awoke from coma last evening."

Last evening. After I left. The samrat had stared at the commander, his spirit lifting with joy and floundering in anguish in the same heartbeat. Had he but delayed his departure a little... "Was that all? Didn't the message say anything else?"

"It did, your honour. It said that other than you, the queen remembers nothing. It seems she is asking for you, Samrat."

She was asking for him.

Vikramaditya tossed in bed again, so he was staring at the ceiling of the governor's vacant mansion, where he had been put up for the night. The traitor, Satyaveda, was locked in a cell, and a new governor for Malawa had yet to be named. The samrat interlaced his fingers over his stomach and sighed. The long and hard ride from the horse station, with the briefest of halts in between for a rushed lunch and a change of horses, had exhausted him, but the news from Ujjayini kept his mind from succumbing to sleep.

Vishakha was awake, and was asking for him. She remembered him—at last. What should he do?

He stifled a yawn.

Vishakha needed him. The message said she remembered nothing but him...

But the Hunas were approaching the frontier, coming back to take what they had lost...

He was her only anchor in a sea of uncertainty. He couldn't let her drift by herself...

But she wasn't by herself. She was surrounded by people who loved her and would take care of her. Dhanavantri, Kshapanaka, Kunjala, the Queen Mother... It was the frontier that had no one else and needed his presence...

But what if the Mother Oracle was wrong about the Hunas...

The oracle had never been wrong. Dvarka had nearly fallen, and the Hunas did not gamble to lose. They would come again...

Darkness.

...hear me, good king... it is ending...

This was the first time in years that Vishakha had remembered him, asked for him...

The Hunas had to be stopped from crossing the frontier. Vararuchi had volunteered to come, but he had insisted on taking on the task of protecting Sindhuvarta. He was here now, and he couldn't leave... *mustn't leave*. The future of Sindhuvarta was at stake...

Darkness.

...last of the leaves fall... be over... thank god you hear me... time is...

He had promised to protect Vishakha. He had also promised to protect his people...

...my promise to you... kept the Halahala safe... great risk to Borderworld...

Darkness. And a smudge of fog wading through it, listless. The smell of decay.

Betaal?

Yes, good king...

Is there something you have been meaning to tell me?

Yes. The tree is dying, and the darkness is moving in. Soon, there will be no Borderworld.

What?

Shukracharya's asura army inflicted severe damage on the tree. Irreversible damage...

Wait, wait, wait... You said there won't be any Borderworld?

Yes, good king. The leaves are falling. The tree is drying up. For us ghouls, it is the end.

No. No, no... It can't be.

It is alright, good king. We are...

No, wait. Everyone knows Borderworld is eternal. Borderworld is indestructible.

Nothing is eternal, good king. Everything has to come to an end, and everything will.

There has to be a way out.

There is none. Borderworld will be destroyed soon...

No.

I wanted to thank you for your friendship and bid you goodbye…

Panic gripped Vikramaditya. Borderworld was in danger. He had to do something. He had to help the Ghoulmaster. He had to wake up…

"Samrat, wake up."

Vikramaditya awoke, staring bleary-eyed, wondering how long he'd been asleep. It was still night, he could tell. As his vision adjusted, he saw two figures by his bed. One was bending over and shaking him gently by the shoulder.

"Samrat," said Atulyateja. "My deepest apologies for waking you, but a rider has come with news from the command centre at Sristhali."

"What is it, commander?" the king propped himself up.

"Earlier this evening, an army of Hunas was spotted gathering along the frontier. The scout report adds that the army stretched to half the width of the desert and ran nearly as deep."

Vikramaditya shot out of the bed. "Where exactly is this army amassing?"

"Over the mountains, southwest of Sristhali, your honour. A day's ride from Udaypuri."

It struck the samrat that he had anticipated this even as he had framed his question. South of Sristhali, the Arbudas were riddled with passes that a determined army would target to cross over into Sindhuvarta.

"The most porous section of the frontier," he remarked, "and the toughest to defend."

Kalidasa

Sky and desert were an identical grey in the murky light of pre-dawn, the dark mass of the Huna army spread out in between, keeping the two from blending into each other. The Hunas were assembled a few miles from the foot of the mountains, where hundreds of fires had been kept burning all night to deter the barbarians from sneaking closer under cover of darkness. With the day set to break, these fires were dwindling, and trails of smoke drifted along the mountain ridges where Avanti's army waited and watched, their flags and banners aflutter in the cool wind. Down below, where paths from the desert led into passes and defiles in the Arbudas, elaborate spiked defences had been put up to retard the rush of Huna horses, and boulders were strategically positioned at the heads of pathways to be launched at horsemen and soldiers who got through the gaps.

"They've been here two days now. What are they waiting for?"

The speaker was a captain of the Imperial Army, the edginess plain in his tone.

None of the soldiers within earshot said a word, though

everyone felt the same nervousness churning in their veins. The anticipation of bloodshed was often much worse than the actual thing; there was hardly time for fear in the latter, whereas the former offered plenty of scope for the imagination to run riot. And the way this Huna horde had been amassing, blotting out the western horizon one regiment at a time, chilled the very marrow in the bones.

"They will make a move anytime now, captain."

The voice was accompanied by the scrunch of feet on gravel, and the soldiers turned to see their samrat draw up beside them, followed by Atulyateja and other commanders of the Frontier Guard and the Imperial Army. The men all bowed and stepped back, giving the samrat and the commanders room at the top of the bluff.

"That army is large enough to launch a sustained attack on our positions," Vikramaditya went on as he observed the Hunas. The wind ruffled his tousled hair, his face was lined with dust from the long ride from Udaypuri, but his eyes were sharp and focused as they swept the desert, probing for insights into the Huna mind. "Judging by the way they are positioned, I imagine they will strike simultaneously all along the length of this border to create multiple pressure points that are easier to breach. And by spreading themselves out, they offer our archers poorer targets, minimizing the damage we inflict on them."

The men looked unhappily into the desert.

"I can't see any catapults," said Atulyateja.

"Siege weapons slow an army down," the king replied. "This one wants to move as swiftly as it can."

"We must do everything to stop them from breaching the border," said a commander.

"On the contrary, we should let them force their way in at a couple of spots," Vikramaditya corrected. Seeing the men gawk in confusion, he asked for a map. Unfurling the square of fabric and spreading it on a rock, he pointed, "We will fall back here and here; these lead to narrow passes where we can pin them down later. But it must look natural. They must believe they have broken through our cordon. Now, thinking that these spots have been successfully breached, the rest of the Huna army will converge at one or the other of these points. That is when we hit them; we get them all bunched together so that our archers can drill them with arrows."

The commanders nodded and conferred, passing rapid instructions to junior officers to set the plan in motion. Messengers were dispatched north and south, so all commanders along the frontline could be apprised of the strategy, and troops were redeployed at the points where the Hunas were to be lured to their doom. With something to do, something to finally keep their minds off the lingering, nerve-racking wait, the anxiety that had seized the men seemed to ebb, replaced by an enthusiasm that came from a sense of being on top of the situation.

But all sense of control went up in smoke the instant the howl issued from the desert.

Heads turned as one and the army of Avanti stared, eyes drawn to a point to the left of the Huna army, where something of impossible dimensions seemed to have materialized all of a sudden, like a towering dust storm. The sun picked that moment to rise over the horizon, and as the men in the mountains watched in horror, the dust storm reconstituted to form a pair of monstrous beings that emitted bloodcurdling cries from their dark mouths, where lightning forked and flashed incessantly.

"What are those?" gasped a commander standing next to the king.

No one knew. No one replied.

"What should we do, your honour?" Atulyateja asked, leaning closer to the samrat.

Vikramaditya's hands were on the hilts of the Hellfires. "Let us see what happens."

Everyone was so busy staring at the dust giants that it took a while for someone to notice the small band of horsemen who were halfway across the desert floor, riding in the direction of the Arbudas. As murmurs spread along the ridges, Atulyateja observed the approaching riders carefully.

"What are they doing?" he wondered, surprise and suspicion rearing heads in unison.

"Should we sound the alarm, your honour?" another commander piped in.

"Hold the arrows," Vikramaditya commanded, his gaze on the advancing horsemen.

As drummers relayed his order along the length of the mountain ridges, the samrat fixed his eyes on one of the two riders at the head of the small party. The figure sat high on his horse, now clearly visible in the sunlight that was flooding the desert. Even at this distance, the king found it easy enough to identify the horseman, his shadow trailing him on the sand, long and grotesque in the slanting sunlight.

***

Shukracharya stood on the steps halfway up to the black crystal throne of the asura lords, so he could see over the heads of the assembled asura generals. There were hundreds of asura men and women crammed inside the court, the high priest noted with satisfaction, all armed and raring to go to war. Right in front were his own sons, Chandasura and Amarka. Looking at them, Shukracharya could tell they were furious at having failed in their mission and were burning with the desire to make amends. Behind him, on the throne, sat the three consort-siblings of Patala.

The high priest raised a hand to arrest the conversation flowing through the wide room. Then, in a voice loud enough to carry all the way to the back, he said, "I shall not waste everyone's time by repeating why we have all gathered here today. Let it suffice to say that our patience has been stretched by the human king, and it is time we educated him about the consequences of antagonizing the asuras."

A roar of approval went around the court, and Shukracharya waited for it to abate.

"Let me also remind everyone here not to take the humans of Avanti lightly. The king is the Wielder of the Hellfires, though as children of Diti, you are protected from those swords and have nothing to fear. However, his nine councilors are the bearers of the Nine Sacred Pearls, and this gives each of them remarkable powers. I have done what I can to weaken the force of the Nine Pearls so that the councilors pose less of a challenge, but I would still be cautious; the last time Indra tried to get the Halahala, the councilors successfully stopped an army of nagas and kinnaras from getting to Veeshada's dagger."

This time, the murmur that went around the hall was more circumspect.

"Moreover, it has come to our notice that Kubera and his yakshas have thrown their weight behind the humans," the high priest announced. Seeing his sons squirm and turn red in shame and anger, he decided to spare them more embarrassment by skipping the details. "We do not know what the yakshas' motive could be, but we can assume they will assist the humans until it suits them. So, be prepared to encounter yaksha magic."

Shukracharya paused to let his words sink in. "Your lords, Hiranyaksha and Holika, will lead you into battle, where your job will be to engage the king's councilors and distract them, so that your lord, Hiranyakashipu, can get the Halahala. To assist you in laying the human city to waste, we will invoke the serpent-dragon Ahi—which my sons will raise with the help of the mantras that Hiranyakashipu has brought with him from Devaloka."

A round of surprised gasps and cheers went around the hall. The high priest waited for the noise to subside before turning to face the throne. Looking at the three asuras lords, he said, "Veeshada's dagger has been in the human king's custody for too long, and the longer it stays with the humans, the greater the risk of the devas, or maybe the yakshas, laying hands on it. That cannot happen. The dagger belonged to an asura. It was an asura who took the Halahala. The Halahala is destined for us asuras. Let us go and claim our destiny. Let us take back what is rightfully ours."

Hiranyakashipu, Hiranyaksha and Holika rose from the crystal throne. Hiranyakashipu took a step forward and raised his fist in the air. "For Patala. For asura glory," he called.

"For Patala. For asura glory," the hall shouted back in a deafening roar.

***

The stream was less than a hundred paces from the Lava-Viratapuri road, but the forest in these parts was so dense that the road couldn't be seen from where Ghatakarpara and Amara Simha sat on a large, flat boulder, their feet up to the ankles in water. Angamitra and his *samsaptakas* were nearby, chatting amongst themselves while their horses drank from the stream or nibbled the grass that fringed the riverbank. A pair of *samsaptakas* kept watch on the highway, though this was more out of habit than necessity, as the forests in the region had been free of bandits for over a decade.

"Phew," Ghatakarpara blew his cheeks out in amazement. "So much has happened since I left Ujjayini. We've been attacked by rakshasas, the Hunas and a monster snake; Queen

Vishakha regained her memory but lost it straightaway; all of us have acquired miraculous powers, and Kalidasa…" he shook his head in wonder, "…Kalidasa has crossed over to the enemy's side. *Unbelievable*."

"And you managed to get yourself kidnapped," Amara Simha chuckled drily. He squinted at the prince. "You're feeling alright?"

Ghatakarpara nodded. Though he still bore signs of exhaustion from the arduous trek across the Marusthali and over the Arbudas, Amara Simha noted that some colour had returned to the boy's cheeks, and his hair looked like it had before—oiled, washed and neatly combed. Encouraged by the presence of his king, Baanahasta—who had hastened from Viratapuri upon hearing about the attempt on Shashivardhan's life—the physician at the garrison of Kasavati had done a commendable job of restoring Ghatakarpara, so he could be well enough to attempt this ride back to Ujjayini. Baanahasta had, of course, offered to have Ghatakarpara shifted to Viratapuri so he could rest and recuperate, while Shashivardhan had wanted Amara Simha and Ghatakarpara to go with him to Kausambi instead.

"Father would want to thank both of you in person for having saved my life," the prince of Vatsa had entreated them over a pitcher of firewater. "And the *vaidyas* in the court can nurse Ghatakarpara back to health. Come with me, please."

Amara Simha had thanked Baanahasta and the prince, but declined them both, insisting that they had to be back in Avanti at the earliest. Shashivardhan eventually gave in, raising his jar in Ghatakarpara's direction. "Brother," he had said, "I owe you my life, and father and I are in your debt. Vatsa cannot ever repay you for what you have done, but I will consider it an honour if you accept the position of Vatsa's chief councilor and military adviser once I have become king." Downing his drink, he had added, "Help me be a good king to my people."

"Why did Councilor Yashobhavi do it?" Ghatakarpara asked suddenly, over the gurgle of the stream.

"Wish I knew," Amara Simha shrugged, keeping a closed face. Piyusha, the bodyguard, had agreed to carry out the killing for money; he had no hidden agenda of his own, nor did he know why Yashobhavi wanted Shashivardhan dead. "I think we will learn the truth once they interrogate him."

"He was always kind and loving towards me," said Ghatakarpara, staring into the water. "I remember him bringing me a leather puppet once… a dancing woman. From the Southern Kingdoms, mother told me. Another time, he got me a small drum all the way from Srivijaya. And on hot afternoons, he would bring *jamun* and *ber* during season. Yashobhavi used to be around a lot, but after I moved to Ujjayini, I saw less and less of him."

Amara Simha glanced at the king's nephew out of the corner of his eye but said nothing.

"Really lucky I happened to arrive just in time, at the spot they'd picked for the killing," the boy said with a shake of his head. "And even more lucky for both Shashivardhan and me that you found us in the nick of time. Otherwise, both princes of the Vardhan dynasty gone…" He looked at Amara Simha gratefully.

"All thanks to Nor'han and his father. The old man gave Nor'han to us on the condition that he would track you to the frontier and no further. But the boy volunteered to come over the mountains into Sindhuvarta—honestly, if he hadn't come, we would never have found you." Amara Simha glanced at the sky. "They had no reason to help us, but they still did."

"I wish I had met the boy."

"I told him you'd want to when you regained consciousness, but he was eager to return home. He was afraid his father would worry if he delayed too much."

Ghatakarpara gave a thoughtful nod. "I would never have thought that I'd owe my life to a Saka."

"I'd never thought I would meet a Saka whom I didn't want to kill," Amara Simha sounded pensive. "Yet, when we were looking for you in the desert and we attacked the fortress where you'd been held prisoner, there were these two women and a boy of three or four in front of me, pleading for mercy. Seeing that child on its knees, begging to be spared, did something to me. I... changed. Don't ask how." He paused to draw breath. "You go into battle with blood in your head. You come out with blood on your hands. Sometimes, battles teach you more about compassion than any religion can."

Ghatakarpara peered at his companion. "You know, you're growing old."

They looked at each other for a moment; then they burst out laughing.

"You also owe thanks to the Mother Oracle," said Amara Simha. "She read the signs of your kidnapping in the clouds... oh, wait, there's something I have to give you."

The older councilor went to his horse and rummaged through the saddlebag. Finding what he wanted, he turned back.

"Here," he said, holding a gold sun-crest medallion by its chain so the sun-crest swung gently from his splayed fingers. "The Sakas had taken this. I got it back for you."

"Thank you," the prince slipped the medallion over his head. "So, I owe the oracle," he said, smiling as he adjusted the sun-crest. "I will remember to thank her."

"And Atulyateja, who deduced that Satyaveda had a hand in your kidnapping. And..." Amara Simha hesitated, "...well, you also owe the girl."

Ghatakarpara looked up sharply.

"From what I gather, she was the one who brought the bangle that you had made for her to Atulyateja, which gave him the lead to Satyaveda," Amara Simha continued. "And Atulyateja tells me she persisted in her search for you—without having the faintest inkling that the man she was looking for was a prince of Avanti and Vatsa."

"She knows now, doesn't she?" Ghatakarpara asked glumly.

The brawny shoulders rose in a shrug. "Your identity could hardly be kept secret from her."

"Was she angry?" the prince scanned Amara Simha's face.

"I don't know. I haven't even seen this girl. You'll have to ask Atulyateja."

"You're right." The boy paused, thinking. "I must go to Udaypuri. I will take two or three of the men and head west—"

"You're not going anywhere," Amara Simha protested. "You're coming with me to Ujjayini. I gave the Samrat my word that I would bring you back—"

"You *have* kept your word by bringing me back to Sindhuvarta," Ghatakarpara interrupted. "Isn't that good enough? Let me go to Udaypuri—"

Amara Simha gave his head a firm shake. "Your mother is in Ujjayini, sick with worry—"

"Mother is always sick with worry about something or the other."

"—and your uncles will want to see you, as will everyone else in—"

"Just tell mother I am fine," the prince turned to face the older councilor. "Tell *everyone* that I am fine. Look, I have to go to Udaypuri. I *must* go—"

"Because of the girl?"

"Yes." Ghatakarpara stared at Amara Simha as if he were a fool. "Why else would I want to go there? I must meet her. I have to—"

"Keep your voice down," the older councilor said. "The men can hear you."

The prince looked over his shoulder, then turned right back. "I must apologize to her for what I did," he whispered fiercely. "I have to tell her my intention—"

"What's her name?"

"What? Oh, Aparupa."

"Okay, listen to me. This Aparupa is the daughter of a traitor, a man who conspired to have a prince of Avanti kidnapped, and helped smuggle the kidnapped prince across the frontier into enemy hands. This man is in custody and will be charged with treason. He will be imprisoned for life, though there is an equal chance he will be sent to the Forest of the Exiles. Do you see the absurdity of the situation?"

"Well, I happen to be the prince who was kidnapped—"

"Exactly."

"—so, if I don't have a problem with this man's daughter, I don't see anyone else having a problem with her."

Amara Simha stared at Ghatakarpara.

"Besides," the prince added, "let's not forget that this daughter assisted in the same prince's rescue."

"You think the palace will—" Amara Simha began, then stopped. "What do you intend to do when you get to Udaypuri?"

"I will find Aparupa and tell her—"

"Get to the point where we assume that she forgives you. What next? What will you do?"

Ghatakarpara gave this a moment's thought. "I will ask her to marry me."

With a deep sigh, Amara Simha stared into the forest across the stream. Overhead, the sun was climbing steadily into the sky, but the forest was still cool.

"I know what is going through your mind," the prince said. "You are thinking that I am being foolish in throwing away a place in the king's council and forfeiting my right to be known as a prince of Avanti. You are thinking that, in all likelihood, I will also cease being a prince of Vatsa, and that I will be letting down so many people in the courts of Ujjayini and Kausambi, none more than my uncles—the Samrat, uncle Vararuchi and King Chandravardhan. You are thinking it is stupid of me to turn my back on a life of privilege only to live with the stigma of being married to a traitor's daughter. You are right, for I *am* being foolish, and this is *sheer stupidity*."

Amara Simha gave Ghatakarpara a sidelong glance.

"You are right," the prince continued with a sad smile and a shrug. "Even Shashivardhan might feel compelled to forget his offer to make me his chief councilor. But you know what? I am willing to go through all of this for the sake of being with the woman I love."

Amara Simha opened his mouth to say something, but Ghatakarpara stopped him.

"You just told me how Atulyateja made a mention of Aparupa's persistence; to her, I was just an ordinary soldier of the Frontier Guard, yet she looked so hard for me. What does that tell you about her?"

The older councilor said nothing.

"What advice would you give a man—*not me*, another man—who knows a woman loves him as deeply as Aparupa loves me? Would you ask that man to forget this woman, or would you tell him to do everything possible to protect her love that is so rare? What advice would you give?"

Amara Simha tried looking away, but Ghatakarpara placed a hand on his brawny arm, forcing him to turn and meet his gaze.

"Thoughts of Aparupa are what kept me going during my flight across the Great Desert. She is the reason I made it through the cold mountains. I must go to her, please. I must convince her that it was never my intention to fool her. I must seek her pardon. I must prove my love to her. Above all, I must find her before it is too late. So, let me go."

"Listen to me," Amara Simha tried to reason. "You are in no condition to go to Udaypuri by yourself. You are yet to recover from your ordeals in the desert and the mountains. You are still weak. Come to the palace so Dhanavantri can take a look—"

"Does mother know about Aparupa? Does uncle Vikrama know? Uncle Vararuchi?"

"They do, I suppose," Amara Simha admitted. "Atulyateja couldn't have kept her out."

"Do you think they would approve of her and me?" The prince noted the older man's silence and nodded. "I thought not. Once I am in the palace, they will find a way to stop me from seeing Aparupa. How would they let me go when so many generations of tradition and family honour are at stake? Which is why I must go to Udaypuri first."

Amara Simha sat with his head sunk in thought. Finally, he turned to the boy. "I understand how you feel about this girl. And if you want to know what my advice to you would be, here it is. Hold her as close to you as possible, for as *long* as possible, because you never know when time will conspire to separate you. But listen when I ask you to come to Ujjayini with me. You are weak, and if something were to happen to you in Udaypuri, I would never be able to look the Samrat in the eye. I would have failed him. Let Dhanavantri nurse you back to health. Then you can go to Udaypuri. I give you my word that I shall do everything it takes to unite you and Aparupa, even if it means earning the ire of the palace. Come with me now, for *my* sake. I will come with you to Udaypuri for yours."

For a long moment, Ghatakarpara sat staring into the water, not saying anything.

"You have my word," said Amara Simha again, giving the prince's shoulder a squeeze.

The boy finally looked up at his companion. Slowly, he nodded.

***

Atulyateja's sword was in its scabbard, balanced across the saddle and his left thigh, his right hand resting lightly on the hilt, ready to draw the blade at the slightest provocation, as he rode into the Marusthali behind his king.

Down by the floor of the desert, the air was full of sand that grated the eyes and clogged the nostrils; overhead, the sun radiated heat, causing sweat to bead on the commander's forehead and trickle down the side of his neck. But the young man didn't seem to notice, for his sights were on the Huna contingent—and in particular, on the broad-shouldered giant he had spent his growing years idolizing. He still remembered the first time someone had introduced him to the man as Ghatakarpara's friend. Placing a hand on his shoulder, the man had stared into his face and said, "When you have a prince for a friend, learn to fight better than the prince. That way, you will keep your self-esteem, and your friendship will be that of equals."

The Huna horsemen, who numbered less than a dozen, had stopped a few hundred paces from Avanti's defences, and there they now waited. Within moments of their arrival, they had sent a message into the mountains, asking the samrat to come and meet them, promising he would not be harmed, while seeking an undertaking from Avanti's troops that they would not attack either. The Hunas hadn't cited any reason for wanting to meet the samrat.

Atulyateja and his fellow commanders had argued against Vikramaditya going to meet the Hunas on the grounds that the barbarians weren't to be trusted, and that the meeting might be a pretext to attempt the samrat's assassination. Vikramaditya, however, would not back down from the dare. Finally, giving in to Atulyateja's protests, he had agreed to let the commander accompany him into the desert.

Seeing the samrat and the commander emerge from the shadows of the mountains, five of the horsemen got off their horses and headed out to meet them halfway. Vikramaditya reined in and dismounted, forcing Atulyateja to follow suit, and the two of them walked towards the approaching Huna quintet. The commander sensed a stillness in the air, a tense silence behind him in the mountains, a similar hush from the waiting Hunas. The quiet was disturbed only by the intermittent lowing of the dust giants and the sound of his sandals scuffing the sand.

When less than thirty paces separated them, the other four Huna warriors drew to a halt, but Kalidasa kept walking until the distance between him and the king had reduced to ten paces. He finally stopped and considered the samrat.

The samrat returned the gaze, staring his former councilor in the face.

Behind Kalidasa, the four Hunas watched with hooded eyes.

By the king's side, Atulyateja observed Kalidasa's hand stray towards his scimitar. He tensed.

The giant's eyes flicked to Atulyateja. They registered recognition, but they went back to the samrat.

Nothing moved in the heat of the sun.

"Some changes since we last met," the Huna spoke finally, his eyes on the king's beard.

"Changes there too," Vikramaditya replied, nodding at the shorn head and the livid scar that marked the *hriiz* on the giant's forehead.

Kalidasa inclined his head. "How is Ujjayini?" he asked casually.

"Holding up."

"It is built from the iron will of men," the giant remarked, squinting at the Arbudas.

His hand went to his scimitar in a flash, and before Atulyateja knew it, Kalidasa had the blade out, holding it easily in his hand. Behind him, the four Hunas drew their swords.

Atulyateja's sword was partly out of its sheath when he realized that the samrat hadn't even touched the Hellfires. He shot a worried glance at his king, who stood straight-backed, legs apart, looking at Kalidasa.

Moving with the speed and grace of a tiger, the giant suddenly went down on one knee and placed his scimitar flat on the desert floor, between him and the samrat. He stayed down, head bowed, and as Atulyateja stared in confusion, the four men standing at the back got down on their knees and laid their swords, likewise, on the ground before them.

Then, almost as one, all five men regained their feet, leaving their weapons lying where they had placed them.

Sweat ran down Atulyateja's brow in rivulets and got into his eyes. He blinked, looking from Kalidasa to the samrat, totally perplexed. What was happening, what were the Hunas playing at, what did—

"This is what I have brought you and Avanti, Samrat Vikramaditya," Kalidasa said, pointing to the Huna army with a sweep of his muscular arm. "And this." He gestured in the direction of the towering dust giants.

What did that mean, the commander asked himself, his eyes growing wide as he listened to Kalidasa, comprehending… but not believing what the giant was saying.

"The Hunas are here as friends, Samrat, to help us in our fight to protect the Halahala."

***

Urvashi had not known what to expect when the deva ushered her hurriedly through the passages and hallways of the palace, telling her that Indra was awaiting her arrival with great impatience. The news of her return had preceded her, brought to Amaravati by the garudas, and the deva had met her the moment she stepped off the moat that bridged the abyss, insisting that she come with him to see the lord of the devas.

Reaching the hall that housed Indra's pleasure chambers, the deva pushed the door open for Urvashi. Walking in, the first thing the apsara noticed were the cushions thrown on the floor amidst a scattering of hastily discarded clothes and jewellery. Curtains hung around the bed located straight ahead, but light from the arched windows filtered through the thin fabric, allowing Urvashi to see the sleeping forms of two apsaras, satin sheets spilling from the bed on all sides. The curtains billowed in the breeze, revealing the bare back of one apsara, the other apsara's hand thrown languidly over the first one's waist in repose.

"Urvashi."

Turning, the apsara saw Indra on a divan to her right, propped up on one elbow, looking at her with eyes that were bleary with a lack of sleep and an excess of *soma*. On a stool opposite sat Narada, his face lighting up with pleasure at the sight of Urvashi. The naga lord Takshaka was also present, sprawled on another divan. Between the three was a small ironwood table over which a cloth had been spread, a *chausar* board tastefully embroidered on the cloth.

"Urvashi," Indra said again as he pushed himself upright before lurching to his feet.

"My lord," the apsara bowed her head.

"What took you so long?" Indra asked with a note of annoyance. "I was starting to wonder if it was the human king who had successfully seduced you, instead of the other way round." He laughed to make light of what he'd said, but since the others didn't seem to see any humour in it, he cleared his throat awkwardly. Taking a fumbling step in Urvashi's direction, he said, "Tell me you have brought us some good news. Tell me I wasn't wrong in thinking you would discover the Halahala's whereabouts."

"I… the human king found out who I was and why I was in his palace."

His hands on his hips, Indra peered at the apsara suspiciously. "What does that mean?"

"I was placed in confinement, my lord. I didn't get an opportunity to learn anything about the dagger."

Indra's face turned ugly with anger and disappointment. "What about when you seduced the king? He would have said *something*… made some reference…"

"I didn't get a chance," the apsara blurted in desperation.

"All these days in the palace, and you never got a chance? Not even *once*?" Indra frowned at Urvashi. "Could it be that you didn't make enough of an effort—"

"I did my best…" the apsara began, then stopped and looked away.

The deva scrutinized her. Then, reading her expression correctly, a look of disbelief coupled with contempt crossed his face. "Vikramaditya turned you down," he sneered. He looked at Takshaka and Narada. "The most desirable and irresistible of apsaras in all of Devaloka, and she fails at the *one* thing she is supposed to be adept at, the *one* thing that qualified her for the task she'd been entrusted." Indra cast a disdainful glance at Urvashi. "What good is an apsara if she can't tempt a man to fall into her arms, mad with passion?"

Feeling the weight of Narada and Takshaka's gaze, Urvashi's cheeks burned with shame and anger. "I tried my best, my lord," she mumbled, swallowing the hurt and humiliation.

"You fail to seduce the human king, and you manage to get

yourself caught and thrown into captivity. Well done," the deva threw his hands up in frustration. "You could have stayed in captivity instead of returning empty-handed, but I'm sure the thought didn't occur to you."

Aghast at the callousness, the apsara stared at Indra. Then, even though a tide of resentment was building inside her, she said, "I have not returned empty-handed. I have brought news for you. The human king is not in Ujjayini. He is at the frontier to fight a barbarian invasion."

"And how is this useful to me?" Indra cocked a critical eye at the apsara.

Urvashi was amazed she had to spell this out. "If the human king is at the frontier, there can be no Hellfires in Ujjayini, my lord."

Alerted to the opportunity that had come their way, the devas and the naga exchanged excited glances. "He would have taken the Hellfires with him, of course," Narada smiled genially.

"Even if he hasn't, there's no one in Ujjayini capable of wielding them." Takshaka rose from his place at the *chausar* board, the game already forgotten.

Indra stood erect, his eyes bright and purposeful, his movements free of the sluggishness that had afflicted him moments ago. "Any idea till when he is likely to be away at the frontier..." he asked Urvashi, his tone less surly, "...how much time we have?"

Urvashi shook her head.

Indra showed his displeasure at the apsara with a mild grimace. "We shall have to make do with what we know," he said, recovering. He faced Narada and Takshaka. "How long would it take to have a full force ready to leave for Sindhuvarta?"

Narada frowned. "Takshaka and his nagas are here already. It depends on who else you want for—"

"The Maruts, the nagas, Tribhanu's kinnaras... at least what remains of them," the deva lord interrupted. "All the deva regiments we can muster, including the Ashvins, who'll hopefully prove to be more courageous this time. Let us strike with such force that nothing remains of the human city once we're through."

"What about Manyu and me?" the diplomat asked. "And Agneyi and her fire-wraiths?"

"I need someone to protect Amaravati in case of an eventuality," Indra replied. "No, what I've asked for should be enough to crush that puny human kingdom."

"It will take a day to get everyone together," said Narada. "Perhaps more."

"Get going then," Indra said, snapping his fingers. "The sooner we're in, the sooner we can be out. We shouldn't be around when Vikramaditya comes back from the frontier." He turned to Takshaka. "You mentioned that the king's councilors..."

No longer listening to what was being said, Urvashi watched Narada leave the chamber. She then turned to stare at Indra and Takshaka, who were busy conferring. She looked at the bed, where the apsaras had slept through the conversation. It dawned on her that she had already been forgotten, dispensed with once she had served a purpose. She had not known what to expect when the deva had hurried her through the palace to meet Indra, but this wasn't how it was supposed to end.

Without a considerate word, without a gesture of gratitude, without thankfulness.

She wondered if she should mention the vyala attack on Ujjayini. She decided against it; they hadn't asked, so there was no need to say anything.

She turned and left the room. No one noticed her go.

***

"I am Khash'i Dur, chief of the *b'wo* Hunas. I offer you my friendship and the friendship of all the Huna tribes of this empty land. We are honoured to meet you, king of Avanti."

Bobbing his head in a token of acknowledgment, Vikramaditya appraised the scarred face in front of him. "A Huna fluent in the tongue of Avanti," he remarked. "Rare."

"I could say I learned the language of your land in anticipation of this meeting, but you'd know it for a lie," Khash'i Dur smiled. "I learned it to understand those I wished to rule."

Even a passing mention of the Hunas' original intent made the atmosphere turn cold, despite the mid-morning heat.

"Why the change of heart then?" the samrat asked. "Why this sudden offer of friendship?"

"Because of everything he told us about you," the chieftain said, gesturing at Kalidasa. Then, remembering something, he smacked his forehead with his palm. "But first, let mc introduce you to my brothers, the chiefs of the other Hunas tribes. *Shy'or* Ba'rh Taha, *shy'or* Gahvi'e and *shy'or* Are'zzh..." One by one, the three chieftains bowed to Vikramaditya. The eldest, a tall man with a flowing grey beard, spoke a few sentences, ending it with another bow.

"Brother Are'zzh says he remembers you having led an attack on his garrison," Khash'i Dur translated. "The garrison fell in half a day, and he says he never saw a better fighter than you." The chief smiled. "He's happy he will not be meeting you in battle again."

Vikramaditya glanced at Kalidasa, who inclined his head in confirmation.

"What did he tell you?" the king asked, nodding in the direction of the giant.

The chief of the Hunas drew a deep breath. Overhead, the sun blazed, and the heat beat down hard on the desert.

"He told us about the swords," Khash'i Dur pointed to the Hellfires with an expression of awe. "What they are capable of doing, how they came into your possession, and what it means to be the one who can wield them. He then told us about the Ancient God who has charged you with protecting the dagger." The chief looked at the king in wonder. "It's not every day that the gods seek the help of humans. That and the swords prove you are special and unique and... *blessed*." He bowed again, and though the other *shy'ors* didn't understand a word, they bowed as well.

"He also told us about how you found him as a child and took him to your palace, where you grew to become the best of friends," Khash'i Dur continued. "He told us about your other councilor... the girl whose father is a traitor."

"*Was* a traitor," the king said. "His crimes are behind him, and he has made amends."

The chieftain spread his arms and smiled. "Like you say, he was a traitor. But you spared his life for the sake of the young daughter. Later, you made her a councilor. What you did for Thra'akha and that girl tell us that apart from being a brave warrior, you are a kind and fair human being. That is rarer and even more unique in this world."

"But instead of being rewarded for all this, you only suffer. Your city has been ravaged, your kingdom is besieged, your enemies abound—so much so that Thra'akha feared sharing his plan to come here and seek our help with anyone in the palace, lest the word spread, and someone tried to stop him."

Vikramaditya's gaze went to Kalidasa. The giant studied his hands and said nothing.

"Thra'akha told us about the queen and your love for her, and how you refused to accept an offer to cure her in exchange of the dagger." Khash'i Dur's expression softened. "It requires great courage not to bend for the ones we care the most about. He told us what you have been put through, and he appealed to us to change our minds about attacking Sindhuvarta. He told us that we should be aiding you in your battles to protect the dagger instead."

The samrat glanced at Kalidasa again, who looked away self-consciously.

The chief looked back at his army in the desert. "The truth is that we don't want to face you and your swords in battle," he continued. "If what Thra'akha says is true—and we have no reason to disbelieve him—we probably won't be around to speak of it if we fought you. Yet, it is equally true that you are in need of allies, and we can be of assistance to you." Pointing at the other *shy'ors*, he said. "My brothers and I hardly took any time to arrive at a decision, good king. Here we are, at your service."

"Your gesture of help is greatly appreciated," Vikramaditya inclined his head. "But to come this far and commit yourselves to a fight that is not yours is not reasonable, unless you are getting something in exchange." He looked shrewdly from face to face.

"I made an offer that I think the throne is in a position to honour," Kalidasa said softly.

The king raised his eyebrows, saying nothing, waiting. However, before Kalidasa could add anything, Khash'i Dur intervened.

"It is plain to me that you are a fair man with a strong sense of justice, so let us discuss the merits of what we hope you will grant us at a more opportune time. What matters is that we are here to assist against your enemies. This Huna army is now yours to command."

"My enemies are the formidable and godlike devas and asuras," the samrat said. "I mean no disrespect to your able warriors, but I don't know how much they can help."

With a sweep of an arm that seemed to encompass half the burning desert, Khash'i Dur said, "You forget the *yah'bre*."

"The what?"

"The *yah'bre*," the chief repeated, pointing to the looming dust giants. "Brought to life from the depths of hell by our *droiba*."

"*Droiba*?" Vikramaditya stared.

"Yes, our priest. He is a powerful man—"

"I know," the samrat interrupted. "You have a *droiba* here with you?"

"Yes," Khash'i Dur looked surprised.

"Take me to him, now." The king's eyes shone with intensity. "I think he can help me."

Shalivahana

Shukracharya's brow was a jumble of lines and furrows knotted in concentration as he stared at the bones lying scattered on the mandala. His eye darted from one bone to the next, deciphering what they collectively said. Dissatisfied, he scooped the pieces up and dropped them back down with a clatter, gleaning information from them.

The high priest sat hunched over the mandala for a long time. Then, with one final roll of the bones, he stood up and left the room in a rush, leaving the bones where they were.

He hurried through the corridors of the palace, which were abuzz with preparations for the assault on Avanti. Asura minions ran from forges with their arms loaded with javelins and barbed pikes; grim asura warriors in armour fell into formation beside enormous *ekashringas*, the war rhinos' backs black with plate armour, their one-horned heads swaying in impatience; mutant war mahishas pranced around courtyards bearing huge axes, while drummers beat a militant rhythm on large *bheris* festooned with auspicious marigold garlands.

Weaving through the crowds, Shukracharya arrived at the chambers of the lords of Patala. He searched through the rooms until he came upon the brothers engaged in heated discussion. Seeing the high priest come through the door, Hiranyaksha turned to him.

"We need your advice, mahaguru. We can't agree over what is better; brother going into the king's palace by himself, or both of us going in. In my opinion—"

"You're not going to the human city, Hiranyaksha," the high priest interrupted. "Your brother and Holika will lead the asuras."

"But why, mahaguru?" Hiranyaksha stared at Shukracharya, astounded.

"Because the bones have just revealed that the human king and his estranged councilor have renewed their friendship." The high priest glared angrily. "It turns out that the councilor was never against the king. He had everyone fooled, including me."

The asura lords looked at one another in bewilderment.

"It doesn't matter," Shukracharya said. "What's important is that the king and the councilor are together, and they are heading back to Ujjayini with a massive army of barbarians."

"And we have to be afraid of them?" Hiranyakashipu raised an eyebrow in disdain. "A king, an additional councilor and a few barbarian warriors?"

"We have to be wary of them, yes," said the high priest. "The councilor, in particular."

"Why?"

"The Nine Pearls. Remember, each councilor represents one pearl..." Seeing the asuras nod, Shukracharya sighed. "By driving the councilors apart, I had weakened the power of the Nine Pearls, but with the councilors slowly uniting again, the pearls will exert their influences over each other and their powers will multiply. Then it will become impossible to defeat the king's councilors." He stared at the brothers. "We cannot let that happen."

"The pearls must stay separated," said Hiranyaksha with a slow nod of realization.

"Yes. By keeping even one pearl away, we can prevent the rest of the pearls from becoming too powerful. That's why, while the rest of us head for Ujjayini, you will take an army to stop Vikramaditya and his councilor."

Shukracharya's gaze pierced Hiranyaksha.

"Stop them," he repeated. "Nothing must come in Hiranyakashipu's way. *Nothing*."

***

"It is so parched out in the desert that even hope shrivels and dies, Vikrama."

Kalidasa sat cross-legged on the hard ground, cradling a big bowl of pumpkin and lentil gruel and staring into the fire, watching the flames dance in the early evening breeze. "I have been at its centre, in villages and towns three or four days' ride from the frontier," he continued. "It is the same everywhere. Dry, hot, barren. Nothing grows in that soil, and water is so scarce, people are willing to kill for it. But here," he spread his hands, "this side of the Arbudas, things are the exact opposite. The land is fertile, water is plentiful." The giant paused and looked at the king. "Is it fair that some have so much, while others have so little?"

Vikramaditya, sitting across the fire from Kalidasa, a bowl in his hands as well, did not reply. Instead, he let his gaze wander over the armies of Avanti and the Hunas, camped next to one another in the scrub-laden plains east of Sristhali. Cooking fires dotted the slowly darkening landscape as the men settled down to an early dinner and a few hours of rest, their horses nibbling on the sparse grass nearby. Cautious interaction had started between the two sides, mostly over subjects of common interest: horses—the warriors all being horsemen—weapons, and now, food. The Hunas, the samrat noted by the size of the two camps, outnumbered the soldiers from Avanti and the Anartas by a substantial margin.

Earlier in the day, the king's impulsive decision to meet the *droiba* had triggered panic among Avanti's troops, and it wasn't until Atulyateja explained the turn of events to an incredulous audience that calm was restored in the mountains. Later, eyes popped at the sight of Kalidasa riding into camp with the samrat, and word travelled at the speed of lightning, so every soldier for miles knew the Hunas had made a friendly overture, and that Kalidasa was no longer to be treated as a traitor.

Calling all horsemen within hailing distance to assemble, Vikramaditya had announced that they—Avanti's riders and the Huna horsemen—would be riding hard all the way back to Ujjayini to help the beleaguered city. The king had also announced that a Huna priest would come with them, though he didn't explain why. The combined force left after a quick lunch, thundering eastward and away from the frontier, so that a curtain of dust rose into the air, blocking them from the infantrymen and archers whom they had left behind in the Arbudas.

"The Hunas are desperate to lead a life that isn't a daily struggle for survival," the giant continued, seeing that Vikramaditya wasn't about to say anything. "The desert wouldn't allow that, so they crossed the Arbudas in search of a better life. But the older kingdoms of Sindhuvarta didn't want to share what they had so much of, what they didn't even *need*. So, the Hunas learned to take what they wanted by force."

"By murdering innocent men, women and children," the samrat spoke at last, levelly.

"In every war, on every side, it is the innocent who die in the greatest numbers."

The king said nothing.

"Even as we sit here speaking, innocent men, women and children are dying of thirst in the desert, while the kingdoms of Sindhuvarta have more land and water than they can use." A bitter smile twisted Kalidasa's lips. "Just because those innocents aren't dying by the sword doesn't mean their blood is not on somebody's hands, Vikrama."

Vikramaditya nodded quietly.

"I am not defending the Hunas, I am not condoning their past brutalities, I am not taking their side," the giant appealed to the king. "I cannot, because although I am one of *them* by birth, I am one of *us* by upbringing. I am *both*. What I am trying to do is take who I am and bridge the gap between the two sides, show how both can coexist."

"I understand," the samrat said.

"Sindhuvarta has vast tracts of vacant land that is ideal for farming," the giant said. "It is land that none of the kingdoms need. The Hunas could settle there and live in harmony with the rest of us. They'd have the land that they want, they would owe their loyalty to Avanti, and the kingdoms of Sindhuvarta could stop living in constant fear of an invasion."

"I see your point, but all the kingdoms of Sindhuvarta have to agree before we can take any decision," the king replied. "Remember, I have to carry all our allies along." He paused and added, "I think Khash'i Dur understands this."

Kalidasa nodded. For a moment, they sat in the gathering twilight, watching the sparks rise from the fire.

"Why didn't you tell me about your plan to strike a truce with the Hunas?" the samrat asked.

"The palace was a dangerous place, and I believed no one could be trusted," the giant replied. "The Healer... he'd been playing a game. He was manipulating us in different ways. I sensed he was intent of driving us apart, so when it occurred to me to cross into the desert to seek the help of the Hunas, I decided to play along and make it appear as if I had gone for good. The hope was that he, or whoever else was watching us, would believe their ploy had worked, and Avanti had been weakened." His face fell and he gave his head a regretful shake. "I had no idea my going away would really weaken Avanti and take it to the brink of a rebellion."

"Vararuchi took your departure very badly. He thought I had compromised Avanti's safety by letting you go over to the enemy. Had I known your real purpose, I could have told him in private and set his mind at rest."

"I am sorry, brother," Kalidasa looked dismayed. "I didn't know who had infiltrated the palace, and I didn't want anyone learning about my plan, even by accident. What two people know is not a secret. But if I had known things would turn ugly with Vararuchi—"

"It's alright," said Vikramaditya, thinking of Vismaya's impersonator and Urvashi in the role of a palace maid. He wondered if there were more deva or asura spies skulking in the palace. "What happened is probably for the best, and Vararuchi is back in the council..."

"I still owe him an apology," Kalidasa said.

A few moments later, he turned to look at Vikramaditya. "Did you really believe I had turned my back on you, that I would never return to your side?"

The samrat considered the question. "One can never be sure, but there was something you did that never quite fitted with your anger at Avanti for what had happened to you all those years ago. Sure, your performance in the Throne Room that day was very convincing—except for one little thing."

"What was that?" asked Kalidasa.

"Remember your councilor's medallion?"

"Yes. I broke it off."

"And?"

"And what? I gave it to you."

"Right. You were furious at what had happened to your

family, you blamed the throne for the injustice, you despised the throne… yet, after breaking off the medallion, you bent and placed it gently on the floor between us. Given your outrage, the natural reaction would have been to fling the hated symbol of Avanti to the ground. Instead, there was loving care and respect in your action, which was completely at odds with everything else you were saying. Whenever I went back to that moment, I felt there was more to what had happened that day." The samrat paused and smiled. "That is probably why I walked into the desert this morning, even though you were the enemy. You could say you gave yourself away without any of us noticing."

"I could never make myself throw that medallion to the ground," the giant replied, chuckling. "Amazing that you noticed such a small thing."

"It's not a small thing," Vikramaditya replied. "It is what marks the truly loyal apart."

"I am sorry for everything," Kalidasa said again, his eyes moist. "Had I shared my plan with you, you needn't have come this far to the frontier, and you could have been with Vishakha right now…"

"You did what you thought was right," the king replied. "Who knows, I might not have agreed to let you risk the journey into the Great Desert. And even if I had, I might still have had to come, had you failed to convince Khash'i Dur and the others. You averted an invasion that would have cost many lives and drained Sindhuvarta's resources. You did well, brother."

The samrat paused, and as an afterthought, added, "You helped get us the *droiba*."

The sound of approaching footsteps made them turn.

"Mind if I join you?" asked Khash'i Dur.

"Not at all," said Vikramaditya, pointing to an empty spot by the fire. "Have you eaten?"

"Yes," the *shy'or* said, running a hand over his stomach. He looked around and smiled. "A week ago, who'd have thought this possible… your men and ours, eating together in peace."

The king inclined his head.

The chieftain squatted. Following a moment's silence, he looked at Vikramaditya. "I regret the young prince's kidnapping. The Sakas never told us they had taken him captive. Had we known…" he broke off. Then, sounding hopeful, he said, "But the Sakas have been informed we're no longer going to war against Avanti, so they've probably let him go."

Vikramaditya sighed deeply and nodded. The fire crackled in the still air.

Khash'i Dur glanced at Kalidasa before turning back to the samrat. "I've been told that you aren't informing your palace about us becoming friends." Seeing the king nod, he looked mystified. "Why not? A Huna army is riding towards your city. The palace shouldn't misunderstand and order your troops to attack us—"

"They won't," Vikramaditya assured him. "I shall send them the news of our truce when we are much closer to Ujjayini. In the meantime, Commander Atulyateja has informed the outlying garrisons, so they won't feel threatened by reports of this army."

"Pardon my asking, but why not tell the palace *now*?"

"Because, as Kalidasa had rightly feared, there may be deva or asura spies in my palace. Two were exposed just this week. I do not want anyone to learn about our plan until it is too late to hinder us. The longer we delay in informing my palace, the less time our enemies will have to react."

"Makes sense," the chieftain agreed.

"This plan of yours…" Kalidasa eyed Vikramaditya over the fire, "…sounds very risky."

"I can't think of a better one. Can you?"

Kalidasa looked away, then back at his old friend. "Will it work?"

"*One* opportunity is all we will get, so we will *have to* make it work."

Khash'i Dur and Kalidasa exchanged ominous glances.

"Even that window of opportunity is closing very rapidly." Cracking his knuckles, the samrat stared into the fire. "We are running out of time, and I have to get to Ujjayini as quickly as possible." He looked at his companions with troubled eyes. "The slightest delay could seal the fate of Avanti forever."

***

A rectangle of lightning flashed in the barred window, a bright stutter illuminating the tree swaying in the thunderstorm outside. The lightning also lit up the rain driving down, so for one suspended moment, the drops were scintillas of light, dazzling like diamonds. Then it was dark again, and what remained was the after-image of window and lightning, and some leftover light for Shanku to make out the faint outline of Greeshma.

"Are you sure you can do this?" The bandit's words nearly drowned in a crash of thunder.

Shanku had lost count of the number of times Greeshma had posed the same question. She nodded before realizing the bandit couldn't see her well enough in the dark. "Yes."

"Even in this rain?"

That was a stupid question.

Yes, she was banking on the fact that she could find her way about in the dark. She had been working on it over the last two nights, using her powers to slip out of captivity and get onto the tree outside, and from there into the compound, then willing herself to flit from the shadow of one structure to the next, from thatched overhang to spreading tree, disappearing here and appearing there, chalking her way slowly around Janasthana while staying concealed from any danavas who might be keeping a watch. She had spent her first outing familiarizing herself with the city, while the second night's focus had been learning to access Shalivahana's palace—easily identifiable by its size and prominence. However, on neither occasion had it rained the way it was now, so she had no way of answering whether she could find her way in the rain. Stupid question, so Shanku ignored it.

"I should go," she said instead.

She thought the bandit nodded his head. "You've got the knife, right?" he asked.

Shanku gripped the dagger she had nicked from a sleeping guard the night before, its contoured hilt smooth and cool against her palm. "Yes," she said, stepping under the window, so raindrops pelted down on her upturned face. "Okay, I'll see you."

"Be careful," she heard Greeshma say. "Don't take the—"

The bandit's words were plucked away abruptly as the councilor's vision tilted and sped upward, through the bars and out of the window in a blur… and Shanku found herself balanced on the branch she had been aiming to land on. She had not accounted for the wind and the rain gusting against her small body, so she was forced to grab the tree's broad trunk for support. She had barely gained stability when she felt the knife slip from her wet grasp—and before she could do a thing about it, the blade fell, struck and bounced off one of the tree's lower branches, before disappearing into the darkness.

Cursing, the girl stared where she thought she had last seen the sliver of the dagger. She could get down and search… but darkness was starker in the interplay between lightning and tree shadow, and there was no point in looking for the knife, she realized. She had barely set out on her mission, and things had already started to slide. Cursing again and blinking to get the water out of her eyes, the councilor took her bearings. To her right was a narrow building that she recognized as a storehouse of some sort, and in another lurching mind-leap, she vanished from the branch and materialized under the building's awning.

On her first night out itself, Shanku had had the option of tracking down the five soldiers whom the danavas had captured with Greeshma and her, but she had put the idea aside as a waste of time. She had only the nights to explore Janasthana without being spotted, and looking for a way to Shalivahana was the priority. Locating the men—she hoped they were still alive—would serve no purpose unless she was able to free them, which she couldn't do. What she could do was find Shalivahana...

Sheltering against the rain—she was drenched already, her hair hanging in clumps and sticking to her face and neck—the councilor stood on tiptoe to get a better view of the buildings across the street. The road itself was churning with rainwater, but the storm was keeping the danavas indoors, which was good. In a wink, she was at the other end of the street, and a moment later, she appeared under a distant doorway, further along the road.

The rain impaired visibility, but because Shanku was relying on her sense of direction and didn't need to see every single step of the way, she navigated the route to the palace with relative ease. Getting in and finding Shalivahana wouldn't be as simple, she knew; the palace was better guarded, and she had no idea where she could start looking for the danava lord once she was inside.

The palace was an imposing structure, its central tower rearing into the lightning-lit sky like a dire omen. Moving with the stealth of a cat, the councilor crept through a thicket of trees, locating herself before propelling her mind-body onto a distant roof. She landed square, perfectly balanced despite the rain and the tricky slope of the roof, but even as she was congratulating herself, the sky behind her lit up with lightning.

And in its staccato brilliance, below her on the ground, she saw a danava guard look up in her direction, drawn by the lightning. The danava's expression changed when he noticed her silhouetted against the sky—and the next instant, Shanku saw him dissolve into a familiar oil-black mass.

The lightning died, and darkness took back possession of the roof and the ground below.

The girl felt something wet and slimy slither around her upper arm, grabbing her.

Throttling the scream that was building in her throat, the councilor mind-hauled herself from the roof, tearing away from what was trying to nab her, blitzing through the rain, vanishing in the dark and reappearing on an inner verandah on the palace's second floor, overlooking an open courtyard. As her vision stabilized, the girl registered rain beating down on the roof, and in the flashes of lightning, she saw water cascading into the courtyard.

She also saw more oil-black shapes spill into the courtyard, searching for her, and over the rain, she heard a multitude of voiceless whispers, sounding like dry leaves blowing in the wind.

Shanku pressed herself to the wall, her heart pounding frantically. She felt her arm where the slimy appendage had held her. She shivered. She had been seen; an alarm had been raised.

Sticking to the shadows where the lightning couldn't expose her, the councilor edged along the verandah and slipped into a passageway, trying to ascertain where she was. The whispers ebbed and flowed, now loud and somewhere nearby, then fading. It struck Shanku that the oil-black forms could also conceal themselves in the shadows, waiting to catch her—

Something latched onto her shoulder. The girl screamed. A cold hand gripped her wrist.

Wrenching herself free, Shanku mind-leaped. She had no idea where she was going, but that didn't really matter anymore as the danavas were on to her. So, casting caution to the winds, she went where she pleased in an erratic, random hunt for Shalivahana. A dark and empty hallway emerged around her that she hurtled through; another empty room, then one full of oil-black shapes that sensed her and gave chase. She mind-leaped into open air, and a splash of lightning showed she was over a rooftop, in a vertiginous fall, the oil-black shapes in hot pursuit...

...and she was exploding through a window, into another dark room.

Another blinding flash of lightning, followed by a crack and roll of thunder that shook the ground under the councilor's feet.

In the light of that flash, a tall figure standing by another window.

Also, in the light of that flash, the tall figure turning... a sword in its hand.

Finally, in the light of that same flash, a dagger in its sheath on a table by Shanku's side.

The oil-black forms burst in after her.

Without wasting a moment, the councilor snatched the dagger, pulling it free of its sheath.

The oil black shapes were close behind, reaching for her.

The figure in front was turning fast now, the sword coming up in an arc towards her.

Shanku mind-leaped, squeezing past the curving blade and sliding in close to the figure. The dagger went under the figure's chin, its point pushing into the figure's throat...

Pressing hard.

Pressing harder.

"Drop the sword," Shanku hissed. And louder, over her shoulder, "You all... get back."

The sword fell to the floor with a heavy clatter. The forms hung back.

"Take me to your lord," she snapped at her hostage.

"You are very good," the figure replied in a voice that sounded like the creak of old branches when the wind sighed in the trees. "You got the better of me."

"Take me to your lord *now*," the councilor insisted. "I won't hesitate to kill."

"You won't kill me. That's not why you are here."

The councilor hesitated, wondering what that meant.

"We know you are not here to do us harm. You have come to seek help for your king, who is protecting the Halahala from the mighty devas and asuras."

Shanku stared at the figure in astonishment, trying to make out its features. "You know all this?"

"Yes. We were watching you from the day you set foot in the Dandaka. If we'd thought you posed us a threat, none of you would have made it so far."

"Why not meet me sooner then? Why the hostility; why were we treated like prisoners? One of my men was killed by—"

"All the men who came with you are alive." Lightning flashed, and the girl got a glimpse of a scarred face, bearded with black-green moss. A crown of thorns rested on the figure's head. "And I apologize for the shabby treatment, but it was a test—to see if you were worthy of our help."

The councilor paused to think about this. "Who are you?"

"The one for whom you've come all this way. I am Shalivahana, lord of the danavas."

Shanku eased the pressure on the dagger and stepped back from the danava. As another bolt of lightning struck close, followed by an ear-splitting crash of thunder, she flipped the dagger around, so it lay across her palms, open and non-threatening.

"Salutations," she said as the thunder rumbled and subsided. "I am Shankubala, councilor in the court of Samrat Vikramaditya. I apologize for intruding like this, but I had no choice, as I had to find a way—"

"I know," said the danava, accepting the dagger. "Things were designed with the purpose of getting you to display initiative. Either you devise a way of reaching me, or you end up being a prisoner in Janasthana for the rest of your life. I see no point in helping those who will not strive to help themselves."

"So, are we worthy of your help, lord?"

Lightning still flashed, but the thunder was receding. The storm had lost its edge too, settling into a steady downpour.

Shalivahana considered the girl, a smile creasing his mossy beard. "You have proved yourself very worthy and earned the respect of the danavas, Shankubala. We will help your king."

***

Rain fell in a silent drizzle, forming soft concentric circles on the water where the reeds grew, close to the riverbank, and away from the swift currents of the Yamuna. The barge eased out of the darkness, pushing past the reeds and breaking the patterns of the rain's ripples, before bumping against the bank. The bargeman manoeuvred the vessel around lengthwise, then called over his shoulder in a low voice.

"We've reached."

Balancing themselves delicately on the gently rocking barge, three figures disembarked. All three had shawls pulled low over their faces to keep out the rain—and keep their identities concealed. Once they were on firm land, one of them produced a small lamp and lit it. As the barge pulled away, the three began their trek, walking single file through the rain and dark, leaving the river behind.

The ground rose sharply as they walked, so they were all a

little out of breath when they finally crested the rise and found themselves in a small copse of *ashoka* trees. They had still to recover fully when, all of a sudden, a voice came from the dark.

"Stay where you are. You are surrounded. Don't run."

More shadowy figures stepped out from behind the trees, while men rose from the sides of the path that the travellers had just taken from the river. Torches were lit, swords and spears glinting in their light. The three travellers counted ten to twelve men spread around them.

"Take your shawls off," one of the men commanded with a wave of his sword. "Now."

The three men threw their shawls off, baring their heads.

"Hold up your hands."

The three complied.

The man giving orders approached them with a torch. He sported the turban of a captain of the Magadhan army. Running a watchful eye over the travellers, he nodded, satisfied.

"They are unarmed, your honour," he called out.

Another figure stepped out of the darkness. Shoorasena.

Walking up to the travellers, hands on his hips, the king glared at the three middle-aged men.

"Which one of you is Gajaketu?" he snapped.

The travellers looked at one another, mystified. "You are mistaken, sir," said one. "We don't know of any Gajaketu—"

"Do you take me for a fool?" Shoorasena sneered. "You come to Pandara by boat under cover of night, you act all mysterious in your shawls, you're obviously in a hurry to get somewhere... but you don't know Gajaketu?"

The three men again exchanged glances. "We are traders who missed our boat—"

"Stop," Shoorasena growled, drawing his sword. "You have one chance to tell me which of you is Gajaketu. Otherwise, all three of you die right now."

The travellers looked at the cordon of soldiers, and then at each other a third time. Then, one of them took a step forward, his face pale with fear.

"Your honour, please let me go," he entreated. "I was forced into this. I had no intention of creating any trouble for you—"

"*You* are Gajaketu?" asked Shoorasena, lifting his sword.

"I am just a soldier of Kosala," the man blurted. He pointed to one of his co-travellers. "*That* is Gajaketu."

Shoorasena spun towards the man who had been indicated. "You?"

The man took a hurried step back. Turning, he tried to break through the ring of soldiers.

It was futile. He was immediately grabbed and held.

"Help," he shouted, squirming and staring into the surrounding darkness. "Help us."

"Quit shouting," said Shoorasena, approaching the man. "No one is going to help you."

"Please... I am sorry, I will go away..." the man babbled. "Let me go, please... *Help*..."

"Shhh..." the king put his finger on his lips and waited for the man to quieten. "Regret," he said, speaking into the silence, "is never a dependable friend. It invariably arrives late, and hardly ever rescues anyone from trouble. Don't waste your breath regretting and whining that you're sorry. It will be of absolutely no use." Shoorasena paused, his expression hard in the torchlight. "You shouldn't have agreed to come here. You shouldn't have mentioned a thing about that morning to anyone, for that matter. None of this would have happened had you just kept quiet; we could all have carried on with our lives peacefully. But no... you had to be a hero."

"Help," the man squeaked in terror. "Please don't hurt me... please..."

"Quiet," Shoorasena admonished. "What choice do I have...?"

"No... please, no..." The man was thrashing about.

"If you stay alive, you will spread your story, and there will always be people to listen."

"*Help...*"

"Shut up," the king growled. "No help is coming. This is where you die, understand? No one saw you arrive. No one knows where you are, so no one will know what happened to you... Your story will die with you—"

"*Shoorasena.*"

The king turned. "Who is—"

A rush of feet from all directions, accompanied by orders that weapons be dropped. The men with the king turned, spears and swords now pointed outward at the darkness.

"You are surrounded, captain," a voice called out. "Put your weapons down."

"What is the meaning of this?" Shoorasena asked, enraged.

As more torches were lit, it became apparent that the copse was crammed with soldiers. Half-a-dozen men pushed their way through to the front.

"What is all this?" Shoorasena thundered, putting up a show of defiance that didn't reflect in his eyes, as he scanned the faces of the newcomers. "I will not tolerate such—"

"Please drop your sword," Commander Shirsa said heavily.

The king stared at the large man with the mop of iron-grey hair. "Have you lost—"

"Enough, Shoorasena," said Councilor Ashrava. "We heard you admit to the killing of King Siddhasena on the palace steps—"

"I did not say anything of the sort... Captain, arrest the councilor..."

The captain dropped his sword, and his men did likewise.

"Fools," Shoorasena yelled. "I will..." he turned to Ashrava. "The musician is lying."

"Yes, he is," the councilor agreed.

The king blinked in confusion. "Then why—"

"He is lying because he isn't Gajaketu, just as these two aren't soldiers of Kosala," Ashrava said. "They are actors whose job was to get you to confess to the killing. It was all a part of Asmabindu's plan to expose you. This whole story about Gajaketu coming here was a trap to get you to incriminate yourself."

"What are you talking about?" Shoorasena bristled.

"Commander Shirsa told you about Kosala trying to smuggle Gajaketu into Magadha," said Ashrava. "What any king would have done is to get Gajaketu arrested and try him for treason against the crown. But *you* did not want him arrested, because *you* did not want the people of Magadha to hear what he has to say. Didn't you just say, 'Your story will die with you'? You tried to have him killed instead, so that the truth would end with him."

"You conspired against me," Shoorasena cast a bitter, venomous glance at the men in front of him. "I shall have this council suspended and all of you—"

"You conspired against our beloved king, Siddhasena," Ashrava interrupted. "The council of Magadha strips you of your powers as king and places—"

Shoorasena launched himself at Ashrava with a roar, but Shirsa and his men were prepared. They parried his attack, surrounding him. "Drop your sword," the commander repeated.

The sword fell to the earth with a dull thud.

"This council strips you of your powers and places you under arrest for the murder of King Siddhasena... and for the attempted murder of Councilor Ashrava."

The king hung his head in dejection as Shirsa's men took him by the arms to lead him away.

"Asmabindu, *that rat*," Shoorasena spat the words at Ashrava. "Do you know he was the one who gave Uttama, Diganta, Bhaskara and Pallavan away? Betrayed them so he could become the governor of Vanga?"

"I know. He is already under arrest."

Shoorasena stared in surprise.

"Once I realized that Pallavan and the others had been betrayed, I traced the captain who had made the arrests at Uttama's mansion. I asked him who all had been there at the time of the arrests." Ashrava looked at Shoorasena in the torchlight. "He mentioned *five* names, but only *four* had died—while the fifth was walking around Girivraja, a free man. And that man had earlier lied to me that he'd been by his sick wife's side the night of the arrests." The councilor turned to leave, then looked back. "The two of you could end up as neighbours in the palace dungeons."

***

Amara Simha's eyes opened. Asleep to awake in an instant, he blinked, adjusting to the dark.

He wondered at the sound that had awakened him. Something that—

There. A faint clink of metal.

Taking care not to make a noise, he turned his bulky frame so he could see behind him. The sound had come from the direction of the trees bordering the riverbank along which the group had encamped for the night.

But for the horses tied under the trees, the councilor saw nothing at first. Then, continuing to observe, he spied a figure moving furtively between the horses.

Amara Simha was on his stomach now, his right hand around the hilt of the short sword that he kept handy, his left braced on the ground so he could spring to his feet. He wondered if it could be horse thieves, though that seemed unlikely—horse thieves kept their distance from military units, and theirs was a fairly large one. Which was why they hadn't set a watch in the first place, thinking it unnecessary so deep inside Avanti's territory.

He was still deciding whether to raise an alarm—or go over and check for himself—when the figure emerged from the trees, leading a horse by the bridle. The councilor rose to a crouch with the intent of accosting the figure when the man's gait struck him as familiar. He paused and sank back to the ground, following the man with his eyes.

The man led the horse up the slope of the riverbank, keeping to the grass to dampen the sound of the hooves. Amara Simha waited for the man to reach the top of the knoll before getting to his feet and darting off in pursuit, staying in the shadows, so he couldn't be seen if the figure turned back to look. Arriving at the point where the riverbank joined the road, the councilor ducked behind a thick tree and poked his head out carefully.

The figure stood barely fifteen paces away, tightening the saddle's straps.

Amara Simha waited, debating whether or not to reveal himself.

The man finally got on the horse and flicked the reins. Amara Simha watched the beast amble away, knowing where it was headed.

It wasn't until the rider had disappeared from view that the councilor plodded wearily back to camp. Stepping between slumbering soldiers, he headed for the spot where Ghatakarpara had spread his bed after the evening's meal. There was enough starlight to make out the prince's sleeping form, lying on a straw mat under a thick cotton quilt.

Squatting beside the bed, Amara Simha peeled the quilt back, knowing he wouldn't find the prince wrapped in its folds. He was right. The quilt had been cleverly rolled up and placed in position, so it looked as if someone was under it.

The brawny councilor heaved a sigh and straightened, pained by Ghatakarpara's surreptitious departure.

Ahi

He sat by the window of the tavern, nursing a cup of weak firewater and looking out at the scale of destruction in absolute amazement.

This couldn't be the outcome of what the kinnaras had done, he thought to himself. Yes, the kinnaras had set parts of the city ablaze, he remembered, but they could not have achieved the level of incineration he had seen since his arrival in Ujjayini earlier that morning. Entire neighbourhoods had been charred and reduced to ashes, and there were hardly any structures standing that had not been touched by fire. This was a burning that was an end in itself, whereas the kinnaras had only been interested in drawing the humans out of the palace so he could look for the Halahala; a plan that had worked fine until the real Hellfires had… *No.*

Matali shook his head to clear his mind of the Hellfires.

Take these with you, so they can remind you of your uselessness, and that you still have a penalty to pay for letting Devaloka down.

Indra's injunction rang like a curse in Matali's ears. The thought of the swords never left him; it haunted him, reminding him of his incompetence and his failure, a failure that he was eager to correct, which was why he had returned to Ujjayini without anyone in Devaloka knowing of it. Desperate to win his master's favour, the deva's aim was to do something unexpected—like finding the dagger, and if that was impossible, finding the real Hellfires, or getting a vital piece of information that the devas could use. He was determined to prove his usefulness and earn Indra's pardon...

"Move to the corner, old man," a voice snapped.

Glancing up, Matali saw four soldiers of the Watch standing by the long table where he sat, glaring at him. Soldiers of the City Watch, the deva thought to himself—*perfect.*

"You're taking up too much space," one soldier said with an impatient wave of his hand.

"Sorry," he said in a raspy voice, scuttling along the bench while pretending that all his joints hurt with age.

The men sat down. The leader rapped on the table to get the keeper's attention. "Four."

Sipping his drink, Matali studied the men. He had considered posing as a Palace Guard or a soldier of the Watch for easier access to the palace, but the risk of being found out was high, as he'd already learned. So, he had plumped for anonymity instead. He had no idea who the old man had been; he had found him gathering firewood in a small forest to Ujjayini's north. After slipping on the man's face, he had hidden the body under a fallen tree in the hope that the man wouldn't be missed, and that wild animals would find him before anyone else did.

And because he couldn't get an entry into the palace, he had come to the next best place for information, a place where tongues loosened easily, where a lot could be learned if one knew how to separate the truth from exaggeration...

The keeper served the men, who downed the contents of their cups at one go.

"Why is this so thin?" the leader looked at his cup with distaste. "All water, no fire."

"Supply is short, sir," the keeper answered with a helpless shrug. "Three local breweries were burned to nothing."

"So, you add more water, but charge the same rates?" the leader grunted. "Four more."

Matali waited until the men were halfway through the second round. "I can't believe this has happened," he said to the man seated next to him, pointing at the window.

"Mmm-hmm," the soldier said, mildly intoxicated and not interested in an old drunk.

"Don't mind my asking, sir, but how did all this happen?"

The soldier stared. "You don't know?" He turned to his mates. "This chap doesn't know what happened to the city."

Three heads peered at Matali curiously. "Where have you been all this while, old man?" the leader asked.

"I was away," the deva was intentionally vague. "Someone told me about some horsemen. Horsemen who were part-horses. They said the horsemen burned everything."

"The horsemen burned *some* portions, but it was the flying beasts that burned everything."

Flying beasts?

"The horsemen were flying?" Matali asked drunken-stupidly.

"Pshaw," the leader tossed his head in exasperation. "These flying beasts are different... like birds, but with five heads. More dangerous than the horsemen, who mostly died..."

The deva nearly sat up in surprise. Like birds, but with five heads meant only one thing—*the vyalas*. That clearly explained the scorching. It also meant that the asuras had been here. The big question was, had they claimed the dagger?

"What happened to the flying beasts?" he croaked. "Did we drive them away?"

The soldiers exchanged gloomy glances that made Matali's stomach knot up in anxiety.

"We wouldn't have made it alive if the yakshas hadn't arrived in time to save us."

Yakshas.

Matali was dumbstruck for a moment. "The beasts were defeated by yakshas?"

"Drove them back wherever they'd come from," the soldier next to him nodded in relief.

"It is good to know the yakshas are around to help if the need arises," the keeper chipped in, plonking a third round of firewater for the soldiers.

"The yakshas are still here?" Seeing the soldiers and the tavern keeper nod, and remembering he was putting on an act, the deva raised his cup. "Thank god for that."

"Thank god, indeed," the keeper said. He pointed at Matali's cup. "You want that refilled?"

"No," said the deva, draining his drink. "I have to meet someone. I should be going."

The asuras had attacked with a force of vyalas, but the yakshas had somehow come into the picture and rescued the city. The yakshas had stayed back, which could mean anything. But as the asuras probably knew this, Indra too had to be informed...

"—am less worried that the Samrat is not in Ujjayini," one of the soldiers was saying.

The deva tensed, an ear on the conversation.

"Absolutely," another agreed. "The Samrat can tackle the savages at the frontier while the yakshas help the council protect the city."

The human king was at the frontier and not in Ujjayini.

Matali could feel his exhilaration mount as he hurried out of the tavern. He had to get back to Devaloka quickly. *No king meant no Hellfires*. Forget the vyalas and the yakshas; *this* was news that could win him back Indra's respect and help him reclaim lost prestige...

Walking down twisting alleyways smeared with soot and ash, past empty shells of shops and homes, the smell of burned and wet debris in his nostrils, the deva chanced to look at the sky, which had been largely overcast all morning. The clouds were, in fact, stacking up, heavy and grey to the north, moving in over Ujjayini on the back of a strong wind.

Deciding it would rain soon and it was best he didn't get caught in a downpour, Matali was about to shift his gaze away from the sky when something caught his attention. He slackened his pace, then came to a complete halt, eyes riveted on a spot where the clouds were moving in a strange pattern, looping and writhing violently from inside. At the same moment, the clouds in the near vicinity rapidly changed colour, reflecting all the shades of grey and black, one after another.

As the deva watched, a portion of the clouds suddenly tore from within, revealing a sinuous black form prowling in its depths. However, it quickly roiled and ducked back into cover, the clouds rearranging themselves over the gaping tear, curtaining the sinister sight from view.

But Matali had seen plenty to turn pale.

Having heard of the theft of the mantras, he could see what the asuras were about to unleash on unsuspecting Ujjayini. And he didn't believe the yakshas could do anything to intervene and assist the humans this time.

It was time he made a swift getaway, he realized.

He wasn't at all keen on becoming an unintended target of Ahi's deadly venom.

***

"It doesn't make sense. Why on earth would Yashobhavi want Shashivardhan dead?"

"I've been thinking about it, and I think I know why," Amara Simha said.

"Tell us then," Vararuchi frowned.

"It's something that Vikrama told us," Amara Simha explained. "You weren't here that day, but..." he looked at Varahamihira and Dhanavantri, "...remember, in this very chamber... the two of you, Shanku, Kshapanaka, me..."

The physician and the engineer furrowed their brows, trying to recollect which day Amara Simha was referring to.

"About Pralupi," the brawny councilor reminded them.

"Of course," said Dhanavantri, smacking a hand into his palm. "It's so obvious."

"What is?" asked Vararuchi, puzzled.

"It's like this," said Amara Simha. "Vikrama told us that Pralupi was hell-bent on getting Ghatakarpara crowned as the next king of Vatsa instead of Shashivardhan. It seems she was pestering Vikrama to intervene and influence Chandravardhan to name Ghatakarpara as his successor."

Vararuchi blew his cheeks and shook his head, but it was Dhanavantri who spoke first.

"I witnessed one of her later conversations with Vikrama," the physician said with a shudder. "She was... relentless and uncompromising."

"Anyway," Amara Simha continued, "to support her case, Pralupi maintained that there were people in Kausambi who were prepared to back Ghatakarpara's succession. When Vikrama asked her who these people were, the one name Pralupi mentioned was that of Yashobhavi."

"Who paid the bodyguards to have Shashivardhan killed," Dhanavantri breathed out.

"But would Yashobhavi go so far...?" Varahamihira stopped.

The councilors exchanged cautious glances, not vocalizing what each of them was thinking: Could Pralupi have had a direct hand in the attempt on Shashivardhan's life?

"She came to me out of spite," Vararuchi broke the silence, "because Vikrama had refused to entertain her. I did wonder what he'd done to earn so much of her hatred."

"What's that?" asked Varahamihira sharply.

"I didn't get an opportunity to warn Vikrama before he left, and since his departure, so much has happened that I didn't get a chance to tell any of you..." Swiftly and without digression, the king's brother detailed Pralupi's late-night visit to the garrison of Musili.

"Her condition was that I make Ghatakarpara king," he said, avoiding the councilors' eyes. "Though it was more like a demand for the favour she was supposedly doing me. The thing is I wasn't the one who sought her help; *she* approached me, yet she spoke as if I owed her."

"And how would you have done what she wanted?" Varahamihira asked.

"No idea," Vararuchi shrugged, looking completely lost. "I was supposed to figure out a way once Vikrama had been humiliated and had been forced to step down as king."

"She is dangerous and irrational," said Amara Simha, running his fingers through his beard. "She will stop at nothing to get what she wants." He looked at Vararuchi. "Did she say what she had planned against Vikrama?"

Vararuchi shook his head.

"The point is—" Dhanavantri began, but before he could get there, the door to the chamber swung wide open. Pralupi stormed in, glaring at Amara Simha.

"Where is my son?" the princess demanded. "Why isn't he in Ujjayini?"

"Your son decided to leave for Udaypuri instead of coming here," Amara Simha replied.

"What's in Udaypuri? And why didn't you stop him?"

Amara Simha hesitated. "He has gone to meet his friends. I tried telling him he should come to the palace, but I think he was keen on going."

"Friends?" Pralupi asked archly. "What friends in Udaypuri could be so important that he'd rather go there than come and meet his mother?" She paused, then spat viciously, "It is that girl, isn't it?"

Amara Simha shrugged.

"And you let him go?" the princess's voice rose to a treble. "You know she is a common merchant's daughter... *a traitor's daughter*. She was probably the bait that hooked him, the cunning little thing that she is. Ensnaring my trusting boy. And what is *he* thinking? Has he forgotten he is a prince by birth? And *you*," she rounded on the councilor. "You too forgot that he is a prince? How irresponsible of you. Your job was to bring my son back—"

"Which I have," Amara Simha interrupted tiredly. "I tried talking him out of going, but it was his choice—"

"You obviously didn't try hard enough."

"He is a grown man, capable of thinking for himself. Short of binding him to his saddle and bringing him in like a prisoner, there's nothing more I could have done."

"You promised to bring him back," Pralupi shook her head, stubborn and unreasonable. "He cannot be with that girl. Someone should get him back. He shouldn't have been allowed—"

"Why does Councilor Yashobhavi want Prince Shashivardhan dead?"

"What?" The princess turned wide eyes on Varahamihira.

"Yashobhavi tried to get Shashivardhan killed in Matsya," the lame councilor said, watching Pralupi closely. "The attempt was a failure because Ghatakarpara thwarted the assassins and saved Shashivardhan's life."

Pralupi's hand flew to her mouth, and she stared at the councilors, one by one, in horror. Pale and trembling, she held herself erect by taking the support of one of the chairs around the council table.

"Where is he?" she asked in a voice that wasn't much more than a whisper.

"Who? Yashobhavi? In Kausambi," Varahamihira replied. "Probably being interrogated."

"Chandravardhan should let him be," the princess said in an agonized voice.

The councilors looked at one another. "Why would Chandravardhan do that?" asked Amara Simha. "Yashobhavi just tried to murder his son."

"Oh, why... why did you do it?" As her body was racked with sobs, the princess crossed her arms and held herself tight, shoulders heaving. "I too wished he were dead, but that didn't mean... oh, you shouldn't have..." she sighed through tears. "You could have waited..." Then, as the pain got too much to take, she buried her face in her hands, turned and made a dash from the council chamber.

Frozen in their places, the councilors stared at the door. As the echo of Pralupi's feet receded, silence once again engulfed the room. The four men said nothing, too afraid to speak.

Why did you do it... Those had been Pralupi's words.

I too wished he were dead, but that didn't mean... oh, you shouldn't have...

You could have waited...

They had all been grappling with why Yashobhavi had ordered the killing, but now, just like that, because of what the princess had said in her anguish, they finally knew.

I too wished he were dead, but... You could have waited... The impatience of a parent.

He did it because he loved the boy, Amara Simha thought to himself, as a father would love his own son.

At that moment, an eerie, unsettling hiss filled the room, seeping in through the very walls of the palace and making the blood run cold in the councilors' veins.

***

With another roaring crash, a second structure crumbled in the eastern quarter, sending more ash, dust and rubble into the warm, stuffy air lingering over Ujjayini.

In the sky, right above where it had just wrought its destruction, Ahi was already fading, its body hidden in the clouds, its plumed head with its slanted, amber eyes and hideous mouth still drooling venom, vanishing right before the councilors' eyes.

"The consolation is those buildings are empty," Vararuchi remarked tersely.

The councilors were on a terrace that offered an unrestricted view of most of Ujjayini.

"We must find Kshapanaka," Amara Simha growled, feeling powerless and frustrated. "She faced that thing down the last time."

They searched the sky for signs of the serpent-dragon.

"How?" Kubera, who had joined the councilors, asked. Seeing his question was unclear, he added, "Did she do it, I mean."

Amara Simha looked at the yaksha. "By shooting it full of arrows and weakening it."

"That's not possible," Kubera shook his head, so the ornaments he wore clinked softly. "Ahi is an elemental creature. It doesn't feel pain, so it cannot be tormented, weakened or subdued with weapons. And it cannot be killed."

"I don't care what sort of creature it is, but Kshapanaka brought it under her control and forced it to flee."

"She couldn't have," the yaksha was adamant. "Whoever summons Ahi controls Ahi, and the only way of gaining ascendency over Ahi is by weakening that control."

"Didn't the Healer say that he had saved Ujjayini by breaking Indra's son's hold over Ahi?" Dhanavantri asked. "I recall the Samrat mentioning this..."

"*That* is possible," Kubera affirmed.

"We will believe a liar like Shukracharya now, is it?" Amara Simha challenged, his eyebrows drawing together in annoyance. "I saw Kshapanaka corner that thing—"

The yaksha was shaking his head again when Vararuchi forced himself into the debate. "Let's understand this," he said. "You say this thing can't be killed. Why?"

"Because Ahi is an elemental serpent-dragon," Kubera explained. "It is made of water, which cannot be destroyed or wounded or held captive. Burn it, and it'll turn to vapour. Freeze it, it'll turn to ice. Its form will change, but that's not dying. The process can be reversed, and it can always become Ahi again. That's what it is doing right now—changing from water to vapour and disappearing, only to reappear in the form of water."

With a pause to draw breath, the yaksha added, "You don't defeat Ahi; you defeat the mind that controls Ahi."

A moment's silence, as everyone made sense of this, still scanning the overcast sky.

"You are here to help," Amara Simha said grumpily. "Can't you do anything?"

"We wish we could, but one cannot fight water."

The serpent-dragon formed quite suddenly from the clouds to their left, the head rearing, so the black and brown feathers ruffled along the length of the sinuous, muscular back. Without ado, it opened its mouth and spat a load of grey venom over the northern district. Buildings collapsed with a grating, wrenching sound as debris mushroomed into the air.

"Anyone living there?" the yaksha asked.

"It depends on the precise spot—"

"The City Watch garrison is located there," Amara Simha growled, interrupting Vararuchi. "There will be soldiers in the barracks."

"Also, the hospices set up to treat wounded soldiers," Dhanavantri cried. "This is—"

Just at that moment, the alarm bells began tolling, though more than conveying urgency, they sounded melancholic and repetitive.

"We can't just stand here and watch that thing destroy our city," Amara Simha snapped. "I'm going to look for Kshapanaka. I believe she can stop this thing."

Vararuchi and Dhanavantri looked at each other. Ahi was already gone in the sky.

"She's probably already on its tail, which is why she is not here," Vararuchi reasoned.

"Good," the brawny councilor said as he turned to leave. "I'll find her and help her."

"She is the only one immune to that thing's venom," the physician reminded him. "There's nothing you can do. Kshapanaka will have to face the thing alone."

Amara Simha stopped and gave Dhanavantri a grudging look.

Vararuchi turned to Kubera. "Can you tell who is controlling Ahi and how?"

"Easy," the yaksha lord shrugged. "It's either Indra's son, Jayanta, or one of Shukracharya's sons, Chandasura or Amarka. Only those with both asura and deva blood can command Ahi, so the choices are down to these three."

"But do you know *where* they are controlling Ahi from?"

Kubera stared at Vararuchi with brightening eyes. "It has to be from somewhere close. Close enough for them to see and direct Ahi..."

"Can you find out exactly where—"

"Yes," the yaksha lord replied. "My yakshas will go..."

Placing his hands on the parapet, Kubera hoisted himself onto it. Even as his foot landed on the narrow strip of stone, his body underwent a striking transformation, and the three councilors stared in surprise at the grey langur seated on the parapet. The langur slipped off the parapet, and using its expert grip, it climbed down the palace wall until it reached a spreading banyan. Leaping onto a branch, the langur lost itself in the foliage; the next instant, a crow's harsh caws broke from the tree. Even as Vararuchi, Amara Simha and Dhanavantri watched, hundreds of crows took flight from the trees surrounding the palace lake and headed straight for the banyan, cawing loudly in response.

The king's brother turned to Amara Simha. "We may not be equipped to tackle Ahi, but we can definitely fight and defeat whoever is controlling the serpent."

***

"How did you know where to find me?"

"The yakshas," Amara Simha replied over the sound of the hooves.

"Oh," said Kshapanaka. It was all the explanation that was needed.

They were riding along a narrow, winding lane in the city's western quarter, making for the south gate, a dozen horsemen of the City Watch coming in their wake. Everyone kept an eye out for the serpent-dragon, which had last been seen spitting venom over the northern parts of Ujjayini.

"The yaksha is right about Ahi," Kshapanaka remarked. "I chased it across the city, I shot it full of arrows... Nothing impacts it. A waste of precious arrowheads."

"Mmm-hmm," the older councilor frowned. "But you stopped it the last time."

"Like Kubera says, it was probably someone else. Remember what the Healer told us in the council chamber about Indra's son—"

"Yes, yes," Amara Simha interrupted harshly, but his face immediately softened. "Sorry, it's just that I thought we had a counter to the snake, and now it's disappointing to learn that we don't."

"We do seem to have found a counter to Ahi," Kshapanaka reasoned. "Isn't that why we are going where we're going?"

"You're right," said Amara Simha as they swung onto an open road that bisected Ujjayini's southern district.

Kshapanaka glanced up. "Best stay close to shelter. We don't want venom falling on anyone even by accident."

Reflexively, Amara Simha nudged his mount closer to the awnings of the houses lining the street, and the riders coming behind did so as well, even though everyone knew this semi-protection would serve little purpose against the serpent-dragon's threat. As if seeking to underscore this, Ahi materialized abruptly over Ujjayini's east, disgorging venom, flattening houses and sending tremors through the city. Kshapanaka cursed as everyone reined in their horses and took cover, watching the snake dissipate into the clouds that now lay thick over the city.

"We must hurry," said Kshapanaka, riding out from under an awning.

"Move," Amara Simha motioned with his battle-axe as he kicked his mount into a gallop. Kshapanaka and the riders responded, and the cavalcade set off in a thunder of hooves.

"Why isn't Vararuchi here?" the woman yelled to be heard.

"Dhanavantri thought Vararuchi coming would leave the dagger too vulnerable. Drawing us away from the palace is a tactic that both the devas and asuras have used before."

Kshapanaka nodded to show she approved.

The road took a natural turn, and as Ujjayini's south gate came into view, the councilors observed a large group of horsemen waiting in the shadow of the gate. On drawing closer, it became plain that the riders were *samsaptakas* led by their commander, Angamitra. The fat figure of Kubera peeled itself from the group and came forward as the councilors brought their horses to a halt. Angamitra joined them, as did two commanders of the Imperial Army.

"Okay," said Amara Simha, once he was sure he had everyone's attention. He looked at the yaksha. "For everyone's benefit, tell us where the asuras are controlling Ahi from."

"The serpent-dragon is being controlled by the asura brothers, Chandasura and Amarka, who are hiding in those hills," Kubera pointed south, beyond the gate. "They are being guarded by a large asura force. We think they may also be protected by some form of sorcery that won't be easy to penetrate."

"Okay," this time Amara Simha addressed Avanti's warriors. "The yaksha lord here says the only way of stopping the snake is by stopping those asura brothers, so what needs doing is pretty simple. Smash through the asura army, find the brothers and kill them. Are we ready?"

"Our regiments are waiting beyond the gate, your honour," one of the commanders said.

"The *samsaptakas* are ready," affirmed Angamitra.

"My yakshas await my signal," said Kubera.

"Let's ride then," Amara Simha nodded. He raised his battle-axe. "*Avanti*," he roared.

"*Avanti*..." those around him roared back.

The battle cry spread to the soldiers amassed outside, and they roared too, as the councilors, the *samsaptakas*, the two commanders and the men of the City Watch poured out of the south gate. Behind them, the yaksha lord switched forms in a flash and took wing as a hawk, sailing over the city's ramparts and soaring above Avanti's army. And behind him rose thousands of hawks, lifting up from the trees and rooftops, and skimming south towards the broken ridges where the asura army waited.

***

Wi'daar... wi'daar...

Breaking somewhere along the army's left flank, the murmur spread like a tide to reach the ears of Khash'i Dur, Vikramaditya and the rest of the company riding at the centre.

Wi'daar... wi'daar...

In the sky... in the sky...

"*Urug... wi'daar,*" a Huna captain reported to Khash'i Dur quite unnecessarily, because the chieftain had caught the murmur and was already staring at the sky.

As were Vikramaditya, Kalidasa and the other three *shy'ors* riding beside him, and half the army, fingers all pointing, eyes gazing upward in curiosity and wonder...

...at hundreds of blazing dots that were rising over the horizon in great arcs of fire and smoke, flooding the southern sky and bursting into brilliance by rivalling the brightness of the mid-afternoon sun.

Wi'daar... wi'daar... The words carried to the very back in awed whispers, and without anyone noticing, the horses dropped pace from a full-paced gallop to a slow plod.

"We have never seen the likes of this," the chief turned to Vikramaditya. "What do you make of it?"

"Whatever it is, I suspect it doesn't bode well," the king replied. "Best be on our guard."

His hand strayed to the hilt of his sword, but Khash'i Dur restrained him by placing his hand on the samrat's arm. Then, glancing at the *droiba* riding behind, the chief nodded. Finally, he looked at the Huna captain.

"*Eb'a,*" he commanded.

"*Eb'a,*" the captain repeated his chieftain's order, motioning the army to a halt.

The *droiba* got off his horse and elbowed his way to the front. He bore a closed brazier filled with burning coals in one hand and had slung a worn cloth bag over his shoulder. The blue paint he habitually wore had run with the sweat, so that the deeper tones of his skin showed underneath.

"What?" Vikramaditya asked, looking from the *droiba* to Khash'i Dur to Kalidasa.

Khash'i Dur looked up at the flaming specks zigzagging along the blue sky, trailing fire and smoke. "Isn't the realm of the Ghoulmaster nearing its end?"

The samrat nodded.

"Time is short, and you must get to Ujjayini," the chieftain said. "Let this not slow you down. We will go ahead with the *droiba*..." he drew a triangle between himself, Kalidasa and the king with his chin, then inclined his head at the Huna army, "...and leave whatever this is to my brothers. They will take care of it."

Vikramaditya glanced at Kalidasa, who nodded back as he eased his scimitar out of its sheath and rode over to a captain of Avanti's cavalry, so that the plan could be communicated to Avanti's troops. Khash'i Dur held swift consultations with the three *shy'ors*, relaying orders, and the three chiefs spurred their horses and dispersed to assume command of the army.

Khash'i Dur turned to the Huna captain. "*Da'aro meke,*" he said, drawing his sword.

Vikramaditya watched the captain raise a ram horn to his lips and blow. As a shrill blast rang across the plain, the horsemen freed their swords and gripped their spears, while the archers nocked arrows into their bows. Meanwhile, the *droiba* left the side of the *shy'ors* and shuffled into the plain, digging a hand into his bag to draw a fistful of sand.

Overhead, more and more dots rose from the haze that smudged the edge of the sky and snaked over the open countryside. They numbered in the thousands now, but they stayed in the upper atmosphere, giving the impression they were heading west. But on reaching some sort of zenith, the ones in front suddenly dipped and started their descent.

Down below, the men drew their breaths and steeled themselves.

The echoes of the horn died away. In the ensuing stillness, everyone's attention was torn between the burning dots descending far over their heads, and the *droiba*, who was walking into the plain all by himself, his headdress of feathers spilling out behind him, fluttering in the wind. By dint of some arcane sorcery, wisps of smoke from the charcoal brazier were banding around the shaman, wreathing his body, writhing like snakes...

Vikramaditya's eyes shuttled from the *droiba* to the falling dots—except they were no longer dots but flaming meteor chunks, descending faster and faster, growing rapidly in size. From the arc of their trajectories, the samrat guessed the meteors would land in the vicinity of where the *droiba* was headed...

He looked from Khash'i Dur to Kalidasa in apprehension. Seeing neither of them lift as much as a finger to intervene, and seized by a fit of trepidation, the king tightened his hold on the reins when he felt Kalidasa's hand on his arm.

"The *droiba* knows what he is doing, my friend," the giant said softly.

Closer and closer the meteors hurtled, hundreds of them now, screaming down, streaming smoke and flames. Behind and above them, more dots filled the sky, many starting their earth-bound fall, a lot more of them still rising to the peaks of their parabolic arcs. The ones closest to the ground were now clearly visible, ragged boulder shapes, cracks showing on their surface, filled with molten fire.

In the plain below, the *droiba* had come to a halt a hundred paces from the vanguard of the combined Huna-Avanti army. He stood facing away, hands by his sides, a grotesque figure with his feathered headdress and spindly legs. The smoke still slithered over him in a loving caress.

Above him, the meteors dropped… lower, lower, lower…

The samrat was beside himself with anxiety when the *droiba* finally stuck his hand out and tossed the sand into the air. The coil of smoke sprang after the sand, wrapping itself, fusing the particles together, catching the crystals in an upward spiral, spinning faster…

…and at the same time, the first meteors crashed into the plain less than a hundred paces from where the *droiba* stood.

Their impact caused the ground to shake, and as meteors landed one after another in an incessant shower, kicking dirt and dust into the air, mighty reverberations rose from the plain. Meanwhile, the earth under the shaman's feet lurched wickedly, erupting towards the spiral of smoke and sand, forming a dense column that drew the *droiba* into its folds.

Dust and dirt filled the air, obscuring the view. The samrat watched the whirling column grow in size before it cleaved into two parts with an ear-splitting shriek of rage that drowned out the rumble of the meteors. The two pillars drew apart and drifted into the plain, recomposing into the *yah'bre* as they went, and from the remains of the dust column the *droiba* emerged, dishevelled and streaked with dirt, but otherwise unharmed. Behind him, meteors continued to rain down on the plain, sending shivers deep into the ground.

"*Hl'a,*" the *droiba* called, beckoning with one hand, the other still balled into a fist.

But Vikramaditya's gaze was already past the shaman, slipping through the curtains of dust to the enormous horned figures emerging out of the debris of the meteors, stepping clear and holding aloft jagged javelins with points that glinted even in the muddied air of the plain; row after row, stretching halfway to the horizon, thousands of figures rising from their meteor shells for combat.

Despite the incensed bellowing of the *yah'bre* that stood in their path, the horned figures didn't so much as budge. Then, as if in response, a dreadful lowing rose from the flanks of the horned army, and a regiment of war mahishas appeared from over a rise, their horns thick and black in the sunlight, their battle-axes arcs of flashing light as they charged at the army of horsemen.

"*Hl'a,*" the shaman waved his hand furiously.

"Come, Samrat," Khash'i Dur yelled as the figures who had arrived in the meteors broke into a run. He kicked his horse in the flanks. "May the *hriiz* ride with us."

To the king's right, Kalidasa raised his scimitar and shouted, "*Kul'a gwede'r.*"

As one, the men raised their weapons high and shook them.

"*Kul'a gwede'r. Kul'a mahek. Kul'a q'ult,*" the Huna horde roared back.

"Hurry, brother," said Kalidasa.

Vikramaditya spurred his own mount forward, the chieftain in front, the giant following. They bridged the gap to the *droiba* in no time, and in a surprising display of dexterity, the *droiba* grabbed the king's arm and swung astride the horse's back, behind the king. But the horned warriors were already converging on the spot, slipping past the *yah'bre*, the tips of their javelins fifteen paces away and closing in, blocking their exit. The Huna horsemen were coming up from behind, and in his peripheral vision, the samrat saw the war mahishas stampeding into the melee as well.

Finding Khash'i Dur, Kalidasa, the shaman and himself at the vortex of the battle, the king reached for one of the Hellfires.

At that moment, the *droiba* threw the second fistful of sand into the air.

A dense cloud of dust enveloped the samrat and the shaman, exploding in all directions in an instant, so it was impossible to see even Kalidasa or the *shy'or*.

"*Oi u'za,*" the *droiba* shouted into the king's ear, shooing him forward with his hand.

The pall of dust was so thick that it was hard to breathe. Vikramaditya had no idea which way to go, but he obeyed the shaman's exhortations and drove his heels into his horse's sides. As the beast broke into a gallop, the lowing of the *yah'bre* and the war mahishas came chasing after him, the breaks in between filling out with the Huna battle cry.

Raise the sword. Raise the storm. Raise the war. That's what Kalidasa had said it meant.

"*Kul'a gwede'r. Kul'a mahek. Kul'a q'ult.*"

***

Emitting another malevolent hiss that made the hairs on Vararuchi's arms stand on end, Ahi reared over the central districts of Ujjayini, its mouth opening wide to spit venom.

Then, convulsing violently, it shattered in all directions, its body losing form and colour as it reduced to a million droplets that rained down harmlessly over the city.

"Did you see that?" Dhanavantri shouted in excitement, wiping the few drops of water on his forehead with his *angavastram*. "You saw that, didn't you?"

"Mmm-hmm," Vararuchi replied cautiously.

"It just broke and vanished," the physician trilled, stepping onto the terrace with more confidence now. "It was about to attack, but someone stopped it."

"Something happened to it, yes," the king's brother was guarded in his enthusiasm.

"I tell you, it must be Amara Simha, Kshapanaka and the rest of them. They must have found the asuras controlling the snake."

"It's a possibility—" Vararuchi stopped in mid-sentence as Ahi reappeared directly overhead, looking straight down at the terrace where they stood.

"Oh no," the physician exclaimed, going pale as excitement and certitude deserted him.

Watching the serpent's head draw back to strike, the councilors were about to make a dash for cover when the monster twitched again.

Then it froze.

The councilors stared, bewitched, as Ahi stopped moving and crystallized, turning into hard ice, white from the inside, light refracting along its surface.

"What's happening—" Dhanavantri began, but stopped on seeing a fissure appear on the ice, accompanied by a loud crack.

The next instant, the serpent-dragon cracked completely and disintegrated into bits of ice that fell to the earth like hail, ice turning to water within seconds before vanishing completely as vapour.

"There, again... see?" Dhanavantri was now literally jumping in delight. "They've got the asuras who're controlling this thing. Nothing else can explain this."

"You could be right," Vararuchi admitted with greater willingness. Before he could complete his thoughts, though, a figure stepped through the door to the terrace.

"Acharya," Dhanavantri called out in surprise and delight.

The chief councilor nodded a greeting and walked up to his fellow councilors, observing the sky all along.

"When did you arrive, raj-guru?" Vararuchi asked.

"I got here around the time that thing showed up," the chief councilor pointed upward. "We had just entered the eastern quarter when it started wreaking havoc. We had a narrow escape and had to seek shelter for a while." He paused. "How are we tackling the snake?"

"It is already being tackled," the physician grinned. "Amara Simha and Kshapanaka led a force against the asuras who are guiding the snake, and it has started behaving erratically. It doesn't seem capable of attacking us anymore."

"It's too early to arrive at that conclusion," Vararuchi said levelly, and Vetala Bhatta was nodding in agreement when Ahi showed up to the north, darting in and out of the clouds. The serpent's body thrashed about, waning in and out of shape until it dissipated into vapour.

"See?" Dhanavantri pointed, looking vindicated. "It is not behaving the way it normally does. It looks as if it is in agony."

The other two councilors were compelled to nod.

"Well, thank god Kubera was able to find out where the asuras were controlling it from," said Vararuchi.

"*Who* was able to find out?" Vetala Bhatta squinted.

"Kubera, the yaksha—" the king's brother stopped and threw up his hands. "Such a lot has happened since you left, Acharya. I don't know where to begin."

"Later then," the raj-guru nodded. "As long as the yaksha can be trusted."

"He and his army saved us from the vyalas."

"And certain death," Dhanavantri added quickly.

"Vyalas?" Vetala Bhatta considered his fellow councilors with raised eyebrows.

"Flying beasts that spew fire. They burned most of the city down before the yakshas came to our aid." Vararuchi paused. "And now they're helping us counter Ahi."

Nodding slowly, the Acharya looked at the sky. "Vikrama is at the frontier, I was told."

"Yes."

"He has taken the dagger with him, I presume."

"No, Acharya. It is here, in the palace. Vikrama has left it in our custody."

Vetala Bhatta eyed the two councilors with misgiving. "What made him do that?"

"He believes we can protect it," said Dhanavantri. "Actually, he believes Varahamihira can."

Giving this a moment's thought, the Acharya said, "Then our job is to protect Varahamihira. We must do everything—" the chief councilor paused and pointed at the sky. "What is that?"

The other councilors turned to see an immense ball of flame scorching the northern sky and heading straight for the heart of Ujjayini.

Hellfires

The asuras swarmed out of the dust, their horns and javelins jutting into the air.

Reining in his steed, Kalidasa leaped to the ground. "Keep going," he called to Khash'i Dur, tossing him the reins. "Be with the king. I will join you."

The chieftain caught the reins with a nod and steered both mounts into the dust.

Gripping the shield that the *shy'ors* had gifted him—identical in design to the one that had belonged to Zho E'rami, they'd said—the giant turned and hoisted his scimitar, feet planted apart, one behind the other, side-on and perfectly balanced.

Kul'a gwede'r. Kul'a mahek. Kul'a q'ult.

The asuras came at him, roaring in bloodlust.

The ones in the lead were six or seven paces away when Kalidasa sprang at them, shield up, his scimitar scything into the javelins with a resounding clash of steel, breaking the asuras' holds on their weapons and skewing their aim. Without a change in momentum, he ducked and went under the lattice of javelins, rolling and coming up fast from below, so the asuras' bellies were now hopelessly exposed. Kalidasa's scimitar flashed, cutting stomachs, spraying blood and spilling guts, and thus the first line of asuras died, screaming in agony.

One of the dying asuras collapsed on top of Kalidasa, but the giant bore the brunt of the asura's weight on his shield. Bracing himself on one knee, balancing the body, he then heaved with all his might, getting to his feet and tossing the body, one-handed, onto the path of the next wave of asuras, their swords and javelins trying to get past his defences. The asuras reeled, disengaging themselves from the body, and using those extra seconds of time and elbow room to his advantage, Kalidasa stepped into the kill. Drenched in asura blood, resembling a spectre from a nightmare, his sword swinging in fierce, bloodied arcs, the giant slashed and skewered the asuras, dropping all four in rapid succession.

The din of war rose all around, cries of rage clashing with shrieks of terror and pain as the Huna army locked with the asuras in a brutal struggle. Somewhere, a horse neighed in panic, the sound swallowed by the lowing of the *yah'bre*. As he strode after Khash'i Dur, from the corner of his eye, Kalidasa saw a young Huna stumble out of the dust with a sword buried deep in his back, and as the air cleared and the plain gradually unfolded, the number of fallen bodies—human and asura in almost equal proportion—came as a shock to the giant. A final volley of arrows sailed overhead, a death swarm targeting the asuras before they met humans in a lethal crush, and Kalidasa noticed that most Huna warriors had abandoned their mounts to fight the asuras on foot.

The asuras were the more formidable of the two, but what the Hunas lacked in strength, they made up in grit and ferocity. They assailed the asuras in packs, one or two fighters invariably sacrificing themselves so the others could move in for the slaughter. Still, the desert warriors were no match for the mahishas, who mowed the men down like grass with their battle-axes, so the plain quickly filled with mangled bodies. But the charge of the war mahishas was countered by the *yah'bre*. They trampled the asuras underfoot and plucked and dismembered the mahishas before gorging on the corpses, their lightning-crammed mouths opening wide in anticipation of the feast. Everywhere, the air was thick with bloodlust, the ground drenched with gore.

"*Iti,*" Khash'i Dur hailed from the right.

"Where is the king?" Kalidasa asked, nearing the chief.

Khash'i Dur pointed to a fresh cloud of dust thirty paces away. "Hurry."

Just then, half-a-dozen sturdy asuras broke through the fighting to assail the two men.

"*Zuh u'za,*" Kalidasa shouted at the chief as he turned to face the asuras.

The asuras had speed and surprise on their side, so the giant took a succession of blows on his shield as he tried to blunt their attack. Seeing he was on the back foot, the asuras came at him hard, pressing in close, hardly giving any room to manoeuvre, while looking for a gap that they could exploit.

With swords and javelins raining down on his shield, Kalidasa stole a quick glance over his shoulder to ascertain if Khash'i Dur had gone after the samrat. What he saw, instead, was a war mahisha wading out of battle, swinging its battle-axe to cleave a Huna's head in two and cut open the back of another—before heading straight for the chieftain. A small knot of Huna warriors tried tackling the mahisha, but the beast swatted them aside and stepped in Khash'i Dur's path, blocking his access to the dust cloud.

Kalidasa was gauging the distance to the mahisha when a javelin gouged his upper arm, sending a bolt of pain up his body. Furious at himself, the giant whirled and backhanded his attackers with his shield, repelling them and making room to swing his arm. A sword sneaked through and grazed his stomach right under the ribs, but finding his assailant within striking distance, Kalidasa gritted his teeth and slashed upward, opening the asura's midriff. Driving the scimitar into a second asura's chest, he was marking his next target when a contingent of soldiers from Avanti came running to assist him.

"Handle them," he panted as he yanked his sword free.

His left arm blazed from the javelin wound, blood mixing with sweat and running down his hand, but ignoring the pain, Kalidasa focused on Khash'i Dur and the mahisha. The *shy'or* had wisely relinquished his horse to gain some agility, but with its bulk and reach, the mahisha had a distinct edge, sweeping at Khash'i Dur repeatedly with its axe. The best the chieftain seemed capable of doing was staying out of its murderous range.

His eyes pinned on the beast, Kalidasa sprinted towards Khash'i Dur. Halfway there, the councilor spied an asura making a run at the chief from the side; without breaking his stride, Kalidasa flung the scimitar in a whirling arc. The massive sword caught the asura on his left side, splitting him almost in half from temple to torso. Bending to grab a pair of discarded javelins, one in each hand, Kalidasa made for the mahisha.

Building up a tempo—and feeling a sudden rush of raw power in his sinews—the giant took half-a-dozen strides and leaped at the mahisha. Seeing him airborne, the beast swung its axe, but Kalidasa was much too fast; even as the heavy, double-headed weapon began its journey, the giant had hurtled into the mahisha, knocking the axe from its hands and sending the beast staggering.

Then, before the mahisha could regain its balance—or recover its senses—the big councilor drove both javelins into the sides of its muscular neck with tremendous force, burying the tips in deep, skewering the shafts right in. Dark blood squirted from severed arteries.

A wretched, high-pitched bleat burst from the mahisha's lips and it toppled flat on its back to lie still, bison eyes staring at the sky, the javelins quivering to a standstill as the bleat yielded to a gasp.

Heaving a deep sigh, Kalidasa stepped back from the dead creature.

"*Zuh thra'akh go.*" Khash'i Dur stared from the mahisha to the giant in disbelief.

Kalidasa studied his hands in wonder, turning them over, clenching them into fists. He could still feel the strange, heady surge of power in them. "Yes, I killed it," he nodded reflectively. A small pause, then, "Let's go."

Walking back to retrieve his scimitar from the asura he'd killed earlier, the councilor turned to take one look at the plain. Both sides were well matched, and the *yah'bre* had come into their own, stomping and pounding at the asuras and mahishas. There was no way of saying how long this would last.

"Let's go," the chieftain called, holding out the reins of Kalidasa's horse.

The giant pulled his sword free of the dead asura.

The two men rode into the dust storm blind, not knowing where or how to find the king or the *droiba*. They floundered in circles, struggling to see and breathe, until a figure materialized from the swirls of dust.

It was the *droiba*. On foot. Alone.

"*A'so sumrat?*" Kalidasa heard Khash'i Dur ask about the samrat.

The councilor caught nothing of the shaman's mumbled reply. But seeing the chief shoot him a look of alarm, he understood there was cause for worry.

"What's happened?" the giant edged his mount closer, listening to his voice quaver.

"Someone attacked them. The *droiba* lost his balance and fell, and when he got back on his feet, the horse was dead—and there was no sign of the Samrat or his attacker."

***

Far below him, the human army of Avanti met the asuras in a thunderous clash of metal and rage, but to Kubera, who was gliding high above the rocky hills to Ujjayini's south, with the evening wind under his wings, the sounds of the battle felt like the roar of the surf, distant and disjointed.

The battle did not directly concern him. The humans would have to deal with whatever the asuras did to stop them, and he knew the result would be far from pleasant. What he was banking on was that the asuras would be sufficiently distracted to miss the multitude of hawks flying into the hills. Once they had their targets in sight—and once they had a measure of the sorcery protecting Shukracharya's sons—the yakshas would change form accordingly and attack... and it would be too late for the asuras to save the brothers.

As the gentler slopes fell away and the terrain became scarred with deep ravines and gullies, Kubera guessed they weren't far from where Chandasura and Amarka were directing the destruction of Ujjayini. The yaksha lord glanced at the hawk flying to his right—the yaksha who had located the brothers' whereabouts—and the hawk blinked and tilted its head to confirm Kubera's thoughts. The yaksha lord returned his attention to the hills, which were teeming with little prey that he could now easily pick out with a hawk's heightened vision.

The hawks had still to crest the first hill when Kubera's attention was caught by a figure standing atop a ravine, etched against the dull browns and greens of the land by a golden radiance. Drawn to it by curiosity, the yaksha sharpened his focus on the figure—and a tidal wave of rapture burst in his head, flooding his senses, rendering him numb.

Kubera grappled with what he was seeing... with his eyes, and in his *mind's eye*. And the more he looked, the more overwhelmed and helpless he became, mesmerized by the beauty of the form...

—*it's a trap*, a voice screamed in his head—

...its exquisiteness, its allure, its desirability...

—*look away, look away*, the inner voice struggled to assert itself—

...but he couldn't take his eyes off her. Instead, he stared, drinking her beauty with his eyes, soaking her into his parched soul...

She was stunning; more stunning than the apsara Indra had brought with him to Alaka, more stunning than any apsara he had ever laid eyes upon. Her skin was the colour of gold, every naked inch of her radiating the warmth of love; her long hair, undone, was a caress in the wind, her breasts and hips beckoning him to their satin-soft shadows and folds. Her blue eyes on his were languid and intoxicating, but they held a promise of ice and lightning that was impossible to resist. Her lips moved, and even at this distance, he could hear his name being gasped in unbridled passion, a desperate moan seeking out the desperation in him...

—"*Kubera*"—

—*no, ignore her, she is not*—

But there was no ignoring her because she was inside his head. She was an enchanting, sun-drenched splash of colour; she was the heady scent of lovemaking; she was the quickening in his pulse; she was the rush of blood to his loins. She was all that mattered, and all that Kubera wanted was to sweep her into his arms and ravish her. She was taking his breath away...

—*she is an illusion*—

Kubera realized he couldn't breathe.

He tried flapping his wings, but he felt paralyzed, powerless.

It crossed his mind to blink and look elsewhere, but that would mean not looking at her, and the thought was too unbearable to consider.

—"*Kubera*"—

Hearing her call his name in love, he allowed himself to sink into her, sink and drown...

He started falling.

On the slopes below, mahishas and *ekashringas* ripped through Avanti's army, sending men and horses scattering in terror. Battle-axes and javelins were red with human blood, and *ekashringas* tore open horses' bellies and gored soldiers to death, stampeding over those who had fallen, breaking ribcages and crushing skulls underfoot. The air was full of the stench of fear as those with weaker wills turned to flee the asura onslaught.

Hoisting his axe with both hands, Amara Simha faced a charging *ekashringa*. The brute came at the brawny councilor at a powerful gallop, its head swaying, tiny eyes narrowed in rage. Amara Simha waited, switching his gaze from the armoured animal to the asura riding it, her javelin pointing at him. The beast was five paces away when the councilor made a sudden feint to the right. The *ekashringa* swung its horned head, tracking Amara Simha, trying to gouge him; the javelin also swerved and thrust, but Amara Simha had already gone in the opposite direction, grabbing the javelin as he dived and rolled out of the *ekashringa's* murderous path. He yanked the javelin hard to unseat the asura, while swiping at the animal's underbelly with his axe. But the broad blade simply glanced off the beast's armour without inflicting even the slightest damage.

Amara Simha and the asura leaped to their feet, grappling with the two ends of the javelin, wrestling the weapon from one another's grasps. A strong and skilled warrior, the asura fought the councilor hard until Amara Simha's grip weakened, giving the asura a chance to drive the shaft into him. The javelin was inches from his stomach when Amara Simha eased out of its way, allowing the tip to slip past him. Carried by momentum, the asura came within his range, and with a powerful sweep, the councilor buried his axe into the side of her head.

Amara Simha turned to follow the *ekashringa* when something landed by his feet with a soft *thup*. The councilor stared at the fallen object, then looked up at the sky.

In another part of the rugged slopes, beset by asuras, Kshapanaka shot a glance skyward. The asuras were thronging around her and she could no longer use her bow effectively, so she had taken recourse to her spear, fending off blows with its shaft as she cut and stabbed, infecting her attackers with venom. Asura warriors screamed and decomposed all around her, but more came in their wake, a relentless press of prodding swords and javelins, wearing Kshapanaka's defences down until, with a great bellow, Amara Simha cleaved a bloodied path to his pupil's side.

"You alright?" he shouted.

"Yes."

Kshapanaka parried two javelins that were thrust at her. Flipping her spear around, she rammed its blunt end into one asura's throat, breaking his windpipe. She was turning to tackle the second attacker when a sword brought that asura down. Kshapanaka nodded at Angamitra, who stood over the fallen asura, his face bloodied from a deep gash over his right eyebrow.

"Noticed the hawks?" asked Amara Simha.

Kshapanaka nodded. Wiping sweat off her forehead with an arm, she looked again, eyes growing wide with apprehension.

The sky was full of the falling birds. Cartwheeling and plummeting, wings flopped open and flailing against the wind, the hawks dropped by the hundreds all over the hills.

"The yakshas were supposed to find and stop the asura brothers..." Amara Simha muttered as his muscles bunched and grew larger, his hair and beard changing colour and growing coarse as he began transitioning into man-lion, "...but something seems to have come in the way of their plan."

***

"He is many, your honour," the first soldier panted, his voice cracking with fear, robbing his words of coherence.

"They are all him," said the second soldier, making a little more sense than the first one. He too panted as he ran alongside Vararuchi, trying to keep up.

Without dropping pace, the king's brother took a sharp corner, *urumi* coiled in one hand, shield in the other. "There are many versions of him... duplicates," he eyed the soldiers. "Is that it?"

"Yes, your honour."

"How many?"

The soldier who had spoken second shook his head uncertainly. "Many..."

"Where are they?" Vararuchi asked, feeling exasperated.

"Some were in the vicinity of the wrestling pits, one was seen in the east market, and the City Watch patrol was ambushed near the moneylender's mansion."

"How many attacked the patrol?" the councilor asked, listening to their feet echo along the deserted lane.

"There were two of them, your honour."

Vararuchi felt a flush of anger on his cheeks. Eight soldiers had died in the attack. Eight men to be avenged.

The lane opened onto a wider road, and the councilor braked on seeing a dozen soldiers of a City Watch patrol approaching from the other direction.

"Anything to report?" the king's brother asked.

"Nothing here, your honour," a stout soldier with a greying moustache replied.

Vararuchi nodded. "Search that section there. We'll look this side."

The patrol did as they'd been instructed, while the councilor and his men turned to follow the road. The three had hardly taken ten strides when a horrifying scream rent the stillness of the empty quarter.

"That way," one of the soldiers pointed in the direction of the patrol they had just passed.

Another shrill cry broke before it was choked abruptly. Voices rose in alarm, shouting.

"Hurry," called Vararuchi, breaking into a run.

Slipping past an old *ashoka* tree, the councilor tore down the alley the patrol had picked. The alley emerged onto a narrow quadrangle, and stepping into the open, Vararuchi stopped short, reeling at the sight that met his eyes.

Six or seven bodies already lay on the ground, sprawled on top of the one another with their heads staved in, blood pooling around them, three with their faces to the darkening sky still heavy with clouds. None of them appeared to move or breathe, and Vararuchi didn't spend time on them. Instead, he focused on the three soldiers who were still on their feet—and on the golden-haired, ebony-bodied figure standing in their midst, towering over the men, ornate antlers branching from its head. A cruel, spiked mace swung from the figure's hand, dripping blood... dripping blood as it swung towards one of Avanti's soldiers...

The blow landed with a *thwack*, opening one side of the soldier's head, spraying fountains of blood into the air. As the man keeled over, one of the two remaining soldiers lost his nerve and fled, shoving Vararuchi aside in his panic to exit the alley, leaving the last soldier to face the giant alone. The figure raised his mace yet again, but Vararuchi was already charging, the *urumi* uncoiling in his fist. Thrusting the soldier aside, he lashed out at the giant, the supple blade snaking towards the massive black torso, cutting through it...

...through it... as if cutting through air... the giant's body rippling along the cut...

...and then the blade had passed the body, through it and out, without leaving the slightest scratch or indent on the giant's skin.

And now, the mace was descending on Vararuchi's head in a crushing blow, the spikes sharp and wicked, primed to break through skin, flesh and skull.

Just as the mace was about to make contact, the councilor got out of its way. The blow sailed through thin air, offsetting the giant's balance and tipping him forward. Vararuchi flashed the *urumi* again at the giant's neck, but the sword once again went right through the black body. Taking advantage of their proximity, the giant drove his barbed gauntlet into Vararuchi's midriff, but Vararuchi was gone, slipping around and behind the giant before the punch could connect. Again, the giant overbalanced; again, the councilor tried to break the back of the giant's neck with the edge of his shield; again, the shield met no resistance. The giant swung his barbed fist, which Vararuchi evaded with ease... The two duelled in the strangest fashion, dancing around one another, lashing out with all their might, but failing to land even a single blow...

As his frustration mounted and he dodged another nasty swipe, the futility of engaging with this thing struck the councilor. Whatever it was, it couldn't be wounded, much less killed, so there had to be a better way of countering it...

Fresh screams issued from Vararuchi's left, where the alley

gave way to the square. Putting distance between himself and the giant, the councilor eyed the mouth of the alley—where the pair of soldiers who had come with him lay flat on the stones, bludgeoned by an exact replica of the giant he had been fighting. Stepping over the men it had just killed, the double focused on the soldier Vararuchi had saved earlier. The soldier stared at the second giant in horror, his mind not registering the mace raised high over the giant's head...

"Get away," the councilor screamed as he leaped across the square to intercept the blow. His shield up, he hurled himself at the giant, aiming for the hand wielding the mace so he could throw the giant's aim... But instead of making contact, Vararuchi went through the giant and crashed against a far wall, falling in a heap, winded.

The sound of the mace connecting with flesh was followed by the crunch of imploding bones, which was followed by a grunt of pain that died in the throat the moment it was born.

Then came the heavy thump of a body striking the ground.

Still out of breath, his body bruised and hurting from the fall, Vararuchi twisted around to see the two giants standing over the dead bodies in the square, looking down at him, lying curled up against the wall...

***

Eyes the colour of hammered gold blazed down into his own as Vikramaditya grappled with the big-shouldered asura for control of the sword.

With height as well as weight to his advantage, the asura exerted tremendous pressure on the sword's hilt, using both hands for greater leverage. The king's knees bent under the strain and his hands shook violently as he fought to keep the broad blade from slitting open his throat. Still, the sword closed in inexorably, the asura twisting Vikramaditya's hands and the king's sweat-stained face contorting in a desperate bid to save himself…

Dust enveloped them like a cloak, dense and impenetrable.

The asura had ambushed them with incredible speed and strength, springing out of the dust, slashing at the horse and bringing it down before the king or the *droiba* had even figured they were under attack. Vikramaditya had fallen and rolled, freeing himself of the horse, but he had still to get to his feet and reach for his swords when the asura came hacking at him. It had taken all the king's skill and a touch of luck to put a lock on the asura's hand.

Drawing on the last reserves of his strength, the samrat slowly forced the asura's hands back. In the hope of stunning his opponent, he then rammed his forehead into his assailant's craggy face. The asura blinked and jerked backwards, his lips split and bleeding, but before the king could seize the initiative, the asura's head snapped forward to butt him right back.

A shower of coloured sparks exploded around the blinding pain in Vikramaditya's nose, and darkness grew in front of his eyes as his legs buckled and gave way. On his knees, holding the asura's hands, stubbornly refusing to let go of the sword, the samrat swayed like a drunk, tasting the blood from his broken nose in his throat, trying to clear his head…

Grabbing his chance, the asura wrenched his hands free of the king's loosening grasp. Then, planting a firm foot on Vikramaditya's shoulder, he kicked hard, sending the king sprawling on his back.

The fall jarred Vikramaditya back to consciousness. Opening his eyes, he blinked at the asura towering over him, ram horns curling up from his forehead, granting him height and majesty. Dust eddied and rose above the asura's head as he appraised the king, a smirk hovering on his battered lips.

"Thought you could escape using the dust for cover?" the asura asked, wincing through his words. "Clever, but not good enough to escape my vision. I can see everywhere. In the dark, in a storm, through this dust. My eyes are special, and that's why they call me Hiranyaksha."

Without warning, with no sign of what was going through his mind, the asura lifted his sword and swung it at Vikramaditya. The blade came down in a flash, but the samrat was already scrambling out of its way; by the time the tip reached him, he was no longer there, the blade swishing through air an inch short of his back. This incensed the asura, and he swung on the reverse with a ferocity that could have taken a head off. The samrat barely managed weaving out of the way.

Hiranyaksha slashed a third time, and again, Vikramaditya twisted and rolled out of harm's way… coming up on one knee, perfectly poised to draw his swords. The blades emerged from their sheaths in a synchronized *seeng!* that cut through all the other sounds of battle, and Vikramaditya raised them to catch and deflect Hiranyaksha's next blow.

Rising with feline grace and speed, he slashed horizontally in quick succession, parrying the asura's sword and slipping under his defence, cutting him on the arm and across the chest, so the asura staggered two steps back in surprise. Taking the opportunity, the king leaped back as well, and the two fighters crouched and stared at one another as dust whirled around them. Small flames licked the tips of the samrat's swords.

"I could fight you till one of us dropped, but I don't have the time," Vikramaditya raised the Hellfires, swishing them in the air.

Hiranyaksha's eyes strayed from the king's bloodied face to the swords—and his pulpy lips twisted in a dark sneer. "Did no one tell you the Hellfires don't work on Diti's children?"

Vikramaditya's hands stopped moving as he looked into the asura's golden eyes.

Remember, the churails *will come only when summoned, and they can tell between their wielder's friends and foes, even in the thick of battle.*

Laayushi's words from all those years ago resurfaced in the samrat's mind. He pictured the abandoned Huna garrison and the small, black-skinned demon standing in the middle of the courtyard, telling Kalidasa and him about the Hellfires...

Vikramaditya didn't take his eyes off Hiranyaksha as he whipped the swords.

There is another thing you must know about these swords...

The flames flared and leaped, growing in length.

When Diti fashioned these swords, she worked powerful spells into them to ensure the churails *of Naraka would never harm her offspring. However, when Diti took the swords to Sage Kashyapa for his blessings, the sage did two things. To prevent their misuse, he willed the swords to obey only those who were truly noble and virtuous...*

The flames were now belts of fire, flowing from the tips of the Hellfires.

Then the sage invoked even more potent mantras to override and annul Diti's spells granting the asuras immunity from the churails*—*

Shocked and confused, Hiranyaksha stared at the swords blazing in the king's hands.

—so that nothing would prevent the wielder of these swords from punishing the asuras if the need arose. Sage Kashyapa kept this a secret from everyone but my master, Paurava, and as the new Wielder of the Hellfires, you too must keep the secret, king of Avanti. So that Diti's evil-born remain complacent and unprepared for the wrath of the Hellfires...

"No."

Sword raised, Hiranyaksha launched himself at Vikramaditya with a yell that was rage, panic and disbelief in equal proportions. But before the asura could cover half the distance, the king flicked one of the Hellfires in his direction. The belt of fire detached and looped, smacking Hiranyaksha flat across the chest and throwing him back. The asura screamed as flames bit into his flesh, burying deep, burning him up...

The samrat whipped the blades, sending bands of fire floating into the air. The dust over the plain thinned and dropped away simultaneously, as if by miracle, and the light grew dark and grainy as eerie shadows masked the sun. The plain came in the grip of a deathly stillness, and combatants stopped warring to gaze up in wonder, watching the fire belts coil and interweave to birth Naraka's three gruesome *churails*. Screaming sound and fire through their open black mouths, the banshees separated and skimmed across a darkening sky like hungry predators.

The *churails* swooped over the battle, singling out the asuras and mahishas for punishment. Hiranyaksha fell thrashing to the ground, wrapped in flames; watching the asura in the throes of death, Vikramaditya's vision dimmed, and he rocked on his heels as pain lanced across his midriff. He waited, doubled over, until his vision cleared... before straightening to examine the cut that ran from one side of his stomach halfway to his navel. The wound bled profusely, and by its appearance, it was deep.

Another wave of giddiness came upon the samrat, and he felt his legs wobble, while his grip weakened on the Hellfires. As he dropped to one knee, Kalidasa, Khash'i Dur and the *droiba* came running to his assistance.

"Brother," Kalidasa exclaimed, taking the king by the shoulders and steadying him.

Squatting before Vikramaditya, the *droiba* studied the cut, probing with his fingers. The king drew his breath in sharply, and the *droiba* said something to the *shy'or*.

"The *droiba* says it's not good," Kalidasa translated. "You must not ride."

Vikramaditya gave his head a tired but firm shake. Then, driving the tips of the Hellfires into the ground for support, he gripped the hilts tight and pushed himself erect, swaying while he regained his balance.

"You cannot go on like this—" Khash'i Dur began objecting.

"I cannot stop," the samrat insisted. He looked in the direction of Ujjayini. "There's no time. For all we know, we might already be too late to save my city."

* * *

Watching the hawks fall, Holika marvelled at the simplicity of Shukracharya's idea.

Ever since the facts surrounding the rout of the vyalas had come to light, there had been apprehension in Patala over the role the yakshas would play in defending Ujjayini. The yakshas were remarkable shapeshifters, capable of taking virtually any form with the help of their unique magical powers, and this made them formidable opponents. As Hiranyaksha had pointed out, "The yakshas can counter everything by becoming its opposite. If we are to succeed, we must first find a way of neutralizing them."

With less than a day to go for departure and a solution still eluding them, the high priest had come to them. "What is a yaksha's greatest weakness?" he had asked.

No one knew, because yakshas didn't have weaknesses.

"But they do," Shukracharya had insisted. "It was a weakness that cost them Devaloka."

"A weakness for apsaras, of course," said Holika.

"A weakness for beauty, epitomized by the apsaras," Shukracharya corrected. "And that is the weakness you will exploit, Holika."

While they had no means of guessing what form the yakshas would assume to enter battle, logic indicated *they* would be the ones to lead the attack on Amarka and Chandasura, slipping through the cordon in disguise while the humans fought the asura army. So, she had waited at the top of the ravine, using spells of her own to project an image of herself—an image where every aspect of her beauty was accentuated many times over, making her irresistible to every yaksha who beheld her, distracting them from their task of helping the humans...

It was plain good fortune that the yakshas had chosen to take the form of hawks. The hawk's superior eyesight had amplified the effect of what Holika had achieved, triggering a sensory overload in the yakshas' minds that they were quite incapable of dealing with. The outcome was that they were now dropping from the sky, spiralling to their deaths—

"Witch Queen, there is a problem..."

Holika turned to find an asura minion behind her. "What is it?" she asked, draping herself with a length of cloth now that her nakedness had served its purpose.

"Chandasura and Amarka are losing control of Ahi."

The sorceress pushed past the minion and strode down the ravine, crossing over to a gradient on the western slopes of the hill. The din of battle fell away behind her. She scaled the slope to where a few dozen asuras guarded a small cavern. Stooping low, she entered the cavern, which was lit by seven lamps laid along the floor, where a mandala of a snake was drawn with charcoal, flour and vermillion. Chandasura and Amarka sat at the centre of the mandala with a small pile of palm leaves on their laps, while a copper basin full of hot water bubbled in front of them. Sweat trickled down the brothers' necks and shoulders in broad rivulets, and their faces contorted in grimaces of concentration.

"What's happening?"

Instead of replying, Chandasura frowned and narrowed his eyes so they were little more than slits on his chubby moon face. Amarka read from the palm leaves, and two threads of steam rose from the copper bowl. Using a sharp knife, Chandasura made an incision on his thumb—Holika noticed that most of the asura's fingers already bore cuts—and let the blood trickle, before extending his hand towards the wisps of steam.

"Follow the trail of your blood and mine," Chandasura growled in suppressed anger. "Follow the hand that guides you. Obey the blood that has given you life, mighty Ahi. Obey, and come to where your blood awaits you."

Holika watched the twists of steam rise from the boiling water, the disparate wisps banding to form the hazy outline of a hooded serpent. The ghost-serpent swayed indecisively, stretching for Chandasura's bloodied fingers before collapsing under its own weight and dissipating.

"No," Chandasura snarled. Amarka too rocked back with a frustrated groan.

"What's happened?" the Witch Queen asked again. "I thought you had the serpent-dragon in your control."

"We did, but something's gone wrong," Amarka replied. "Ahi has stopped responding to our commands."

"Are you sure you've got the mantras right?"

Chandasura turned to peer at the sorceress with his hostile, slit eyes. Holika nodded.

"Perhaps someone or something has gained influence over the snake," said Amarka.

"Who could it be? And how did they do it?"

"No idea."

"It must be the yakshas," Chandasura grunted. He looked at Amarka. "Let's try again."

Amarka began reading the mantras as Holika exited the cavern to survey the hills, watching the last of the hawks fall from the sky. She gazed at Ujjayini next, lit golden by the declining sun, and in stark contrast to the brooding, overcast sky. Ahi spasmed in the clouds fleetingly, as if seeking an escape.

The yakshas had come to the hills as hawks, but could some of them have stayed back in the city to deal with Ahi, Holika wondered. And did the yakshas' magic have the potency to take control of the serpent-dragon? She doubted it. Nothing was powerful enough to stop Ahi, and the mantras that guided it were with Chandasura and Amarka.

Yet, someone was forcibly taking control of the snake and had to be stopped.

Knowing Shukracharya could easily find the culprit using the bones, the Witch Queen set off in search of the high priest. But before she had covered half-a-dozen yards, her attention was drawn to a strange sound that appeared to come from a great distance, yet was loud enough to quell the roar of battle from the other side of the hill. She paused, locating the sound.

A distinct screaming-howling.

Her expression turned grim as she finally pinned its source.

An immense black cloud of what appeared to be smoke was swirling and swerving from the south, blotting out half the horizon, moving fast and low over the land and heading straight towards the hills and Ujjayini.

An immense, soot-black cloud of oil-smoke, screaming-howling into battle...

Failures

How many versions of him are we dealing with?" asked Dhanavantri, staring down at the palace causeway, where three of the antlered lookalikes prowled.

"Nobody knows, your honour," the captain of the Palace Guard sounded frazzled. "There are so many of them, it's impossible to tell."

The windows along the length of the gallery were lined with archers, arrows fitted and ready to be fired, while in the hallway below, soldiers of the Palace Guard waited behind the sealed palace door, on their guard, but fraught with nerves. The causeway was scattered with arrows that had been shot at the three apparitions when they had shown up at the palace, none of the missiles having had the slightest effect.

"And they all came out of that ball of fire?"

One of the ebony-bodied giants strode to the palace door and hammered on it irately with his mace. The sound of metal on metal boomed through the palace, but the door held. The giant turned and stalked off down the causeway, stopping to look back at the palace.

"I am not sure, your honour," the captain answered the

physician eventually, eyeing the three giants warily. "There's talk about them multiplying... one becoming two. Some soldiers say they saw the thing split—"

"Like the horsemen who attacked us in the beginning?" Vetala Bhatta considered the captain shrewdly.

"A bit, your honour... but with one major difference. Those horsemen were real and could be killed. These doubles are all mirages that are impossible to maim or kill."

"Hmmm," the raj-guru said thoughtfully.

"Keep the palace door barricaded and all the windows on the lower floors firmly shut," the physician instructed. "And bring us any updates you get."

Once the captain had departed, Dhanavantri assessed the chief councilor. "Okay, what's on your mind?" he said, dropping his voice. "Let's hear it."

The Acharya looked at the physician. "You remember the horsemen who multiplied." Seeing Dhanavantri nod, he continued, "I was right about them being controlled by one, common brain—that is how they all fled in fear when Vikrama went out with the Hellfires."

"I remember."

"The captain said soldiers have seen these things split," Vetala Bhatta pointed out. "What if it is the same with these giants, what if they too are influenced by a single mind?"

"What if they are?" the royal physician asked. "Vikrama isn't around to terrify that mind with the Hellfires, so how will it help?"

"I could try to take control of that mind and get it to do what I want."

"It didn't work with the horsemen, remember?"

"It worked with Daipayana," the raj-guru countered. "I saw the whole Magadhan army march into the Ghost Marsh under Daipayana's command. It's definitely worth a try."

In no time, Vetala Bhatta had his spear in one hand, the other hand clenched to his chest as he stared at one of the antlered heads on the causeway. Eyes closed, he whispered the mantra, and the skulls at the end of the spear glowed—

—The Acharya was pitchforked into a viscous darkness that reeked of blood, and a terrible rage filled him—

kill kill kill kill kill

—When he tried to extricate himself from the thing's mind—

kill kill kill kill kill

—he realized that the rage was submerging him—

kill kill kill

—It came as a shock to him that he was hearing the voices of all the things roaming the city, their collective rage—

kill kill kill said it would be hidden kill kill find the councilor kill kill

The chief councilor opened his eyes with a gasp, his face hot with anger, sweat running down his forehead and neck.

"Are you alright?" Dhanavantri looked at him in concern.

Vetala Bhatta nodded.

"So... what happened?"

"These things are empty shells," the raj-guru replied, pointing at the giants on the causeway. "Other than rage, they are devoid of emotions. They are predisposed to killing, and their only purpose is to take lives. They are manifestations of some terrible sorcery, which is why they cannot be killed. And because they have no minds, they cannot be influenced, and they feel neither pain nor fear."

The physician stared at the chief councilor in horror. "They are unstoppable?"

"I won't say that," the Acharya said. "I am certain they are replicas of an original, and if the original can be found and stopped, these can be stopped too."

"How do you know about—" Dhanavantri began.

"I heard his thoughts too. He is looking for something that's hidden… must be the Halahala." Vetala Bhatta paused. "Let me find him."

Shutting his eyes, the chief councilor again reached into the mind of one of the giants on the causeway.

kill kill kill kill kill

Ignoring the rant, the Acharya sent his mind out, seeking the voice—

kill kill kill kill kill

—from all the other rage-infested voices—

kill kill kill are soldiers kill kill take my chance kill

The Acharya latched onto the words, and suddenly he saw a passageway open in his mind…

…now is the time to attack… now is the time to kill… kill kill

Vetala Bhatta's eyes blinked open and he stared in astonishment, recalling what he had seen. A passageway. A familiar passageway, one that he had walked along many times.

A passageway on the second floor of the palace.

Whoever it was whose mind he'd been inside *was already deep within the palace.*

…now is the time to attack… now is the time to kill…

The chief councilor turned to Dhanavantri in alarm, but at that very moment, the apparitions on the causeway turned and made a rush at the windows on the lower floor. They swung their maces hard at the old wood, and in what sounded as one, explosive splintering, all the three windows that had been assaulted shattered and caved in…

The antlered lookalikes barged through the ruins of the windows and set foot in the hallway, roaring with bloodlust.

***

"But Indra already knows about the human king's absence from the palace."

"He does?" Matali blinked at Narada. "Who told him?"

"She did," the diplomat pointed over the deva's shoulder.

Matali turned to find Urvashi by the door that led away from the hall. "You... are here?" he mumbled in surprise. "I thought you were somewhere in the human king's palace."

Somewhere in the human king's palace... the apsara said to herself as she stepped out of the shadow of the curtains.

"Where is our lord?" Matali asked, looking back at Narada.

"He has left for the human city to claim the Halahala. I am surprised you didn't run into him on your way here. Once Urvashi brought the news..."

But Matali was no longer listening, as he felt resentment build against the apsara. By bringing the news of Vikramaditya's absence ahead of him, she had ruined his plans of pleasing Indra, and now she stood here looking superior—

"How did you learn about the human king?" he snapped harshly at the apsara.

"By staying back in the palace instead of disappearing the way you did," Urvashi said levelly.

Matali's eyes narrowed. "There's no reason to be so pleased with yourself. All you have done is send our lord straight into harm's way."

"What do you mean?" Brihaspati asked in alarm, trundling forward on his bow legs.

Seeing Urvashi shoot him an apprehensive glance, Matali sneered. "As I was leaving Ujjayini, Ahi made an appearance," he paused for effect. "The asuras must have sent it to devastate the humans, but we mustn't forget that Ahi will not discriminate between humans and devas." Looking at Urvashi, he added, "Let us hope our lord does not run afoul of the serpent-dragon while it is reducing the human city to dust."

"Are you certain it was Ahi..." the chamberlain began in his whiny manner, but Urvashi had already turned to head back the way she had come.

I thought you were somewhere in the human king's palace.

Matali had been to Ujjayini, but he hadn't bothered to check her whereabouts—*somewhere in the human king's palace*—or find out whether she was alright. It was possible he had tried and failed—or that it had been impossible to even try—but Urvashi doubted this very much. When he had been exposed, Matali had vanished without a trace… had left Avanti without as much as a reassurance that the devas would be back for her. She had been abandoned, left to her fate. And no one in Devaloka seemed to have missed her enough to attempt a rescue. Had it not been for her own initiative, she would still be a prisoner in Ujjayini, instead of walking free in Devaloka…

But was she really free in Devaloka? Or was she a mere puppet, a slave to the whims and fancies of Indra? Urvashi thought back to what the deva lord had said about her, the day she had returned from Ujjayini: *The most desirable and irresistible of apsaras in all of Devaloka, and she fails at the* one *thing she is supposed to be adept at… What good is an apsara if she can't tempt a man to fall into her arms, mad with passion?*

Then there were Vikramaditya's words, overheard from the back of a chariot: *I don't know how you treat your women in Devaloka, but in Avanti, the dignity and honour of our women is sacrosanct…*

Even when her duplicity had been discovered, the human king had been decorous: *The kingdom's enemies are held in the dungeons, but that is no place for women. You will remain in the palace as a prisoner of Avanti, but you will be accorded the dignity a woman deserves.*

Whereas the deva lord, to whom she had pledged her life and loyalty all these years, had been disparaging of her faults: *You fail to seduce the human king, and you manage to get yourself caught and thrown into captivity… You could have stayed in captivity instead of returning empty-handed...* That was the welcome she had got after putting herself on the line to help the devas find the Halahala.

Walking along the galleries of the palace of Amaravati, the apsara considered the worth of her allegiance to Indra. The deva lord said he loved her, and she had always believed him. But meeting Vikramaditya had forced her to re-examine the notion of love... love that was selfless, kind and respectful. Love that was soulful.

Can you be her, the only woman I have ever loved?

Urvashi felt a twitch of guilt as the samrat's words reminded her of Avanti's queen. She had taken advantage of the woman's affliction to escape and return to Devaloka—for what? For the devas, who thought so little of her, who cared for nothing beyond their unbridled lust for power?

Guilt welled and washed over the apsara like a sick tide. She had betrayed the trust of the woman Vikramaditya loved, only to come back to Devaloka, so she could contribute some more to the king's misery by having yet another destructive deva army march to his kingdom. The human city had already suffered greatly because of the devas' and asuras' greed. And now with Indra on his way and the asuras unleashing Ahi...

Urvashi paused to stare out of a window, appalled and ashamed at what she had done.

***

The *ekashringa* was less than a dozen yards from Kshapanaka, her back to the charging beast while she battled three asuras, when the *chakram* sailed towards the rhinoceros in a looping arc, its edge glinting in the dying light of sunset. The weapon flashed over the *ekashringa's* heavy snout, cutting into the base of the animal's big horn and shearing it right off. A shrill, ear-splitting squeal of anger and agony burst from the beast's lips, but far from slowing down in confusion, the incensed *ekashringa* kept galloping, heading straight at Kshapanaka, now even more intent on mowing her down. However, a second *chakram* came whirling in the wake of the first one, this one expertly aimed at the bend in the rhino's knee, which left the knee joint unprotected every time the beast folded its legs in gallop. This second *chakram* struck the beast true, slicing through tendon and bone, and the *ekashringa* collapsed in a pile, its butchered leg buckling under a mountain of muscle and plate armour.

Hearing the beast crash right behind her, Kshapanaka turned on instinct, taking her eyes off the asuras she was combating. The asuras were also distracted by the rhino's spectacular fall, but seeing that Kshapanaka's attention had been diverted, two of them sprang forward, their swords and javelins stabbing at the councilor's back.

Neither weapon covered half the distance to Kshapanaka.

Both asuras halted midway into their lunges, eyes and mouths opening wide as if in parody of one another, their weapons slipping from nerveless fingers. One of them coughed and looked down at his chest in wonder, staring at the point of the dagger that protruded from under his breastbone, oozing blood down his belly. The asura yelled as the dagger was ripped from his torso, and he went weak and dizzy with pain, falling face forward in the mud where his mate joined him in a moment. Together, they journeyed into the afterlife, leaving Shanku to stand over their dead bodies, bloodied knives in both her hands.

Having recovered his poise, the third asura lashed out at Shanku with his sword, but the girl vanished, and the weapon swept harmlessly through empty space. The next second, she stood behind the asura, slipping one arm over his shoulder, bringing a dagger up to his throat and slashing it open in a flash. Simultaneously, the second dagger slid between the asura's ribs, stabbing him in the heart.

"Shanku," Kshapanaka exclaimed as the asura crumpled at Shanku's feet. Pausing, she stared around her. "What's this... smoke?"

"The danavas," Shanku smiled.

Kshapanaka stared at the swathes of oil-black sweeping along the battlefield, then turned to Shanku, her eyes bright with excitement. "You've brought them."

Instead of replying, the girl switched both knives to one hand, plucked another *chakram* from her belt and curled it past Kshapanaka's shoulder in one easy move. Surprised, Kshapanaka spun around to find a mahisha teetering behind her, battle-axe raised to strike her down. The *chakram* was buried almost all the way into the mahisha's torso, and as it tipped forward to crash on its chest, the *chakram* went deeper, snapping the beast's spine and emerging from its back covered in blood and gristle.

"Wow," Kshapanaka's eyes widened in wonder. "That was some—" But Shanku was gone. Kshapanaka shrugged, still smiling, and turned to stare at the oil-black shapes looping and swooping as they first singled out the marauding *ekashringas* and mahishas for attack.

Impossibly absurd though it seemed, the massive beasts were ensnared in skeins of oil-black, their movements constricted. The oil-black tightened and coagulated around the struggling *ekashringas* and mahishas, forcing the beasts to a standstill, after which, one by one, they were ingested into the densely swirling masses. When the oil-black patches unravelled, there was no sign of the beasts, every one of them permanently lost in the oil-black.

Once the rhinos and war mahishas were neutralized, the danavas turned their attention to the asuras, who had begun sensing that the battle was slipping away from them. All ambitions of mounting a counterattack crumbled in the face of an emboldened push by the humans, led by the man-lion, Amara Simha, who fought his way forward by flaying asuras with his axe and tearing them to shreds with his claws. Shanku blitzed from one point to another, too fast to be cornered, her daggers faultless in their hunt for targets, while Kshapanaka waded into melees, turning asuras into piles of rotting flesh with every slash and thrust of her spear.

And around them, oil-black shapes lunged and swallowed asuras alive.

Then, out of the writhing mass of warriors she stepped, cleaving through curtains of oil-black with her chain-blade, glowing golden-orange in the last light of day, so it felt as if she was on fire.

Out she stepped, brandishing chain-blade and sword, calling to mind a spectre of vengeance.

Holika.

The sorceress went straight for Kshapanaka, the chain-blade snaking through the air to wrap around the councilor's spear; Holika yanked on the chain-blade, wresting the spear from Kshapanaka's grasp and casting it off with a flick of her wrist. Pinning an icy gaze on the councilor, the Witch Queen circled her target, the chain-blade coiling over her head as she prepared to deliver a killing blow. At the same time, she parried an attack that came from her left, using her sword to cut down three soldiers of Avanti.

The chain-blade's tip darted at Kshapanaka, but the councilor responded with speed, picking a fallen sword and using it to deflect the attack inches from her face. But before she knew it, Kshapanaka was defending herself against a barrage of blows, the sorceress the more efficient of the two with the sword. Driving the councilor back, Holika used the chain-blade to attack and maim close to a dozen soldiers of Avanti who were within striking distance.

A mass of oil-black materialized to Kshapanaka's left and slipped between her and the Witch Queen, smothering the latter. But the chain-blade whipped back and attacked the oil-black, ripping it until it fell away, recomposing into the gnarled and bearded figure of Shalivahana. The lord of the danavas rolled out of the chain-blade's way, dodging its stabbing tip before grabbing the chain tight, looping it around his forearm for leverage. The blades bit into his bark-like skin, but Shalivahana retained his grip on the chain, holding the sorceress back as Kshapanaka dived to retrieve her spear, so she could block Holika's strikes better.

Caught between the councilor and the danava, for a moment, the Witch Queen seemed to be at a loss, struggling to free the chain-blade while parrying the probing tip of Kshapanaka's spear. Sensing an opportunity, Angamitra rushed to Kshapanaka's assistance, but just then, Holika's lips moved, invoking spells. And before everyone's eyes, she changed, projecting an image of herself that drew from the deepest fears of those facing her, building on those fears, exaggerating them—so that she assumed a different terrifying form in the eyes of each person beholding her.

Kshapanaka staggered back, seeing Vishakha go up in flames, heat causing her skin to bubble and burst, her hair falling off in sizzling clumps, her face melting like wax as she screamed out Kshapanaka's name…

Angamitra froze at the sight of a girl of around ten standing in front of him, soaked to the skin, water dripping from her lank hair. Her flesh was pale from having been submerged for a long time, and her lips were blue and cracked as they whispered to him, addressing him in a dialect of Viswapuri as 'brother'…

Amara Simha looked in Holika's direction... and stared as his long-dead wife stretched out a hand to him. She was ashen faced, her lips colourless, eyes without her habitual spark of life and laughter. She held a baby in the crook of her arm, also ashen faced, its lips colourless, its eyes closed, never to open...

As a deathly hush fell over Holika's immediate vicinity, the sorceress seized the moment to strike Kshapanaka's spear out of her way and lunge at the councilor, her sword aimed straight at Kshapanaka's bare throat.

***

The Halahala is safe in the hands of the humans.

Vetala Bhatta rushed up a flight of stairs and turned into a gallery that led to the southern wing of the palace.

This fight must end. The humans mean us no harm. We must turn back.

As he traversed the gallery, the raj-guru paused to see if the thoughts he had been trying to plant in the mind he had tapped into were taking effect. He listened...

must find the councilor who is protecting the dagger and

Grimacing at the outcome of his efforts, the Acharya renewed focus, generating an avalanche of thoughts which he directed at the mind...

The hunt for the Halahala is futile. Vikramaditya will never yield the dagger. Not to the devas. Not to the asuras. To none, other than the Omniscient One himself. Nothing will be gained by battling the humans. We must let them be and return, for the Halahala will be safe in their custody...

The Acharya paused once again, listening... and his mind filled with a view of a hall in the southern wing. The possessor of the mind was heading for a passage...

dagger is not far... can feel it... so near...

Vetala Bhatta's heart did a little somersault as he realized where the owner of the mind was; two passageways and a set of stairs from where Varahamihira—

The dagger is not important, he screamed at the mind, hoping the urgency would drive his thoughts through the barrier that was impeding them, stopping them from getting through... *We must not fight the humans... They will never surrender the dagger...*

Swerving to his left, the Acharya hurried down a passage that served to connect the east wing to the section of the palace where the intruder was...

will take the Halahala back to Patala... In the chief councilor's vision, the mind's owner was nearing the end of the first passageway and turning into the second... *to defeat Indra...*

Realizing he was making absolutely no inroads into the mind, Vetala Bhatta turned into a hall that was situated midway between the gallery that led to Varahamihira, and the stairs that the asura—that it was an asura was plain now, as the mind had envisioned defeating Indra—would take to come down. Viewing the stairs from the approaching asura's point of view, the raj-guru turned and braced himself, his eyes on the stairs...

kill kill kill kill

The monosyllabic thoughts of the giant replicas suddenly swamped the Acharya's mind, and he thought back to the scene of utter violence he had witnessed in the palace's main hall as he had left to chase the intruder. The clones had gone completely berserk, killing soldiers of the Palace Guard, the hall echoing with screams of terror—

—and now the echo of footsteps.

The asura appeared at the top of the stairs, a daunting sight, his skin black as the night, tresses and beard cascades of molten gold, an exuberance of antlers on the head, haughty and unrestrained. The versions outside were exact doubles, but to Vetala Bhatta's eye, this asura somehow appeared larger in size and even more intimidating.

I must go back. I must leave the humans alone... The Acharya flung thoughts the asura's way in the hope that something would permeate that arrogant head...

What is this old human doing... Is he the councilor guarding the dagger?

The chief councilor saw himself in the asura's mind, standing in the middle of the hall, spear in one hand, the skulls glowing red... and he felt a burst of contempt for himself... *The old fool will have to die if he dares to stop me, Hiranyakashipu...*

Watching the asura descend the stairs, his spiked mace trailing on the steps, ringing dully as it struck every stair, the raj-guru was overcome with dread—and the absolute certainty that he would fail to stop the asura from getting to Varahamihira.

must go back... cannot defeat the humans...

The asura was now in the hall, approaching him...

"Stop," said Vetala Bhatta, raising a hand in command.

To the chief councilor's surprise, the asura slowed.

"You can't go any further," the Acharya said, seeing himself in the asura's mind. He felt the asura's disdain and anger bubble inside him as he heard the asura snort in derision.

Then, taking long strides, the asura came at him.

Vetala Bhatta brought his spear around, gripping its shaft with both hands, its tip pointed at the advancing asura. But even as he was bracing himself against the attack, the asura swung his mace with such speed and violence that the spear was knocked from the raj-guru's hands. The weapon flew and landed on the floor with a heavy clatter, and Vetala Bhatta stared at it in surprise...

Turning his head, he looked at the asura, knowing his

time had run out. That the mace would find his head next, shattering it to a pulp—

The asura raised a foot and kicked the councilor on the chest.

Air rushed out of the Acharya's lungs as he was lifted and hurled backwards, the hall a dizzy whirl of movement, his torso wrenching in pain where the asura's foot had landed. In a moment, though, other pains competed for his attention as he crashed against a wall and fell to the floor, his shoulder, back and knees on fire. Rolling onto his side, he curled into a tight ball and lay quiet for a moment, allowing the darkness to engulf him as pain shot through his body in vicious shards.

foolish enough to stop me

Hearing footsteps depart, Vetala Bhatta pried his eyes open. The darkness ebbed to reveal the floor of the hall right by his cheek, its expanse stretching away from his face, its smoothness cool and hard on his skin. His spear lay half the way across, well out of his reach.

The raj-guru turned his head painfully to see the asura's feet walking away, heading towards Varahamihira. He knew there was nothing he could do to stop the asura.

Get out of there, he screamed, searching for Varahamihira's mind. *The asura is coming. Get out, get out...*

Then, as another idea struck him, the Acharya changed tack.

Varahamihira needs help, he cast his thoughts as wide as he could, seeking Vararuchi. *Come back to the palace, wherever you are... come back. The Halahala must be saved.*

***

With a vehement hiss, Ahi broke through the clouds.

Scrambling to his feet, he ran down the lane, craning his neck to look at the sky, seeking out the snake. He turned one corner, then another—and suddenly, it was there, above him. Light from the setting sun shimmered along the length of the serpent's body, its feathers blowing in the wind as it reared, its mouth open, tongue greedily licking the air. It coughed, bringing up venom—

—but his hands were already up, fingers flexing... choking... crushing... squeezing... sweat breaking out on his brow as he wrestled with the form of the snake...

The serpent fought back, growing in volume, fattening with water, rising over the rooftops, even more impressive and even more determined to play havoc. The acidic venom rolled grey and viscous in the pit of its mouth, which reeked of decaying flesh, and the snake rocked its head back to spit.

He wrung his fingers tight, constricting the water molecules in the serpent's body, burning it up...

...and Ahi shuddered and disintegrated into vapour, its venom dissipating before it could do Ujjayini more harm.

Exhausted from his efforts, Ghatakarpara slumped against a blackened wall.

For a long moment, he leaned quietly, getting his breathing back under control. Mopping the sweat with his forearms, he rubbed and flexed his wrists and fingers, working the strain and soreness from them and getting the circulation going before straightening to scan the sky. At last, he turned his gaze to the west.

A troubled frown crossed the prince's face. Soon, it would be dark, and seeing into the clouds would be impossible. How would he know where the damn snake was when it showed itself?

Maybe he should get to the palace, he thought to himself; someone there might have a clue... Ghatakarpara shook his head. The palace was unlikely to know what to do about the snake. If someone did, they would have done something already. So, he would have to deal with it...

It was made of water, he remembered Amara Simha telling him about the serpent while they were on the road from Kasavati. *Your uncle saw the thing come out of the sea and destroy the whole Huna fleet.*

The moment he had set his eyes on Ahi, the prince had been sure it was the same snake, back to haunt Ujjayini. And recalling Amara Simha's words about the thing being made of water, he had taken a chance, reckoning that he might be able to control it. The gamble had paid off, and though the monster was hard to bend to his will, he had been able to keep a check on it, preventing it from destroying more of his city and taking any more lives.

What Ghatakarpara had failed to take into account was the toll the effort would take on him. Tired and yet to fully recover from his flight across the desert and over the northern Arbudas, the prince felt sapped from his struggle with Ahi. The confrontation had drained him of every ounce of energy, his legs were wobbly where he stood, his head reeled every time he made a sudden move and his pulse felt weak at his wrist. Yet, fighting the urge to drop against a wall and fall asleep, he had persevered, pursuing the snake across the city—

The hiss came again, boiling through the clouds, filled with hate.

Doubled over, one hand trailing the wall for support, Ghatakarpara stumbled the length of the alley, keeping an eye out for Ahi. He turned a corner, and faced with a dead end, he picked his way back until he was in a wide street. Catching a glimpse of the serpent's tail, he chased it around another corner and up another street. Finally, reaching an open square where the townsfolk sometimes gathered for the spring and harvest festivals, he looked up to see Ahi in the sky.

Again, the snake opened its mouth to spit venom over Ujjayini, and the prince fought it again, forcing it to change its form, this time into watery ice that melted almost at once and sluiced over the city's northern district, flooding a pair of narrow alleys with ankle-deep water. But almost at once, all that splashing water drew back together into a staggering column that reared over the rooftops, and in seconds, Ahi fashioned itself back into existence.

Throwing his hands up, the prince squeezed with all his might, and the serpent bucked and writhed, struggling to break free, its amber eyes simmering and reflecting the fire of twilight. Man and elemental snake fought as the night stole across the sky like a great scar, before Ghatakarpara, with a superhuman wrench, compelled Ahi to disintegrate into a fine mist over Ujjayini.

Even as the serpent vanished, Ghatakarpara wilted under the effort, his legs giving way, so he had to grab the charred trunk of a small tree to keep himself from falling. Holding the stump, he swayed drunkenly... then he let go and collapsed by the tree's roots, too tired to rise.

The sun slipped below the far horizon, and darkness came rushing at the young prince.

Destroyer

Straining with all his might, one hand raised, the palm thrust outward, Varahamihira fought to keep the energy shield intact between himself and the fearsome asura. With eyes crazed with greed, the asura went at the shield tirelessly, managing to rip the film open a couple of times, but Varahamihira quickly fused the rips back before the giant could force his way through. Still, the pressure of keeping the shield from coming apart was intense, and the councilor's arm and shoulder hurt as he balanced awkwardly on one leg and the crutch.

Get out of there, Vetala Bhatta's telepathic shout in his head had shocked Varahamihira. *The asura is coming*

Shocking or not, the urgency in the Acharya's voice had been unmistakable, so he had left his hiding place, dagger tucked safely in his belt. Escaping into the hall, he was still thinking of safer places when the asura had accosted him, rushing at him like a black thunderstorm.

Centring his energies, Varahamihira pushed hard, propelling the energy shield forward and out. The impetus took the asura by surprise, repelling him. His face clouded in anger at the councilor's defiance, but gaining control of his temper, the giant smiled a cunning, hateful smile instead.

Varahamihira blinked as the asura shifted and ebbed in the gathering gloom; then, as he watched, a shadow detached from the asura's body and stepped away. Before the councilor knew it, there were two antlered asuras facing him, the second a spitting image of the first. Another shadow separated from the giant, then a third, and suddenly, four identical antlered asuras were fanning out, surrounding Varahamihira from all sides.

The first of the replicas came at Varahamihira, mace raised and swinging.

The councilor hopped to counter the attack, casting the energy shield, blocking the rush.

Another double moved in from the opposite direction.

Hobbling on his crutch, Varahamihira motioned with his hand to create another energy shield between him and this assailant.

The third and fourth asuras entered the fray at the same time, coming in from two sides.

Sick with fear, the councilor frantically cast energy shields to hold the asuras back. One, two, three, four; the asuras attacked each shield with fury, and even as he watched, more shadows divided from the original to form replicas… six, now seven of them in number. All seven formed a ragged circle around him, attacking the crackling shields and tearing them down with their maces and gauntlets faster than Varahamihira could rebuild them, all seven of them edging closer with each blow, looking for gaps to squeeze through…

You will discover the limits of your power only when you use it to its full extent, the samrat had said to him before leaving for the frontier. *Have faith in your power.*

The councilor whipped his hand in front of him and across, executing a full spin using his crutch as a fulcrum. Immediately, a wall of buzzing energy sprang up all around him, reaching from the floor to well over the uppermost tip of the asuras' antlers. Again, he spun, generating a second shield within the confines of the first one. He created a third, then a fourth energy wall, then paused with exhaustion to assess how his handiwork stood up. The walls reinforced each other, dulling the effects of the spiked maces—

But almost at once, more asura replicas manifested, attacking the walls with fervour. And as the councilor watched in horror, the shields began stretching and coming apart.

The hall was now steeped in shadow, purple-grey twilight framed in a pair of windows, so Varahamihira missed sighting the figure until it was up by the wall of energy, striking at the asuras. Seeing the supple flash of an *urumi*, Varahamihira let out a sigh of relief, but as the facsimiles turned on Vararuchi, the *urumi's* blade going through their bodies without leaving as much as a nick on them, Varahamihira's hopes sank. Still the king's brother assailed the replicas, harrying them, darting in, then leaping away, dodging their blows and staying just beyond their reach, drawing them away from Varahamihira...

As the defensive energy shields tore and dissipated, Varahamihira shot his hand out and pivoted to raise another wall, but midway through the manoeuvre, his crutch tangled with his leg and tripped him up. The next moment, the councilor was flat on the ground, pain rippling across his chest and exploding from his chin as he lay face down, too tired to get up.

He turned to look for Vararuchi through the sparks flying before his eyes, but the king's brother was outside his range of vision, though he heard the scurry of feet and the thuds of the maces as they struck the floor. He looked up at the thinning energy walls around him, and at the feet of the asuras who were striking the walls. Rolling to his side, he felt the dagger in his belt. It was still there... although he didn't know for how much longer.

Turning again, he took in the torches that had appeared at the door at the end of the hall.

One of the palace attendants, Varahamihira thought to himself, here to light the lamps.

Only, no palace attendant in his right mind would be wandering about the palace lighting lamps when there was a battle raging in the corridors and the chances of getting killed were exceedingly high. Must be soldiers with torches then, looking for—

But these flames were unusually shaped for torches, longer than normal, and strangely curved so that they resembled... *the blades of swords...*

The aches from the fall already receding, his excitement barely contained, Varahamihira watched the flames arc and weave in the darkness, forming fluid belts of fire. He sensed the stillness in the hall as all the asura manifestations paused as if in a trance, drawn to the flames and the dark, silhouetted figure wielding them.

The hands holding the swords went still, the swords pointing downwards, the belts of fire spilling to the floor in coils. But the very next instant, the flames flared, lighting the samrat's bearded face from below, shiny with sweat, his eyes cold and hard on the asuras lined up in front of him.

Varahamihira didn't see Vikramaditya move; all his eyes detected was a blur of motion and light as the Hellfires spun and belts of flame lashed out in quick succession, knitting in the air like a pair of snakes dancing around each other. Before the councilor even knew it, a horrific wail rent the air as a *churail* raged over the hall, black mouth open and vomiting green fire.

The *churail* lunged and came screaming at the asuras ranged around the protective wall of energy. Varahamihira folded his hands over his head and cowered, certain that he too would be incinerated, but except for a strong force of wind, he felt nothing. Lifting his head, he saw that other than the samrat, Vararuchi and a lone, antlered asura—the original, Varahamihira suspected—the hall was empty. The last remaining asura stood rooted, staring at the *churail* as she looped to the hall's ceiling and turned back…

"This is not possible," Varahamihira heard the asura's whisper in the momentary silence that filled the hall. "I am Diti's son—"

The *churail's* mouth unhinged as it faced the asura.

The asura shook his head in disbelief. "No…"

The asura took to his heels as the *churail* launched itself at him in a shrieking rage. He was halfway across the hall, headed god knows where, when Varahamihira observed a flame leap from the banshee's mouth and envelop the asura. The asura crashed to the floor, writhing and screaming in pain and terror. Picking himself up by a supreme effort of will, he made a blind dash, wrapped in green fire, so only his antlers showed at the top. Reaching a window, the giant threw himself out of it, arms and legs kicking as he went down into the lake in a fiery blaze.

Varahamihira picked himself up gingerly, a dull pain in his chin where it had hit the floor.

"Are they all gone?" Vararuchi asked. He peered out of the window, though it was too dark outside to see.

"I think they are," said Vetala Bhatta, who had appeared at a door on the opposite end.

"The dagger," said Vikramaditya, approaching Varahamihira, the Hellfires already dimming in his hands. The *churail* had disappeared overhead. "Is it safe?"

"Yes," the lame councilor breathed out in relief and drew the slender blade from his belt.

Sheathing one of the Hellfires, the samrat took the dagger. Holding it up so its obsidian hilt glowed in the dull light, the king contemplated the Halahala swirling seductively in the hilt's black depths, iridescent blue flecked with gold and silver specks.

Vikramaditya's eyes narrowed. "Now to destroy this thing forever."

***

Holika was almost fully into her lunge when she felt herself being pulled back violently, the tip of her sword stopping just short of Kshapanaka's throat. The sorceress strained, slashing desperately to bridge the tiny gap, but the thing that had her in check was strong, hauling her back hard. It took the Witch Queen a moment to realize that it was the danava restraining her with the chain-blade—and though she could have freed herself by letting go of the weapon, she was loath to lose it. So, she wrestled, off-balance, one part of her mind wondering why the danava had not been influenced by her spells.

Then, she remembered. The danavas had no emotional attachments, so they had no yearnings and harboured no regrets. Hence, her manipulative spells had failed to rouse feelings in them.

Whipping her sword around, the Witch Queen attacked Shalivahana, who kept his grip on the chain-blade as he blocked her blows with the other hand. Shalivahana tried getting his vine-tentacles around the asura to put her in a bind, but Holika swiftly hacked the vines away. The two fought hard for leverage, neither succeeding in getting the better of the other.

The sorceress had just managed lopping off another of the danava lord's tentacles when she felt a sudden hush descend around her. At almost the same time, a faraway wailing came to her ears. Glancing around, she was surprised to see that the asuras, danavas and humans had all ceased fighting and were staring towards Ujjayini. Releasing her hold on the chain-blade, Holika stepped away from Shalivahana. She turned to the north, and her eyes flew open at the spectacle of the *churail*s sweeping across the sky, spewing fire.

Although she knew the asuras were protected from the *churails*, the sight of the apparitions sent a shiver down the Witch Queen's spine. She was still wondering how the *churails* had appeared over the city—had the human king slipped past the cordon laid by Hiranyaksha?—when the three banshees swerved and headed in the direction of the hills. The fighting had come to a standstill, all eyes pinned on the approaching *churails*. Realizing she wouldn't get a better opportunity to strike down her opponents, Holika heaved her sword and turned on Kshapanaka... when a cry of fear broke over the hills. Holika turned to see the banshees open their mouths and spray fire on the battlefield. The asuras and war mahishas instantly caught fire, whereas the human and danava fighters were left unscathed.

Shocked with disbelief, the sorceress stared as the *churails* set the whole asura army on fire. Seeing the asuras flail and fall, their screams rending the evening air and drowning out the wails of the banshees, Holika's mind went back to the stories that had been narrated about the Hellfires, generation after generation; about how Diti had made sure that the asuras would be immune to the *churails*.

All stories. All lies. All wrong.

With that realization came fear. Fear that clutched Holika's heart in an ice-cold grip, freezing her into inaction. All she could do was stare at the oncoming *churails*, one of them heading straight at her, the mouth opening wide, flames boiling up...

Somehow, the Witch Queen got herself to turn and break into a run. But the flames followed in hot pursuit, burning the skin on her back and neck.

***

"Borderworld is dying?"

The Acharya's words echoed in the stunned silence of the hall.

Vikramaditya nodded. "The banyan that sustains Borderworld was irreparably damaged during the asura attack," he said with a touch of sadness. "Its fall is inevitable."

Someone had brought torches in and lit a few of the lamps. In their light, the councilors could see that the samrat was exhausted. A crude dressing covered a wound he had sustained on the stomach, but the king had refused to let Dhanavantri look at it, insisting it must wait.

"The Ghoulmaster sought me out to tell me Borderworld was nearing its end, and to bid me goodbye." The king considered his council. "Any time now, Borderworld will cease to exist."

"And you want to take the Halahala into Borderworld?" Vetala Bhatta stared.

"When Borderworld ends, everything inside it will also end. It is the perfect opportunity to destroy the Halahala, once and for all." The samrat winced, feeling the dressing on his wound tenderly. "It is too late to save Borderworld. But at least we can shield the other three worlds from the Halahala and the insanity it is capable of inciting."

The raj-guru, Vararuchi, Varahamihira and Dhanavantri exchanged uneasy glances. "It doesn't sound like a good time to go into Borderworld," the physician observed.

"It is our best chance at getting rid of the Halahala," Vikramaditya was persuasive. "We lose this chance, and we are stuck with the dagger, and the devas and asuras will never leave us in peace. They will keep coming back for the Halahala, and this city and its people will pay the price of their greed. Ujjayini will be devastated, and the hopes and dreams of its people will come to a sad and terrible end. We cannot let that happen. If we have to free ourselves from a constant threat of war, we must destroy the Halahala now."

The silence extended as the councilors thought about this.

"How do we know Borderworld hasn't ended already?" asked Vararuchi.

"We don't, but for all our sakes, let's hope it hasn't," Vikramaditya replied.

"It is too dangerous," Varahamihira said with a shake of his head. "What if Borderworld ends with you still inside?"

"It is a chance we must take," the king was adamant. "It is our only hope for peace."

Another meditative silence. The samrat looked at the faces around him in exasperation. "The more we debate this, the harder it will be for me to get in and come back," he said.

"We were entrusted with the dagger so we would protect it," Varahamihira said thoughtfully. "By destroying it, would we be breaking our word to the Omniscient One?"

"The Omniscient One placed the Halahala in our safekeeping *because* he couldn't see a way of destroying it," said Vikramaditya. "Don't forget that the Halahala was always meant to be destroyed, and the Omniscient One would have done so, except for Veeshada's cunning. Our task was to protect the dagger from falling into the hands of the devas and the asuras. If I can place the Halahala in Borderworld in time, we will have succeeded in keeping our promise to Mahadeva."

"You are grievously injured," Dhanavantri protested. "You are in no condition to make the journey into Borderworld, Vikrama. It can be extremely perilous."

The samrat placed a gentle hand on the physician's shoulder.

"The last time I was there and in trouble, you brought me back," he said. "If my life is in danger, I believe you can bring me back again. And then there is Vishakha. She's been asking for me, so somebody try stopping me from coming back to her." He paused and his face softened. "How is she?"

"She is well," Dhanavantri said. "Just don't keep her waiting too long."

Vikramaditya studied the dagger, the contents of its obsidian hilt concealed in his grip. Then, with a nod at the raj-guru, he said, "Let us do this for Ujjayini."

***

Watching the *churails* scream and circle overhead, staying as inconspicuous as possible even though darkness lay thick over the land, Shukracharya scuttled frantically up the slope to the cavern from where his sons were guiding Ahi. He knew they had lost control over the serpent-dragon, but he also knew the meddling councilor was no longer capable of interfering with Ahi...

There was so much he knew now, so much that the bones had told him.

He wished he had asked the bones about the Hellfires earlier. He hadn't, because he had never thought it necessary; because, like everyone else in Patala, he'd believed in the stories. So, he had watched in horror as the *churails* had assailed the asura army. Shocked numb by the sight of the burning and fleeing asuras, he had rushed to the bones for explanations, and explanations and answers he had got in plenty.

Kashyapa had nullified the mantras Diti had cast on the swords. Kashyapa and Paurava had kept this a secret, as a result of which...

Hiranyaksha was dead. Hiranyakashipu and Holika had fled Ujjayini. The asura armies had been routed, with help from the barbarians from the west and the danavas from the Dandaka. The Nine Pearls had come together despite his best efforts, even though the young boy was at death's door.

And Vikramaditya had once again prevented the asuras from claiming Veeshada's dagger—

—which was now on its way into Borderworld.

Vikramaditya was intent on destroying the Halahala, the high priest fumed in disbelief as he crested the slope and the mouth of the cavern came into view, a slice of dim light in the night. Vikramaditya was intent on making sure that the asuras never got ascendency over the devas. He was going to deny the asuras the chance to reclaim Amaravati, he was going to deny him, Shukracharya, the pleasure of seeing Indra and Narada and Brihaspati—mainly Brihaspati—and all the other devas grovel before him...

There were too many scores to settle with the devas, so there was no way he would let the king get away with his plan.

Chanting a mantra under his breath, Shukracharya made his way to the cavern. Entering it, he saw Chandasura and Amarka seated before the ghost-serpent, which swayed over the bowl of bubbling water.

"Is the snake back in your control?" the high priest asked.

"Yes, father," Chandasura replied. "For a while it wasn't—"

"I know," Shukracharya waved his hand brusquely. "The human you were against is probably dead, so it doesn't matter. What I want you to do is take full control over Ahi and destroy the city. Start with the king's palace. At the end of this, nothing must remain of the humans."

"Yes, father," said Chandasura.

The high priest extracted a knife from his waist. Completing the *sanjivani-mantra* he'd been uttering, Shukracharya slit his wrist with the knife, severing the veins so the lifeblood flowed down his hand, dripping off his fingers and spattering on the cavern's rough stone floor.

The knife dropped from the high priest's hand as he collapsed and entered Borderworld.

Amarka and Chandasura didn't turn to look at their father's body, slumped by the mouth of the cavern. Sweat dripping off their brows, they repeated the mantras that kept Ahi in their command. As more strands of steam rose from the water and latched onto the ghost-serpent, the apparition thickened and reared, its hood fanning out, its mouth open, so the sick smell of rotting flesh spilled and washed against the walls of the cavern.

Outside, hidden by the night, Ahi slipped through the clouds over Ujjayini.

Sacrifice

Do you know a way of controlling Ahi?"

"What?" Jayanta gawked at Urvashi stupidly.

"You were the one who brought it out of its slumber. You must know of a way..."

Jayanta poked his head out and surveyed the gallery. It was empty, except for the apsara standing at the door to his chamber. His eyes narrowed suspiciously.

"Father has sent you, hasn't he?"

"Father...? No... I came on my own accord."

The prince assessed the apsara for a moment. "What do you want with Ahi?"

"I want you to stop Ahi."

"Stop?" Jayanta blinked in surprise.

"Yes, stop Ahi."

"From doing what?"

"From destroying the human city."

The prince looked suspicious again. "What's so special about the human city?"

Pushing past the prince, deliberately brushing her bare shoulder against the prince's arm even though she detested the touch, Urvashi sailed into the chamber. Turning around, she crossed her hands, so her breasts pushed up, catching Jayanta's leering eye.

"That's of no concern to you." The apsara stared at the young deva. "Can you stop it?"

Jayanta's eyes trailed the curves of Urvashi's body. He looked at her eyes, which stared back at him defiantly… but also held a promise that he had never seen before. His pulse quickened in an instant.

"The mantras were stolen by Hiranyakashipu," Jayanta offered a noncommittal shrug.

"I know. But I thought you might still know how to control the snake." Urvashi paused. Once she'd said what she was going to say next, there would be no going back, she realized. "I… am willing to grant you the love that you seek—if you can do it."

Jayanta gaped at the apsara like an idiot. Then, remembering to breathe, he shut his mouth and swallowed. Wetting his lips, he began closing the door. "I might be able to—"

"*Right now.*"

The prince stopped; the door was halfway shut. There was steel in the apsara's voice.

"I want you to stop Ahi *now*," she repeated. "Everything else will follow."

Giving it a moment's thought, Jayanta nodded. Closing the door, he looked around the untidy chamber. "I have the lamps, charcoal and flour, but I'll need vermillion—"

"How will you stop the snake if the asuras have the mantras?" Urvashi asked.

A smirk appeared on the prince's face. "That's what they think…" He turned to Urvashi, his expression suddenly wary. "You are certain you're not here at father's bidding?"

"No," the apsara insisted. "Do you think he would send me here with my love on offer?"

"Can't put anything past him," the deva sneered. "Father would go to any lengths to get what he wants. To answer your question..." rummaging through a trunk, he extracted seven lamps, "...the asuras don't have the mantras."

"What?"

"Sorry, they do," Jayanta explained, "but not *all* of the mantras."

Keeping the lamps to one side, the prince cleared the floor to draw a mandala with charcoal and flour. "When Brihaspati ordered me to hand him the mantras, I surrendered only half of the palm leaves and kept the rest with me," he said. "I did not want to part with the mantras entirely; the one thing I have learned from father is that you never give away power. No one had set eyes on those mantras in a thousand years, so there was no way Brihaspati, or anyone else, would know the mantras were incomplete. What Hiranyakashipu took away from here were the mantras that can control Ahi *in part*... but not fully."

Jayanta surveyed the serpent-shaped mandala he had drawn with pride. Then, looking up at Urvashi, he said, "Only I have the mantras to control Ahi fully." Walking over to the apsara, he took her chin in his hand, smearing flour on her cheeks. "Aren't you pleased I am here for you when you are in need of aid?" He kissed the apsara hard on her lips, biting them with passion, panting into her, his hands spidery and running amok all over her body, groping, gripping, squeezing...

Urvashi pressed her palm to the deva's chest. "Later," she said, licking her lips and hating the stink of stale *ganjika* on her tongue. She looked into his crazed eyes. "Ahi first."

Reluctantly, the prince drew back.

"What about the mantras that Hiranyakashipu took with him?" the apsara asked. "Don't you need them?"

"They are here," the prince tapped a finger to his head self-importantly. "Don't forget, I have raised the snake once already." He started placing the lamps along the mandala. "Why do you want the human city saved?" he probed suddenly.

"Does it matter? I am here for you."

"Mmm-hmm," said Jayanta, plonking a copper bowl in the centre of the mandala. "Did you know that father wanted me to raise Ahi too?" he prattled. "Had he asked graciously, I would have, but being gracious is not one of father's admirable traits." He chuckled. "Though now I am glad he wasn't gracious. Otherwise, how would I have helped you..."

Why do you want the human city saved?

Urvashi turned the question in her mind as she tuned out the deva's chatter. Where could she begin explaining? Did she herself understand her motivations? Yes, there was her disillusionment with Indra. There was her admiration for the human king. There was the remorse she felt for her behaviour with the queen. But was all this enough for her to set aside her loathing for this worm of a prince and offer herself to him in exchange of his help? And to what end? She didn't know for certain that Jayanta's intervention would prevent Ujjayini's destruction. She didn't even know if the prince was lying about the mantras, so he could even be taking advantage of her...

You said you could become whoever I wanted you to be, Vikramaditya's words suddenly came back to her from the queen's bedchamber. *No, Mithyamayi. We mustn't change like that for love; it wouldn't be love at all. If anything, it is* love *that changes us, transforms us, makes us better than who we are. When you understand this difference, you would have understood love.*

Urvashi stared in front of her unseeingly.

"What should I do with Ahi once it is in my control?"

The apsara looked from Jayanta to the mandala. The lamps had been lit, and everything was ready.

It is love that changes us, transforms us... makes us better than who we are.

"Send it back to where you brought it up from," she replied.

The king had been right. She had finally understood, and *he* had made her understand.

The prince settled down before the copper bowl. "Do you know where Ahi is right now?"

Letting out a sigh full of longing, Urvashi nodded. "Somewhere over the human city."

***

Another section of the palace's north wing went down with a deafening crash, sending tremors along the floor under Vararuchi's feet as he sprinted down a corridor. The roar of tearing masonry channelled down the passage, snatching away the councilor's words egging Varahamihira to keep up. The older man hobbled behind as best as he could, but there was no question of catching up with the king's brother, who had turned the corner and disappeared from view.

Reaching the turn, Varahamihira saw the terrace to his right crowded with palace hands and guards, jabbering as they leaned over the parapet and pointed downwards or craned their necks to stare at the sky. The lame councilor jostled to the front to see debris from the collapsed walls still raining into the palace lake, though the full extent of the damage was hidden by the dark. The lake's waters slapped against the palace walls, the agitation slowly subsiding.

"—the snake."

Varahamihira turned to see that Vararuchi had pushed his way to his side. "What?"

"It's confirmed," Vararuchi shouted to make himself heard over everyone. "It's the snake."

Varahamihira nodded, and they both searched the black sky. Neither could see anything. No stars, no constellations, no moon, no Ahi.

"Any injuries or casualties in the palace?"

"We might find someone trapped while clearing the rubble," Vararuchi shrugged. "Can you stop it from inflicting more damage? With your shield?"

"It depends. First, I must be able to see it. Second, I must be in the section of the palace that is under attack. Third, I don't know if I can create an energy shield large enough."

"You've got to try. The thing has taken down three sections of the palace already."

The sound of something liquid splashing into the lake issued from their right, followed by the hiss and sizzle of scalding water.

"The snake spat into the lake," someone shouted.

"If it gets the causeway, we'll be stuck here for a long time," Vararuchi muttered. "Come. It's somewhere that side."

They went along winding corridors and up open galleries, chasing the serpent, but when they got to where Vararuchi had thought Ahi would be, there was nothing. They gazed at the sky, scanning—

A scream. Followed by another crumbling, shattering noise.

The councilors turned to see a segment of a faraway roof cave in. Dust mushroomed in the air.

"There," Vararuchi pointed at a nebulous, serpentine form hanging over the palace.

Focusing on the form and seeing it rear back, Varahamihira realized that the snake was preparing to spit venom again. Instantly, he flung his hand up, casting a shield as wide as he could, but the width of the shield barely covered the terrace on which they stood. The serpent spat again, and another part of the palace erupted, dust and debris shooting into the air, the aftershocks sending cracks up the outer walls. The snake itself vanished into the night.

"It's not working," Varahamihira said woefully.

"The palace won't hold up if this goes on for much longer," Vararuchi growled. "We must move Vikrama somewhere safer."

"We can't disturb him until he's back from Borderworld," Varahamihira reminded him.

"But he's too much at risk here with this thing..."

Vararuchi pressed his fingers to his temples in order to focus, when the hiss broke directly overhead. The councilors looked up, their hair standing on end, their mouths dry with terror. At first, they saw nothing but the black sky. Then, slowly, the fuzzy outline formed from the surrounding clouds, and Ahi became a distinct shape, swaying gently.

"The shield," Vararuchi whispered.

Varahamihira felt the age in his bones as he lifted his hand; the very air seemed to resist him, reminding him it was a bad idea. But still his hand went up.

Then, unexpectedly, the clouds parted in the east to let the moonlight through.

And in that pure, milk-white light, the councilors saw the elemental snake in all its glory. The moonlight reflected off and refracted through its shimmering body, its open hood punctuated by the slits of its baleful eyes, burning from within and blood-orange in colour. Its mouth was a dark pit from which a forked tongue darted out, greedily licking the air.

The serpent rose over the terrace. It stared down at the councilors. It drew its head back.

"The shield," Vararuchi hissed urgently.

Varahamihira tried to remember how to cast the shield, but only fear came willingly.

Ahi drew to its full height, ready to spew venom on them.

"Use your shield," Vararuchi screamed under his breath.

Ahi swayed...

...and thinned...

...and lost form, weight and density. It lost its malevolence too.

Ahi evaporated.

All that remained was the beautiful moonlight.

"Something happened to it," Varahamihira marvelled.

"I think… it died," said Vararuchi, his shoulders slumping in relief.

Somewhere in the city, an alarm bell started ringing.

"Now what?" said Vararuchi, both surprised and vexed.

Within moments, a second, then a third bell joined the tumult. Exchanging worried glances, the councilors strode indoors, where they ran into a flustered guard.

"Ujjayini is under attack," the guard needed no prompting. Struggling to keep the fear from his voice, he added, "It's the same snake-faced things that came a few nights ago, digging up from under the earth."

"Any sign of the half-horses?" Vararuchi snapped.

The guard mumbled indistinctly, his words drowning in the strident blare of a trumpet that cut through the din of the alarm bells, which were now tolling all over the city.

"That was an elephant," Vararuchi exclaimed, cocking his ear and looking at Varahamihira, who had turned to face Ujjayini. The old councilor's face appeared pale in the dim light.

Varahamihira's lips moved slowly to form a single word. "Indra."

***

The water in the copper bowl was perfectly still. Not even a hint of a ripple, no sign of steam.

"Where did the thing go?" asked Amarka, frowning at the bowl.

"It just fell back into the water and disappeared—like it had died or something," Chandasura growled, looking all around him, then up into the roof of the cavern, as if expecting to see the ghost-serpent hiding there, playing truant.

"Let's try again," Amarka said gruffly.

As one brother recited the mantras, the other made yet another incision on his finger and dripped blood into the bowl. But nothing happened. The ghost-serpent refused to be tempted.

"Is it working?" asked Amarka, beginning to sound flustered.

"Focus on the mantras," Chandasura snapped. "Let me do my job."

They stuck at it until Chandasura finally dropped his hand in vexation. "It's of no use," he grunted. He felt the side of the bowl. "Even the water has gone cold." He shoved the bowl in anger, and water splashed onto the floor. "Must be the same human councilor, the one father mentioned."

"Father said he was probably dead," Amarka gave the matter some thought. "No, it's not him. He struggled with Ahi. This is someone who has a lot more authority over the serpent." He got to his feet.

Emerging from the cavern, the brothers surveyed the sky. A half-moon illuminated the clouds in soft hues of silver.

"Nothing," said Amarka in a tone sharp with disappointment. "Ahi's gone."

"Aargh," Chandasura rumbled with impotent rage. "What are we to do—"

The sound of something heavy dropping on very light feet interrupted Chandasura, followed by a deep, menacing snarl. The brothers whirled around to see the moonlight fall on a bulky figure standing in the coarse scrub of the hills. The figure stepped into the light coming out of the cavern.

A man-lion.

Acting in unison, the asuras charged at the beast. They were powerfully built and incredibly strong, but neither of them was prepared for the fury with which the man-lion leaped at them, tawny arms raised, claws open, slashing down first with the right hand, then the left, in quick succession...

The brothers staggered back, Chandasura mauled across his broad, yellow face, his left cheek and mouth torn open, Amarka's right shoulder and chest in ribbons and bleeding. Chandasura rallied despite the pain, his massive fist driving into Amara Simha's chest, surprising him so that Amarka was able to sneak past the councilor and dart inside the cavern. Chandasura took another swing at Amara Simha, but the councilor sidestepped this time, swiping at the asura's exposed belly, cutting flesh and muscle.

Amarka emerged from the cavern with their maces, one in each hand. Seeing the man-lion's back turned to him, the asura rushed into an attack, his mace raised, all set to bury its spikes deep into Amara Simha's back. But something tripped the asura up, sending him sprawling. Alerted by a feline's sharp instinct, Amara Simha turned to see Amarka flounder towards him. Grabbing the asura by the hair, the councilor yanked him forward and threw him to the ground, then turned in time to dodge another of Chandasura's blows aimed at his face. With a roar that echoed over the hills, the man-lion closed his jaws over Chandasura's arm, clamping down so hard the asura screamed in agony, the bones in his muscular forearm cracking under the pressure.

Releasing his hold on Chandasura, the man-lion switched his attention to Amarka, who was staggering to his feet. But even as Amara Simha stepped forward, hand up and claws opened to smash down on Amarka's head, chains magically appeared around the asura, binding him captive. Amarka thrashed around to free himself, but the chains were sturdy, so all he did was trip clumsily and fall again at the man-lion's feet.

Amara Simha knelt by Amarka's side, set to club the asura to death, when suddenly, he felt a restraint on his arm. The councilor snapped around to see a chain slipped around his wrist as well, its other end held by Kubera.

"You said you wanted them as prisoners," the yaksha reminded the councilor.

A snarl escaped the man-lion's lips, but his arm slackened and his shoulders relaxed. As the chain eased and vanished, Amara Simha got to his feet.

A yaksha brought a lamp from the cavern. The light fell on the figures bound in chains.

"Exactly what we came looking for," Kubera said cheerily. "Shukracharya's sons."

"Why side with the humans, yaksha?" Chandasura asked with a bitter scowl. When no reply was forthcoming, he bared his teeth in anger. "You have come in our way two times in a row. The yakshas will regret this, I promise."

Kubera smiled in response. "You should be more concerned about *your* welfare right now. Shortly, you will face the Wielder of the Hellfires, and you have come in *his* way too many times for the meeting to be pleasant."

Chandasura gritted his teeth but said nothing.

The yaksha who had brought the lamp whispered something to Kubera.

"It seems we have a surprise inside," the yaksha lord said, pointing to the cavern.

Approaching the figure on the floor, Kubera and Amara Simha bent to examine the face; its identity was plain to both of them by the eye-patch that covered the left eye.

"Is he dead?" the man-lion asked.

The yaksha checked for a pulse beat. "He is, but again, maybe he is not."

"What does that mean?"

"Shukracharya has mastered the *sanjivani-mantra*, which enables the dead to return to life."

"Let us take him too then," Amara Simha grunted. "If he does come back to life, I will derive great pleasure in killing him all over again."

***

The wind tugged at Vikramaditya as he fumbled through the murky blackness, blind for the most part, so he had to bank on his hearing—and his memory—to find his way forward. His feet dragged over piles of dead leaves, their scrunch underfoot sharp in his ears, muffling the distant creaking of an old tree. Despite the wind, the air was stale and smelled of decay. Here and there, shafts of weak, grey light splintered the darkness from above, and in these pools of illumination, the samrat saw tatty trails of mist float over a thick carpet of yellowed banyan leaves.

"Ghoulmaster, where are you?" Vikramaditya called out, cupping his hands to his mouth. "Answer me, please."

The wind whistled, and the tree creaked.

The king took ten steps before stopping. "This is your friend, Vikramaditya. Where are you?"

Silence. And then a dry, tired whisper. "Greetings, wise king."

Vikramaditya turned to see Betaal step from the semi-darkness into a beam of grey light. The ghoul's hair of flames had dwindled in strength and colour, dancing dull yellow in the wind, and he stooped under some unseen burden set on his shoulders.

"What brings you here at a time such as this?" the Ghoulmaster asked.

The samrat looked into the darkness around them. The tree creaked louder than before.

"I was wrong to bring the accursed dagger into Borderworld," he spoke in a tone heavy with deep regret. "I should never have involved you. This is my fault. I brought this upon you and Borderworld, and I can't set it right. I am sorry, my friend."

The ghoul drifted a little closer to Vikramaditya. "Don't blame yourself for what's happened, wise king. This is how it was meant to be; this is destiny. Borderworld would have ended, one way or the other. You did what you thought was right, and I am pleased Borderworld played a part in protecting the Halahala and honouring your promise to the Omniscient One. If you were to ask me again, I would put Borderworld at your disposal all over again." With a pause, he added, "This is what friends are for—to help each other whenever the need arises."

The king nodded slowly.

"Is this why you came all the way?" Betaal stared curiously. "Just to say sorry?"

Vikramaditya looked at the Ghoulmaster for a moment. "No, but first tell me... Is there *no* way of saving Borderworld? Can't *something* be done to stop the tree...?"

Betaal was shaking his head. "Listen, wise king," he said.

Incapable of bearing its weight, the tree groaned, an exhausted, grating sound, a death lament.

"There is no way of undoing the damage the tree has suffered," the ghoul said "Nothing can stop the tree from falling, nothing can save Borderworld."

Vikramaditya nodded to say he understood.

"In which case, with your permission, there is one more thing Borderworld can do to protect and keep the other three worlds safe." The samrat slowly slipped the dagger from his belt. "In its destruction, Borderworld can offer the other worlds security from the Halahala."

The Ghoulmaster looked at the dagger, then back at the samrat. "You don't need to seek my permission, wise king. I already said I would put Borderworld at your disposal again if need be." With a hint of dry humour in his voice, he added, "And it is only fitting that Borderworld destroys the thing that led to Borderworld's destruction."

Betaal stretched a bony hand at the king. "I will be happy to rid you and the three worlds of the Halahala's burden."

It was Vikramaditya's turn to shake his head. "The idea is to be rid of the Halahala, not you."

"I don't understand."

"I've also come to take you with me."

"Where?"

"To Avanti."

Betaal stared at the king. "To the world of the humans? Why?"

"I cannot let you stay here as Borderworld collapses around you. I cannot stand and watch while you quietly go away. What kind of friendship would that be?"

The Ghoulmaster was quiet for a moment. "This is very kind of you, wise king," he said at last, "but I must decline. This is my world; I belong here. This is where I have lived, and it is here that I must die."

"The world that you speak about no longer exists, my friend," said Vikramaditya. "Your ghouls are all gone, and nothing is left of that world. This isn't your world. If you choose to die here, it will be for nothing. Come with me, instead—"

"And do what?" asked Betaal. "What would I do in your world?"

Before the samrat could answer, the rending sound of wood being torn apart issued from the dark. The ghoul glanced over his shoulder, then looked back at the king.

"Not much longer before the tree falls," he said, twitching his skeletal fingers for the dagger. "Give me the Halahala and leave."

"No," Vikramaditya said adamantly.

"This is no time to argue—" Betaal began, then stopped as he looked behind the king.

Vikramaditya turned to see a figure lurking in the shadows. His features were hidden, but his build was familiar, short and stocky, an ironwood *danda* in one hand.

"We meet again." The figure stepped into the light, taking stock of the king and Betaal. "Give me the dagger."

The samrat shook his head. The same instant, wood wrenched and twisted violently, followed by a rumbling crash. Shivers ran through the earth, and a gust of wind propelled dead leaves into the air.

"Give me the dagger," Shukracharya demanded sharply.

"Never," said Vikramaditya.

"You fought with great courage and determination to earn my respect," said the high priest. "Let that be good enough, human. Don't be greedy. Accept your defeat with grace and hand me the dagger, so we can get out of here while we still have the chance."

"The only way anyone will ever get out of here is without the Halahala."

"Enough," Shukracharya spat in anger. "Give me the dagger *now*. I command you," he began casting a spell, "give me—wait... what—?"

Vikramaditya sensed a presence close behind, but by the time he could react, the dagger had been snatched from his hand. Spinning around, he saw the ghoul draw away, putting distance between himself and the king.

"What are you—" the samrat began, but Betaal was already addressing the high priest.

"You want the dagger, do you?" he asked, as another enormous cracking and tumbling sound emerged out of the darkness, as though something was falling in on itself. Betaal waved the dagger at Shukracharya. "If you want this, you will have to come and get it from me."

The samrat stared as the Ghoulmaster turned and slipped out of the light, fleeing towards the dark… from where came the sounds of chaos and collapse.

Vikramaditya was still coming to grips with the turn of events when the *danda* landed hard on the back of his head. He reeled under the stunning blow, his vision darkening and going splotchy as Shukracharya shoved past him in his pursuit of Betaal. The high priest swung the *danda* once again, lower this time, cracking it against the king's knees.

Coherent thought whooshed out of the samrat's mind and he buckled and fell, his head in the leaves, their rustling loud in his ears, accompanied by the pounding of Shukracharya's feet receding into silence.

Halahala

There, to the left. Heading towards the causeway."

"God, it is… *huge*."

Listening to the rising apprehension in the men's voices, Vararuchi sprinted along the gallery, *urumi* swinging from one hand, a shield in the other. He tried to catch a glimpse of what the men in the gallery below him were looking at, but it was too dark outside and the angle was wrong.

Heading towards the causeway.

Fighting the urge to slow down and see for himself, the councilor kept going to the mournful toll of Ujjayini's bells.

"Take your positions by the windows," a captain ordered a group of archers.

Rushing down a flight of stairs, Vararuchi had to take care not to trip over two soldiers sprawled on the steps, the first with his head smashed in, the other's face mangled beyond recognition. The palace was full of dead bodies scattered here and there in the aftermath of Hiranyakashipu's assault; there had been no time to clear the place between that and the attacks by Ahi, and now, Indra.

The councilor crossed the atrium in five bounds and shot through the main door, just as the elephant resumed its trumpeting. Running down the causeway, he peered across the lake, striving to locate the beast from its call—when suddenly he discerned its moving shape, a hulking shadow in the surrounding darkness, loping by the lake's edge with big, belligerent strides.

He was still only halfway across when the animal swerved into view at the other end of the causeway. The light from the palace was weak, and the moonlight was mild and diffused, but what the moon and lamplight failed to reveal, the imagination readily filled in, accentuating the beast's proportions so that without him even realizing it, Vararuchi dropped pace, staring at the mammoth in astonishment and suddenly feeling defenceless. The sense of vulnerability only heightened as the elephant drew closer and the councilor counted the six curving tusks, the beast's ears flapping in anger as it rolled its trunk and trumpeted, intimidating in sound and size.

And then, he noticed the figure seated on the animal's back.

Calming his nerves and taking a hold of himself, the councilor broke into a run again. There was no way he would let Indra set foot in the palace—

Something large and nimble leaped at him from the lake.

Vararuchi sensed movement out of the corner of his eye and heard the slosh of water sluicing away before the thing had even set its feet on the causeway. Without sparing a moment's thought, and going purely by instinct, the councilor lashed out with his *urumi*. The stroke was randomly directed, but the supple blade connected, slicing through flesh. The thing slipped and fell on the causeway before toppling back into the water.

The king's brother had barely caught his breath when three more shapes shot out of the water and landed on the causeway. Two in front of him, one behind.

The things attacked Vararuchi almost simultaneously, swinging their swords at him, but the councilor parried their blows with his shield while ducking out of harm's way. He swung his *urumi* at them, missing completely once, but slashing one of the things in the reverse swing... and then, as the moon came out from behind a cloud, be noticed the horned snake heads of his attackers.

The snake-faced things that came a few nights ago, he remembered the guard saying.

Their blood makes our flesh decay, he recalled Varahamihira saying.

Blocking an attack with his shield, Vararuchi leaped from the creature he had just wounded. This was going to be tricky, he realized. He couldn't let their toxic blood touch him, even by accident.

Dodging a swipe aimed at his midriff, the councilor shot a glance at the elephant, which was striding towards the causeway, its progress unchecked. Vararuchi gripped his shield tight and spun hard, driving the shield flat into the snout of one of the snake-heads, shattering it. Using the momentum, he kicked the creature back into the lake before it could bleed. Again, he rocked back on one foot, then leaped past the second creature, slamming the shield into the side of its head and shoving it hard into the water. The third snake-head poked him, stabbing him on his right forearm. Pain shot along the length of his arm, but the councilor quickly turned and socked the shield's edge into the creature's snout. Sending it into the water with a splash, Vararuchi turned to confront the elephant, when five more shapes emerged from the lake, swords and spears pointing his way...

The mammoth was thirty paces away. Plotting all the conceivable moves he could make and reviewing each conceivable outcome in his head, Vararuchi hoisted his shield as he prepared to plough right through the line of snake-heads in front of him. Bracing himself for impact, the councilor was about to break into a run when—

—from the shadows of a pair of *saptaparni* trees growing by the lake's edge, a figure stepped out.

Straight onto the elephant's path.

His back to the palace and the causeway, his legs planted firm, the figure faced the advancing mammoth.

Vararuchi stared at the familiar broad-shouldered figure, at his heavily muscled back and the curving scimitar that the man wielded.

The elephant trumpeted, petulant at such an open sign of defiance.

The snake-headed creatures paused at the sound. Their heads snapped around to look behind.

In an effort to threaten the man standing in its way, the mammoth swung its head from side to side, its tusks now less than twenty yards from him, carving up the night air. The earth shook with every stomp of its feet, the vibrations carrying down the causeway to where Vararuchi stood. The councilor watched Indra raise a heavy sword over his head, blue currents buzzing and rippling along its broad blade...

The man with the scimitar stood his ground with rock-like resolve.

"Watch out—" the councilor called in warning, but Indra's sword was already descending.

Vararuchi watched, spellbound, as lightning surged from the tip of Indra's sword, a ragged, coruscating line of light, leaping at Kalidasa, its glare throwing the shadows all the way back, so that for a fraction of a moment, time appeared to come to a standstill around Vararuchi, the mammoth, Kalidasa and the five snake-heads on the causeway.

The bolt leaped at Kalidasa, burning the air in its path, leaving a scorched smell in its wake. It leaped at Kalidasa's chest, murderous in intent, powerful enough to strike down the broadest of trees...

But the lightning bolt never reached the giant's chest.

His mouth opening in amazement, Vararuchi followed Kalidasa's arm as it whipped up the scimitar, pointing it straight at the bolt, which struck the blade and exploded into a shower of sparks. Rings of blue current ran up the scimitar and appeared to vanish into its hilt, even as the impact of the bolt sent Kalidasa staggering back three steps. The giant stood with his head down for a moment, shaken, the scimitar still pointing at Indra, its tip wavering a little—and then, to Vararuchi's disbelief, Kalidasa lifted his head to lock eyes with the deva, the scimitar steady and solid in his grasp.

The deva swung his sword at Kalidasa again, but this time, nothing happened.

No bolt of lightning. No smell of burned air.

Flipping his grip on the scimitar, Kalidasa raised the weapon over his head so its tip pointed straight down. Fascinated, Vararuchi watched the giant drive the blade hard into the ground, barely a foot from where he stood, burying its point deep into the soil...

Five streaks of lightning emerged from the spot where the scimitar had pierced the earth. The streaks spread like dazzling fissures, radiating outward and tearing a zigzag path towards the elephant, which was already backing away, trumpeting in fright as the ground between it and Kalidasa started caving in. The mud sank swiftly, forming a trench, and the mammoth almost got dragged in, extracting itself and withdrawing to safety under dire threats and curses from Indra.

As the ground finally settled, Kalidasa and the deva stared at each other across the width of the trench.

Yanking the scimitar out of the ground, the giant lifted his left hand and shook his finger at Indra, warning and admonishing at the same time.

"Never," he roared.

Five bolts of lightning came down around the causeway in rapid succession. Blinking in their light, Vararuchi saw five hulking figures where the lightning bolts had struck. The figures had horns on their heads, and bore jagged-edged swords. Their eyes were white and luminous like moonlight.

Consolidated thunder crashed over the palace, loud enough to shatter the eardrums.

Snapping out of his spell, Vararuchi looked at the snake-heads, who were still rooted to their spots. Discarding the *urumi* and drawing his *katari* from his belt, the king's brother burst into a run, the *katari* aimed at the first snake-head.

***

For all his skeletal appearance, the Ghoulmaster was surprisingly strong.

He kicked and heaved against Shukracharya as they scuffled for leverage, rolling on the ground and sending the leaves scattering, the priest's forearm locked around the ghoul's scrawny throat, the other hand trying to pry the dagger free. But Betaal resisted, clawing at Shukracharya's face as he twisted and tossed around, keeping the dagger just outside the high priest's reach.

With a grunt, Shukracharya tightened his grip around Betaal's throat, but the ghoul dug in and writhed, freeing himself from the priest's grasp. Scrambling up, the ghoul lunged in the direction of the void that was opening up in front of them, spreading like a stain, darker than all the darkness around it, the pitch-black of nothingness from which neither light nor sound emerged.

Shukracharya threw himself after Betaal, grabbing him, hauling him back, and they both landed hard on the ground. Shukracharya felt the air rush out of his lungs, his ribs jarring on impact, but the ghoul was already wriggling free. Applying all his might, the priest dragged Betaal down and pushed himself over the ghoul, pinning him, but Betaal's hand was already raised and drawn back...

...the dagger aimed at the expanding blackness...

The priest flung out a hand in desperation.

Clamping the ghoul's bony wrist hard, he jerked the hand back, stopping Betaal from flinging the dagger into the void. Then, yanking even harder, he wrenched the hand all the way back, so the arm dislocated at the shoulder.

With an agonized scream, the Ghoulmaster let go of the dagger.

Shukracharya was onto the dagger in a flash, snatching it up in one swift grab. Feeling the smooth, hard obsidian hilt against his palm, a thrill of elation went through the high priest's body. His eyes glowed ecstatic—finally, *finally*, he had Veeshada's dagger in his hand.

The black emptiness rolled in, gathering momentum as it gained mass, its edge no more than twenty paces from the high priest and the ghoul.

Scurrying to his feet, Shukracharya turned to head back the way he'd come.

He took two steps—when a hand grabbed him by the ankle from behind, tripping him.

The high priest fell face forward. The dagger slipped from his hand and went spinning.

Shukracharya watched the dagger strike the ground, bounce and roll away. He reached out to catch it, but his balance was off. He missed. The dagger skittered out of reach.

Kicking himself free of Betaal's grasp, the high priest scrambled onto all fours and made a lunge for the dagger—

—but Vikramaditya beat him to it.

The samrat bent and picked the dagger from his feet.

Shukracharya's eye narrowed in dismay. The king straightened, wincing a little, but his grip was firm on the dagger. The deva and the human stared at each other...

Despair wrapped heavy hands around Shukracharya's shoulders as he saw the resolve in the samrat's eyes. The Halahala was not going to be his after all, the realization finally dawned—

"Don't do it," the high priest wheezed in a voice ragged with anxiety. "It is too precious to be destroyed, king. It is... *Don't.*"

His eyes locked on Shukracharya, Vikramaditya drew his hand all the way back. Putting all his strength into the throw, the samrat hurled the Halahala at the incoming void.

"*No...*"

Shukracharya watched the dagger sail over his head. He turned and chased after it, his hands stretched and flailing, but the king's throw was powerful and well directed.

"*No...*" the high priest wailed, slipping and stumbling on the brink of the void.

Spinning through dead air, Veeshada's dagger disappeared into the blackest of black.

***

Swathes of oil-black, almost impossible to distinguish in the dark, swooped through the city, swallowing nagas, kinnaras and devas whole. The yakshas switched form—poisoned arrows, fireballs, sneeze-inducing pollen—to disorient the kinnaras and the Ashvin cavalry, and the Acharya successfully got the fear of the *churails* to germinate in *one* Ashvin's mind, sowing panic through the entire Ashvin force. Kshapanaka combed Ujjayini's streets, hunting down nagas and kinnaras, while outside the city, the Hunas, along with soldiers from the imperial garrison of Musili, ambushed the rearguard of the deva army, the *yah'bre* stomping a path through the devas, crushing them underfoot and destroying their morale.

And Shanku coordinated these multiple attacks against Avanti's aggressors by mind-leaping from one part of the city to another, conveying information, sharing strategies and serving as a guide when required, so that between the yakshas, danavas and human warriors, Ujjayini was well defended, and the devas failed to gain any ascendency.

"I'm running low on arrows," Kshapanaka called out over the pealing of the bells, unleashing another volley at a unit of nagas she had intercepted in an alleyway with Shanku's help.

"I'll find you some," Shanku yelled back from the terrace of a nearby building. She sprang to the ground and strode over to inspect a dead naga. "You're sure I shouldn't let this thing's blood touch me?" she asked, eyeing the dagger she had buried deep in its head.

"Absolutely. Unless you want to see your flesh rot right before your eyes."

Running a hand over her empty belt, Shanku made a face. "I'll also need to look for daggers for myself then." Turning to Kshapanaka, she said, "I'll be back soon. Don't go so far that I can't find you."

The next instant, the girl was in a street in the deserted eastern section.

She mind-leaped three streets to a City Walk picket in the hope of finding soldiers there, but then remembered that that portion of the city had been evacuated. The picket was empty. She mind-leaped again, this time close to the palace. Standing on the steps that led to the flower market, she surveyed the area, but except for two dead half-horses—bodies burned black, limbs twisted in agony—there was nothing there either.

Shanku was about to leap again when five bolts of lightning blazed down almost in unison, lighting up half of Ujjayini. The next instant, five loud cracks of thunder shook the city in one intertwined explosion of sound. Cringing from the noise, the girl tensed, realizing that the lightning bolts had struck close to the palace; she also recognized their pattern from a night similar to this one, when she had first mind-leaped—

She mind-leaped. And she stared at the figures by the causeway.

At the five horned rakshasas with eyes like quicksilver. At the short figure of Vararuchi, who was slaying a group of snake-heads at the head of the causeway. And at the giant—who took a bolt of energy that a rakshasa had hurled on his chest, before flinging the bolt right back on his assailant. Shanku watched the air curve and warp around the bolt's trajectory, hitting the rakshasa so hard his bone armour cracked. The rakshasa fell back in surprise, and the giant hoisted his scimitar and charged at the rakshasa...

Shanku realized she was grinning to herself.

I'm running low on arrows. Remembering her errand, she shook her head, still smiling.

She mind-leaped... and found herself in the southern districts. Empty streets. Shuttered shops and houses.

The girl smacked her forehead, remembering. The city armoury, of course...

Almost in no time, Shanku was back to where she had left Kshapanaka, two quivers full of arrows slung on each shoulder and eight knives of assorted sizes in her belt. She sped from street to street in search of Kshapanaka, but the queen's sister was nowhere to be seen.

Another mind-leap brought Shanku to a street that bordered the spice market and the square where the harvest festivals were held. The street was empty, but a figure lay crumpled at the foot of a small, burned tree. Curious, the girl approached the figure, her expression changing as she recognized the familiar build and the long hair concealing the face. Kneeling down, she brushed the hair back.

Ghatakarpara.

Shanku pressed two fingers to the prince's neck, checking for his pulse. She hardly felt a beat, and the boy's skin was discouragingly cold to the touch. She looked around once, then got up and blitzed—

—from street to street until she found Kshapanaka creeping along an alley, bow drawn.

"Shhh," Kshapanaka pointed her chin at something hidden in the darkness at the far end of the alley.

"Here," Shanku whispered, shrinking into the shadows and thrusting the quivers at the other woman. "I must go. I found Ghatakarpara lying on a street near the spice market."

Kshapanaka stared. "Is he alright?"

Shanku shrugged. "I must go." She mind-leaped.

She knelt and propped Ghatakarpara until he was in a sitting position. Then, struggling with the boy's weight, she got him to stand, leaning him against her shoulder so that he didn't fall right back. He slumped on her unhelpfully, his hands flopping, his head lolling, and his knees giving way. The girl tried her best to ignore the voice that kept insisting this was not going to help save the prince.

Remembering the lifting and carrying techniques she had seen Kalidasa and Angamitra teach young *samsaptaka* cadets, Shanku took a deep breath before hoisting Ghatakarpara onto her back. She staggered, her legs wobbling under the strain, but she quickly regained her balance by spreading the prince's weight more evenly across her shoulders.

Breathing in again, she focused her mind on a safe spot deep in the palace.

She made a mind-leap for the Labyrinth.

***

"I'm only slowing you down, wise king. Go, and let me be."

"I'm not leaving this place without you," Vikramaditya gasped, hitching Betaal's good arm around his shoulder tighter for better leverage and helping him off the battered boat that had ferried them across the stale, slime-infested waters of the Kshipra. The ghoul's other arm dangled limp and useless by his side.

"Why?"

"Why not?" the king replied, shuffling-dragging the Ghoulmaster up the moss-covered steps of Ujjayini's bathing *ghats*. "How is sacrificing yourself in Borderworld going to help?"

"What will I do in your world?"

"I don't know," the samrat answered truthfully, peeking over his shoulder. The void was right behind, the Kshipra already disappearing into black, so the faint moonlight ended just yards from the water's edge. "But leaving you to die in yours is not the answer."

They took the steps two at a time, looking back every so often to see if the void was gaining on them. They were nearly at the top, close to the gaping hole where the city's western gate had once stood, when the king missed his footing and stumbled. The ghoul let out a yelp of pain as he too fell, his broken arm striking the steps.

Recovering his balance, the samrat held Betaal. "I am sorry."

"Not your fault, king," the ghoul grimaced. "You are injured. You must go ahead—"

"Not without you," Vikramaditya held on stubbornly, helping Betaal up the last few stairs. Slipping past the crumbling ramparts, he cast another look to see that the void was skimming up the *ghat's* steps, closing in on them quickly.

They rushed through Ujjayini's streets, avoiding puddles and potholes, tripping over exposed tree roots. Vegetation flourished everywhere, the houses gone but for a dilapidated gate here or a tumbledown wall there. Trees cast gloomy shadows, making it impossible to tell natural darkness from the destructive void that was chasing them.

"How do you intend taking me into your world, Samrat?" the ghoul asked. "Moving between worlds is incredibly hard—"

"But not impossible," Vikramaditya said between breaths. "You've done it before."

"That was against my will… and with the aid of powerful sorcery."

"And I have a powerful sorcerer who can make it happen again." The samrat looked at the Ghoulmaster, who was staring at him in suspicion. "There is a *droiba* waiting in my palace to help in your transition." Seeing alarm spring to Betaal's eyes, he chuckled. "This *droiba* is a friend of Avanti. He will not harm you, that's a promise."

The ghoul fell silent. They slipped through the dark city until the remnants of the palace came into view. Most of the walls had fallen away and many of the roofs were missing; what was left resembled an empty ribcage, moonlight shining right through the vacant spaces, softly illuminating the white mist that was rising from the surrounding lake. The scene was ethereal and translucent, the causeway providing the only sense of solidity to the landscape.

But even as Vikramaditya and Betaal hobbled onto the causeway, its rotted wood splintered and collapsed under their weight. They fell, and as they got back on their feet, Betaal looked over his shoulder and drew his breath in sharply. The samrat looked too—

—to see the causeway disappearing four paces behind them.

There was no lake or city in sight. Just the black void.

"Hurry," shouted Vikramaditya, breaking into a run.

"I can't," the Ghoulmaster said, falling on one knee.

"You can," the king screamed again, pulling Betaal up by the elbow. "Hurry."

They ran, a blind and desperate run with the ravenous void in pursuit, gobbling up every last bit of Borderworld, removing all trace of the realm of the ghouls. They ran, knowing they couldn't outrun the void. They ran, because they had run so long that it was foolish to give up now...

They ran, because there was a door in front of them. The door to the palace. Heavy and made of iron, now rusted.

With the black void a hand's reach from their backs, Vikramaditya threw himself at the door, pushing hard with his shoulder. The door resisted... then, with a groan of complaint, it began swinging on its hinges, creaking...

The samrat pushed with both hands, and the door parted—

***

—opening wide to let Samrat Vikramaditya step out of the palace and onto the causeway, Hellfires burning in both hands.

The samrat strode down the causeway, eyes fixed on Indra, fingers curling over the hilts of the swords, gripping them tight. The deva lord was at the other end of the causeway, squaring off with Vararuchi, neither warrior gaining an upper hand. To the right, Kalidasa was battling the Maruts, hammering them into submission with fists and sword even though he was vastly outnumbered.

Crossing the causeway's midpoint, Vikramaditya gave one Hellfire a wristy flick, causing the flames to taper and flare, forming a belt which the king cracked in a wide sweep, a whiplash that reflected off the lake. The motion and glare of the belt caught everyone's attention—and the tussle by the causeway drew to a halt.

Indra stared at the figure of the advancing king... and at the flaming swords in his hands.

As a quick stab of apprehension ran through his heart, the deva took two steps back.

"Is that fear that I see in your eyes, deva?" the king taunted for everyone to hear. "Where is the famed deva bravery now? Where has *that* disappeared?" Stepping off the causeway, Vikramaditya held one of the Hellfires up like a torch to see Indra's face better in the dark. He pretended to study the face before shaking his head in disappointment. "No courage here, no nerve. What next—are you tempted to turn and run?"

The deva's eyes narrowed in spite.

"Ah, finally, something other than simple fear," the samrat smirked. He lowered the sword. "Alright, here's the deal. You don't deserve to be treated fairly after all that you have done, but just to make this an even contest, a more equal fight, I will not summon Diti's *churails* while fighting you." He shrugged and looked at the deva questioningly.

Indra eyed the king with suspicion.

"You have my word."

A twisted smile creased the deva's face. "I believe you," he nodded. "I will fight—"

Without warning, he charged at Vikramaditya, his bone sword raised and swinging.

The king barely had time to raise his own sword and block the blow, which was aimed at his head. Steel and bone rang out loud, and the impact of the strike sent Vikramaditya stumbling, and Indra sprang forward to deal the king another blow. The samrat parried, almost losing his hold on one of the Hellfires. Not wanting to give his adversary room to recover, Indra swung again and again, pushing Vikramaditya towards the causeway. The king was so busy dodging the deva's blows that he had neither the time nor the opportunity to attempt a counterattack.

One foot on the causeway, barely a yard from the lip of the lake... and still being beaten back by the deva, Vikramaditya breathed in and analyzed the pattern of Indra's attack: a swipe, another swipe, a lunge forward... Steeling himself, the samrat staved off the swipes and the lunge. Then, as the next set of swipes began, he abruptly stepped a little closer to Indra.

Swipe. Block.

Swipe. Block.

The deva lunged, the bone sword driving at Vikramaditya's midriff, where the cut from Hiranyaksha's sword had reopened and was bleeding again. The king pulled back, but not so quickly that Indra lost the incentive to persist with his attack; instead, keeping within range, Vikramaditya drew the deva into the stroke, the sword's tip dangerously close to his stomach, enticing Indra to stay with the thrust and strive a little harder.

And sure enough, committed to the stroke, believing he could nail his enemy if he stretched himself just a bit more, Indra leaned into the thrust—

—and overbalanced.

Spinning on his heel for momentum and leverage, Vikramaditya launched a furious assault on Indra. He rained a flurry of blows with the Hellfires, slashing high and low, alternating between short jabs and sweeping cuts, rattling the deva's bone sword and cutting through his defences to inflict searing wounds on his forearms. He lashed out without cease, not stopping to catch his breath, not slowing to give his arms rest...

And with every blow, Indra was repelled backwards. The deva stumbled and dropped to one knee, but Vikramaditya was relentless. Indra raised his sword to fend off the blows, but the samrat leaped in the air, twirling full circle and bringing both Hellfires down on the upraised sword.

The bone sword cracked and shattered.

Indra stared at Vikramaditya in shock. The king looked down at the deva in anger, his chest heaving from the exertion, the Hellfires held halfway up, smouldering slowly.

Indra's eyes went to the Hellfires, then returned to the king.

"I should kill you now, except that you are defenceless," the samrat said through gritted teeth.

"You and your honour," the deva sneered. "Come on, do it."

Vikramaditya stared into the cold, blue eyes.

"Do it," Indra challenged. "*Do it now, or I will return for Veeshada's dagger.*"

"Veeshada's dagger doesn't exist anymore," a familiar voice came from across the trench.

Vikramaditya looked up to see Shukracharya in chains, standing next to Amara Simha. Two other heavily built figures were also in chains, while a fat, bejewelled figure stood to the left of Amara Simha.

"Mahaguru Shukracharya," Indra remarked with a dry smile. "What deceptions do you intend planting with that little lie of yours?"

"It is not a lie, lord of Devaloka," the high priest called out. "It is the absolute truth. That man standing in front of you..." he pointed with his head, "...has done us both in, defeated both of us."

Confounded, Indra looked up at the samrat. "What do you mean?" he asked, turning back.

"He has destroyed the Halahala, deva."

"You expect me to fall for that one?" Indra scoffed, glancing at Vikramaditya.

"I was there when he threw the dagger into Borderworld. Neither Borderworld nor the dagger exists anymore," the high priest said.

"What happened to Borderworld?" Indra gaped. "Why doesn't it exist?"

Seeing Shukracharya keep mum, the king smiled sardonically. "Tell him," he goaded. When the high priest still didn't speak, he said, "It was *his* and the asura army's doing. In their lust for the Halahala, they destroyed the Ghoulmaster's tree, the tree that sustained Borderworld."

He looked at Indra. "If you are wondering, it was I who left the Halahala in Betaal's custody, and Borderworld paid the price. But never again, for I have destroyed Veeshada's dagger. No one can claim the Halahala anymore, no one can threaten to destroy any of the three worlds."

The lord of the devas gazed at the king in astonishment. "You... *destroyed the dagger?*"

Vikramaditya nodded. "And now, I have to decide what to do with you."

His eyes went from the deva to the high priest as he spoke. "I asked you to leave us in peace and never return to Avanti. Yet, you came back." His gaze returned to Indra. "I told you I would never part with the Halahala, but you didn't listen. You tried to take my wife from me, my brother from me..." the samrat's voice went through an angry inflection, "You sent your half-horses and snake-heads to burn my city. You came back when I had warned you to keep away. And you," he went back to looking at Shukracharya, "*You* destroyed Borderworld. You took my friend's home away, so he had nowhere to go and I had to bring him to Avanti. In your greed, the two of you sent your armies to destroy my beloved Ujjayini..." The Hellfires raged hot in his hands. "How must I punish you?" he thundered. "*How?*"

Silence stretched around the causeway.

"The asuras meant you no ill will," the high priest spoke at last. "Remember, it was my desire to cure the queen fully and to help you in whatever way we could. All the asuras ever wanted was the Halahala... but now that we cannot have it, we will bother you no more. Let us go our way in peace."

The king looked at Indra, who stared right back. "You are a deva," the deva lord said heavily. "I cannot believe you destroyed the dagger instead of giving it to the devas. But whatever is done cannot be undone, which goes for the suffering you and your city have endured as well. I regret that, but it was all for the Halahala. There was nothing personal in any of this."

A bitter smile played on Vikramaditya's lips. "There is talk of peace now, and apologies are being offered. I assume it is expected of me to reciprocate by letting bygones be bygones and being magnanimous... that I be the bigger person and let my noble nature dictate a course of action." He paused and his hands fell wearily to his sides. The glow of the Hellfires dimmed. "I let you leave the last time around. I will give you a chance to leave again," he said. "Take your armies and rid yourselves of my city as quickly as you can. Put as much distance as you can between yourself and Ujjayini."

He pinned his gaze on Shukracharya. "Go," he said as a thin, cold smile turned the corners of his mouth. "Go," he said, switching back to Indra, "*—before I change my mind.* Go now, *go.*"

Shukracharya's eye widened in alarm as he beheld the samrat step back to allow Indra to get to his feet. The deva strode away, motioning to the Maruts to follow, but the high priest kept an anxious gaze trained on the king. Then, as the chains came off him and his sons, he spun around and elbowed through the assembled yakshas and human soldiers, muttering under his breath.

"Hurry," he egged his sons. "Let's get out of here."

He broke into a run, and Amarka and Chandasura did likewise. "What is the matter, father?" asked Amarka, drawing level.

Instead of offering an explanation, Shukracharya shot a backward glance at Indra, who was still mounting his elephant. "Fool," he snapped, waving at his sons to keep up.

Amara Simha and Kubera watched the high priest and his sons disappear into the dark before exchanging dismayed glances. By the causeway, Vararuchi stepped towards his brother.

"We can't let them go—" he began protesting, but he paused when his eyes met the samrat's. Vikramaditya nodded as he went past and stepped onto the causeway.

Vararuchi turned to see Indra astride the mammoth. Five bolts of lightning arrived to take the bruised and battered Maruts away. Kalidasa slowly sheathed his scimitar.

Vikramaditya trudged down the causeway, scowling in pain and counting his steps.

Do it. Do it now, or I will return for Veeshada's dagger.

All the asuras ever wanted was the Halahala... but now that we cannot have it, we will bother you no more.

It was all for the Halahala. There was nothing personal in any of this.

The samrat had crossed the midway point and was nearing the palace door. He slowed... and came to a stop. He turned to look at Ujjayini. Indra's elephant was still in sight. Shukracharya was nowhere to be seen.

I let you leave the last time around... I will give you a chance to leave again.

His grip tightened on the Hellfires. The swords caught fire instantly.

Take your armies and rid yourselves of my city as quickly as you can.

"Arise, sisters of Naraka," Vikramaditya whispered.

Put as much distance as you can between yourself and Ujjayini.

"Arise and annihilate those who mean ill of the one who wields these swords." The words left the king's lips in a caress as he swung the Hellfires and whips of flame erupted, looping and coiling in the air.

Go—before I change my mind.

One, two, three... the whips rose as though caught in a swirl of wind, pirouetting around one another, knitting in and out over the palace, fusing together—

In a wink of an eye, the *churails* were in the sky over Ujjayini.

The sight of the banshees evoked a wild cheer around the lake. Almost at once, the cheer was interspersed with a roar of voices and stamping of feet.

"Avanti… Avanti… Avanti… Avanti…"

Fleeing through the city's darkened streets, Shukracharya and Indra looked up, startled, their expressions turning from panic to terror…

"Avanti… Avanti… Avanti… Avanti…"

The roar spread through Ujjayini, quick as wildfire, as the *churails* went screaming after the enemies of the kingdom, three avenging spirits on a quest to deliver fiery justice.

"Avanti… Avanti… Avanti…"

Vikramaditya pushed the door open to enter the palace. He felt astoundingly tired. He wanted to lie down… down… down… He slipped, but hands grabbed him, arresting his fall.

…down… down… down… His eyes closed.

"Vikrama."

He opened his eyes.

He looked into a face that he had been dying to see since that night Atulyateja had given him the news. *It seems she is asking for you, Samrat.*

"Vikrama," Vishakha whispered, smiling at him, her eyes filled with tears. "You came back."

Vikramaditya realized he was lying on the floor, his head on Vishakha's lap. He noticed the Acharya looking down at him, and he saw Dhanavantri appear and kneel by his side.

The samrat smiled up at the queen in contentment. He reached for her face, and she took hold of his hand, pressing it to her damp cheek. "You came back from the frontier," she repeated.

Vikramaditya sighed.

"I would have come back from death's door just to hear my name on your lips, my love."

Epilogue

Vararuchi crouched behind the shield, low on one leg, the other extended forward, only his eyes showing above the shield's rim, intent and watchful. His right hand, bent sharply at the elbow, clutched a *katari*, its point unwavering as he assessed his target. Springing nimbly into the air, the councilor jabbed the *katari* at his imaginary opponent, blocked a blow with his shield, executed a twirl and stabbed low a second time, before drawing back into a crouch, shield up against his chest.

The sun had yet to rise, and the light in the mud pit was still a dull grey as the councilor slowly stood up, sweat running off his lean, oiled torso. Flexing his shoulder muscles and wringing out a crick in his neck, he walked to a row of weapons laid to one side. Putting the *katari* down, his fingers flitted over an assortment of blades, deciding which to pick. Finally, the councilor selected a thin, long sword with a curved blade.

"Why not this one?" a voice called out.

Vararuchi turned to find Kalidasa standing by the entrance to the mud pit, scimitar in hand. As he walked into the enclosure, the giant held the sword out to Vararuchi.

"You wanted me to surrender this," Kalidasa said, offering the hilt to Vararuchi. "I couldn't at that time, because I still had battles left to fight. But now..." he motioned, urging the other councilor to take the scimitar.

The king's brother gazed up at the giant, studying the *hriiz* on his forehead thoughtfully.

"This is the sword that stopped Indra's charge into the palace," he said. Placing a hand on the hilt, he pushed the blade away. "It is best left in the hands of the one who wielded it so effectively for Avanti."

Kalidasa resisted for a moment, then nodded.

A lopsided smile touched Vararuchi's lips as he considered the Huna. "I should never have doubted your loyalty to Vikrama. I am sorry."

"No." Sheathing the scimitar, Kalidasa took a step closer to the king's brother and held him by the shoulders. "If there is room for an apology here, that apology must be mine. I did you grave injustice, but my objective behind all those accusations was not to—"

"I know, I know," Vararuchi interrupted. "Vikrama told me everything. You don't need to explain yourself or apologize. You acted keeping Avanti's interests in mind; whatever you did was for Avanti's good."

"I almost made enemies out of brothers," the giant's hands dropped to his sides and he shook his head ruefully.

"Yet, it was the three of us who stood there two nights ago, fighting Indra and protecting the palace." Vararuchi gave Kalidasa's arm a reassuring squeeze. "Unbreakable is what we are."

After a moment's thought, the giant grinned and drew his sword. "Practice?" he asked.

"Sure." Eyeing the scimitar, Vararuchi replaced his sword with a broader, heavier one.

Walking to the end of the mud pit, Vararuchi turned to face Kalidasa. The giant dropped to a combative crouch, but the king's brother just stared at his opponent with a serious expression, the sword limp in his hand.

"I am sorry," he said.

"For what?" Kalidasa frowned from the opposite end. Slowly, he drew himself erect.

"For what happened that afternoon in the garrison of Lava." Vararuchi dropped his eyes. "Your father, your sister... your family." He looked across at the giant. "It was war, but it was also wrong."

Kalidasa stared at the other councilor for a long moment. The sun was showing through the branches of the trees that surrounded the mud pit.

"It was wrong, but it was war," the giant said. "It was also a long time ago, and we must all move on." He smiled. "I lost one family that day, but I found another here in Avanti. I have nothing to complain about." He crouched and gripped his scimitar.

"Come, let's practise."

The king's brother nodded. Taking two steps forward, they began circling each other.

***

"How do I even begin thanking all of you for coming to my kingdom's aid?"

"You don't, Samrat Vikramaditya," said Kubera with a shake of his head. "Please don't thank *me*, at least. I owed this to you after what my yaksha did to the queen. The regrettable part is that I sanctioned that attack without caring to understand Indra's motive, or learning the least bit about you." He hung his head in shame. "Nothing can make up for my stupidity, for which I am deeply apologetic, but helping you was a small attempt at putting things right." He paused to look at the samrat gravely. "Knowing what the devas and the asuras wanted and seeing that they were prepared to go to any extreme to have their way, we yakshas decided to step in to assist you."

Shalivahana, who lounged next to the yaksha, nodded. "I couldn't agree more," he croaked in his old, tired voice, his scarred face hardly betraying any emotion.

"Saving this city from the vyalas and Ahi was anything but small," the king insisted.

"The vyalas, yes... But to be entirely honest, we had no part in stopping Ahi, though that was our intention when we left the city's gates," said Kubera.

Vikramaditya looked at the yaksha in confusion. "I don't follow you. I thought—"

Kubera pulled a rueful grimace. "Before we could even get to Shukracharya's sons, we came under Holika's spell," he said, going distinctly red in the face. "We were... rendered helpless. We recovered only after Holika had fled from battle, freeing us from the effects of her spell."

"I heard about her spells," the king said. "My councilors saw some horrible things... like dead people..." He looked enquiringly at Kubera.

"Something like that," the yaksha mumbled and shifted in his seat uncomfortably.

"The Witch Queen's powers are impressive," Shalivahana agreed.

"It's fortunate that none of those powers worked on you danavas," the samrat smiled in relief. "Amara Simha tells me that it was your arrival that turned the tide of the battle our way. Who knows what course that battle might have taken—what course this whole campaign to protect the Halahala may have taken—had you not agreed to come to our support?"

"Your councilor, Shankubala, was quite persistent," the danava's moss beard cracked open in a small smile. "I'm glad we came, though, for I have the good fortune of getting to know not just you, but also Kubera, and..." he leaned to look at Khash'i Dur, seated to Kubera's left, "...the brave chief of the Huna tribe. It is not every day that those who helped safeguard the Halahala get to sit all in one place. I am honoured to be here."

Vikramaditya smiled and took in the airy chamber where they were seated, overlooking the lake. Early-morning sunlight filtered through lace curtains and splashed on the white marble floor. Ujjayini was steeped in the aftermath of strife, cocooned in a fatigue that was one-part relief at having survived the ordeal, one-part grief at the losses borne and one-part the slow renewal of hope and order.

"And you, my friend," the king said as his gaze settled on Khash'i Dur. "What can I say to you for having come all the way from the Great Desert to fight a battle on my behalf? And the *droiba*... I didn't need his assistance to enter Borderworld as the Acharya had returned, but without the *droiba*, we could never have rescued Betaal from Borderworld."

"You address me as 'friend'. That is enough," the *shy'or* waved his hand unassumingly.

Vikramaditya gave a thoughtful nod. "I shall confer with the kings of Sindhuvarta soon. Until then, you and the men who rode with me can settle in Avanti. Vararuchi and the raj-guru will ensure that the land you are provided is fertile and hospitable."

As the chief bowed his head, the samrat looked at the yaksha and the danava. "Destiny brings us to unbelievable places. Look at us. Until a while ago, I thought the danavas existed only in stories. I hated the yakshas for what had happened to Vishakha. And we," he gestured to Khash'i Dur, "were sworn enemies. Yet, danavas, yakshas and Hunas have helped me keep my word to the Omniscient One..."

"It is not destiny but karma that brings us to unbelievable places, Samrat," said Kubera. "It is your karma that brought us all to this moment. Your grit, your determination, your willingness to hold out against all odds. You inspired us to come to your aid, and we all came willingly."

Shalivahana and the Huna chief nodded in agreement as Vikramaditya bowed in response.

"I take it that you want to go back," he said to Kubera.

The yaksha nodded. "Your city is beautiful, but I am afraid I miss my Alaka very much." He looked at the samrat. "Why don't you come with me and see its beauty for yourself?"

"My city is destroyed and needs rebuilding," the king smiled back. "But I will come soon."

"You are welcome to visit Janasthana as well," said Shalivahana. "All three of you." His lips rearranged in a smile. "It's a promise that you will be treated a lot better than Shankubala and her men were."

As everyone got to their feet, Khash'i Dur spoke with a twinkle in his eye. "I could invite you to the Great Desert, but I am not sure you would want to come to that merciless place."

Vikramaditya went to the chieftain and took him by the shoulders. "I would never turn down an invitation to a friend's house." With a pause, he added, "Thank you for everything."

A footfall was heard by the door. Turning, the samrat looked at the palace hand in enquiry.

"Your honour," the man spoke. "Councilor Dhanavantri sent me to let you know that Prince Ghatakarpara has returned to consciousness."

***

"I thought it was the yakshas who were responsible for controlling Ahi." Vetala Bhatta stared in surprise at Ghatakarpara's sallow face looking up from the pillow. "It was you?"

"Maybe it was actually them," the prince replied. "I assumed it was me—"

"No," said Vikramaditya. "Kubera just admitted that the yakshas didn't manage doing a thing to stop the snake." With a note of pride, the king added, "It was very brave of you to take on Ahi all by yourself."

"How did you do it?" Varahamihira asked, leaning on his crutch eagerly.

"The boy must rest," Dhanavantri tried to intervene, but Varahamihira brushed him off.

"Go on, tell us."

"Amara Simha had told me about Ahi on the way back from Kasavati," Ghatakarpara replied. "He'd said the snake was made of water, so I thought I should try and see if I can control it." He paused to take a slow breath. "It wasn't easy. But I tried right up to the point where I lost consciousness."

"You did very well," Varahamihira exclaimed. "You destroyed the darn thing."

The prince smiled.

"Watching it disintegrate and disappear was such sweet relief," Varahamihira shook his head as he relived that fraction of a moment. "It was about to get Vararuchi and me when it melted in the moonlight and was gone."

"Okay, enough for now," Dhanavantri insisted, waving his hand. "We can talk later—"

"Wait," the prince called, one hand raised. "You said there was moonlight?"

Varahamihira paused. "Yes."

"Can't be," said Ghatakarpara, puzzled.

"There certainly was. I wasn't alone. Vararuchi was there as well, as were more than a dozen palace guards. We all saw the snake vanish in the moonlight."

"But," the prince paused, "the sun was still setting when I lost consciousness, and there was no moon in the sky. I am certain of that."

The samrat and the other councilors looked at one another.

"I have a question," said Amara Simha, stepping forward, "and it has nothing to do with Ahi." He frowned at the prince. "What were you doing in the streets of Ujjayini? Weren't you supposed to be somewhere around Udaypuri?"

Ghatakarpara dropped his eyes guiltily.

"We all want to know," said Vikramaditya in a gentle but firm tone.

The prince looked from his uncle to Amara Simha. "I am sorry I disappointed you by leaving the way I did," he said. "I wasn't thinking straight. But along the way, I realized that I had let you down. So, I turned around and made my way back. I was heading for the palace when the snake appeared in the sky, and I decided to try and stop it."

Amara Simha nodded. Before Dhanavantri could urge them to leave, the Acharya spoke. "We really must let the boy rest now. Come..."

Leaving Ghatakarpara in the care of a junior physician, everyone filed out of the room. Out in the gallery, the samrat turned to Dhanavantri. "He looks tired."

"He will be fine," the physician replied. "Don't worry."

They trooped down the corridor. Varahamihira broke the silence, speaking partly to himself. "The snake was around spewing venom long after the sun had set."

"When Kubera and I found the asura brothers," said Amara Simha, "it was plain that they had lost control of Ahi. The snake was nowhere in the sky."

"If Ghatakarpara was unconscious, and neither the yakshas nor the asuras had control of Ahi, what caused the snake to disappear?" wondered Vetala Bhatta.

It was Vikramaditya who answered. "The possibilities are endless," he pointed out. "We may never learn the truth behind the serpent's mysterious disappearance."

***

"This is my oldest friend from childhood... and also my newest," said Vikramaditya.

Vishakha took a tentative step forward, peering up at Betaal's wrinkled face in the light of the torches. The ghoul's hair of flames had burned low and hung in smouldering patches over his face, so he had to part them with his bony fingers to look at the queen better.

"And this must be Queen Vishakha," he said in his old, cracked voice as he bowed.

Vishakha stared into the Ghoulmaster's black, empty eyes for a moment, then bowed. "I am sorry," she said, "but I don't remember you either."

"That is because we've never met before, my queen."

"Oh," Vishakha looked at the king, confused.

"The idea was to introduce you to one another," Vikramaditya explained. Addressing Betaal, he said, "How is your shoulder, my friend?"

The ghoul jigged his right shoulder up and down without any discomfort. "Your physician is blessed. He fixed me back in no time."

"Indeed," the samrat admitted, his hand straying to the bandage covering his midriff. The cut had almost healed, while the pain had all but disappeared. "His touch is bringing relief to so many people in Ujjayini." He looked at the surrounding darkness. "Are you comfortable here in the Labyrinth? It is the only place where sunlight doesn't reach, so..."

"Except that I have nothing to do here, I'm fine," Betaal replied. "Sure, I can go where I like once the sun has set, and I'm thankful. But I just sit here during the day doing nothing." He paused. "The boredom is killing me as I feared it would, wise king."

"Why don't you help us?" said Vikramaditya, after thinking for a moment.

"In what way?"

"You are nearly as old as the Ancient Gods. You have seen and experienced so much, learned so much about life. Why not share everything you have learned by way of stories? There is so much we humans can learn from you."

"Stories..." the Ghoulmaster turned the idea around in his mind. "I'm too tired to write."

"You don't have to. Narrate them to someone, and they will write it. I will get someone from my court to—"

"No, no..." Betaal said emphatically. "Here's what I will do... I will tell *you* the stories, and you can do whatever you want with them. This way, I will get to meet you now and then."

"Alright," the samrat said, smiling. "We have a deal."

"And guess what?" Betaal rubbed his hands together at his own cleverness. "I will make these stories interesting and challenging... worthy of your wisdom."

On their way back from the Labyrinth, Vikramaditya and Vishakha went past the palace bath. Walking hand in hand, the king glanced down at the bath... and he paused, shaking his head.

"What?" Vishakha asked, looking concerned.

"I remembered..." Vikramaditya tightened his hold on Vishakha's hand. "There's something I have to give you."

Entering their chambers, the king went to a chest from which he extracted a small box made of ironwood. He brought the box to Vishakha, opening it slowly for her.

"My ring."

Her face beaming with delight, the queen took the jade jewel out of the box. Turning it to the light, she studied her name, artistically inscribed on its green surface. "I lost this in the palace bath once, and you found it for me. I thought I had lost it again." She slipped the ring on her finger.

"I took it from you after you fell the second time. I thought I'd give it to you whenever you recovered... that's what I had done the first time as well." The samrat looked away. "There were times I was afraid this ring would never leave its box again."

Vishakha raised a hand and caressed Vikramaditya's cheek lightly. Her eyes were moist.

"Thank you for keeping this safe." She dropped her hand to inspect the ring again. "This ring is important to me. It was a gift."

"From whom?" the samrat probed.

"From mother."

Vishakha stopped, surprised at her own words. She looked at Vikramaditya, who was staring at her in excitement.

"You remember her?"

"Yes... a little," the queen replied, after some deliberation. Her face brightened. "It's slowly coming back to me. I remember father too, and... my little sister."

The king held her by the shoulders and peered into her face. "Sister?"

Vishakha nodded. "Kshapanaka."

Her eyes widened and she looked at Vikramaditya in enquiry. "*That* Kshapanaka?"

Grinning and pulling her by her hand, the samrat led Vishakha out of the chamber and down a couple of passageways until they reached a heavy door. The king knocked.

Kshapanaka opened the door, her face registering surprise. "I wasn't expecting of you..." She began, then stopped on seeing the expression on Vikramaditya's face. "What is it?"

The samrat's grin widened. He looked at Vishakha and gestured towards the councilor.

"Kshapanaka..." the queen said in an awed voice. "You were so small..."

The councilor's eyes were glistening pools of tears as she smiled and threw her arms open to her sister. "You've remembered," she whispered through trembling lips.

Vishakha sank into Kshapanaka's tight embrace. Tears ran down the younger sister's cheeks. She squeezed her eyes shut, weeping with joy, before opening them to look at Vikramaditya.

"She remembers me," she exhaled gratefully between shivering sobs. "She remembers."

***

"I am told Pralupi departed for Vatsa this morning."

Vikramaditya nodded.

"I'm presuming she didn't bother bidding you goodbye," said Vararuchi.

Vikramaditya shook his head. "She told mother last evening that she was leaving."

The brothers rode on in silence. To their right, workers were dismantling the empty shells of three burned-out buildings. From all around the city came noises of walls being broken and buildings being razed to the ground as the rebuilding of Ujjayini began in earnest. Citizens who still had houses to return to were filing through the gates in a trickle, and a few markets had come up, selling produce from nearby farms. Wood and stone depots had sprung up, and a royal decree had been passed, putting a cap on the prices of both commodities to prevent hoarding and profiteering. Meanwhile, a steady stream of corpses—human, kinnara, naga, deva, asura and a few yaksha—were being taken out of the city and cremated, so the air smelled of smoke and burned flesh when the wind blew from the west and the south.

"We should have asked her to leave a long time ago," Vararuchi remarked. "Her place is in her husband's house." The councilor paused and sneaked an awkward glance at his brother.

"The palace is hers too," the samrat reminded him. "It would have been wrong to have asked her to leave against her will." If he caught the implication in Vararuchi's look, the king made no mention of it.

"She hatches conspiracies against you, she makes your life miserable," Vararuchi shook his head in wonder. "How can you be so patient with someone like her and not want to see her punished?"

"What choice do I have? She is still my sister, *our* sister." Vikramaditya turned his horse into a narrow lane. "And for people like her, no punishment is greater than being denied the very thing that they have been hankering after all their lives."

"She must be mad at Ghatakarpara's decision," Vararuchi followed his brother in.

"She hates it, but with Ghatakarpara's departure from the palace, it must have finally dawned on her that she's played her hand and lost," the king answered.

"She didn't ask you to intervene one last time?"

"I made it clear to her that I wouldn't stop him from going," Vikramaditya shrugged.

Vararuchi was silent for a moment. "You didn't tell Ghatakarpara, did you?" He looked at the samrat. "About... Yashobhavi?"

Vikramaditya shook his head. "It is a rumour that I can't prove or disprove. If Ghatakarpara is to learn about Yashobhavi, it has to be from his mother."

"It is probably best if none of this comes to light," the councilor reflected. Remembering something, he turned to the king. "Have you heard the latest from Magadha?"

"Mmm... Shoorasena has been charged with murder, and Kapila has been placed under arrest in Tamralipti—"

"That's old news," Vararuchi grinned. "Since Magadha now doesn't have anyone with direct royal lineage to sit on the throne, they are debating the possibility of turning the kingdom into a republic."

"Like Vanga?" Vikramaditya shook his head and smiled. "The irony of it all."

Vararuchi chuckled. Looking around, he noticed that they had emerged onto a road that skirted the old cattle market. "You know Sharamana," he said, changing the subject suddenly.

Vikramaditya blinked. "Who?"

"Commander Sharamana. The garrison chief of Musili."

"Oh," the king nodded.

"Ever since he heard how you went out of your way to rescue his family from the half-horses, he's been deeply ashamed. He wants to offer his apologies... for rebelling against the throne. Not just him, the commanders Suhasa and Ajanya also seek your pardon. So does Pulyama." Vararuchi looked at the samrat pleadingly. "You will pardon them, won't you? They're not at fault. If it is anybody's fault, it is mine. I incited them."

"They have nothing to fear," Vikramaditya assured him.

Vararuchi let out a sigh of relief. After a pause, he asked, "But why did you do it?"

"Do what?"

"Help Sharamana's family? Sharamana had risen against you, his family had refused to heed your orders... they even refused to acknowledge you as the king of Avanti." Vararuchi shook his head. "In your place, I would have decided they didn't deserve to be rescued."

The samrat smiled. "Father once told me that the cardinal rule of kingship is that the people can abandon their king as they wish, but a king can never abandon his people. As a king, I have a duty towards *all* my people—I cannot discriminate between those who support me and those who don't, or those of love me and those who don't. If Sharamana's family was in trouble, it was my responsibility to protect them. Until I am king, they are my people. This is a burden that every king and every parent has to bear."

Vararuchi studied Vikramaditya for a while.

"Father was right," he said at last, nodding in appreciation, "when he said that you were born to be king."

***

"You will never become a king. Don't you realize that?"

"I don't want to become one, mother."

"How dare you say that?" Pralupi had glared at him. "It is all I have wanted for you."

"No, mother. It is all you have wanted for *yourself*, and that is causing you all this hurt."

"Where did you learn to talk back like that?" she had hissed. When he didn't reply, "You will lose everything if you go. Your place in the council, your royal title, everything. This palace will disown you, spit you out—"

"The Samrat said I could remain in his council for as long as I wanted, and I would always be welcome in the palace."

Seeing Pralupi shake her head irritably, his resolve had strengthened. "Even if uncle hadn't said all that, I would go, mother. It is by *not going* that I will definitely lose everything."

Ghatakarpara squinted in the harsh sun of the frontier, surveying the bedraggled cluster of houses that made up the hamlet of Balipura, clinging to the side of a small hill. It was a little past noon, and the houses were all shuttered, the windows closed to keep the day's heat out. There wasn't a soul stirring anywhere, the land flat and open to the east, the barren Arbudas rising to the west.

The prince spurred his horse, and in minutes, he neared the first set of houses. He sniffed the air searchingly before passing on, riding along the wide, mud-paved lane that served as Balipura's main road. He rode slowly, sniffing all the while until his nose detected the delicate fragrance of *aguru*.

My grandfather makes the best incense in all of Malawa, he remembered Aparupa once telling him.

Ghatakarpara drew to a halt before a large house from where the fragrances of *goparasa* and sandalwood joined that of *aguru* and lifted into the still midday air. The house was walled off from outside, the only visible entry through an old door made of heavy wood. The door was latched shut from inside.

Dismounting, the prince crossed to the door and pushed at it. It barely budged. He knocked.

There was no response.

He knocked again, harder. Then he pushed the door repeatedly, rattling the latch inside.

"Who is it?"

Ghatakarpara's world went still. So still he could hear his heart beating in his chest.

"Aparupa?" he called in a hushed, disbelieving voice.

"Who is it?" the voice repeated, with a note of uncertainty.

"It's me."

Silence.

"Aparupa… I have come for you."

Silence.

"Open the door, Aparupa… please."

Silence.

"I have left everything and come to be with—"

"You lied to me."

Ghatakarpara leaned on the door in desperation, hands rolled into fists, pleading.

"I am sorry for everything, Aparupa, but I can explain—"

"Go away."

"Please listen to me—"

The sound of a door shutting. Heavy, decisive and permanent.

"Aparupa, please... just listen to me..." Ghatakarpara knocked on the door. "I am here for you. I am not returning to the palace... You are all that matters to me..."

The boy had no idea how long he stood at that door, cajoling the silence behind it. When he finally stepped away, sick and miserable at heart, his shadow was no longer stumpy underfoot; instead, it leaned along the wall at a crooked angle, a lonely human shadow among a hodgepodge of angular roof shadows.

Unable to decide what to do next, unwilling to turn away, desperately hoping Aparupa would relent and that the door would suddenly open for him, he stood staring—

"Aaaaaa... aaau..."

Ghatakarpara turned to see Dveeja on the road behind him. The man's eyes were bright, and he looked happy to see the prince.

"Uuuh... aaaii..." he mouthed, grinning. "Aaaa..."

"Dveeja," the prince looked at the man in anguish. "Aparupa doesn't want to see me."

"Aaai... uuuu...?" Dveeja looked at the prince, his face crumpling with concern.

The boy nodded, feeling the weight of the world in his chest. "She is not willing to listen to me; she won't even open the door." He hung his head in dejection.

"Uuuu... uuh..." Dveeja grabbed the prince by his arms and shook him. "Ai... aaaa..." he beckoned, waving his hand as he started moving to the side of the house. "Aaaaa..." he called, looking back, making sure Ghatakarpara was following.

Turning a corner, they followed the wall to a small stone well at the back of the house. A narrow door had been built into the wall next to the well. Bending low, Dveeja slipped past the door, motioning to the prince to do likewise.

Once inside the compound, Dveeja led the way to a side door, which was also closed.

"Aaai..." he called. "Aaa... uh..."

Footsteps.

The door opened to frame Aparupa in a rectangle of semi-shadow. She stared at Dveeja and then at Ghatakarpara. Her eyes were red, as if from crying, and her lips quivered with rage. "Why is he with you?" she demanded.

"Aparupa—" the prince began, but the girl cut him off, snapping at Dveeja.

"Tell him to leave immediately." She turned and went into the house.

Dveeja turned to Ghatakarpara and motioned with his hand to the boy to wait. "Aaah... uuuuu..." Pointing to himself, he indicated that he was going in. "Aau... uuu... aai?"

The prince nodded.

Dveeja went in, shutting the door behind him. Ghatakarpara stood in the sun, unmindful of the heat as he tried to listen for sounds from inside. He thought he heard Aparupa's voice once or twice, raised in anger, but he couldn't be sure, though he did hear Dveeja once from an upper-storey window.

Time passed and the prince was tiring. He hopped from one foot to the other, afraid to leave the spot, when he heard footsteps approaching again.

The door opened, and both Aparupa and Dveeja stood inside, looking out at the prince. Ghatakarpara looked at the girl's stormy eyes and realized he'd rather sink and drown in them than float elsewhere in the world.

"I went to Udaypuri looking for you," he said. "No one knew where you were, so I took a chance and came—"

Aparupa rushed out of the house and threw her arms around the prince, crushing him in her embrace as she burst into tears against his chest.

***

"Are you going to be wearing that hideous thing for the rest of your life?"

Smiling politely, Kalidasa stole a glance at the palanquin bearers, noticing how all four of them were struggling to keep a straight face, pretending not to have heard a word of what the Mother Oracle was saying.

"Why would you inflict something like that on such a handsome face?" the crone went on, clearly enjoying herself. She'd been back in her element the moment the palanquin had left the palace, and now that they were in the open countryside, she was virtually unstoppable.

"I was just… following Huna tradition, mother," Kalidasa replied, looking sheepish, his hand unconsciously touching the *hriiz*. The skin around the scar was pink and puckered.

"By no means does it look like a scorpion." The woman leaned out of the palanquin and peered up at the giant riding beside her. "Do you know what a scorpion looks like?"

"He is a poet, not an artist, grandmother," Shanku said, laughing. "Stop teasing him."

"Right. I hope he's learned his lesson then and sticks to poetry," the oracle cackled as she settled back in her seat.

Kalidasa rolled his eyes good-naturedly and looked at Shanku, who grinned back.

"Is it that bad?" the giant asked in an undertone, referring to the *hriiz*.

The girl glanced at it and shrugged. "It'll take getting used to." Seeing Kalidasa's expression, she laughed again. "It's fine. You know grandmother is exaggerating."

Without anyone noticing, the two councilors dropped pace, allowing the little convoy to go ahead. They were to the northeast of Ujjayini, the city already lost behind in a fine mist of rain, riding to the spot where the Wandering Tribe had freshly set up camp. The afternoon air was cool, the sky evenly overcast.

"Tell me something," said Kalidasa. "When I left Ujjayini, everyone seemed convinced I had broken all my ties with Avanti. Even Vikramaditya believed so, to some extent." He fingered the sun-crest medallion around his neck, which he had got back the day before. "Did you also believe I had left for good?"

Shanku gave this so much thought that it felt as if she hadn't heard the question.

"Honestly, I couldn't make myself believe it," she said at last. "All evidence pointed to the fact that you were not coming back, but anyone who knows you would realize there was no way you would turn your back on the Samrat. So, despite everything everyone said, I thought you would return. Which is why I never lost hope."

Kalidasa nodded. They rode in silence, the horses' hooves thudding softly on the muddy trail.

"I would never turn my back on you," the giant said shyly. "You must know that."

"I do. Which is also a reason I never lost hope."

"What are you laggards doing?" the Mother Oracle hailed them. "Hurry up. I'm getting bored here."

"Oh god," Shanku groaned. The councilors spurred their mounts forward and drew abreast of the palanquin. "Happy?" Shanku asked.

"Can't keep up with an old woman, is it?" the oracle looked at them shrewdly. She then poked her head out and called out to Brichcha, who was riding some fifty paces in front. "What have you thought about your daughter's future, old man? In case you haven't noticed, she is nearing marriageable age."

"Grandmother," Shanku muttered under her breath, trying to shush the woman.

The old warden reined his horse in and turned. "You're the one good at predictions, so why don't *you* tell me?" He smiled cheekily at the old woman, grinned at his daughter and flicked the reins to get his mount moving again.

"I don't predict the future," the oracle mumbled. "When will the idiot understand that?"

"Some family, this one," Kalidasa shook his head at Shanku in amusement.

The party topped a rise. Ahead of them lay a green valley, and at its centre, like flowers in full bloom, was a profusion of yellow and red tents. The oracle leaned the other way and pointed, excited to be finally back among her people. "Isn't that the most beautiful sight in the world?" she called to Brichcha, who nodded wisely in response.

"Speaking of the future," Shanku glanced at Kalidasa, "Aren't you going back to writing poetry now? It's been a while since you wrote anything."

Kalidasa nodded slowly. "Yes, but I want to take a break from poems. I am thinking of trying my hand at a play."

"A play?" Shanku's eyebrows went up. "You have a story in mind?"

"I was thinking of a love story about a king and a queen, where the queen loses her memory. The king is broken and—"

"And?"

"Maybe I will switch the roles around," Kalidasa thought aloud. "It'll be the king who will forget the queen, and the story will be about her struggle to win back his love..."

"The woman's perspective?" Shanku smiled in approval. "So much better."

The End